RETRO

THREE WOMEN'S LIVES
A TRILOGY

This boxset includes The Boatman's Daughter, Live A Little (Initially published as Brioche), and Diana's Story.

Retro

Three Women's Lives
A Trilogy

Rosemary Blake

Acknowledgement

Cover by SelfPubBookCovers.com/Arpibookcovers

Interior formatting by Kari of KH Formatting

With thanks to Denise who listened and supported as I wrote and to my early readers: Jenny Cooper, Margaret Mills, Kay Jaques, Julia Starr and Mo.

For an up-to-date list of books by this author check out the website www.rosemaryblake.co.uk

DEDICATION

This book is about dilemmas that women face throughout their lives and how they are affected by popular events and attitudes. It is dedicated to my grandchildren who will be making their own life choices in the years to come.

THE BOATMAN'S DAUGHTER

BOOK 1

CHAPTER ONE

The dutiful daughter who never made waves, Imogen was nervous about delivering her news. She'd been ringing round suitable adverts in the 'Flats to Let' column of the paper. Now Mum arrived shrugging off a dripping raincoat and anxious to get the shopping inside.

'Let me help you,' Imogen sprang up to take the bags.

Dulcie Best sank down thankfully into a kitchen chair still wearing her ridiculous plastic rain hat. 'Oh yes, what a relief,' and then she looked up from the kitchen table in alarm, 'What's this you're doing Imogen?'

Imogen was sure that she flushed, but she carried on regardless, 'It's time I moved out.' She hadn't wanted to look at Mum but now she stole a glance.

Dulcie sighed, 'Look, we've tried to bring you up properly. You can have some fun now you've finished college and you're a lot better off under our roof.'

'I need to be independent and work out what makes me happy. Lots of my friends have already left home.' Imogen looked around the gleaming kitchen and felt a moment of panic that she may lose the argument and see this house become her prison.

'You're still so young,' Dulcie ripped off the rain hat angrily. 'I left my parents' house when I got married, and if you live here, your dad could put a word in for you at the bank.

Then you could get a nice boyfriend. We'd like you to have a family and settle down around here.' She blinked quickly to clear the tears that had sprung to her eyes.

Imogen batted away any sympathy for her. If she let herself feel for her mum, she may find herself giving in. Anyway, Mum and Dad didn't rely on her, they had their own lives.

She had a hazy idea of the life that was out there, garnered from sitcoms like 'the Liver Birds' and 'Man about the House'. She felt exhilarated and at the point of take-off. Each new choice would affect her whole future (now where had that idea come from – teachers perhaps?)

As an only child she had been expected to be a high achiever and so she had learned to plan towards goals. She did that, spreading the local evening paper out on the bedroom floor to plan her move.

> *'Wanted: attractive young girl to work as barmaid. Includes evening and weekend work.'*
>
> *'Friendly lady receptionist required for hotel'*
>
> *'Efficient young miss needed as soon as possible for a position at Kent & Minster advertising agency. Secretarial skills and excellent references essential.'*

That sounded like her. She would apply. Now for somewhere to live.

Alone, like an imposter walking those leafy Victorian streets, she had trundled her suitcase from the bus stop. Not sure how much further there was to walk, she dawdled, savouring the importance of the occasion. But it was also because she felt apprehensive.

Set behind gates and high stone walls each solid house had some novel design feature: a pillared portico or decorative eaves. Aha, she reached a familiar gloomy house with a peeling wooden gate hanging slightly ajar. It was half-hidden by a sprouting laurel hedge topping a stone wall. She had had an appointment there three days earlier, with Tony. Surprisingly young to be the owner of a sprawling house with rooms to rent, he seemed easy going and warm.

'There's plenty of room. Just me and Anita. You'll like Anita. She rents the attic. 'Tony flicked back his sweeping fringe. 'You're welcome to bring your friends in too. I like having people round, so the more the merrier. Put some money down in advance, then you can move in whenever you're ready.'

Now she used her key in the heavy door for the first time and called a tentative 'hello'. She could hear distant movement and smell a faint reminiscence of meals past. Overcome by a dread of meeting whoever was there, she decided to go to her own rooms and settle in. She surveyed the small living area which was almost filled by an enormous armchair, bordered by bookshelves and a bay window. She had an adjoining bedroom with central cast-iron bed which was dwarfed by high ceilings and a heavy dark wood wardrobe. Hmm nowhere to lay out her toiletries; she'd need to remedy that.

Leaving the suitcase on the bed, she sat on the window seat and took in the view. The window was at the side of the house so the outlook was onto dense bushes, and a variety of birds hopping through spindly flowers and thick ferns. Craning her neck to the right she could see part of the front wall and the path.

'Breathe' she told herself. 'It's new but it will be OK. It's home now.' This had to work out because she'd taken such a stand to go there. She felt guilty that she had foiled her parents' plans for her. The enormity of what she had done, suddenly hit her and she felt a bit shaky.

'Knock, knock,' called a female voice. 'Can I come in?'

Imogen rose to her feet and rushed to open the door. 'Oh yes, yes of course. Hello I'm Imogen.' She took in the slender girl with dark outlined eyes, pale lips and long, shiny dark blonde hair. She took a step away from the doorway to welcome her in, 'Are you Anita?'

'That's right. I was curious to meet you. I've brought a housewarming gift.' she said proffering a broad green bottle.

'Mateus Rose. Thank you that's so kind.' Imogen said unconsciously adopting her mother's mannerisms. As Imogen hadn't unpacked, they arranged to go up to Anita's attic rooms.

'I've got a kettle in my room, because it's so far down to the kitchen.' Anita said. They sat on bean bags in a corner and Imogen took a quick look around at the eclectic decoration: a peacock feather, a fan, macramé hangers and 'far out' posters mixed in with elegantly discarded clothes and hats. An array of half-burned candles were lodged in the necks of wine bottles, with glaciers of wax creeping down the sides. This was the bohemian life that she dreamed of.

'You're giving me a lot of inspiration for my room.' she said.

'Oh I'm glad you like it.' Anita said 'It feels like home, although sometimes I'm away. I'm an actress and I have to go where the work is – sometimes on tour. Of course, at other times I'm doing odd jobs while 'resting'. I do a bit of waitressing here and there. Anyway, tell me about yourself, what do you do?'

Imogen filled Anita in on her background and about hoping to start a new job at Kent & Minster. Imogen didn't easily let her guard down, but Anita seemed so open and enthusiastic that she felt able to talk about anything with her. She'd soon forgotten any homesickness… until she realised the time.

'Oh sorry, I must nip down to the nearest phone box and call Mum to let her know that I'm here safely.' But they arranged to get together often and it felt like a relief to have got to know someone in the house.

She banished her unease about leaving home and worry about the new job, by thinking about Anita's life. She had got what Imogen wanted… success. Imogen pictured her as the curtain fell taking the applause and being met by autograph hunters. She admired Anita's nerve in breaking into the world of acting, her self-assurance and the way that her room reflected her personality.

By the time Imogen visited with Anita again, she'd bumped into Tony a few times. He was always busy and sometimes had people with him. The previous evening they'd encountered each other in the hall.

He'd shouted, 'Hey, I'm having drinks and dinner – Thursday evening about eight. Be there or be square,' before laughing and making for the front door. Was he serious? What were the other guests like? What do people wear?

'Are you going to the dinner party?' Imogen asked Anita.

'No I've got a date that night. But you'll enjoy it – it's a regular thing with Tony. He just enjoys being host and his friends are always good fun.' She stopped and Imogen felt Anita's hand on her arm. 'Just don't worry so much – really. I've been through lots of dodgy situations and that's not one of them.'

They had been chatting about fashion. Anita loved thick winged eye liner and she had brought out back-copies of Cosmo. to show Imogen the make-up in the adverts. While leafing through magazine pages she started to talk about roles in the theatre.

'Actresses are expected to be decorative. From comedies where I suddenly lose my top, to trendy musicals with mass nudity. I audition for jobs where I'm a pretty murder victim, a saucy waitress, someone's girlfriend. I tell you, being good looking means that I get work – but what kind of work?' she dropped the magazine and sighed. 'There's more,' with eyes lowered and head averted, she said, 'auditions are dangerous. Some men see you as goods on display. They try to justify touching you or asking you to undress, by saying you need to be relaxed and open-minded for the part.'

On hearing Anita's problems, Imogen felt moved that she was prepared to confide in her; unfortunately it also seemed to confirm all of her mother's warnings about the world.

She continued, 'one elderly guy phoned to tell me that he was deciding between me and one other girl. He invited me to come for a second try out. We met in a hotel lobby and there was no sign of the other girl. I was wary, but I also wanted the part. In the lift he pinched my bottom and I just giggled.' She shrugged 'I couldn't act offended when he could offer me the job. But he was holding the audition in a hotel bedroom.

'While he sat on the bed, I started my audition piece. I was unnerved by his eyes burning into me. For a moment I hoped that perhaps he was impressed by my performance. But he got up, moved towards me and murmured "Perhaps we'll try something else". He was leaning over me. I could feel his breath and just felt the urge to escape. I was wearing a mini dress and he slid his hand under it. I felt him touch my thigh. I don't even remember getting out of the room. I felt so dirty. I ran through the hotel reception with mascara running down my face. Wondering how to get home without anyone suspecting what had happened. I'm freaked out now. I have to force myself to go to any more auditions.'

Imogen noticed tears were seeping from the corners of her eyes and creating glistening, mascara darkened, wet patches just in front of her ears. She ignored them and jerked her head back.

'I bet you think I'm stupid and naïve.' Imogen shook her head not knowing what to say. 'But this is my ambition. It's what I've always wanted to do. For years, my mum managed to find the money for drama lessons for me.' She made a face 'I just don't know what I can do'.

'Oh God I'm so sorry,' Imogen said. She found herself trembling slightly, 'you must have felt awful. You weren't to know that he was so slimy.'

'Tch I've upset you. I didn't mean to lay all that on you.' Anita apologised. 'It's just it's been bothering me for weeks. If anything it gets worse. I feel angry with him – I just want to get back at him, but no one will want to hear what happened. It's seen as a hazard of the job.'

Imogen put her arm around Anita's shoulders, 'Is he married? Could we tell his wife? Could we tell the papers?' she said. Anita gave a shrug with a wry smile. 'Professional suicide'.

'If you are upset like that again come and talk to me about it. Girls need to stick together.' Imogen said, recognising that she was privileged to be a part of the respectable world.

They sat talking into the early morning. Anita felt optimistic about her current boyfriend.

'I haven't known Skipper for long, but he's lovely. He's so considerate. He's young but knowledgeable and he makes me trust that not all men are bad.' she said. 'We just met casually at a canal side pub, but he's such a romantic. He likes Elton John and T Rex just like me – sometimes he sings to me. And – unlike most men – he takes the time to listen.' She picked up a biro and doodled his name in fancy lettering on the magazine. 'He says he might have some contacts who could put in a word for me with theatre directors. He meets them in his work. Sorry I'm going on…have you got a boyfriend? I could find out if he's got a friend for you.'

'Ooh I'm not sure about a blind date,' Imogen gave her a half smile. But this did stir her interest. She felt that there was something missing. Now that she had left home she hoped to meet someone special…someone who would be there with an arm around her. When she saw couples spending time together on long summer evenings, she became wistful and wondered if it would ever happen to her. Maybe she needed to learn how to flirt?

Anita had lent her some magazines from her pile. Perhaps she should approach this like any other project and study hard? She glanced at some of the straplines on the covers:

> *'Exactly how to get over being a shy girl – and bloom.' Interesting.*
>
> *'Secrets of male sexuality to help you win that Man.'*
>
> *'Update on Estrogen, the Hormone that Makes Women more Curvy, more female and more responsive to men.'*

This was another perspective; one where girls took charge of what happened to them. The opportunities were exciting but overwhelming. In the meantime, the weekend stretched ahead. She was used to being part of a family and now she faced getting to know new food shops, getting clothes ready for her new job and possibly taking a Sunday walk around the area. It wasn't appealing. She almost decided to get on a bus home. 'Surprise, I thought I'd come and see you' she would say as she rounded the front door. Then she realised that they would probably be out, and the house would feel just as empty as her new rooms. And if they were there, they would sense that Imogen couldn't hack it however cheerful she tried to appear.

Chapter Two

Imogen watched herself in the mirror, spinning to make her daisy-scattered maxi dress swirl around her legs. She had long legs and short hair; you could describe her as gawky or as Mia Farrow gamine. She practised a bright smile and a nod. How was she expected to act at the dinner party? Had Tony got romantic intensions towards her? She liked his breezy confidence, but a romance with someone who was your landlord could be complicated. What if you broke up? Tony's friends were probably older than her and she worried about what they would think of her. She would keep quiet and observe. This was the safe strategy, but she had vowed to start to take life by the horns. What time was it – three minutes to go? She had prepared much too early. So of course, when she did venture along the hall, listening for voices, she was the first to arrive.

'Make yourself at home. The leather sofa will get crowded later. Try the suspended chair,' Tony gestured. 'What can I get you to drink?' Two social traps: deciding what drinks would be available in the first place, and hoisting herself into a swinging bubble contraption. Bambi from the Baby Cham commercial sprang to mind. While Tony disappeared to get her drink, she tried steadying the chair with one hand while launching herself backwards into it. After a small amount of swinging she was sitting demurely by the time that Tony reappeared.

Then two men with almost identical Ringo-style haircuts arrived. 'Brought this dude,' the one called Mark said, handing Tony a bottle. He wore an informal waistcoat and loon pant look, right out of a New Musical Express advert. Dave, the other, had gone for a sports jacket. 'Bet you're waiting for Janice.' Tony elbowed him in the ribs. Imogen took note to look out for Janice. Tony barely had time to introduce the two men to her when two girls, Sue and Janice, piled through the door.

'What new dish are you going to shock us with today?' Sue giggled 'I still can't get over being given deer to eat.'

'Venison.' Tony corrected with a mock stern expression.

'And I hope someone will look after us this evening if we end up tipsy,' Janice added, with a glance across at the boys. Noticing Imogen for the first time, Janice turned to her, and indicating Tony and Sue, she said 'We make up the three musketeers – sit in the same office'. Everyone was smiling and as Imogen slid out of the swing to join the others at the table, she felt the camaraderie.

'Not sure where Vic and his wife are.' Tony passed round nibbles 'I gave him a map so that they could find us.' He went on to describe the rich smells and cosmopolitan accents of Soho where he regularly visited little Italian cafes and delicatessens. 'So I found some real coffee and I've made real Spaghetti Bolognese.'

'I've had Spag. Bol., but out of a tin.' Mark said.

Just as Tony, with Sue's help, was putting starters at each place, the latecomers arrived.

'Really sorry – we got held up. This is my wife Barbara everyone.' Vic ushered a diminutive, curvy woman in white hot pants, ahead of him to the table.

Well most of them knew each other, so Imogen let the conversation flow over her. Although Mark didn't work with them, he seemed to know Tony from years before and he was confident and jokey. Janice sat next to Dave and played with his cuff link. Imogen wondered how close their relationship was.

'So, what do you think of Women's Lib.?' Sue turned to Imogen. 'Are you planning to have a family or do you have more exciting plans?' Imogen didn't realise that the conversation had taken this turn, so the question put her on the spot.

'I don't know. I'm about to start a new job. I haven't got a boyfriend so I'm not thinking of a family at the moment.'

'It will come sooner than you realise,' said Barbara. 'I mean, it is lovely to have a nice home, but I want to get back out to work. I feel like a cabbage.'

'Do you think women can have it all?' Sue pushed on.

Tony rose to clear the table, 'Exciting changes for women,' he said, 'pass the plates everyone'.

Dave leant in to direct his gaze at Imogen and Sue. 'How you fit babies in with careers? Yeh, I think some people are planners and some people just let it happen. But you know, if you just let it happen, y'might never reach your dreams.'

'But you need to know what your dreams are first.' Janice pursed her lips looking pointedly at Dave, and Imogen wondered if there were some friction there.

The conversation got quite philosophical. Tony talked about doing something creative – cookery, interior design or being an artist.

'The complete opposite of working in accounts then. Why didn't you train to be a chef, or something like that, when you left school?' Vic said.

'My dad's a strong character.' said Tony. 'I was sent to boarding school and he made it clear that I ought to do something like accountancy or become a barrister. At the time, it seemed simpler to do what he wanted than to come up against him. I didn't believe in myself enough I suppose.'

'That's the key, believing in yourself.' said Mark.

Imogen surprised herself by adding, 'And taking a risk.'

'So are you a risk taker?' someone asked her. She explained her home situation and found herself discussing her Mum's life. 'She's a good example of what we're talking about. She's got a full social life and she's into decorating the house in a big way, but is she happy? I can tell that she expects my life will turn out just like hers… I think that's why I've broken away.'

Tony looked downcast, 'Value them while you can Imogen. Mine are gone now and I often wish that I could have got to know them better…'

The mood was lifted by the Spaghetti Bolognese. They were pasta novices and boy, did they find it hard to eat. Initially feeling awkward, Imogen found herself giggling. Tony demonstrated the swivelling around a fork method, but she resorted to chopping off short pieces and using a spoon.

Hmm the mess involved led to a discussion of 'The Exorcist' and all the latest films. Tony suggested that they look out for something that everyone would like and go as a group. People were loosening up which was probably the effect of alcohol combined with good food and company.

'Oh man,' 'Wow,' they greeted the dessert which was carried in with a flourish. Tony had made a gateau topped with piped cream, pineapple rings and glace cherries. The sides were lined with Ladyfingers biscuits.

'You put me to shame in the cooking department.' Barbara said.

'Must be a poof.' Vic directed at Tony and laughed.

Around the room there was an immediate widening of eyes and stilling of hands. Vic was new to the group and glanced around at everyone. There was a flush of pink on Tony's neck but he concentrated on serving out slices. 'Um sorry, just a joke.' Vic added.

Imogen found that she had been holding her breath until the silence was broken by an over-hearty, 'Well this looks good. I'll be wanting seconds.' from Mark and they moved on.

They had all shared information on family circumstances and their views on life, but this incident cemented Imogen's view that trusting people too soon was risky. She felt sorry for Tony who had put so much work into the evening, but he seemed able to brush it off.

There was still some light in the sky when people began to leave and the stifling hot day had been replaced by a pleasantly cool evening. There was a hubbub of voices wishing each other goodbye and they all said that they hoped to see Imogen again. She was just offering to help with the dishes, when Sue came hurrying back in looking panic-stricken

'Oh no. I've locked myself out of the car. I don't believe it'.

'Don't worry, it isn't the end of the world' Tony put his arm around her and Imogen said, 'There must be something we can do'.

Sue came to the party with Janice, but now she was alone. Imogen reflected that you can suddenly feel very alone when something goes wrong.

'Here we are. I'm sure we'll be able to do something with this.' Tony appeared, waving a wire coat hanger. While they went into the street to do some lock picking, Imogen threw on a butcher's apron hanging on the back of the kitchen door, filled a bowl with hot suds and started on the washing-up.

Judging by this group Tony's workplace seemed friendly, she hoped that she would find the same in her own new job.

Chapter Three

Imogen opened a window and gulped in air before washing her hands at the row of basins. She had been at Kent & Minster for an hour and this was a good chance to excuse herself and take stock. She'd been shown to a seat at a shared desk. Well that was good, as there were people to show her the ropes. She'd been given the company handbook and brochures to read. They weren't riveting. But this was just the beginning; she was nervously excited to see how the job panned out. She thought she'd been recruited because she had shorthand and typing skills, but as yet, there was no typewriter on the desk.

Lynette sat opposite her. She had an easy friendliness which helped to quieten Imogen's first day nerves. That morning Imogen had been deliberating about the correct outfit for the office, but Lynette's style, based on a Jamaican colour palette, showed that there was no uniform. Sitting beside the window Lynette's skin glowed copper in the bright light. She wore a tightly banded head cloth and metal bracelets shifted on her narrow wrists as she waved her arms in conversation.

Sitting on Imogen's right was Margaret in a Crimplene suit, who explained that she had been a clerk for the agency for fifteen years. 'I'm the office mother figure. Come to me if there is anything you need to know' she said. Margaret offered to take Imogen from desk to desk on the open-plan floor to introduce her to other staff. Imogen wasn't able to remember many names and felt a bit like an awkward child standing at Margaret's side, while she chatted to each group.

Back at their desk, Lynette explained that they all put ten shillings into a kitty for coffee. 'It comes round on a trolley in about half an hour'. No sooner had they dealt with that, than a sharp suited young man appeared to tell her to make her way up to the boss's office. She had been told that she would be working directly for Ian Fraser even though he hadn't been at her interview.

The smooth lift doors parted onto a carpeted foyer furnished with low-level leather and chrome seating. There was a potted rubber plant next to a teak coffee table strewn with magazines. Beyond was a large office obscured by a bronzed glass wall. Ian Fraser waved for her to push through the glass door.

He was certainly attractive. As she entered, he leaned back in his chair resting his ankle on his knee, stretching the suit material and revealing a fashionable Cuban heel boot. The few lines around his eyes and a slightly receding hairline showed that he wasn't as young as he at first appeared. Imogen sat on a low chair which was at the other side of his desk. This placed piles of papers in letter-trays between them.

'Welcome,' he said in a soft voice with a trace of a Scottish accent, 'tell me a bit about yourself and why you want to work here.'

So this was just an introduction, even so, she wished that she had prepared something to say. Summoning her wits, she started by explaining about her secretarial training. She told him what she knew about advertising and praised the agency's reputation.

'Yes, interesting' he said, glancing out of the window and then lighting up a cigarette with the ornamental lighter on his desk. 'Sorry, do you smoke?'

'Er no.'

'But tell me what makes you tick? A young girl like you – what do you want out of life?'

She laughed; this was something that she wasn't sure about herself. She explained that she'd just left home and waffled some more. Imogen felt her heart-rate rise and her palms growing sweaty. She ended by saying that she was ambitious.

'Good, great.' he jumped up moved round to the front of his desk and sat on the corner. He was now quite close and there was the musty trace of tobacco mixed with aftershave. 'Let me explain the cutthroat world of advertising. It's not all about being creative, success means winning clients and standing out. I see you as a valuable asset. And you might be surprised by this,' he narrowed his eyes at her, 'but I'm going to suggest that you apply for jobs with our competitors. To get ahead we need information on them and on which clients they're chasing.'

Imogen found it difficult to take it all in. At first she thought Mr Fraser was asking her to leave and then… 'Are you suggesting that I could be a sort of spy?'

He laughed and nodded. 'That's putting it in a dramatic way! It's an exercise in gathering information and I need someone bright and lively to be able to do it. If you want to get ahead this will shoot you there.' Then he seemed to realise that she wasn't jumping with enthusiasm. 'But this is your first day. Start off by doing some desk research on other agencies. And I need you to get to know us. Spend some time in the office.' He threw his hands open expansively, 'Listen, I get my wife to hold occasional gatherings. We ask directors and trusted business partners. There's one tomorrow evening in the Boardroom. If you think that you will fit in...' he paused, 'I'd like you to join us. You need to get to know us better.'

When Imogen got back to her desk, subtle questioning revealed that Lynette and Margaret knew nothing of evening events in the office. She concentrated on asking more about the other staff as she was conscious that she was still 'the new girl'. Lynette told her that a group regularly went into the nearby pub at lunchtime for drinks and sometimes organised evening bowling or ice skating.

'Do you go?' Imogen said.

'I go at lunchtime. Come along with me if you like.' Lynette said.

It sounded a good idea. Imogen was tempted to confide in her about the meeting with Ian Fraser and ask for advice, but it felt wrong to jeopardise an opportunity that – who knew – she may be interested in.

*****

The journey home was long enough for Imogen to mull over the extraordinary day.

She wondered whether Ian Fraser was playing some kind of game or living in a fantasy world. Attending the evening event and meeting others may give her more of an idea on that.

She glanced at other people in the carriage. A smart woman in a belted mac sitting opposite and an older man who'd stored a briefcase at his feet. Probably they had mundane, slightly boring jobs. How would it have played out if she'd turned to the man next to her and asked, 'Have you heard much about spies in your workplace?'

She also wondered, 'Why me?' Had she seemed to be a natural liar or someone who enjoyed deception? Imogen wanted to believe that she had integrity, despite the occasional white lie to Mum and Dad. So how did this fit with her own principles? And trying to get a job with a competitor seemed daunting or should that be exciting? It certainly meant that she wouldn't fit in with the Kent & Minster team. She let herself imagine what her parents might think. They would be wary and her father would want to check out the details. But she knew that he valued 'getting on'. He might well tell her to ignore the loss of potential work friendships and take the challenge.

Chapter Four

The lift opened to the sound of murmured voices and the strains of Elton John, one of Imogen's favourites - so she took this as a good omen. She opened the Boardroom door to see a small gathering of people; some standing around the polished table in the centre and some sitting on sofas at one end of the room. Few people noticed her arrive, which was a relief as she didn't want to make a grand entrance. One person who had been sitting on the periphery of a group did turn around. He was a young man in a velvet jacket and smart flares and he approached with a smile.

'Hi, I haven't seen you here before. I'm Peter Lawrence.' he said reaching to shake her hand.

'No I'm new. I just work in the office - I'm Imogen Best.' She winced; never say you are 'just' anything.

'Come, grab some vol-au-vents before they've all gone.' He gently placed his hand in the small of her back. It felt that he had claimed her and made Imogen feel more secure. They joined a group of three women and a man beside the buffet. They were talking about the threat of power strikes and how the government should deal with it. Imogen felt that it was best to just not think about politics so she put on a polite listening look. Worries about electricity cuts meant that there had been a run on buying candles and various people discussed where they had found some on sale. She spotted Ian Fraser across the room. He made eye contact and gave a small wave but then turned back to the people that he was talking to.

Pete turned to Imogen and asked, 'So what do you think of Kent & Minster?'

'It's all very new. It's interesting to mix with a lot of people in an open-plan office,' she said, 'but how are you involved? Are you a director here?'

'Far from it, I'm a supplier. I work with Ian, Jim and Nigel, particularly when they want to entertain customers. I can provide river and canal boat cruises. And I work with the same caterers that they're using tonight.'

'Oh I see. I'd thought that this was staff members and their families,' Imogen said in surprise.

'Well I'm practically family I'm so close to them, 'he said, 'there isn't much that goes on that I don't know about.' She filed this in the back of her mind to consider later, as she wasn't sure whether to believe that he was party to all of the company secrets.

'And you've got a boating business?' she added.

Peter launched into a description of the characters on the water and various amusing incidents that had occurred around boats. There was an intensity to their conversation and to the positioning of their bodies that must have discouraged others from joining them. The original group drifted farther away. Imogen barely noticed as she was flattered by Peter's attention.

Eventually Ian Fraser appeared. Peter seemed to stiffen slightly but both men kept up a friendly manner.

'I need to introduce our new girl to a few people. I'm sure you understand. I'll deliver her back. It's looking as though you don't want to let go of her.' Mr Fraser winked at Peter, who pressed his lips together tightly but waved them on, turning towards the cocktail waiter.

Mr Fraser led Imogen to meet his wife Valerie and two directors of the company. Valerie seemed amiable and easy going but the directors acted older and more pompously than Ian Fraser. Imogen couldn't imagine them being involved in underhand dealings. But she reflected that maybe she was naïve; maybe even her father didn't turn a hair at deception in the business world. If she had felt closer to her father, she may have considered asking him.

Mr Fraser became caught up in an exchange with someone beside him and Imogen found herself floundering for conversation with one of the directors, Nigel Jones. He was questioning her about her home life and her father's profession, and she began to feel uncomfortable at how one-sided it had become. Eventually she inclined her head towards the buffet table and said 'I promised to join someone over there. Excuse me'. She felt herself blush as she saw him glance over his shoulder in that direction and laugh. She thought 'oh no, I'm sure he thinks I'm trying to just help myself to more food'.

'Well I am honoured to see you again. I thought I may have been talking too much.' Peter slid back to her side. 'Old Fraser's been showing you off then. I reckon you're a valued new recruit to the stable.' he said. She didn't like being compared to a horse, but maybe he was trying to tip her off to the way that the company viewed their employees, or at least, their female employees.

'Before you run away into the night. Can I see you again?' he asked, 'We can go to a new Italian pizza place.'

Imogen had had a few cinema trips with boys from college, but hadn't been on a 'proper' date and she had never tried pizza. She felt a frisson of interest at the chance to join cosmopolitan night life. She smiled, 'Thank you I'd like that.'

'Next week then? We can meet under the clock at the station.' Pete said getting his diary out of his top pocket.

CHAPTER FIVE

Imogen banished the feeling of homesickness and began to feel that she belonged. Most evenings, Tony or Anita offered to share meals and eventually a cooking rota developed. Tony had the largest rooms and after work they invariably gravitated to his dining table or to the garden seating area. They became a family group; each taking a role. Imogen gave herself permission to talk freely with them. She shared her questions about life and even tried out a few wise-cracks, that seemed to go down well. Anita, when not out with her boyfriend Skipper, brought gossip from the theatre and Tony acted as a good listener and social event organiser. On occasion Tony lost his affable exterior and told them how unbearable he found the greyness of a career in finance.

Imogen had not seen Ian Fraser for a few weeks. The company was divided into the 'upstairs downstairs' world of a Victorian household. She felt as though she had been invited briefly into 'upstairs' but she much preferred the fellowship of 'downstairs' and chose to ignore his plans for her.

In the office she still managed a passing smile across at Lynette and Margaret, but her induction involved sitting with people who worked on the advertising campaigns. They were brash and confident. Some of them were flamboyant art school types and others were graduates who paraded their intellectualism. She was surprised at the way that they took her to the heart of the group and as she laughed along with their banter, she began to develop her own off-the-cuff retorts.

She valued the outings to the lunchtime pub and developed a taste for garlic bread. There was quite a crowd, but she usually engineered a seat beside Lynette. She was drawn to Lynette's calm demeanour and willingness to see the best in people. They often lagged behind, talking on the way to the pub and as they arrived last, they sat at the edge of the group of colleagues or on stools nearby.

'He's a bit of alright,' one of their friends called across to Lynette, nodding to indicate the group of young male office workers who were standing behind Lynette and Imogen.

'You want to get in there,' an office boy shouted. The young men didn't turn around, feigning a lack of interest. Imogen noticed that Lynette shifted uncomfortably on her stool.

'They're just idiots.' Imogen said quietly in an aside.

'My family are quite religious – Pentecostal.' Lynette answered looking across in disgust at the Kent & Minster group. 'People here act differently from the way I'm used to. I think, they think I'm some sort of tart.'

'I know what you mean. We're expected to take it all in good part but it's embarrassing. It's the same when I'm walking past building sites. I don't like getting all the catcalls either. They seem to think you're on show for their enjoyment.' Imogen replied.

'You haven't thought about boyfriends yet either then?'

'Well I have thought about them.' Imogen admitted, grinning. 'I've been invited out on a date in town. I'm meeting him under the station clock.'

Lynette looked interested, 'My father's very strict. He would never allow that. He would want to vet him first.' Then she added, 'Be careful, make sure that you stay in public places.'

'That's just what my Mum says.' Imogen said with a laugh, but she didn't resent Lynette's judgements, she recognised that she was speaking as a friend.

Imogen also found herself spending time with Clare and Judith. They had joined the company at a similar time and she was flattered that they consciously involved her in their discussions. They invited her to join them at the nearby Wimpy Bar. She treated herself to the Brown Derby (a doughnut and whippy ice cream confection) and she listened to their chatter rather than initiating conversations. She was weighing them up; they exuded a knowing cynicism as though they were both in on a secret. Clare had planned a career as a journalist but had called at Kent & Minster on the off-chance, and landed a job. Judith hinted that she had joined the company through a friend of her family.

When Imogen described them to Tony he insisted on referring to them as 'the twins' but she was sure that they must be distinct when you got to know them. Clare introduced her to the modern classics. Imogen made a point of reading any book she mentioned; she enjoyed stretching her mind through their discussions. Judith had less to say, but she was into music like 'Yes' and 'Jethro Tull', and at one time she grew quite animated in a discussion on Eastern religions. 'Like the Beatles' trip to India' Imogen thought.

They were stashing their handbags into desk drawers ready to start the day when Clare said, 'D'you want to form a team for a pub quiz? It'll be good, we like to test ourselves.'

'Oh I don't know. I haven't been to university. I'm not sure I'd be any good,' Imogen said.

'You seem to have a good general knowledge and we need another person to make up a team. We'll answer most of the questions,' Clare shrugged, 'although you could swot up on something like flags for us. Should be a good night.'

Imogen was worried that she would show herself up, but remembered that she'd resolved not to shy away from cementing new friendships. So she promised to think about it.

That evening, while delicately scooping a rather good lemon posset contributed by Tony, she waved her spoon in the air casually and asked, 'Well what do you think, is it a mistake to go to a pub quiz with Clare and Jude?'

'How do I know . . .I wouldn't join one,' said Anita.

'No, you wouldn't… unless they were asking about playwrights.' mocked Tony. 'Don't listen to her Imogen.' Anita gave his arm a shove and stuck out her bottom lip.

'I think the twins have taken a shine to you. Go for it.' He added.

'Mm, yes they have. Though we don't have much in common. They've asked me to learn flags.'

'Well there you are then. I'm sure we've got an illustrated encyclopaedia in one of the bookshelves. I'll test you if you like'.

***

On a warm and humid evening Clare and Imogen strolled through the 'heritage area' of town. There was a light drizzle. The wet cobbles of the street shone with reflections from cast iron streetlamps. Imogen began to feel as though she were in a 1930s black and white film. Occasionally figures hurried past on the way home from work, all looking down as the middle distance was misty. Clare linked arms with Imogen and it felt as if they'd formed a close bond. Clare had been to quizzes in the past and shared information on the type of teams that entered. Without interrupting the flow of conversation, she ducked down to a litter bin. As she bobbed up again, she quickly stashed a paper package from the bin to her handbag.

'Err sorry, what were you doing?' Imogen stopped in her tracks.

'No don't stop. Keep walking.' Clare urged glancing around. As they moved on she said, 'Judith and I know that Ian's already talked to you.'

'What – well even if he has, what has that got to do with the bin?'

'We're all in the same boat. We don't need to keep secrets - we can support each other. I probably ought to have talked to you about it before tonight. Picking up the money is part of what we do.'

'What?' Imogen was open mouthed. 'Explain what you mean. Ian did talk to me about joining another firm. He asked you that too?'

'Yes, Judith and I have both worked with other companies for a few months. This is part of it. Once Ian has information on members of staff in rival companies, he uses it to his advantage. He also does a bit of arm twisting based on things that we find out.'

'It looks like you're blackmailing people to me.' Imogen said.

'Not us - Ian is. We're collecting information. It's how business works and it's made us very important to the company. Why - does it bother you Imogen?' Clare frowned sideways.

'I've been keeping an open mind about Ian's suggestion, but I don't think he'd fully explained.' Imogen said.

'No, I think he lets you get the lie of the land first. It's quite exciting work really and it shows that he thinks you're capable and intelligent. There isn't really any risk. Before they were married, Ian's wife Valerie worked like us and look where she ended up.'

'Well that position is filled.' Imogen stared fixedly at the cobbles, 'I don't know what to say. I wasn't planning on this when I did a secretarial course. It's flattering I can see, but surely you can't relax in the team when you have to lead a double life.'

Imogen wasn't sure what Clare's motive was in talking to her. Why did they need someone else to be complicit with them? She wondered if Ian had set Clare and Judith up, to induce her to 'join the club'. If there were at least three people working like this, were there more? And if several people were involved, how was it possible for them all to achieve advancement in the company?

'What's in it for you? Have you and Judith seen any reward as a result of this?'

Now it was Clare's turn to look disconcerted. 'Look I hadn't realised that you weren't really on board. Let's wait until Judith can talk to you too. We should discuss it after the quiz.'

'You haven't been upfront with me. I'm questioning what kind of friends you really are,' Imogen said and with that she tucked her head down to her chest, hunched her shoulders and turned to rush down a nearby passageway that led to the high street.

She heard her name being called and she sensed that Clare was following but, increasing her pace, she managed to disappear into the mist.

Chapter Six

After leaving Clare, Imogen arrived home to find the house empty. Being in her familiar room felt like returning to a nest. She had so enjoyed being a carefree office worker that she'd shelved thoughts of Mr Fraser's offer. It had been flattering and also struck her as unreal. She blamed herself for ignoring the situation. Deep down she had known that Mr Fraser would expect some commitment from her. Now Clare's actions had thrust the situation in front of her face. She felt tarnished by the dubious aspects of what Clare and Judith were already involved in.

They were new friends and she'd believed that they genuinely accepted her into their circle. Part of her resented them but, she reasoned, they hadn't meant her any harm. As she always hated to let anyone down, she also felt guilty for running out on the quiz evening.

Well, asking her to walk with Clare while she collected the money, must have been their way of making sure that she was part of it all.

She woke every two hours throughout the night, filled a glass of water, leafed through a magazine, and leant on the windowsill watching birds pecking for worms at dawn.

With sore eyes and a fuzzy head, Imogen started the day badly. She had decided to pretend that nothing had happened, unless Clare approached her. After accepting a stronger than usual coffee from the trolley, she made her way over to Lynette's desk.

'Hello Imogen, you OK?'

'Could be better. I didn't sleep well. I thought I'd come over for a chat. It's a bit hectic on that side of the office,' she sat down beside Lynette. 'Actually, I wanted to pick your brains. What do you think of Mr Fraser? Clare and Jude do some work for him and I think he may want me to do some direct work. There just seems something odd about it.'

Lynette pursed her lips. 'Well we all work for him you know. But no…. I understand what you're getting at. I don't know what's going on and I think I'd rather not know. Those two act shifty and they disappear every so often. We've had other girls who've done the same thing and no one makes a big thing of it. In the end they move on permanently.'

'Oh' Imogen said gulping coffee.

Lynette nodded 'Yes, whatever's happening doesn't seem to be good for the girls involved. I'm glad I've been left to sit here and get on with my work. I like being here. If you can avoid getting wrapped up in anything, I would do if I were you.'

Imogen folded her arms on the desk and smiled at her, 'Thanks Lynette, I wish I'd spoken to you earlier. It would have saved me a sleepless night.' She rose to her feet again, 'better get back over there. We'll get together later, OK?'

There was no chance to get together with Lynette that lunchtime as she had some clothes to take back to Etam, but Imogen instinctively realised that she had an ally there.

On the way home, Imogen called at a corner shop for a bar of chocolate. She had to buy something to make sure that she had change and she snapped pieces off with her teeth as she headed for the nearby phone box.

'Hello Mum. How are you? No I'm OK, just wanted to hear your voice. It's been a while.

Yes I love my rooms I'm settling in well.

Oh yeh, I am eating well. My housemates do a lot of cooking so I haven't had to do too much so far. I've been getting to know people at work too. I'm still finding out what the company's like.'

'Yes I'm still learning about the job. I haven't done any typing yet. Oh, sorry I hadn't realised you were going out. Yes, yes I'll speak to you another time. It's OK don't worry. Have a good time.'

She clicked the receiver back onto its rest. The pile of change that she'd had ready was unused. She wasn't even sure whether she would have gone on to explain the situation. There was no real situation – nothing had really happened to her. Maybe she should follow Lynette's advice and keep her head down, but she did have to decide how to work with Mr Fraser and the two girls.

***

It was Saturday the next day, bright outside but shadowy in the house. Imogen was lethargic. She indulged in some eyebrow plucking and then leafed through her pile of magazines. A quiz caught her interest 'What kind of woman are you?' Grabbing a pen, she ticked her way down the questions and read:

> *'You are led by a strong desire to experi-*
> *ence the world. You know what is right for*
> *you and you are determined to go for it.*
> *You will be drawn to travel, adventure and*
> *the men who share your passion. Embrace*
> *life, make choices for yourself and don't*
> *settle for second best.'*

It felt like a personal message confirming that she was on the right track. She didn't want to go back to being confined by her own anxieties and with renewed energy she leaped up to seek out life.

The back garden beckoned. A slight breeze barely moved the bushes and there was a sharp, sweet scent from the buddleias crowding the path. The laziness of the afternoon was emphasised by the droning of a plane overhead. As Imogen rounded the corner of the house she detected Tony by the tinny output of his transistor radio.

'Oh there you are,' he called 'I thought you were going to sleep all day. Come and sit out here with me. I've got peanuts and cans of lager, if you get yourself a glass.'

Sitting with him in the shade of the parasol she dug her hand into the large bag of peanuts.

'What's been going on? I know you went on a date – anywhere decent?' he said.

'With Peter, yes. He took me to a pizza bar down in a cellar. I hadn't tried pizza – I know you've been to Italian places.'

'Well, what did you think?'

'Oh it was good. Mmm a lovely crust and gooey cheese. I've never tasted anything like it before. We sat at these long benches. It was quite dim down there and there were stubby candles all along the middle of trestle tables.'

Tony laughed at Imogen's enthusiasm. 'Sounds great. And what about him? Did you click with him?'

'He seems nice. There was a jazz band so there wasn't much chance to have a good chat. I wonder what he thinks of me. He seems to be confident in any situation. I wish I were… I wasn't sure what people drink. I ordered port and lemon.' Then she smiled, 'anyway, he put his jacket round my shoulders on the way back to the station and walked with his arm round me. Just before we got there, he pulled me into a doorway and we had a long kiss.'

'Glad to hear it's taking off.' Tony put on a mock serious tone, 'I think I should meet this young man of yours.' Then, 'No really. Is there another date on the cards?

'Even better. He's invited me to dine on his passenger boat.' Imogen huffed a laugh, 'How about you Tony? Any dates lined up?'

'Oh you know me. It doesn't seem to happen. Playing the field at the moment.'

She was curious, but before he could add anything else, Anita's voice sounded out, 'I thought I'd find you both out here.' And she flounced up to the table in a flowing cotton sun dress and a wide-brimmed straw hat.

'Well hello, we never get to see you nowadays,' said Tony.

'Have you been out with Skipper again?' Imogen said and smiled up at Anita.

'Yes again, I'm afraid so folks. I'm addicted to him.' She danced around the table swooping up a handful of peanuts as she went.

Striking a pose she launched into a Music Hall parody, swishing her dress from side to side,

'Daisy, Daisy. Give me your answer do. I'm half crazy, all for the love of you.'

She stopped, gave a sweeping bow and said, 'It's such fun when he's around. And it's a relief to be with him after all the prima donnas in the theatre. He makes me feel special.'

'What's he like?' Imogen prompted.

'Oh it's just… he listens to me. He encourages me. He has a good sense of humour. Sometimes he gets a bit moody, but don't we all? He's got a lot on. He knows lots of people. So he'll get to hear about productions and put my name in front of the right people.

Imogen kicked off her sandals to bury her bare feet in the cool grass. 'That's good.'

'Yes it's good to see you so happy, poppet.' Tony got up, gave her a hug and made for the house, 'Let me get you a glass.'

'It's serious then?' Imogen looked at Anita who had taken a seat opposite. Anita smiled and raised her eyebrows.

As soon as Tony was back, Imogen took the opportunity to collar them about her work problem. She explained about walking with Clare to the pub quiz and Clare's sudden cash pick-up. She shrugged, not sure whether she had overreacted but knowing that it had upset her. She explained what Ian Fraser had offered. 'I need to finally decide whether I'm going to get involved in all that.'

'Hmm it affects your future there,' Tony agreed, 'I just wonder what'll happen if you don't get involved. I don't want to scare you...but you'll be a threat to the company now that you know so much.'

Imogen bit her lip. She just wanted the problem to go away.

Chapter Seven

Pete repeatedly visited the deck in anticipation of Imogen's arrival. It wasn't time yet, so he made himself go check that everything was perfect and to speak to the chef and waitress. He paid them in advance so that they could leave after the main course.

Imogen approached the gangplank, rattling the chains on the 'Closed' sign.

She hoped that she looked the part for a special date. Cute short hair which revealed the curve of the nape of her neck. A smart navy and white mini-dress with matching shoulder bag and patent leather sandals.

Handing her on board Pete said, 'You're looking wonderful.'

Imogen smiled at him but she felt aware that she was probably blushing. Being on his territory, made her feel less in control.

'Ever been on one of these before? My pride and joy… well, this was one of the first goals I achieved. Let me show you around.'

Imogen scanned the carpeted lounge and restaurant area. She really wanted to make a connection with Pete and thought back to what she did know about boats. 'No I haven't ever been on anything like this before. But I'm very interested. I studied the industrial revolution at school. You know, all about the development of inland waterways – aqueducts, James Brindley, horse drawn narrow boats. Of course, this is bigger than that.'

Her eyes darted around taking in the highly-polished walnut surfaces and the expansive windows onto the water. She was drawn forwards towards a table laid outside on the bow. It looked magical. She was acutely aware of Pete putting his hand on her elbow as though to guide her. He gestured towards the table laid with a linen cloth and cutlery, which was under an awning strung with fairy lights. They glimmered dimly in the early dusk.

'Look just for you,' he said and was rewarded when Imogen smiled in his direction.

'I thought we'd start out here. We may need to move inside if the midges appear later.' He drew a chair back for her and took another opposite.

'It's a beautiful evening.' she said.

They sat watching waterside cyclists passing the pub, moorhens darting in and out of the far bank and, closer to them, the occasional splash of a fish leaving a ripple in the still water. The waitress appeared carrying plates of fanned melon.

'I wanted to do everything properly this time,' Pete said. 'Chef has made Boeuf Bourguignon for the main course. Bit of a change from pizza.'

'Well I loved the pizza,' Imogen said, 'and I'm sure I'll love this too, but I'm happy whatever we eat. I'm used to my mother's cooking…Sunday roasts, shepherd's pie. You're very sophisticated.'

'Oh, I got used to fancy food when I entertain business colleagues, but I'm used to the basics too.' He poured some wine into glasses, 'Tell me more about your home life?'

'There's not much to tell,' Imogen shrugged and wondered how to explain a life that would sound mundane but had felt like prison. 'My dad works in a bank and Mum and Dad have quite a busy social life – cocktail parties, dinner parties. Then there's just me. I went to a girls' school and then on to do a secretarial course at college. After that, I wanted to escape.

'We have a nice house and Mum's very house-proud. She likes browsing around department stores and shopping for finishing touches. She just doesn't seem very happy and I felt a bit guilty when I decided to move out.'

'What kind of place do you live in now?' Pete asked.

'I've just started sharing a house with two others. I'm lucky because I get on with them, so there's always someone to talk to.'

'So although your mum has a busy social life, you worry that she might feel lonely without you.'

Imogen was stunned that he had recognised that she felt that way. She looked at him with renewed interest. 'Yes, she's a busy person and she doesn't really talk about her feelings. She doesn't get excited about much, and she and dad never really talk to each other.' Imogen sighed, 'I can't do much about it. Though it has made me determined to do something with my life. I don't know what, but I want to feel that I'm achieving something worthwhile.'

'I'm sure you will. I can see you've got the beauty, the brains and the determination.' Pete looked into her eyes. 'I admire your ambition'. His compliment seemed genuine and Imogen felt pleased, but she hesitated, thinking about the confused situation that she'd got herself in at Kent & Minster. She resolved then and there, to speak to Ian Fraser at some point to make her position clear. Remembering Pete's close links with them, she chose not to mention the company. The Bourguignon arrived at an opportune moment.

Light was beginning to fade and the fairy lights gave soft colour to everything on the table. A family of swans floated nearby and spotting them, Pete brought out a bag of food that he'd kept for them. The air was filled with the peeping of the fluffy cygnets.

They leant side by side over the edge of the boat to get a better look. 'I suppose you know they pair for life,' Pete commented, and Imogen wondered whether he was trying to indicate his own dependability in relationships. 'Appreciating nature is one of the advantages of living by water.' he said.

'But you don't live on this boat, do you?' Imogen said.

'No, I have a traditional narrow boat moored nearby. I left the family home when my mum decided to go into residential care. She's had M.S. for a long time and as a small boy I was her carer. My grandmother was around for a while, and she was great. She looked after us both, but after she died, it was just me and Mum. It meant that I missed some school and didn't take many exams. I lost touch with people who had been friends when I was young. They all moved on, went to university or got careers.

Pete reached for Imogen's hand and squeezed it. She returned the squeeze and he leant in for a kiss. It seemed like a romantic film. She responded passionately. After several minutes they pulled apart having heard jeering shouts from the bank. Some young lads had pulled up their car and spotting the couple they started to catcall. 'Just a Mazda rotary sedan,' Pete commented. 'I aim to have a sports car –an Aston Martin or a Jag. I'm planning to drive past all those lads from school who did apprenticeships and went on to college and show them that I've made it. Is that something you want – a boyfriend with a good car?'

Imogen thought for a moment. 'Well I'm certainly looking for someone who's going places.'

This prompted Pete to tell her about his business interests. He told her that he had managed to gain a good reputation and become part of a trusted group of businessmen. He was able to offer entertainment to them and their clients. He talked of having a variety of rented premises in the city. All the money that he had made in the early days had been put into buying this boat, which had launched his entertainment empire. Imogen didn't bother to listen to all the details, she got the general idea. Pete's face lit up when he was talking about business and she was attracted to his energy.

'I suppose you noticed the girl that shouted over to me when we were leaving the pizza bar?' he suddenly faltered.

She frowned 'What err yes. . . '

'She is involved in the entertainment industry but nothing really to do with me. I don't really know her. Don't you worry about her.' Imogen looked at his expression to discern what his worry was on that score, but he was unreadable.

They retired to the well-lit lounge area. The riverside seemed almost black when viewed through the windows. Staff had left a Pavlova on the servery. They shared the dessert in comfort, with feet tucked under them, on the banquette seating.

'My mum would love to meet you. Will you come with me to visit her?' Pete said. Imogen was flattered to be asked and agreed to meet him on the following weekend.

At the end of the evening he held her arm along the gangway and they let themselves into the ticket office on the bank to phone a taxi for her journey home.

Chapter Eight

Imogen paused in front of the mahogany framed mirror to fluff up her hair after being out in the wind. Peter strode forward, familiar with the nursing home routine. He laid down a bunch of flowers on a spindly side-table to sign the visitors' book.

An assistant was crossing the hall, she smiled and called, 'I'll get your mother for you. She'll be pleased to see you'.

They sat in the conservatory. Pete felt like a cat presenting its owner with a newly caught mouse; he knew that meeting Imogen would make his mother happy.

Mrs Lawrence slowly fixed her gaze on Imogen. 'I'm so pleased to meet you dear. I've heard a lot about you.' She took the wrapped flowers from Imogen. 'It was good of you to come. And thank you for the beautiful flowers.' She turned a few more degrees to face Peter, 'Peter dear, could you get a vase for these?'

It was awkward when he had gone. There was a short silence. Imogen looked around 'It's sunny. Nice to have a conservatory, out of the wind'.

'Yes it's a good place to sit.' said Mrs Lawrence. 'Have you known Peter for long?' and not stopping for a reply she went on, 'He was a lovely little boy. He's so caring. So giving. I can hardly believe that he's all grown up and doing so well for himself now.'

Imogen recognised a mother's pride in her son but wasn't sure what to say in answer. At that moment Peter returned. They arranged blankets around Mrs Lawrence's legs for a trip around the gardens. They made it quick as it really was windy.

When they had settled her back down, Pete gave his mother's appearance a shrewd appraisal to check that they were looking after her properly. She never moaned and she was always keen to hear news. 'We've just had a date on the pleasure boat Mum. I got the staff to stay on and cook something just for us.'

'Oh that's nice.' Mrs Lawrence responded looking at Imogen, who then carried on the description of their evening together.

'Oh, it sounds lovely. And what do you do dear? Perhaps you can work for Peter's business?' Mrs Lawrence said.

'Oh I don't know about that Mum, never mix business with pleasure. Besides Imogen moves in the world of big business. I met her at a directors' party in an advertising agency.'

'Oh that's nice' she responded again, 'I know young girls like to have a good career behind them nowadays before they stop to have a family.' She smiled and nodded at them both. They instantly picked up her inference.

'Early days to be thinking that way,' Peter smiled at his mother, 'but who knows?' and he winked at Imogen.

The train journey home was a pleasure; they were together, they'd had a stamp of approval on their relationship and they had enjoyed the countryside. It was another world from the unrelenting brick and traffic of a city.

After seeing Imogen to the end of her road, Pete walked home whistling. He saw marriage material in her. He was expert at flirting with the 'birds' who used his river boat cruises but he needed to gently tame this little bird. He could imagine himself showing her off at corporate events and completing his image by having her beside him with her hair blowing in an open topped car.

His Mother was so thrilled to picture his future as a respectable husband and father. He was uncomfortable that he didn't fit her expectations, but he could make it happen. From that day on, he would live up to her ideals. Had anyone been in the vicinity they would have been surprised to see him suddenly punch the air and let out a whoop. He decided that he would phase out some of his shadier business ventures and concentrate on the side of business that would make his mum proud.

***

When Imogen pushed open the door to the house, she sensed that Tony had been waiting for her. She instantly felt an irrational guilt that perhaps she had been out while he was bored and would have liked company. One look at him banished that idea. His body was tense with a taut expression and ashen face. 'Have you talked to Anita?'

'No why?'

'She's gone. What did she say the last time you saw her?'

'I don't know. What do you mean she's gone?'

'I haven't seen her for a few days, and she hasn't paid her rent. So I let myself into the attic for a look…some of her stuff is still there, but most of the important things have gone,' he said, his voice speeding up.

Imogen followed him into his rooms. 'You think she's done a runner and she's trying to avoid paying you,' she asked indignantly.

'No, it's not that,' Tony said. 'I know her better than that. She would have just asked for longer to pay if she couldn't find the money. No I'm worried about her.'

Imogen was still in shock at the sudden turn of events. She could see that Tony needed her to stay level-headed as he was upset, but Anita had come to mean a lot to her too.

'You know, I haven't seen her either. Not since the last time we ate together - on Wednesday was it? I just thought she was busy with rehearsals.' Imogen sank down onto the sofa beside Tony, 'If she was going away, it's not like her to not tell us both.'

'I didn't notice anything out of the ordinary. Did she to seem OK to you?' Tony ran his hand through his hair. 'Should I tell the police? No they wouldn't listen, after all she's taken some things with her. They'd just say that she's chosen to go away, or even to do a flit without paying.'

Imogen laid her hand on Tony's slumped shoulder. 'Oh dear' was all she could think to say.

He let out a deep breath, 'You see, I was talking to her about my personal life. Now I'm worried that it's made her react badly. I'd hate to have caused this.'

'I don't know the details, and no,' Imogen shook her head quickly, 'I'm not going to ask you for details. But you're being hard on yourself. Anita felt at home here. I can't imagine that she'd have gone away because of anything that you said to her. You two are as close as family. We ought to make enquiries among her friends. I wish I'd asked her for more details. Does she have any family? She didn't mention any.'

'A mum, but she died a few years ago. I'm not sure about a father. I got the impression that he might have disappeared when she was a child.' Tony said, squaring his shoulders, 'Right, we know she had a boyfriend – Skipper. And we do know where she worked and the names of some people that she talked about.' He rummaged through a nearby drawer and pulled out a notebook and pen. 'How do we get in touch with Skipper? Let's write down everything we know: names, addresses.'

The plan was that they would each phone the workplace of the other to plead illness. So, hoping that no one from Kent & Minster spotted her, Imogen started detective work.

***

She felt out of her depth; she knew that Anita was part of an upcoming show and the theatre seemed an obvious place to start, but she had never considered visiting a stage door before. She wasn't sure what to expect, she had assumed that the door would be secretly tucked away, but it was directly off the pavement at the side of the theatre. The entrance was beside a stack of metal crowd control barriers leaning against the wall. She rang a doorbell and waited. After a long time a young man appeared and Imogen explained the situation. She felt that she was being severely scrutinised and hastily added a lot of additional information to prove that she was indeed a friend, not a fan.

Eventually he said, 'The Company are rehearsing at the moment. If you want her, I should try the rehearsal studios. You could see her in the break. It's in walking distance.' and he gave her directions.

She felt drained from the stress of talking her way into getting information, but gathered new resolve. The walk from inner city to the industrial outskirts allowed her time to think about life so far. She felt a little annoyed at Anita, after all she thought they were close, so why had Anita not confided in her housemates?

A double decker bus sped past and she wished that she'd thought to look up the route and the position of bus stops. On the way, she called at a newsagent for a can of drink and sat on the wall of a railway bridge to rest. It wasn't restful, as there was the rumble of trains beneath her and the rush of traffic behind her. An assortment of people walked the pavement behind and she felt strangely vulnerable, so she decided to move on.

Further on, new age hippy shops and alternative book shops had opened in the run down and cheaper streets of town. She lingered by shop windows to examine Indian saris, crystal balls, packets of joss sticks and mirrored wall hangings. High up on a side street she spotted a small sign for the studios. It was over a single door in an old brick factory building. A couple of young girls in denim were huddled together on the doorsteps. They watched her but made no comment as she picked her way past them.

Inside, she heard muffled piano music and thumps from the floor above. After mounting a narrow, dirt-edged staircase, she found herself confronting a group of hippies; long haired, in suede embroidered waistcoats and wide-flared trousers. They brought to mind musicals like Godspell. They were ranged around benches in the middle of the room and glanced at her with disinterest. Imogen made herself approach them and explained her mission to the man sitting nearest. He blew a stream of smoke through his nostrils and resting his fag on his knee said, 'Are you having a laugh? We are all big enough to look after ourselves here. So, one of the chicks is missing. It's a bloody nuisance. Where is she? Your guess is as good as mine.'

As she was turning to go, another guy who had been talking in a small group turned his head and drawled 'Hey - You could try her agent.'

'Oh thank you,' Imogen said, and hurried back down the stairs, almost falling at the bottom step.

Back at the house, she found Tony with a pile of papers and booklets strewn around him on the couch.

'You look a bit down – no luck? I'm looking for clues.' He gestured through the kitchen doorway to the percolator bubbling on the stove, 'How about a coffee?' Shaking her head, she sank down on the pouf in front of him and told him about the theatre crowd.

'Yes, the theatre agents should have been a lead. She keeps the phone number for her agents, Stan Morrison Associates, in this pile. I phoned them. They weren't at all interested - but after a lot of badgering they admitted that she hadn't turned up for a recent casting. They suggested I tried her at home,' he laughed ruefully. 'Well we know she's not here. But look, we've got an evening paper and a Yellow Pages here. We ought to work our way through and see if there are any clues.'

'You mean she might have made some notes in the margins.' Imogen said lifting the Yellow Pages onto her knee.

Chapter Nine

They found the train times to York scribbled down the side of a shopping list. Following a hunch, Imogen tracked down the number for the theatrical digs that Anita used. Mrs Thorpe, the landlady, had sounded particularly discomforted to be questioned by a stranger, but after some hesitation, she'd admitted that Anita was there. Imogen asked to speak to her but was told that Anita was out.

'If you're friend enough to travel all the way here, you can try visiting. I'm saying nowt more than that. It'll be up to her to decide whether she wants you here, love.'

They decided that they'd both go to York to see Anita that weekend. On the train they shared a Tupperware of sandwiches and watched the rural landscape rush by. Working together in a crisis had brought Imogen closer to Tony. She thought about his disclosure that he'd talked to Anita about something private. Had he had suggested a romantic connection and been rejected? No, it was probably something else. Tony and Anita were more like brother and sister and she felt a twinge of jealousy that they were so close.

And what was going on with Anita? She hadn't mentioned a job in York and it was unheard of for her to miss a casting or to miss rehearsals. Imogen had admired her for being able to bounce back after life's disappointments and now her heroine had fallen short. She gave a shiver. You never knew what difficulties people were facing. She wanted to be able to stand up and be counted on to help… if Anita wanted her support.

York station: a beautiful example of Victorian architecture but busy and noisy. They purchased a street plan at a kiosk and made their way to Mrs Thorpe's. There they were met by a tiny lady wearing a wrap-around overall with bias binding edges and front ties.

She gave them a quick grin and gestured 'Go on up.'

A smell of cigarettes, cooked cabbage and damp clothes hung over the stairs. As they made their way up them, Mrs Thorpe bellowed from below 'Anita, someone to see you'.

Anita had heard the warning. She couldn't quite take in what it meant. And then people on the stairs. Opening the door, she was astonished to find Tony and Imogen. Imogen in front was faced with Anita standing immobile holding a packet of biscuits in one hand. Her hand shot to her mouth and the biscuits went flying. It provided a distraction as they helped to scoop them up.

When they were finally settled, Imogen on the bed and Tony on the dressing table stool, Imogen asked, 'What're you doing up here?' just as Anita said, 'How did you find me?'

After a pause, 'We've been so worried about you' Imogen said.

'I wish you could have told us something.' Tony added.

Indecision flitted across Anita's face, 'I'm sorry. I had a problem. I just didn't know what to do, but I didn't want to talk to you about it. I didn't want you to think badly of me.'

She sunk to the bed beside Imogen and hung her head, her long blonde hair covering most of her face. Then she glanced quickly at both of them.

'It's been awful - I thought I was going round the bend with worry. Since Mum died, I've sorted things out myself rather than turning to other people. In the end, this seemed a good bolt hole. Mrs Thorpe is the nearest thing that I've got to a mother, and she's been ever so good.'

They both leaned in so close that they could almost touch her. Imogen glanced at Tony, he had a pained look and she felt the same. How awful that Anita had had to face her problems alone.

There was a silence while Anita took a deep breath. 'I know you care about me, but I've got myself into a mess. It started when I realised my period was late,' she gave a rueful smile in Tony's direction, 'sorry Tony.'

'I panicked. I saw an advert in the paper for the British Pregnancy Advisory Service and took the number down. When I visited them, they explained that testing would take some time as they have to test on rabbits. When I went back, I had a difficult interview with them as I realised that they're an agency for abortion. I wasn't sure how I felt about that. I needed time to think it through.'

'I had no idea. You seemed OK.' Imogen felt almost physical pain at the shock of this admission.

Anita flicked her hair back. 'I'm good at seeming OK, but underneath I was in turmoil. You see, I'm not sure of Skipper. I haven't known him for long. I worked out that if I told him, he might 'do the right thing' and offer to marry me, but I can't see myself as a wife and mother. I'd be forever in his shadow. It wouldn't be the right thing for me.

'And if I didn't marry him and I had the baby, I wouldn't be able to go on tour. It'd be goodbye to my acting career. I've pictured myself having no money and my child would be known as the child of a single parent family. I know all about that – it's happened to me.'

'You poor thing, so you had an abortion.'

'No, I don't think I can go ahead with it. I contacted Social Services. The Social worker talked about Mother and Baby homes and giving up the baby for adoption. I can't bear that either,' she wrung her hands and screwed up her face 'anyway, I visited one near here. It's just an ordinary suburban house - not all that scary. The Matron showed me round. There were a group of pregnant women all sitting at the dining table smoking. They just turned and looked at me. I can't face joining them – but I think soon I'm going to have to.' Anita began to sob, and Imogen put her arm around her shoulder. 'I've racked my brains for a way that I can carry on as an actress and bring up a child. I wish my mum were here.'

Tony's eyes met Anita's and he looked full of sympathy. He glanced around like a caged animal, 'Come on, you need to get out of this room. Let's go for a walk and find a café.'

While they were trying to walk along the narrow pavements of York, three abreast, Imogen explained how they had found Anita. They turned into a tiny corner café and sat at a table in the window. They ordered coffee, although Anita admitted that she couldn't stomach coffee anymore and so she sipped a glass of orange juice.

Tony laid his hands face down on the table. 'I've been thinking. I don't want you to have to live without your baby or go through an abortion, if you don't want to.'

'Thank you.' Anita said.

'I'm prepared to step in and support you. No,' he said putting his hand up as she opened her mouth to answer, 'I don't mean I'm going to marry you and be the father. I mean that if Imogen and I are there for you...if we really commit to parenting with you, you will be able to have a life and it will be much better for the baby too.'

He turned towards Imogen, 'I'm not sure what you think?' This was all new to Imogen and she wasn't sure what to say.

'What? I can't ask you to do that.' Anita said.

'Look, from my point of view, I hate working in accounts. I'll give up my job and be at home. That way you've always got back up. I've got some savings so I can do without an income

for a short while. Maybe I'll start some work based at home -
so I'll help out financially as well.'

Anita began to look interested. 'I think I'd need to find out
whether Skipper can support me and the baby too.'

'Of course. And if you do want to marry him in the end,
I'll understand. But if you don't – then don't think you'll be on
your own.' Tony said covering her hand with his.

Imogen felt that this was a time to pull together and she
admired Tony's resolve, 'And of course I will be there for you
too.' She said.

There was lots to talk about. They wanted to get back and
Anita agreed to come home with them. They stayed on in the
café while Anita went back to talk to Mrs. Thorpe and to pack
her things.

'I'm thinking about all this. It'll be wonderful to be able
to support Anita…whatever she wants to do. The trouble is
you know, we can't foresee what might happen in any of our
futures. It's such a big commitment.' Imogen said.

Tony sighed. 'I know' he said and smiled at her, 'you may
want to get married and have children of your own. But let's
worry about that when it happens. Anita might get together with
Skipper or find someone else one day. But I can honestly…
well, I can honestly say that I can build my future around Anita
and her child – if she wants me to.'

'It's hard to get my head round it,' Imogen said shaking
her head and then Anita reappeared.

Chapter Ten

Peter, walking around in a bubble, was unaware of the few shoppers in the street. A nearby mother cut into his thoughts, snapping 'Keep up, will you,' to a child dangling from her hand. He had an irrational feeling that she ought to realise that something momentous had happened to him.

Only a few days ago, he'd been in high spirits as he thought about Imogen. He had been busy at work. He'd swung round the door of the ticket shed where the new temp, Jonathan, was taking a telephone booking. Jonathan caught his eye and gestured for him to sit for a moment.

When the call was over Jonathan said, ''Bout a quarter of an hour ago, we got a phone message. They called from your Mum's nursing home. They said not to worry, but I should get down there, if I were you.'

Pete scooted down to the station straight away. He had spent most of his time beside his mother's bed since then. Sleeping in a chair overnight, he had woken fitfully and listened to her ragged breathing. Karen, one of the care assistants on shift, had offered him a sympathetic smile and made sure that he had sandwiches from the kitchen. His eyes had filled with tears.

Mum didn't have the energy to speak. She knew he was there, and they squeezed each other's hands. He put everything else out of his head and tried to find encouraging things to say to her.

He thought back to his childhood. She had always seemed to be old and using a wheelchair, but she must have actually been quite young then. It'd been the two of them against the world. Understanding how to keep her feeling happy had made him the person that he was now.

When he was in Senior School he had begun to feel different. Kids he'd played with in school were now bunking off together at lunchtime and meeting up in the evenings. He'd been left out of all that. Lads around him were talking about apprenticeships and Graham who lived a few doors away was going to technical college. Pete had missed a lot of school and he felt hopeless about his own future.

Eventually even Graham dropped away. One evening just before the mock exams, Pete had been nipping to the chip shop. He'd savoured the chance to be out in the street. Crazy that the chip shop was the highlight of his life at that time, he thought. It had been raining and the reflections of the streetlamps shimmered on wet pavements. The shop windows were all lit and there were a few people still splashing off buses and making their way home. Peter remembered coming close to the chip shop and then spotting a group of lads ranged around a car; some of them in silhouette in the headlamps. At first, he couldn't make it out but it was a little Triumph Herald and he recognised some of the lads' faces. Someone was sitting in it bleeping the throttle. Pete decided to slip past unnoticed.

Greeted by the warm chip smell, gleaming metal counter and Ted the shop owner he should have been slavering with anticipation of a treat but he felt uncomfortable ('discombobulated' as mum would say, he thought affectionately.) Tucking the newspaper package in his jacket to stay warm he shot out into the street again. They were nearer to the shop front now. Surely some of them would know him. Pete looked straight at them. Some took a glance then looked away. Then there was Graham on the edge of the crowd - he'd been grinning at something. He dipped his head at Pete, said in a low voice 'Alright mate' and turned back to the group. It had felt like a body blow.

He had walked home that evening knowing that he would always be an outsider. His stomach felt heavy and then it began to build up into an anger that he could hardly swallow. That was the first time that Pete became determined to show them.

And so I will show them he thought. I am a success now – who needs exams? He had looked at Mum and despite his affection for her, his mind was on the day when he would drive past the lot of them in an Aston Martin and watch them wonder where he had come from.

Mum had felt guilty at asking him to be a carer. He was glad that he'd been able to bring Imogen to see her; then his Mum could feel reassured that he could go on to be happy. He had hoped that one day Mum would meet his children.

Pete left her side to find the staff room. He needed to know what was going on. A nurse in a darker uniform left the huddle and took him into the office. So Mum had developed pneumonia. They were hoping that different antibiotics may work.

Mum succumbed to the illness. The treatment hadn't worked, had it? So his dreams of being able to show Mum what he'd made of himself had come to nothing.

As he'd grown up he had become hardened but despite that he couldn't stop the tears. He waved away the staff – even when Karen came on shift.

They'd offered him his mother's things in three black plastic bags. He was furious, both that her life had been reduced to some bags and at the thought of having to carry them away with him. Now he had a funeral to arrange. He had slammed out of the nursing home, brooded on the station platform and paced the streets nearer home.

He shook himself back into the reality of the street. 'Damn, damn, damn', he hit a phone box, then regretted it. While clutching his throbbing fist he wondered about making a call. He could phone Imogen at work. He didn't have any change, but he could make a reverse charge call. No, bad idea. A surge of anger hit him even harder. Now he didn't know where he was going, or why he was doing anything.

He headed into a familiar part of town. He didn't want Imogen to see him like this, but there were women who worked for him who may offer some comfort. Head down, fists clenched, he dared anyone to get in his way. This was the moment to buy that sports car. He pictured driving past the technical college, the local factories and pubs. It would be intensely satisfying to make eye contact with those young men stuck in their boring careers.

Chapter Eleven

Despite Imogen's relationship with Pete being relatively new, she allowed herself to dream of a future with him.

She wasn't sure how that would fit with supporting Anita and the baby. Besides, she hadn't had much to do with babies and she was apprehensive about an uncharted change in her life. But she did like the idea of seeing Anita and Tony as her new family. At least for now, they were an important part of her life.

They had begun to make plans. They gathered around the dining table in Tony's room. Anita had made a list of the baby equipment they would need. Imogen poured through the classified adverts in local papers and then they used Tony's 'phone to contact advertisers.

'Coffee?' Anita offered, getting up with an exaggerated pregnant woman's slowness, 'I think our throats are getting dry.'

While the coffee brewed Anita said, 'Skipper usually contacts me at the theatre. I should think he'll be wondering where I am. Now we're sure of our plans, I think I ought to tell him about the pregnancy.'

'Yes, it's only fair,' Imogen tilted her head slightly, 'but what if he wants to be involved as a father?'

'That would be perfect, as long as he doesn't expect me to do the domestic bit. I'd like him to meet you, as you're going to be part of the baby's life.' Anita said. 'I need to find out what he thinks. You know, I'm a bit scared of how he's going to react. He seemed a bit unpredictable at times… could you come with me Imogen?'

'Of course,' Imogen nodded.

Imogen would be keen to meet Skipper and to form her own opinion of him. She felt protective of Anita; like the sister she had never had. And taking an interest in Anita's life took her mind off the nagging worry about what to do at Kent & Minster.

Chapter Twelve

The day was overcast. Anita led Imogen down steps under a road bridge onto the canal bank and then they walked. The canal water looked black, reflecting dark, abandoned warehouses along its banks. Imogen was keen to see Anita's boyfriend, but worried about the outcome of the meeting. She wanted to be supportive, so she didn't draw Anita's attention to the depressing surroundings.

While walking along the towpath they discussed tactics. 'Would you like me to leave once you know that Skipper is OK with it, so that you can have a private talk?'

'No, I don't think so. Well…I don't know. If I do, shall we have a secret sign?' Anita suggested. 'We're nearly there. The moorings are just after the built-up area.' Sure enough, the towpath followed the back of residential gardens edged by hedgerows. Tufts of grass and dandelions appeared along the route. People were working on some of the boats but they ignored walkers on the towpath. They stopped beside a narrowboat, smartly painted in green, decorated with traditional flowers and gold scrolls.

'Here it is.' Anita waved with a flourish as though it were her boat. 'I'll hop on and knock.' She confidently held onto the corner of the roof and stepped onto the stern. She knocked and called 'Skipper, I'm here – with a visitor.'

'Skipper!' she looked across at Imogen 'Maybe he's asleep or showering.' They gave him some time. He can't have failed to hear her and to feel the movement of the boat. Imogen was struck by how quiet the area was, she could hear water lapping and bees buzzing. While they waited, her doubts increased but Anita seemed confidently at home there.

Eventually Anita said, 'I've got a key. I'll just go in and take a look.' Before Imogen could voice her doubts about entering Skipper's home, Anita had disappeared. 'It's OK, I'm sure he'll be back soon,' she called through the open door, 'Come on in and we'll wait.'

Ducking her head through the door and negotiating two small steps, Imogen was curious to see inside. Anita was already standing in the galley area filling a battered kettle from a thin spout by pressing a pump beside the sink.

'Make yourself at home, sit down' she gestured to a bench seat covered by a red tartan blanket. Imogen chose to stand and get her bearings. This was obviously a bachelor pad. There were discarded margarine cartons, a yellow cardboard Vesta curry packet lying on the side, and an array of socks hung from an 'A' frame dryer. She felt uncomfortable. The inwardly sloping walls either side of her head made her feel claustrophobic.

'I'm not sure about this. Don't put the kettle on for me. Something makes me feel uneasy about the place. I'm intruding.' She turned and emerged onto the deck again blinking in the brighter light. She was going to leap back onto the bank but as she looked up, she was amazed to see Pete standing a few feet away.

'Imogen.' he yelled in recognition, scratching his head. She stopped. At that moment Anita burst out of the door barrelling into her back. The space was barely big enough for the two of them.

Pete did a double-take and Anita glanced nervously from one to the other of them. She started speaking 'Thank goodness - we were looking for you. I've brought my friend to see you.'

Imogen came to the realisation that this must be Skipper. Pete looked stunned. 'Yes, we already know each other, but I wasn't expecting to see you.' he said, his eyes flicking between the two of them.

'I've meant to be in touch. I've just lost my mother.' He looked down, 'It's taken up all my thoughts - it's been bad.'

Anita was anxious to get her message across and failed to notice that he was actually addressing Imogen. She jumped off the boat and stood on the rough grass in front of him.

She was near enough to lower her voice to a normal level 'I've got some news for you. I thought you should know.' Pete didn't respond.

'I'm going to have a baby.'

Then realisation of what he had said reached her. She stopped and took a step backwards. 'Hang on... You know her?' Anita looking wildly at Imogen. Imogen felt a stab of pain in her stomach at the realisation that they had both been taken in by this man. She looked at Anita with compassion, but she had no idea what to say and wondered how Pete was going to deal with the situation.

Pete looked at Imogen and addressed her 'You know me, you know I've got future plans.' Then he closed the gap between himself and Anita and said 'Crazy bitch. You're nothing to do with me.'

Anita looked crushed. Imogen stepped in 'So you're Skipper' she sneered at him. 'Don't think we want anything out of you. You're despicable. Anita has come to tell you about her pregnancy – and this is how you treat her.'

His jaw stuck out and he whipped round to Anita again, 'I've no intention of supporting you. I don't get into messy situations. Have you found out about abortions?'

'Never mind,' Anita spoke quietly concentrating on the side of the boat rather than on him, 'I've worked out what I'm going to do. I am going to have the child. I'm not on my own. Imogen and my housemate Tony are with me all the way.' she said raising her head defiantly.

'You'll be tapping me for dough.' he said.

'You ought to pay something, but no we can manage.'

'Don't you understand, you stupid girl. I don't want a child in my way! I'm going places round here.'

Anita began to quietly cry. Which seemed to infuriate Pete further. He clenched his fists and gritted his teeth, 'Just get rid of it. You think you and your mates are going to take it on. I know that it won't be the last I hear from you.'

'Skipper. . . ' Anita extended her arms towards him.

'No! Don't think I'm going to let this happen. You've no idea what I can do. He faltered 'And Imogen,' his gaze softened as he looked at Imogen, 'well, Imogen has a future with me.'

Time had stood still for Imogen, she felt like an onlooker to the unfolding drama, but this galvanised her. It was astounding that he could believe he could split himself: treating Anita so badly and hoping at the same time to keep Imogen's respect. She strode up to join Anita. 'I've got no future with you.' she said 'We're sticking together. Don't you worry. We'll be OK.' Anita shrank behind her.

Pete became aware that others on the canal bank were taking notice. 'You're tangling with the wrong person here. Get out of my way.' and waving them away like annoying insects, he jumped on board and disappeared inside his boat.

They hurried back towards the road, each occupied with her own thoughts. Imogen was marvelling that this could be the Pete that she'd been close to. On the passenger boat he had seemed so gentle. They'd fed the swans and she relived their kiss. She realised that he'd just said that he'd lost his mother and that must have been terrible for him, but then it dawned on her all over again that he wasn't who she had thought he was. She was angry that he could be such a user and annoyed that she'd let herself be duped by him. Well if she had been misled, that was nothing to the rejection that Anita had suffered.

She wondered if Anita fully realised that 'Skipper' was Pete.

'He's quite a disappointment.' she said softly and they went on to compare their experiences of him. It seemed that part of Anita was also reluctant to let go of the supportive Pete that she'd known.

'Maybe he'll change his mind when he has time to think about it.' Anita said, but she turned her head and wouldn't look at Imogen.

Chapter Thirteen

Pete would never miss a business meeting but now he had. He needed time to sort this out. How had everything gone wrong? There had to be a way to get it back on track.

He was an information hoarder and he knew that information was power. A habitual method was to collect gossip. He hadn't used the library in years, but now he went to look at the Electoral Roll. He sat at a heavy table in the Reading Room only briefly noting the elderly men already ensconced with newspapers. It took minutes to look up Imogen's street and to find their names: Anthony Kirkham, Imogen Best and Anita Tomalty. He needed a hold over one of them: a debt, a secret, some way he could persuade them to his way of thinking. Pete was best placed to find out these things. He knew a lot of people and he could ask around. He needed to know what Tony looked like, so he'd keep an eye out. It wouldn't be hard to find out where he worked, where he played… It was important to put time and resources into making sure that his own interests were protected.

What he hadn't realised was that Tony was also thinking about him. Some days later he'd visited the ticket office.

'Morning' Jonathan turned around quickly, 'Someone visited first thing this morning. He was asking the crew who you were and they sent him in to see me.'

'What did he want?'

'Seemed OK. Said he was an accountant, so I thought something to do with the business. I said you'd be down at Hanson Street today, if he wanted you. I hope that was OK?'

'Never do that again.' Pete said through gritted teeth. 'You don't just send people to see me without asking first. What did he look like?'

The description Jonathan gave, and the profession fitted Anita's Tony.

'See you, then.' Pete said - they'd be having words later. He went straight down to Hansen Street. The double-fronted shop was boarded up with a small sign indicating Pete's business. He went down an arched passageway to the side and then through a yellow painted front door. There was the familiar face of Betty, the Hansen Street receptionist. She had known Pete for years and her tightly permed Rita Hayworth hair style and deep red lipstick never altered.

'Hiya love,' she greeted him.

He nodded at her and said, 'How's it going? Everyone OK here?'

'Can't grumble.' She nodded over to the girls. They spotted him and crowded round. There was a small space left for him on one of the settees up against the teak lined walls. He enjoyed being centre of attention when he visited. He was so used to seeing them in their skimpy playsuits that he didn't notice anymore. One offered to get him a cuppa tea.

'Thanks Tina, two sugars… you remember.' He had a soft spot for Tina. She had been with him a fair while and you could have a half decent conversation with her. He always made a point of chatting to each girl. It was important to keep up morale and he prided himself on being a good, fair boss. He let Betty take control of any shirkers. He wanted to come over as the soft one - until there was real trouble.

After a final word with Betty, time to make money. 'I'll be in the back in the office. I'm expecting a Tony Kirkham. Check his name and send him through, will you?'

He'd sorted through the post and checked on the safe before he overheard Tony making enquiries with Betty. She brought him to the door.

'Er you don't know me but…' Tony said.

Pete advanced towards him in two strides. 'Think I do. Tony, good of you to pay me a visit. We can have a talk man to man.' He enjoyed having the advantage in this exchange.

Tony hesitated. He seemed reluctant to move any farther into the office. 'It's taken some tracking you down, but I wanted to come to meet you. I'm Anita's friend and I wanted to make sure that everything was clear.' he said.

'Come in, sit down,' Pete said. 'I'm sure we can get everything clear.'

Tony sat in the wooden chair in front of Pete's desk and cleared his throat. 'Anita and Imogen have both been upset by the way you treated them.'

Pete hoped to keep Imogen separate in this current situation. He was originally pursuing her as an attractive accessory on his arm, but now she had got under his skin.

'Now, c'mon,' he said, 'there's two separate issues here. I wouldn't hurt Imogen for the world. It's just a pity she got caught up in… well we've got something going, Imogen and me.'

'Really, well what about your future child?' Tony's chin jutted out and he looked Pete in the eye.

'Look mate. Anita got it all wrong. We were having a good time. It happens. A lot of girls I meet, they work for me here or even do escort work with businesspeople. Anita didn't have a steady income. I could've helped her out.'

'She didn't even know about this business though, did she?' Tony asked looking around the office. 'Look, I'll get to the point. I heard what happened when they visited you. It sounded as though you'd been pretty shocked when you heard the news for the first time. So I wanted to talk, once you'd had some time to think. I must admit…I wasn't expecting to be talking here.'

'So you decided you were going to take on the problem – tracked me down.'

'The girls told me about the boat business, obviously. They're too upset to want to go another round with you, so it was up to me. Look – it's not about money. I just wanted to give you a chance to be part of your baby's life.'

Pete tipped back on two legs of his chair and steepled his hands. 'Aah I see, you wanted to open up lines of communication.'

'Yes.'

Pete crashed his chair onto all four legs again. 'Well mate. If I wanted to open up communication, I could do it for myself. But as you're here – get this straight. I don't want a baby hanging about. I don't want to be contacted about a baby – at all, get it? She won't manage by herself.'

'That's what you think, but we are going to step in, Imogen and me. We're going to support Anita and look after the baby when she has to work.'

'Why can't you keep out of other people's business? You need to just step back from this. I'm warning you. You. . .' he sneered 'You aren't fit to look after a baby. I know all about you now Mr Tony Kirkham.' Pete's eyes gleamed. 'Let's just say, associates of mine have seen you in and out of certain back street clubs, you're well known among the queers.'

Tony looked stunned. 'What, what d'you mean?'

'I suggest that if you don't want me to drop a word in a few ears, you'll stop meddling. You've got a job in a respectable firm. I'm sure you want to protect your reputation. So sort out Anita. You need make sure she gets rid of it.'

'You realise I could also drop the word in a few ears about your seedy businesses.' Tony countered.

'Could you indeed?' Pete said. 'I think you'll find some people know and yet don't know, if you get my meaning. And you'd be publicising Anita's pregnancy too. Would she thank you for that?'

Pete got up from his desk and walked around to stand next to Tony's chair. 'You can go now. If I'm bothered again, you'll regret it – know what I mean?'

He prodded Tony on the shoulder with his forefinger. Tony got up quickly, 'I see there's no point in staying any longer.' He made for the door, out past Betty, through the door with the spyhole and down the passageway.

The encounter hadn't lasted long, but the world had changed for Tony. He felt almost incapable of walking. He had always been able to keep his private life private. Should he talk to Anita and Imogen?

CHAPTER FOURTEEN

Imogen and Anita were loaded down with shopping bags when they caught sight of Tony on the far side of the garden. He was hacking at a lilac tree. His arms were scratched and bleeding and he had twigs in his hair.

'You've developed a hate for shrubbery?' Anita called across. Tony turned looking agitated and said, 'I'll follow you in.'

They had piled the bags on the table and were stashing tins in cupboards when he appeared. He looked like a doctor about to deliver a verdict.

'C'mon what's eating you? Anita asked. 'Sit down and let's talk.'

They sat on the sofa while Tony strode the room. He threw his grubby gardening gloves on the coffee table. 'Well, I tracked down your Pete.' He described finding the massage parlour and Pete's refusal to accept his baby.

'Hard to believe.' Imogen said, 'This is appalling.' She glanced at Anita, 'Never mind, we don't need him.'

'That's not all. He's been doing his homework.' Tony said. Imogen was alarmed to see him drop to his knees on the floor in front of the sofa where they were sitting. 'He's planning to make life difficult for me too.' He said. He looked stricken and stretched his arms out to encompass them both in a group hug, hiding his face from view. Imogen was taken aback, but made a quick decision that she could cope with this level of closeness. It wasn't like Tony and it worried her.

'What do you mean?' Anita said.

'He's absolutely determined to take control. He's threatened to expose me, if I don't persuade you to have an abortion… or have the baby adopted, I suppose.' Tony said to Anita. 'He's found out - that I go to gay clubs. I know you didn't tell him Anita. He's been snooping around and of course his 'business interests' are in that area.' He raked his fingers through his hair.

Imogen was temporarily stunned. What were the implications of this? 'At least it isn't illegal any more' she said.

'Could he do you harm?' Anita said.

'Physically, I don't think he would. But by spreading news about me…

I should think so. People at work wouldn't be positive.' he said grimly. 'I don't imagine that I'd stand any chance of promotion. I hope friends would stick by me, but some people could get threatening about it.'

'If only we hadn't gone to see him. I'm sorry I've brought this on you both.' Anita said looking close to tears.

'Oh, but we had no idea what would happen,' Imogen said.

'Let me get you both coffee and cake,' Anita got up and made for the kitchen.

Tony turned to Imogen, 'It's not just me. Once he talks, I wonder if other gay men may be at risk. Pete could be dangerous. Somehow, I need to make sure I'm out of his way.' He gnawed on his fingernails.

Imogen was absorbed in thinking about how their worlds had been thrown into the air and shaken. The question was not only how to soothe the hurt but how they were going to survive in the future.

'We need to find the courage to stand up to him. We can't let him win.' She said.

'You know, you're right. If I 'come out' to people myself, he can't hold it over me. It's going to be difficult. I might lose some friends. I could be the butt of gossip, but I was planning to leave work for the baby's sake anyway, so that will get me out of the firing line.'

Imogen grinned at him. She was thinking of a new way that they could take control of their own destinies. After all, her own career was already threatened and rising in the corporate world was a minefield for women.

Once Anita had handed mugs around, Imogen decided to test her idea out on them. She worried that they'd think it was a whim, but she really thought it had a chance.

'Look there's something I'd like to ask you,' she said in a rush, 'Since I've had problems at work, I've been thinking about starting a new business. One of my own ... or even of our own? Could we work together on a hotel or a bistro?'

Anita stopped with her mug halfway to her lips, 'You're full of surprises!'

'Yes, that came out of the blue.' Tony looked at her and smiled.

'Between us we have the skills. It would mean that we could work flexibly around childcare. We wouldn't be so reliant on other people's judgements. We could do our own thing.' Imogen added.

Tony reached to grab a pad of lined paper from his briefcase beside the sofa. 'Thanks for being so supportive guys. I'm feeling hopeful already. If I'm at home, I can work on the start-up stage. Let's work on a Business Plan.'

Imogen was amazed at the speed that they had taken up her idea and begun to look at the practicalities.

'I think a bistro, as you are good at cooking, Tony,' said Anita.

'Yes, but I'm an accountant. I wouldn't be doing the cooking,' Tony said. 'Let's consider every aspect. I've got money to invest and I could mortgage this place, but it needs to be thought through. We need to look at what is already here and at the right location for a bistro or hotel'

'Of course, we could start a theatrical digs.' Imogen thought of recently seeing digs in York.

'Not enough money in it. We want something upmarket. How about something that includes a cabaret – Anita? That would interest you?'

Anita's eyes lit up. They were full of optimism and excitement at limitless possibilities. 'It looks like this might be an answer for us.'

Chapter Fifteen

All three housemates now spent their evenings chattering about the future and planning the practicalities of it. Tony brought home a lined accounts book and talked them through costings and sales projections. They used weekends to scan estate agents' windows for suitable business properties. It came down to size and location: they were shown an extended 1930s suburban house which was too small and badly designed, a Victorian Gothic red brick building with fifty five rooms which seemed out of their reach, and an elegant white painted villa with large grounds which needed converting into a hotel. It was a chance to test out their decision-making process and how they collaborated together. They learned to play to each other's strengths and their bond grew.

Imogen diligently arrived daily at Kent & Minster, but she saw it as a short-term job now. She wasn't making an effort with the group, so she allowed herself to revert to being reserved. Judith had initiated an uneasy detente by offering a friendly smile when she passed her some work, but Imogen was no longer involved in Judith and Clare's lunchtime trips.

She gathered her newfound courage and asked to speak to Ian Fraser. It was startling how quickly she received the summons to his office – he must have been waiting to hear from her.

She stood just within the doorway of his office. 'I'm sorry.' She faltered, 'I didn't want to tell you this, but I don't think I can work for you against your competitors. Of course, I was flattered to be asked, but I just don't feel that it's me.' She decided that she wouldn't mention Clare and Judith or blackmail at all.

'I'm disappointed. You're making a big mistake by throwing up this chance. I don't think we were wrong in our evaluation of you – you were capable of doing it, you know. Well, I'm sorry,' he shook his head. His expression looked a lot less kindly than his words. 'We won't stand in your way and you'll always get a good reference from me. Good luck.' he said waving her to the door.

Of all the office staff, Imogen valued her connection with Lynette and Margaret. She recognised that Lynette had been a solid friend to her and that she would miss her when she left. Imogen decided to invite Lynette to join her for lunch in a department store café.

They were lucky to grab a table so Lynette sat down to keep it, while Imogen queued for sandwiches and drinks. As Imogen deposited lunch for both of them on the table and stashed the tray beside her seat, Lynette said, 'Oh thanks. And, well thanks for inviting me. I thought you went out at lunchtime with Clare and Judith quite a bit.'

'Yes, but things changed… I spoke to you before about working for Mr Fraser. You see, they work for him and I'm not going to.'

Lynette looked down and said 'mm.' There was a lot she didn't understand but she didn't ask more. 'You OK? You've been quieter lately.'

'Yes it's been on my mind. But I went to discuss it with him this morning. I'd been getting stressed as I couldn't decide what to do about it. So I feel a lot better now. And Lynette, I wanted to let you know that I'll be leaving.'

'Oh no, not you too.' Lynette frowned and reached for a napkin to wipe up spilled coffee on the Formica tabletop.

Imogen glanced around to check whether they could be overheard. There was a general hubbub in the café. She went on to explain that their boss was a hard man under all his charm. 'He would probably make it difficult for me at work now. I certainly wouldn't get the interesting jobs to do. He didn't say anything intimidating to me, but somehow I felt a bit scared. Silly I know.' She added quickly.

'That's too bad. Don't get me wrong. With your shorthand and typing I'm sure you'll get another job easily, it's just I'll miss you.'

'I know… I'll miss you too.' Imogen said. 'We must keep in touch.' People always said that, but they seldom did. However, there was a genuine attachment with Lynette. It was more than being able to gossip about work and she hoped that they would stay in touch. They carried on to talk about their hopes for the future. Lynette confided that she thought there was probably an unspoken prejudice against black people at the agency as she never seemed to be the one to get opportunities for different work. She was looking into correspondence courses with a view to changing her career. Imogen was annoyed on her behalf as she guessed that she was probably right, but she felt pleased that Lynette hadn't let it hold her back. In turn Imogen told her about the hotel. It was the first time that she had told any outsider about their plans and it made them seem more real.

She'd be able to invite Lynette to cocktails in her own hotel bar and show her around a hotel dining room with wall lights and crisp white tablecloths. A wistfulness came over Imogen. She hoped that it would all work out. She would do everything in her power to make it happen.

Lynette broke into her thoughts. She looked at her watch, 'Oops, we need to do a fast walk back to work.'

Being a few minutes late back from lunch would not ordinarily be a problem and so the girls weren't too anxious. They walked quickly, but with sideways glances at shop windows. Lynette noticing berets, handbags and chunky jewellery, Imogen now noticing wicker magazine racks, hat racks and umbrella stands. A few hundred yards from Kent & Minster Imogen stopped. A red sports car, top-down was just pulling out of the car park.

Pete had come to see Ian Fraser. He half hoped to catch Imogen in passing, but part of him was unsure of her reaction. Having failed to persuade Ian Fraser to come out for a spot of lunch he'd decided to take his new toy for a drive. He had yet to find anyone from his old school but there was always the chance that he may be seen by someone who mattered.

Recently Pete had been feeling empty inside. He'd been motivated to make his mum proud. Now that she had gone, he didn't even get a buzz from business success. He'd believed that Imogen would enhance his image, but now that she'd rejected him, he realised his feelings had been deeper than that.

Suddenly he became aware that Imogen was there. She was there, on the pavement to his right. Wearing a polka dot dress with a white collar, she embodied all that he believed a smart young woman should be. She was with someone he didn't recognise, but it was definitely her. He found himself holding his breath. He drew up to the curb, pulled on the handbrake and leapt over the door to get to her. Imogen would know what buying this car signified. He was keen for her be impressed and pleased for him. His face showed his excitement.

Imogen realised that he was aiming to get to her, and she hurried to the entrance, her companion keeping step. Just as they turned through the gate posts, she glanced over her shoulder and shot him a look filled with scorn. Pete's mouth remained open as though he'd been frozen while calling her, and his eyes filled with tears. He turned, his shoulders slumping and slowly opened the car door to drive away.

Chapter Sixteen

It had been pouring with rain all day. Water hitting the window at full force and running down the glass, a stream pouring from a breach in the guttering and gurgling down the drain. Imogen delighted in the fresh atmosphere and the drama of the storm. So much had been happening, that she instinctively felt it was time to spend a day taking stock. She indulged in reading and playing soothing music on the record player.

It was twilight at 9.30, she made cocoa and took it to bed. This was when the thoughts came rushing in and she twitched and shifted under the covers. She must have slept, because the next thing she knew she had leapt off the mattress and taken two steps across the floor, her heart pounding. The neighbourhood was quiet. The rain was over, and moonlight flooded the floor casting light and shade over tufts of carpet. There was a shuffling noise outside her door; she quietly eased it open.

'Oh hello,' whispered Anita in the process of carrying a bowl of cereal towards the stairs.

'Hello – want to come in?' Imogen spoke softly.

Anita herself, hadn't been trying to sleep. She was still dressed in one of her new Mothercare smocks. The baby bump got in the way of sleep so she avoided going to bed until she couldn't stay awake any longer.

Once inside, Anita raised her voice to a normal level. 'Can't sleep?'

Imogen switched on a table light. 'A bit lonely. Coming to terms with what Pete did – and he's done it to all of us.'

Anita sat crossed-legged on the big armchair spooning cereal and milk and nodded. 'What seemed like the perfect boyfriend - just gone. We need to remember, he wasn't a perfect boyfriend. There must have been signs of what he was like – perhaps I blocked them out.'

'You know, he took me on a visit to his mum. I thought he was wonderful with her, and the staff seemed to love him. Huh, we know he could show people the side that he wanted them to see.' Imogen said. She was conscious that this was the father of Anita's child, 'I'm sorry that I was 'the other woman'.'

'Not your fault… I should have gone and got on the pill. What a fool, I didn't want to face the family planning clinic. Now I'm going to be known as an unmarried mother. People'll cross the street to avoid me. I'll never get a boyfriend now.' She put her bowl down on the floor and laughed to relieve the tension, 'And now I'm going to get fat!'

'True friends won't turn against you. Have you got any family?'

'Yes I've got a little sister in America, I never hear from her, and quite a few aunts and uncles in Ireland. I'm afraid I know their views on premarital sex.' she said.

'I think we need to go and buy you a ring. That'll help.'

'It will when I'm out and about with a pram. Though it would get complicated if we let people think that Tony's the father. Thankfully, theatre people aren't judgemental…'

'And being hotel proprietors will mean we can work out our own lifestyles. Even that's stressful at the moment for me.' Imogen threw up her hands 'It's as though my life has suddenly veered off course. Mum and Dad always said "Get a steady job and settle down. You know, "don't sit on a cold step you'll get a chill in your kidneys" "Never a borrower or a lender be", "Wear a coat, you'll catch cold." And when I left home, I knew they thought "you'll come to a bad end." So I saw my future mapped out: falling in love and then becoming a housewife with two children, living in a nice house. Don't get me wrong, what we're doing is exciting – really exciting. But it's a risk. I'm feeling jittery at the moment.'

Anita gave her a squeeze 'Not such a risk though – getting tied up with an accountant!'

At that moment, they heard the front door. They hadn't realised that Tony was out, but now he was arriving home. They listened as he moved into his own rooms. Since Pete's accusations they both conjectured about where he'd been.

'It was a surprise, hearing about Tony. I hadn't even known of anyone being homosexual before.' Imogen said.

'It's not unusual in the theatre. Has it bothered you?'

'I'm still getting used to the idea. I don't know anything about it. He didn't seem girly to me.'

'No, he doesn't need to be, y'know'.

'And I wonder what it means for us. But he's still the Tony that we know, isn't he? He's lovely…and partly…well, I feel sad for him. He'll never have a normal life.'

'A pity he'd had to go to seedy areas of town,' Anita said 'but it is harder for Tony to find love. It's driven underground. Have you heard - things are getting more open? A few years ago there was a march through London, started by activists, and it seems to have carried on. People are saying ''we aren't prepared to hide anymore." so perhaps it'll all be OK.'

'And he's our Tony. We'll stand up for him.' said Imogen.

'That's the spirit.'

Anita smiled and glanced at the moonlit leaves through the window. 'It feels peaceful tonight, as though nothing can hurt us. I love the moon. She's feminine, watching over us. I'm thinking of baby names. Diana is of the moon.'

'She was a Roman Goddess' said Imogen.

'Yes I'm thinking of mythical names and heroes. Helen too, and for a boy – Hector or Zeus?'

'Apollo, Jupiter,' Imogen laughed.

'Well maybe James for a boy. But I think this is Diana,' Anita patted her bump. 'It won't be long now. But I am worrying about the hospital and the birth.'

'Would you like me to be with you?'

'Oh, thank you. That means a lot to me. Soon I'll need to get a case packed ready. It hasn't seemed real until now. But there's actually going to be a baby in this house. I worry about what sort of a parent I'll be too.'

'What was your own childhood like?'

'Mum was always busy trying to work and look after us. She got no help at all from our Irish relatives. She felt like an outsider and I felt their rejection too. Often she just cried with tiredness and didn't have time to talk to me. I hope I can shelter my baby from that feeling. But then, I knew she loved me, she gave up so much of her life for her children.'

'That's it. It takes love and understanding. You've got that. You'll make a fantastic mother.' Imogen said. 'At least you'll have something to love,' she added casting her eyes down with a tiny smile at the corners of her lips.

Anita touched Imogen's shoulder and looked her in the eyes, 'We'll all love the baby.' she said emphatically.

Chapter Seventeen

The ward's doors swung open and Imogen looked across the beds for Anita. She was over by the window where they'd wheeled her the night before. Anita's eyes were half closed and she looked almost as white as the pillow that she was resting on, but when she saw Imogen, she threw her arms open and put on a wide smile.

'Well hello, I've brought magazines and fruit. Where shall I put them? 'Imogen busied herself around the locker, 'didn't know what you wanted, but Tony can bring in whatever I missed when he comes in later.'

'Oh, I'm glad he's coming' Anita said in a low voice 'and could you contact the theatre crowd for me please, some of them might visit? Have you seen this?' She nodded to the other beds where new mothers were being visited by husbands and parents. 'I feel intimidated'.

'I don't blame you,' Imogen said with a wry smile 'but you'll soon be home. Now let me have another peek at little Diana.' She moved around to the transparent cot.

'Hello, my lovey. You're so beautiful.' she cooed leaning over it. The previous evening, she had held Anita's hand throughout. She had been gripped by the experience of that primal struggle, staged in a white impersonal room, from which arose a tiny creature. Diana was now a small person with little pursed lips, delicate closed eyelids and tiny lashes.

'I see flashes of Skipper in her.' Anita said.

'Oh, but I'm sure she's got your chin and her hair is wispy blonde.'

Anita settled back down on the pillows, 'I'm glad we bought all those baby books. I need L plates. But the night nurse was friendly, she's helped me with breastfeeding. They say I can go home in a couple of days if the feeding's working out.'

'Oh fingers crossed then. We're all ready for you at home – we're getting a lot of supplies moved from the house to the hotel. Tony's collected our van and he's driving over the hot air hand driers, new basins … oh and lots of other things.' She realised that Anita was distracted. 'Sorry, you must be tired.

Anita smiled at her, 'Well you must be tired too. You were up in the night with me. But, the house and the hotel seem a million miles away. It's just four of us in this room, feeling a bit sore. We're all caught up with what to do with babies, at the moment.' Imogen squeezed her hand, but then they both attended to the cot as with squeaks and twizzling fingers Diana was awakening.

***

Since the start of labour, Tony had spent an anxious time wondering what was going on at the hospital. He was relieved when Imogen finally walked in the door with news. She had gone back to visit again and he wanted to get a lot done before it was his turn to go to the evening visiting. He had been loading and unloading the van and driving to and from the hotel all morning. He was dusty and sweaty despite the chill in the air.

While negotiating the front path carrying large boxes, he became aware of someone passing him on the way to the door. When he'd deposited the boxes in the van, he saw her knocking and waiting - a tall woman wearing a winter coat edged with fur and a floppy, felt hat.

'Can I help you?' he re-entered the gate. She looked unsure. 'I'm looking for the people who live here. My daughter, Imogen…' she said.

'Oh hello. Yes, she does live here. Come in.' he said. He ushered her inside, noticing that she was pulling a case on wheels. He showed her into his living room and offered to take her coat. Once she'd removed the hat he took in wavy brown hair framing a long face, an exceptionally wide mouth and a high forehead.

'Wait a moment, I'll just go and lock the van'.

Mrs Dulcie Best took the opportunity to cast an eye over the room and peer out of the window. She wondered where Imogen was and who this young man was. Perhaps he was Imogen's boyfriend. She felt it was a breach of etiquette to just turn up on someone's doorstep. Sometimes she could be haughty when she actually felt embarrassed, so she would tread carefully, she didn't want to alienate Imogen's friends.

'I'm afraid Imogen's still at the hospital.' Tony said.

'Oh no, what's wrong.'

'No it isn't her. Anita had her baby last night. So, she's visiting.'

'Anita, shares with Imogen? I don't know who everyone is.' she gave a small laugh.

'Oh sorry,' said Tony running his hand through his hair, 'I'm Tony.'

'Please call me Dulcie,' she answered reaching out to shake hands. Tony went on to tell Dulcie that Imogen had supported Anita through the birth. Dulcie wondered where the father was and bit her lip at the thought of Imogen having to deal with a girl who'd got herself pregnant out of wedlock, but said nothing. Then she asked,

'So where's the other girl who shares with them?'

'Tony laughed, 'There isn't another girl, just me. I bet Imogen will be surprised to see you.'

Dulcie was resentful and also a little hurt that she had known nothing of Tony, but she was too polite to let it show. She had had a long and emotional journey and wanted to find a way to recharge her batteries.

'I made a spur-of-the-moment decision to get away, just for a while at least', she flushed slightly. 'I'm not sure what I'm planning to do at the moment. I'd hoped that Imogen would be pleased to see me. I thought perhaps she'd find room for me at least for a few days.'

Tony glanced at her suitcase. 'We've got spare rooms here, let me help you settle in.' he said reaching to pick up the case. Tony gave Dulcie a tour of the house and entertained her until Imogen came back. He told her about their hotel.

'It's a large white stucco house not far from the university, ideally placed. It was originally the home of a nineteenth century industrial magnate. The servants' bells are still there, all lined up in the scullery. We're installing more bathrooms with luxurious sunken baths and we want efficient heating. Then the girls are talking about shag pile rugs and tiffany lamp shades. We're aiming at the top end of the market.'

Tony's face had become animated and Dulcie found herself drawn in to share his excitement and pleased that Imogen was part of it.

'Everyone has a car now. So we're going to have the front and back gardens asphalted over, so that there'll be a good sized car park. It's quite a challenge, particularly when there's a new baby arriving home soon.'

At that point there was a rattle at the hall door and Imogen appeared. By then, Dulcie was sipping a glass of white wine and had kicked off her shoes. Imogen's heart missed a beat, but she managed to maintain her composure. 'Hello? Why are you here Mum?'

'Hello, darling. I'm sorry I'm such a surprise. I wanted to see you though.'

'Imogen threw herself into the swing chair and sprawled a bit. She felt it was disrespectful, but she was tired and slightly resentful at having to deal with her mother at that moment.

'Well yes, it is a bit sudden. There's been a lot going on recently. I've just come back from visiting my friend. She's had a baby.' Her face softened and she said to Tony, 'Such a sweet baby. She's looking all around her and snuffling against Anita.'

'Yes, Tony told me, he's very kindly been keeping me company. He's told me about the hotel too. You must tell me all about it. We've got a lot of catching up to do.'

Tony leapt up and gave Imogen a sympathetic smile. 'I've organised a bedroom for your mum. You look bushed. I'm going to put some soup on for you both before I set off.'

'Oh thanks.' Imogen realised she was pleased to see her mum, but her mind was full of her current life. It was hard to assimilate her new life with the old.

Chapter Eighteen

While Tony busied himself getting ready for the hospital, Imogen's thoughts had been racing. She wondered what had happened between her parents and in the absence of any information she imagined the worst. She felt affection for her mother, but it seemed very inconvenient that she had turned up now.

'Now we're on our own – d'you want to come into my room?' Imogen said. Dulcie followed her down the passageway. Imogen sat down on the window seat cradling a mug, leaving the easy chair for her mother.

'I'm sorry Mum. I realise you must be disappointed that I'm sharing with a man.'

'Well he seems a nice man, at least,' Dulcie studied the floor and spoke in an uncharacteristically small voice.

'And you've found out that Anita's had a baby.'

'Yes that certainly isn't ideal, but I'm glad it isn't you.' Dulcie looked her daughter in the eye. Look, things have changed for me. I haven't come to check up on you, even though it might look as though I have. There are things I want to explain.'

Imogen frowned as her mother went on, 'I haven't had your advantages and education. I've tried to do my best and build a good life. I tried to make sure that you use your advantages and make a good career and marriage. I thought I knew what

85

a good life was, but mine hasn't been so easy.' She shook her head. 'I know it probably didn't look awful to you, but I've felt increasingly lonely. Your father, he's often busy, not at home enough. If I try to talk to him, he doesn't listen.'

'Isn't that sometimes just a part of life?' Imogen said.

'Well that's just it. What life? I've got friends, but they're self-absorbed, competitive even. If I talked to them about how I felt, they'd store it all up to gossip about. I've been keeping up a front. I don't do anything that actually means something.'

'Well, what do you want out of life Mum?'

Dulcie threw her hands into the air. 'I mean, I know what I enjoy doing – I enjoy planning and designing…'

'Yes I know you plan the house decoration.'

'I do,' Dulcie nodded at Imogen, 'but it isn't enough.'

Imogen had also felt isolated when her father was at the office and her mother was absorbed in changing the house around. She felt touched that, finally, her mother was talking about feelings with her.

'It came to a head last week when Ted, well your Dad, came across me standing at the sink crying and he said "If you're going to get like that, you need to see the doctor" – with no thought in his head, that maybe it was him, not me.'

Imogen smiled slightly. Yes, Dad did lack emotional perception. And this was like the pieces dropping into place. She had tried to find her own path in life, and her mother's admission that being a middle-class housewife was not enough, confirmed that she had been right.

'Anyway, I did get to the doctors. He offered me Valium – the housewives' panacea. We're all on it you know. I spoke to a few more sympathetic people too. The vicar – well he partially understood, but he seemed keen on my coping with it as it is. Then I spoke to Stephen, you know, John and Marilyn's son. He's a very intelligent boy. I found he understood the search for something else. But - that got me into problems with

Marilyn, who seemed to think that I was trying to seduce him!' she raised her shoulders in exasperation.

Suddenly she reached across and held her daughter's wrist 'So I'm getting older – time is passing me by. I'm not asking to share your life – that wouldn't be fair. But I am asking you to be there for me while I work out what to do next.'

'Oh, Mum.' Imogen held her mother's hand. 'Does dad know you're here?'

'He's away at a conference at the moment. I'll phone him and explain. Don't worry about him – I know he won't be at all upset.'

'I think he'll miss you, you know. It's really sudden Mum, but I think I understand what you're talking about. I've been looking at my own choices and what's best for me too. And, of course I'll support you.'

Imogen got the chance to tell her mother about Kent & Minster and about Pete. Dulcie listened and nodded solemnly. She made no comment and didn't add her own opinions. Imogen was overcome with gratitude for that. They talked. Imogen put on the table light and her eyes began to feel gritty. They were both yawning and decided to call it a day.

'I'm glad we've been able to talk,' said Dulcie standing up. 'And you know, I think I could help with the baby and with the hotel. Only if you'd like me to, of course'.

True to her words, Dulcie acted as cheerleader when Anita arrived home. They had been looking forward to her arrival and Tony had even hung a Welcome Home banner along the hallway. Tony had gone to collect her but when she walked in she was clearly exhausted and looked pale.

'I'm not sure where to put the carry cot. She'll need quiet but I want to be able to see her.' was her first concern.

'Sit down and relax. I'll lay out all the baby equipment.' Dulcie said. Over the days she washed out Babygros, made sure that the grocery shopping was done and sat with her while she fed Diana, offering advice and reassurance. An additional room was prepared as a nursery on the ground floor and Anita spent most of her time, with Dulcie, in there. Hormonal changes seemed to have hit Anita and she spent some of the early days in tears. She was less irritated by advice than Imogen would have been and appreciated having a mother figure around.

Imogen was pleased that her mother was occupied but worried about her parents' split. She made a point of telephoning her father and he seemed to be coping but it was hard to really know – he was a 'buttoned up' man. They were so busy, that she made a promise to see him when she could.

Imogen's relationship with her mother changed. She thought she had broken away and yet, particularly at first, Dulcie occasionally slipped into anxious mother role and tried to 'suggest' how Imogen should handle situations. But she noticed that Dulcie often visibly caught herself and made a conscious effort to treat her as an adult. At times, Imogen even felt a twinge of unease when she realised how close Dulcie was becoming to Anita and Diana. As an only child, she had never had to share her mother before. But it was a passing thought as her days were taken up in an exhausting race to hit deadlines on the new hotel.

Dulcie found herself remembering when she was wrapped up in caring for Imogen as a young baby. It was bittersweet to contrast those times with Imogen now as a bright young woman. She wanted to know how Anita, Tony and Imogen had got together and whether Tony had any other role in the girls' lives apart from being a landlord. Imogen explained that he was gay. Dulcie was initially astounded, but she even took that in her stride. She began to relax. Outwardly it showed, as she swapped her formal suits and her dresses with bows at the neck, for flowing skirts and tie-dye fabric bandanas.

Dulcie's support allowed Imogen and Tony to spend most of their time at the hotel which had been named the Lunar

Hotel in honour of Diana (Goddess of the Moon) and because, of course, it was painted white. They project managed building work, interior design and staff recruitment. Diana was a four-month-old by the time they started to plan a grand opening. She smiled, loved reaching for rattles and pulled faces at them while blowing bubbles. There was a stream of visitors from the world of the theatre and so there was no shortage of people to entertain and dote on her. Tony, Imogen and Dulcie all vied to play with her whenever Anita needed time to herself and this gave Anita chance to feel involved in the hotel too.

'I bet Ted would love to see his granddaughter,' Dulcie said absently one day, while dandling Diana. 'Oops, what am I saying? Diana isn't his granddaughter.' She laughed.

But Pete didn't try to come near.

Chapter Nineteen

Shopfitters and electricians were hammering and trailing cables across the floor, but the launch night of the Lunar Hotel was approaching. Imogen had invited local dignitaries and tourism representatives, Anita was able to persuade Alec King, a popular soap actor to make an opening speech and cut the ribbon. Tony had organised a string quartet to play in the bay window of the hotel lounge and had been in touch with the media.

They erected a small stage at the opposite end of the lounge from the bar. Dulcie had got thoroughly involved and worked hard placing tables and chairs around the room and supervising cleaning. The team decided that they would provide a night of entertainment. Preparation for a show was enjoyable but time was short and individual acts had to fit in make-shift rehearsals whenever they had the time.

So much planning was involved that mealtimes at the house were suspended and people dropped in for a quick sandwich or toast. They always had the time to stop for baby talk with Diana and a catch up with Anita before rushing back to work. There was a buzz of excitement mixed with apprehension in the air, but Imogen privately knew that it was going to go well.

The appointed day arrived. Last minute details were finished just in time. Deep red velvet curtains, which had been tied out of the way, were swagged over the windows and secured in tiebacks, coverings were whisked off the leather chesterfields and the chaise longue. The string quartet began to tune up and staff arrived to change into their uniforms for the first time.

As the guests started to draw up, Dulcie readied herself to take coats.

'May I welcome you to the Lunar Hotel. Please make your way to the bar, where the management team are waiting to show you our facilities.' She was in her element.

She wasn't a soap fan, but she recognised Alec King from photographs in the Radio Times.

'Our special guest. It's such a pleasure to have you here. I know Anita's dying to see you again. Let me show you where she is.' Anita passed Diana across to Imogen to hold for a while and took Alec off to show him around the hotel.

Soon the room was full and buzzing with voices. It was finally happening. Flashbulbs popped as journalists took photographs. Tony had invested in a Polaroid Land Camera which took instant pictures. It fed out a square of photographic paper. He waved the paper around for a few minutes for the picture to develop and then was able hand photos to groups of guests.

Eventually the musicians stopped and laid aside their bows. Alec King took the stage, tapping on a glass to signify that he was going to speak.

'Ladies and gentlemen, thank you for coming. What a privilege it is to see a historic house such as this, turned into a sumptuous hotel. What a delight to meet a group of dedicated people who followed their dreams and worked together to make the magic happen. I hope you will all spread the word about the Lunar Hotel. I understand that you are going to see more of the team as they entertain you now. So, without further ado I invite you to enjoy the show.' and with a dramatic sweep of his hand he reversed off the stage.

Tony walked quickly centre stage, pulling a small table. He'd changed into top hat and tails and he performed magic tricks culminating by pulling a string of silk scarves out of the hat. He had a further surprise – he'd invited a drag act to provide entertainment. They were dressed as elderly ladies, one with a blue rinse and the other carrying a large handbag. They had a hilarious routine based on one of them mishearing the other and involving double entendres. Imogen felt sure that she recognised the taller of the two. As they brushed past on leaving the stage she realised that it was Vic, from Tony's dinner party.

It was Imogen's turn next. She had had misgivings about dressing up, but after a lot of coaching from Anita, she'd been reassured that she was sensational as David Bowie singing 'Star man'. They'd coaxed her hair to stand up and set it with hair spray. Grease paint created the trademark zig zag on her face. She'd imagined having to compete with a hubbub of noise at the bar, but the audience were appreciative. She was delighted by applause and even whistles at the end of her performance.

Then Dulcie did her bit, by offering a rendition of a comic verse. Last of all, Anita and Alec King performed a scene from Pygmalion with Anita as Eliza Doolittle. It was a great success. Anita was smiling with tears in her eyes when she left the stage. For her, it was a first foray back into acting and the theatre.

Imogen fell into bed exhausted but happy that night. It was the start of feeling exhausted and happy every night. The hard work had begun. They took time to get to know their new staff and make sure that everything ran efficiently.

A routine developed and the hotel office became a regular meeting place where they reflected on successes and ways to improve. It was large enough for each person to have a desk and the walls grew an accumulation of posters, reminders, motivational slogans and press cuttings. An incongruous pile of children's toys filled one corner. One afternoon, Dulcie joined them in the hotel office where they were looking at the monthly figures. She didn't usually get involved in the figures, so they were surprised to see her there.

'I wanted to catch you all.' she said. They looked up expectantly and she moved to stand next to Imogen's chair. 'I want to thank you', and she paused slightly, 'thank you from the bottom of my heart for welcoming me into your lives.' She scanned their faces. Imogen felt concerned at her mother's uncharacteristic emotion.

'In recent months, I've been learning to make my own decisions about what suits me. I've realised from you Tony, that being yourself and damn the consequences will make you truly happy. So, I've been thinking about how I can live a life where I can be myself.' then her eyes dropped to Diana who was sucking a rusk and she smiled.

'And Anita, I admire you for sticking with Diana. You're a brave and wonderful mother.' Dulcie laid her hand on Imogen's shoulder. 'The way that you've all worked together shows what a difference that can make.'

'Well thanks' Anita spoke up looking puzzled at the turn of the conversation.

Dulcie went on, 'Oh, I imagine you are wondering where all this has come from, but you see, now is the time to for me to leave.'

'To leave?' Imogen interrupted, 'Where…?'

'You've successfully launched your hotel, and I've been thinking and reading magazine articles and newspapers. We've got friends in France. So I'd like to go there. And I've found out about a small group of people who've just started communal living in France. They share their lives and eat meals together. Actually, I'm wondering whether I should join them. It's really exciting.'

'Oh, no, we'll miss you. It won't be the same without you' said Anita and other voices joined in.

'Well I'll miss you all and particularly, I'll miss seeing little Diana growing up. But you will all come over to France for holidays, won't you?

She turned to Imogen, 'I've been so inspired and proud of you. I am going to look forwards now – not back. But can you keep an eye on Ted for me Imogen?' she said with a twinkle in her eye.

LIVE A LITTLE

BOOK 2

Chapter One

So, you want this to be our last session,' Nicole uncrossed her legs and leant forward with concerned professionalism.

The therapy room with its low coffee table, box of tissues and deep, wing chairs had become a refuge for Dulcie. She pulled her gaze back to her therapist, 'I've learned a lot about myself, but I can't justify the expense of coming.'

'Getting over a divorce is a gradual process, but you are on your way through it now. There's an end in sight.'

'Yes, I feel that. I really do. The loneliness has been the worst. I thought that moving to a commune would provide me with a ready-made family, but sometimes you are at your loneliest in a crowd.' She glanced out of the window at the lavender hedges and pergola posts outside; her idea of a classical French garden. She recognised that she distracted herself when emotions got awkward, so she continued hurriedly, 'Well I know that the solution is to extend my friendships to outside the commune and then I'll feel at home in the town too. . . I'm determined to try.'

'And you talked about your daughter?' Nicole prompted.

'I don't think I will go back to visit. I'm going to make myself settle here. It won't do to rely on Imogen. She's got her own life to lead.'

'I sincerely wish you well, Dulcie,' Nicole exuded warmth, 'and it's time now to draw our session to a close.'

***

As she stepped onto the street, Dulcie felt lighter for having unloaded her feelings, but also anxious about the challenges to come. Nicole's broad suburban street reminded her of the wealthy suburban life she had left behind in England. She was soon window shopping in the narrow streets of the town centre again. Emerging at the town square she was tempted to wait a while, so that she could meet some of the children from the commune as they left school, but no it was too hot to hang about for long, and besides, the teachers would wonder who she was.

She dodged traffic to cross over the boulevard périphérique before climbing the hill that led home. The walk gave her time to reflect on what had driven her to seek counselling. Being married for so long had made her feel like a spare part in her husband's life. It wasn't Ted's fault any more than it was her's; he'd been caught up in living his life too.

What would he be doing now? Probably in some meeting or finishing off at his desk in time to get home. He would barely notice a difference now that she'd gone. She would stay single now. Who'd have her anyway, she gave a derisory laugh to herself. She felt too old for all that and not ready to pick anyone else's socks off the floor ever again.

The chateau was ahead; home to a mixture of retired people, hippies, and also professional people who idealised an alternative lifestyle. But Nicole was right, there was more to the world than this insular commune.

Chapter Two

The advantage of living at the gatehouse on the boundary was that you could come and go without drawing any comment. Through the grand chateau gateway, she had a gate in a privet hedge into her own garden. Someone had dropped a note through her door, as she stepped over the doormat she bent to pick it up. It could wait for her on the extending table against the wall. The smell of paint still lingered, so she touched the wall tentatively. It was dry. She and her neighbour, Roger, had replastered all the walls and then, yesterday, she had rollered a coat of white paint. The windows were tiny and the resulting darkness provided welcome escape from the sun. Dulcie sank into a fireside chair with a sigh. She kicked off her shoes and closed her eyes.

A low rumble in her stomach reminded her to eat. She idly glanced at the note on the kitchen table. 'Heavens,' there was a jolt of shock. It was a notice about an additional community meeting that evening, 'Another! I don't believe it.' She grabbed her bag and ran.

***

Perspiring from heat and moving at a pace, she pushed open the doors to the communal meeting room. People were already seated so she found the nearest wooden chair. She dug into her bag for something to wipe her brow before looking around. Chair legs grated on flagstones then there was a hush.

This expectant pause before announcements always made Dulcie's stress level rise. She concentrated on the ornately carved roof and the arched windows above. It was like being in church.

'Today, I want to talk about how the locals see us.' This was Jane, with her bouncy page boy cut now appearing serious and pacing the floor.

'The people in the town look at us, and they see us as the outsiders on the hill. We can't let them see us as enemies or worse – weirdos. They have a lot of power. In fact, the mayor is able to make decisions on what we are allowed to do.'

'The French, they are all ignorant,' a well-built man across the room seemed to explode with vehemence, 'why should we want to be a part of their town? We should be self-sufficient.

This was uncomfortable. Most of the residents in the chateau weren't fluent French speakers, whereas Dulcie had perfected the language at a Swiss finishing school. As she lived at the gatehouse, she interacted with the locals more than anyone else. Do they know that I am always going to the town? My way of life often clashes with theirs.

Maggie, the white-haired founder of their group, arose from her chair and raised her voice to say, 'Sit down please, Jane'. Maggie slowly surveyed the circles of residents of her chateau, named 'Le Manoir de Calme'.

'Thank you, Jane. Let us take a moment to centre ourselves. I want all of us to look inside and question our own part in this.'

Dulcie found it extremely hard to centre herself, she actually felt her heart thumping.

Jane went on to speak about a recent visit to the town. As she entered the square from a passageway she had encountered a communal feast. There were men, women and children at a long table under the trees. Jane had felt like an intruder.

'No one from the chateau community was invited.' Despite lamenting the situation, Jane seemed intent on emphasising the cracks between the chateau and the town.

The meeting had moved on. Roger, a skinny young man with a family who lived in a static caravan nearby, slowed down the pace of proceedings in his languid way, 'Yeh man, there is a rift.' he had stroked his wiry beard, 'Our boy, Ziggy has been walking home from school by himself, and some of the French kids threw stones at him.'

Sheila beside him, nodded slowly, 'Yes, Ziggy's being bullied during the school day too. Some of the French children call him names cus he's English. We're cool if he wants to stay at home and run free in the woods, but it's not about that. There's a wider issue guys. It's something we should look at.'

Poor Ziggy. Dulcie was glad that he was playing with the other children outside, he would be mortified to hear the group talking about him. He was a quiet child; Dulcie just wanted to hug him to make it better. She identified with him; they both felt like outsiders.

The conversation on the French versus the English had continued. At least Ziggy's parents were sending him to school, a couple of other children who were new to the Community were not attending a school.

She stood up and said, 'I'd like to support Ziggy. Perhaps I could liaise with the school so that he feels better about it.' A few people seemed to nod in agreement. Roger and Sheila smiled and shrugged. They were so laid back that she saw that as enthusiasm on their part. As she sat down again, she noticed Jane narrowing her eyes at her. Oh dear she didn't want to get on the wrong side of her.

Jane gave a tight smile, 'Well that dealt with for the present, I will share some ideas that I have for the future. I'll put them to the vote, of course,' she scanned the room. 'I've been thinking that we could use some of our land for tourist lodges. The resulting income would create a sustainable community.'

Looking around, Dulcie noticed raised eyebrows and even a few sharp intakes of breath. She hoped that the majority felt like that because, to her, Jane seemed to be trying to change the ethos of the commune. If the idea went any further, she would have to speak out against it.

By taking a stand she might risk losing the support of some of the community, but she knew that she was well-liked. Her nickname among the children, Ceci, was evidence of that. Would she be able to gather public opinion behind her if she needed to?

Chapter Three

The next morning, she mulled over Ziggy's problem at school while spreading butter on day-old French bread. It had lost its soft springiness. She ripped at the tough crust with her teeth; it was still palatable with plenty of butter and jam. Chewing helped her to think. Maybe she should have a chat with Ziggy. Dulcie identified with children.

When her own daughter, Imogen, had been small, Dulcie met up with other young mothers for coffee mornings while the children played. When Imogen worried about fitting in, Dulcie had invited some of the school children to tea. But of course, their house and toys had been a treat for visiting children. In contrast, Ziggy's family had a mobile home which rested among the ivy and nettles in the woods around the chateau. How would local schoolchildren see that?

Dulcie wrapped a crocheted shawl around her shoulders against the chill of the spring morning. She was carrying homemade cakes as a gift for Ziggy's family. She followed a hard-packed earth path winding through a froth of wild, white garlic and spindly silver birch saplings. As her maxi-skirt brushed the foliage, a strong garlic smell arose. The path led in the opposite direction to the chateau. Dulcie kicked at discarded cans and stubs from roll-ups. Littering, eugh, how it spoilt the green of the countryside. The dilapidated green-painted mobile home was in sight.

Ziggy's sister Anise, a rounded child with untamed hair, came running straight at her legs. Dulcie stopped to ready herself for the force of a small girl wrapping herself around her knees.

'Ceci, Ceci you're here. Come and see what I'm doing.' Anise grasped her by the hand, almost dislodging the tin of cakes. 'A fairy house, over here. Come and look,' Anise rounded her eyes and gave an exaggerated look of wonder with all the skill of a street performer drawing in a crowd.

Tall grasses and plantains stretched to fill the space below the mobile home and tendrils of ivy wound up its sides. Anise had made a nest out of vegetation. Dulcie squatted down to Anise's eye level to admire a family of clothes peg dolls set in a circle of stones lined with moss, while the little girl jumped up and down beside her.

'Ooh, you are a clever girl. They're going to be cosy in there. Are you going to make them a play area too?'

Anise made to run off to do just that, as Dulcie said, 'Wait, where's your brother?'

'Ziggy – don't know.' Anise said, at the same time peering out into the woods.

Sheila stepped down from the caravan door, looking tousled. She could be pretty if she combed her long hair, 'Oh hi,' she said. 'She isn't bothering you, is she?'

'Of course you aren't bothering me, are you Anise?' Dulcie answered looking at Sheila. 'Is it OK if I have a chat with Ziggy?'

'Yeh go ahead. You're our surrogate auntie Ceci.' Sheila came forward to touch Dulcie on the shoulder as they looked around the clearing.

'There's a group of children bombing round the woods. I hear them every so often.'

Dulcie held her hand out to Anise, 'Shall we go and have a look for him?'

Roger had followed Sheila out of the van and now sat on a large tree stump. He rested his arms on bony denim-clad knees and, taking a clay pipe from his pocket, he poked strands of tobacco into the bowl.

He squinted up at Dulcie, 'You're fantastic with Ziggy, you have a chat with him.' he pulled Anise towards him, 'I'll keep little ears out of the way.' He ruffled Anise's hair.

Dulcie nodded and was about to look around when she noticed Ziggy, a lanky boy of nine or ten with long dark hair, skulking around the side of the caravan.

'Hello, I didn't see you there.'

He shrank back quickly. 'We were going to take him to school, but you know how it is, by the time we'd got up it was too late,' said Sheila. 'He isn't in a sociable mood today.'

'Well, I've brought cake.' Dulcie held the tin out. Both children ran up eagerly and snatched at slices as though they were starving. Dulcie just stopped herself from correcting them, that wouldn't help her to get alongside Ziggy.

'See my house,' Anise said to her brother.

He looked reluctant but glanced in that direction. Dulcie moved over to where the pegs were lying in the grass.

'You could make something with the other pegs,' Dulcie suggested and picked up the peg bag nearby. She sat down and began to slot pegs together. Ziggy joined her and snatched up five or six. He watched what she was doing. She zoomed her peg model around his head, 'a plane.' He laughed and relaxed into playing.

'I'm going to make another house.' Anise announced.

'You come and do it over here with me then. I'd like to see.' Sheila called to her. Anise skipped over and left Ziggy and Dulcie working in silence. Dulcie glanced at the top of his head as he bent over a complicated design, his long hair tucked behind his ears to keep it out of the way.

'How do you get on with the French children? she said.

'It's okay,' he said in a small voice but his movements with the pegs became more rapid. He started to bash one peg into another.

'They're having a fight,' she suggested.

'Yes, a fight. Like Xavier and Laurent at school,' Ziggy said.

'Are they your friends?'

'My friends don't play with me now. I didn't know it was PE yesterday and we needed our shorts. I hadn't got mine with me, so the teacher made me do PE wearing my pants. The others all laughed.' There was a break in his voice. He speared the two pegs upright into the ground saying, 'When they laughed, the teacher took me to find some spare shorts. But then they called me names for the rest of the day. They used to call me 'Rost bif' when I first started school; that's what they call the English.' He looked up at her, 'and they laugh at my hair.'

'Remember to be proud of who you are Ziggy and hold your head high. That will show them that they aren't winning – but it isn't nice to feel left out.'

'I don't want to go tomorrow.' He screwed up his face. Dulcie felt her own eyes pricking. She wasn't sure what she could say to him.

She took a handful of pegs. 'Look, this crowd all feel safe now because they are in a group and they are all joined against this person.' She held up one wooden peg which she'd adorned with moss. 'We'll call him Mossy - and if Mossy acts strong and doesn't show he's scared some of the weaker ones,' and she separated off a couple of pegs from the bunch, 'are just as likely to go over to Mossy's side. I think you could win your old friends over to your side again. What do you think?'

Ziggy pursed his lips and looked at his own pegs. He needed to believe that it would work. How could she give him the courage to try it?'

'Looks like you are making something good with your peg,' she commented, 'is it a fence?'

'No, it's going to be a house.'

'What can you say to the other children at the school?' she asked. Silence – so she suggested, 'How about "stop calling me names. If you stop, we can play together again." And then suggest a game straight away so that you can all move on. Shall I teach you to say that in French?'

'I can speak French now,' Ziggy screwed up his eyes, 'but what if they ignore me?' he looked up mischievously, 'I could hit them?'

She glanced to her side and noticed that Anise had shuffled closer, intent on listening.

'That might work,' Dulcie said, 'but it might make it worse, and get you into trouble. Could you tell the teacher what has been happening? It's the teacher's job to make sure that everyone gets on together.' He nodded vigorously. She got up and put her arm around his shoulders looking across at Roger and Sheila. 'I'll tell you what, speak to the children about it tomorrow. If we need to get the teacher involved, I can go in to see the school with your Mum and Dad – if they'd like.'

'Sounds like a plan, eh Ziggy?' Roger said. 'Thanks, Ceci, perhaps I could have some of that cake now.'

Chapter Four

Dulcie often collected letters from a large metal mailbox affixed to the entrance pillar of the chateau. She had to screw up courage in case she found a letter from her husband's solicitors. The marriage split had seemed civilised but he was becoming more vindictive. This time, the postman was on his way to deliver to the box. He parked his yellow 2CV van on the grass verge. A fit young man, he covered the distance between them in a few swift strides.

'Bonjour Madame,' he called.

'Bonjour,' she smiled automatically. This was the first time that she had encountered him and she stood back to let him unlock the box.

He lowered his sack to the ground and seemed to sense her reticence.

'I have to put them into the official box,' his brown eyes crinkled in a grin, 'You expect a letter?'

'Yes,' and Dulcie sighed, 'I'm Dulcie, Dulcie Best. But call me Ceci for short, everyone here does.'

'Gilles Joubert,' he said, shaking her hand firmly.

She noticed his tanned complexion, a result of an outdoor occupation.

'You speak good English.' Dulcie said.

'Thank you. I lived in England for several years and my mother also lived in England for some time, before she married my father. She taught me English from when I was a child.'

'Good to meet someone from my home,' Dulcie said, 'whereabouts did you live?'

'I lived on a farm in Somerset. We are a farming family, so I went there to know English farming methods, Madame.'

Dulcie threw her hands up, 'Ceci, please. And what a small world. I know Somerset well. My father and his wife live there and so I've visited. Look, would you like to come inside for a cool drink?'

He glanced down at his watch, 'I have a moment, thank you . . . Ceci.'

He delivered some letters into the box and then followed her along the narrow path through her vegetable patch to the door. There was a faint aroma of smoke from her fire and of coffee, a reminder of her breakfast. She sat him in one of the fireside chairs and dragged a small table close, then reached up to lift glasses from a shelf on the dresser. Gilles glanced around the room. It had the low ceilings and thick walls of a nineteenth-century French cottage. Dulcie had made it feel cosy and the walls were adorned with her own artwork.

'Charming, I can see you know how to make a home.' he said.

'I've always enjoyed arranging rooms. This house has been a bit of a challenge and I haven't had a lot of money. So it's "make do and mend" as they say in England.'

He laughed and waved towards individual items, 'Plants in old pans, pink painted chairs. I think it is quite English. People would be surprised to see how. . . how homely it is.'

'People? You mean the people in the town?' Dulcie's voice was muffled as she bent to retrieve a bottle of homemade lemonade from a bucket of cold water which she used as a cooler.

'They think of the group of English people living up on the hill as "hippies". They imagine that there are wild parties with people dancing naked.'

Dulcie jerked a laugh, 'I suppose a group of unrelated people sharing in a community is a hippie idea,' she said, 'but there's such a variety of different people of different ages here.' She laughed again, 'if only they knew . . . in fact, to make this work, people have made rules. It isn't all about freedom.'

He looked at her appraisingly, 'You fascinate me. You have had the bravery to start this new life. A community in a chateau is not for everyone. So what made you come here?'

Dulcie took a quick intake of breath, 'Oh you know, I'd just split up from my husband, Ted. My daughter was starting a new life for herself.'

She was pleased that he recognised her bravery but she felt a flutter in her chest. Perhaps the rapid changes in her life had affected her more than she realised.

'I saw an article about a Commune in France, so I went to stay with some friends who live near Carcassonne. I enjoyed spending time with them and then I came over here to view the chateau. I had to decide whether I wanted to join. On the whole, the community works well and I love seeing the children running around freely.'

'So you are never lonely.' He noticed the tabby cat that had been curled up on a low stool. It opened its eyes and raised its head to blink at them. 'And of course, you have a friend here.'

The cat seemed to realise that he had noticed it and lithely sprang to the floor then wove backwards and forwards along his shins.

'My cat Oscar. He doesn't take to everyone, but he seems to trust you.' Dulcie smiled at him and took a sip of her drink. Maybe she also trusted him? He had a direct gaze and his interest flattered her.

'What about you?' she said, 'You come from a farming family and yet you work as a postman?'

He grinned, 'Ah, it suits me. I get out to meet the community. I am also the mayor.' Dulcie was amazed, he seemed young to be a mayor. He carried on, 'At the moment, my father is busy on the farm and he doesn't need a lot of help from me.' His slight blush drew her attention, 'I know, I sound as though I want to know everyone's business, but I have a goal.' He sat forward and looked at her intently. 'I can see changes coming. The English love to go to Spain on holiday but I think our tourist industry will soon grow too. So, I want to develop our town to cater for an increase in tourists . . . and our own farm? When my father retires, I will develop our outbuildings to house them.'

His energy increased as he spoke.

'I can see you are passionate about it,' Dulcie said. 'It's quite a long-term goal.'

Gilles smiled. 'For now, I am enjoying meeting my customers. And I have had the chance to meet you.'

This sounded like flirtation, but she felt that he was being sincere. She wasn't sure how to respond so she chose to ignore the comment.

'Can I offer you some cake?' she changed the subject.

'No, no thank you. I have to continue my deliveries.'

'She looked at his hands holding his glass. Brown skin, large knuckles, sinewy wrists and a smattering of tiny hairs, made golden by the sun. She hadn't closely examined a man's hands since Ted, her soon to be ex-husband.

There was a knock at the door. They both turned to look, and Dulcie strode across to see who it was. Her heart quickened, yet she knew that there was no need to be embarrassed about having a visitor.

Jane a small plump figure clutching a black accounts book stood at the door.

'Oh, come in,' Dulcie said and stood back to let her bustle past. 'Jane this is Gilles. Gilles, Jane.'

The open door admitted a shaft of sunlight which highlighted dust motes dancing in the air and made the rest of the room look shadowy. Gilles stood up brushing his fringe back from his forehead and extended his hand to greet Jane. He looked enormous in such a small room.

'I will go now,' he said to Dulcie, 'but I will see you again.'

Jane stood tight-lipped and watched as he edged his way past her to the door. When he had gone, she said, 'the postman.'

'Yes, he comes to the chateau daily, but we introduced ourselves today,' Dulcie said and then wondered why she felt the need to explain herself. 'Won't you sit down.'

This was the first time that Jane had entered the gatehouse since it had been renovated. She was a relatively recent incomer to the community, but she'd paid a premium to rent an apartment in the glamorous chateau building, close to the rooms that their founder, Maggie, owned.

She looked around, 'You've worked hard,' she said finally. 'I'm making a tour of the residents to make sure that the accounts are all up-to-date. I know you have only paid half of the initial down payment and I wonder if you can tell me when we can expect the other half?'

Dulcie screwed up her eyes to work out how to formulate an answer, 'I thought Maggie dealt with all of that. I made my agreement with Maggie when I arrived.'

'I know. And Maggie is lovely. She's getting older now, though. We mustn't take advantage of her. We must share the burden, so I will be organising budgets from now on. I'm collecting towards our next few communal meals too. It makes it easier to buy bulk when we've got a good amount in the coffers.'

'I see,' said Dulcie. 'I can certainly offer my share of the food money, but I've explained to Maggie, I'm waiting for my divorce to be finalised. There won't be any financial problem once that's all done.'

'Hmm, you need to take control there,' Jane said. 'I divorced years ago. You need to make sure that you know what's in your name.' She glanced down at the lined pages of her book, 'I'll make a note to follow up later.'

She stood to leave. Dulcie was dismissed.

Chapter Five

Dulcie considered the contents of her wardrobe. She was so used to wearing floaty skirts and scarves in her new life, but she needed something more subdued to fit this occasion. She was determined to find a solution to the shortage of money. After all, fluency in two languages had got to be an advantage to an employer. She needed to visit the town to hunt for a job. She managed to break into a march despite the steep road edged by rough grass and strewn with loose stones.

Elderly men moving slowly around a boules court in the centre of the town square shaded by spreading plane trees, tall houses with arched windows and with arching undercrofts. In one corner of the square, there were tables shaded by parasols. It would seem a charming scene to a tourist but was ordinary life for Dulcie. She had enough experience of approaching townspeople to know that she had to approach with sensitivity.

She headed for the largest business. Hotel Chez Inez had once been a series of houses lining the route of a major road leading from the square. All of the buildings had now been painted a dove grey to unite them. Someone with an eye for colour had painted the wooden shutters in cornflower blue and installed white roll-out sunshades over the windows.

Dulcie stepped over the front door threshold and blinked to get her eyes used to the dark. The reception area was tiny, with a high hotel desk in one corner. She tapped her palm on the chrome bell.

A small woman appeared. She had a lined face and hair tied in a scraggy knot at the nape of her neck. Dulcie said, in french, 'Are you Inez?' she was met with a blank stare. 'Could I speak to Inez?'

The woman disappeared, leaving her to examine the wooden panelling, which had a build-up of nasty wax polish in each panel corner. She was contemplating a plastic flower arrangement on a side table when a large balding man appeared. He told her that he was the manager.

'No Inez,' he shook his head and wagged his finger backwards and forwards, 'Claude.'

Dulcie explained that she was looking for work and that she had experience of helping out in her daughter's hotel. Claude frowned slightly but led Dulcie through an industrial-sized kitchen and into a smaller room smelling of carbolic where there were mops in aluminium mop buckets, piles of new yellow dusters, crates of tiny soaps, and of hotel-branded matchbooks.

'Can you work in the morning – early?' he said, frowning at her.

Dulcie rose to the challenge, smiling brightly. 'Yes anytime.' It appeared that they were short of staff and behind on the cleaning, so he asked if she could start immediately for a try-out. Dulcie agreed and looked for somewhere to leave her handbag. Donning a nylon button-up overall with handy pockets and lapels she was launched into the role of cleaner. Claude led her up a carpeted staircase to formally meet Arlette, the elderly woman that had met her in reception. He told her that Arlette would explain what to do. Arlette ushered a tall ungainly girl to meet Dulcie.

'C'est Jeannine.'

Dulcie barely had time to greet Jeannine before she was handed an industrial vacuum cleaner and left alone to vacuum one of the bedrooms. The pokey rooms had metal bed heads, scrappy curtains and busily patterned wallpaper. At least, the double windows led onto very pretty wrought-iron balconies. Dulcie's vacuum was heavy, and she could only move it around the bed legs by stopping to haul on the hose. She couldn't get it to pick up matchsticks and hairs that had become woven into the long tufts of the carpets. She swept them up by hand and put them into her overall pocket for want of anywhere else.

Arlette appeared, surveyed the carpet with an upturned nose in a stereotypic Gallic way. She showed Dulcie how to sweep a cloth over the bathroom, clean the toilet and replace soaps and toiletries from a cloth bag that she carried with her. They went back into the corridor to examine the contents of the cleaning trolley. It was loaded with piles of towels and linens. Dulcie understood that tomorrow she would be taught to strip the beds and remake them.

She had only managed to visit two rooms when they hurriedly gathered everything onto the trolley and shoved it into a lift small enough to carry two people who knew each other well. It was time for a break and the women made use of brewed coffee in the kitchen. Dulcie preferred milk in her's, so Arlette opened a kitchen cupboard to collect a handful of individual UHT milk pots.

They asked where she had come from, and she told them a bit about the chateau. This was such a contrast to the quiet rural life there. Dulcie sat on the padded top of a fold-out step stool while Arlette occupied the only chair. She looked around and tried to picture this as part of her daily routine from now on. Jeannine seemed much more amenable than she had at first appeared and launched into an animated discussion on hotel cleaning. It comprised discovering men standing naked in their rooms and finding condoms in unusual places. She had a cackle of a laugh which exposed a mouth full of rotting teeth. We seem to have hit it off, Dulcie thought.

Arlette, who had disappeared for a time, came back to tell Dulcie that it was time to finish her trial. Dulcie left Jeannine with promises to see her tomorrow. She was accompanied down the stairs by Arlette.

As she was leaving Claude appeared behind reception and waved her over to him. Claude gave her a small smile that didn't reach his eyes,

'Pardon madame, you are too slow. Please don't come back tomorrow.' Dulcie found it hard to breathe and her head momentarily went blank. She felt weak at the knees from all the unfamiliar work.

'Payment for today?'

Claude sighed dramatically. He slid down to reach under the counter, took out a receipt book and wrote something. He handed her a flimsy sheet from the tear-off pad with a logo made up of arrows around the globe. He'd scrawled an amount on it, but she couldn't make out what. He handed her a 20 franc note from the till. She took it from the tips of his fingers, turned and left without a word.

She barely noticed where she was walking as she left. She was still processing what had happened. She hadn't had long enough to prove herself and surely anyone can be a cleaner? Her eyes grew blurry. She dabbed a fingertip into the corner of one eye. I am not crying.

'Hello,' she heard a voice at her shoulder. She spun around immediately. It was Gilles but this time he wasn't wearing the post uniform. He was more casually dressed in jeans and tee-shirt.

Dulcie bent her head slightly. She hoped that there were no traces of tears. 'I didn't see you. Wait a minute, I think I've got something in my eye,' and she dived into her bag for a handkerchief.

'Are you alright?' His voice showed his concern.

'I'm alright, really.' She took a step back, 'but thank you for noticing. Things have been difficult. I went to get some work at the hotel here. Apparently, I'm too slow to be a cleaner.' She shrugged and gave a thin smile.

'Claude's place, Oui?' he said.

'Oh, so you know him?'

'Not well, but I have heard things about him. Pfft, it is a good thing that you didn't carry on working there. There are better jobs than that. Let me buy a coffee for you,' he hooked her arm onto his elbow 'and have you eaten?

Chapter Six

Gilles pulled out one of the bent-wood chairs and waited for Dulcie to sit. She felt herself relax as she laid her forearms on the table. They were sitting under a parasol at one of the pavement cafes that Dulcie had often passed but never used.

'Gilles bienvenue.' The smart waitress came over to them with a beaming smile. Her sophistication in a navy-striped, open-necked shirt, with smooth blonde hair swinging around her shoulders, caused Dulcie to have a flash of envy. She felt at her lowest.

She remained seated while Gilles and the waitress became involved in an animated conversation. He eventually turned back to the table as they were handed menus.

'That's Marin,' he gestured after her. 'We know each other since school days. Marin helped me in the elections.' He picked up his menu card, 'So what would you like to eat?'

Dulcie suddenly didn't feel hungry. Everything seemed an effort.

He noticed her face, 'I'll order for you? A steak haché on brioche – to build you up. A chocolat chaud, hot chocolate,' he smiled, 'and the same for me.'

When the food arrived, she had to admit that he'd made a good choice. She was starving. It was good to put down her worries for a while.

'So tell me more about your life at the chateau?' he said, 'Some of the children come down here to the school.'

'Mm, poor Ziggy does. He has had some problems fitting in. I had a chat with him. I hope my advice works.' Dulcie grimaced.

'I wonder . . .' Gilles tapped a finger absent-mindedly on the tabletop, 'is there some way of getting our school children to be interested in England and the English. A project or. . . peut-etre, we could ask people from the chateau to come in to help teach English?

'But Ziggy, in the end, you can only give advice and let him learn for himself. I had some trouble at school because I was so tall. For a while they called me "giraffe". I played up to them and so they thought that I liked the name – that I was funny.'

'Ahh, I am imagining you as a boy in short trousers,' Dulcie said.

Gilles pulled a face, 'Don't imagine it too much!'

Dulcie said, 'You know, we are learning about how to work with other people all our lives. Look at the chateau community 'Le Manoir de Calme'. It is an experiment in how people blend despite variations in their lifestyles and beliefs - and it isn't always calm.'

'How do they get over differences?'

'I think we are still learning how to do that. We are quite a new group and we need to keep on engaging in the debate, so that we get it right in the end.'

Dulcie had finished her brioche and dabbed at her mouth with a napkin. She made the decision to confide in him, 'I admire Maggie for buying the chateau and having the vision. She's getting older though and new people are arriving. We need to keep her vision going.'

He nodded, his eyes shining with interest.

She was glad of a listener, 'I am beginning to realise that if I want what's best for the community, I may have to stand up and say what I think.'

'You could become a role model and keep the vision going. But some people hide in a group. Just like children at school, people can easily lose their sense of personal responsibility and act mindlessly when they get into a crowd.' Gilles frowned.

Dulcie sighed, she looked up at the frill on the edge of the parasol which had been caught by a slight breeze. Maybe she didn't have the mental energy to tackle such a complex problem after all. 'I suppose that's true; like football crowds,' she said.

'And rioters,' Gilles added,' and everyone. Have you seen the English news? The Yorkshire Ripper murders. They are happening so often. And it's another example of the way people feel safe in their own group. At first, they weren't panicked because they thought that prostitutes were being murdered. It was only when the Ripper attacked someone who, how do you say this, was respectable perhaps - wasn't a prostitute that they panicked because he was killing people like them.'

Dulcie suddenly couldn't breathe. Was Imogen safe? She's running a hotel and that means anyone can get into close proximity. 'Oh dear, we're depressing ourselves.'

I'm sorry,' said Gilles, 'I see everything in political or sociological terms.'

'Of course,' she realised, 'I imagine you are always thinking about how you would tackle the same problems if they happen over here.'

Gilles looked at his watch, 'That is true. I see that the people at the chateau are turned in upon themselves. It makes for,' he paused in thought, 'it makes for an intensity, where everything becomes more grave than it should. I think you need a friend outside the community.' He reached across and covered her hand with his own.

Dulcie sensed that this implied more than casual friendship. He seemed a genuinely kind person and would be useful to have in her corner. This new friendship was what she had been talking about in counselling. She took her other hand and covered his.

As though he also saw the unspoken change in their relationship, he commented, 'There will be gossip. Can you deal with gossip about us?'

Dulcie couldn't avoid a slight rise in her voice. 'Let them. I can't let them ruin my life. The problems have started. Jane, you saw her in my cottage,' she jutted out her chin, 'she likes to help our founder, Maggie. She has been nagging me about the remainder of my payment for the lodge. You see, from my point of view, I agreed terms with Maggie at the beginning and she is willing to wait until the money from my divorce comes through, but now Jane's turned into the Gestapo.'

'Not a term we use lightly here.'

'Oh no you're right, sorry, but she is so interfering. I suppose she wants to find a role for herself. She wants to change the whole nature of our community too. She's talking about developing a holiday camp idea.' She caught his eye abruptly, 'I suppose she will want to talk to you about it, in your capacity as the mayor.'

'Explain, what do you think about it Ceci?'

'I can see that you want to make way for tourists, but I believed that we were trying to build a place of calm, sharing, community and understanding. You can't do that if new people are swarming in all the time.' She bit her nail impatiently, 'Of course, we also want to make group decisions, so it isn't up to me. Maggie is getting old and I think she's lost her sway over the community. I fear I am going to have to stand up and make my feelings known, to try to influence opinion.'

'I understand. Tourism can bring advantages but not if it changes your chateau.' He softened his voice, 'I'm glad that you warned me Ceci.'

He caught sight of Marin and dealt with the bill. 'Now, cherie Ceci, let me drive you home.'

Chapter Seven

Sudden heavy showers had turned the grass a vibrant green and water dripped from the leaves. Dulcie had been tucked inside her cottage throughout the showers. She had spent days painting at her easel, and it put her into a wonderfully calm state. Where could she sell paintings of the French countryside? English people would really appreciate them. Last summer she visited large brocante sales in local town centres and this sparked another idea. She could buy quintessentially French furniture from markets and take it to London to sell. She would focus on selling to interior designers. She could take the paintings too. Her spirits lifted, excited at launching a business venture.

Now the rain had stopped, it was important to get out into the community. She wondered about finding waterproof boots, and then gave up the idea. Walking through wet grass in sandals would feel delightfully refreshing.

The world of the chateau had changed while she had been busy. A stranger was walking across the courtyard. A middle-aged woman in floaty black clothes; she reminded Dulcie of a crow pecking along the ground. Maybe she had dropped something. Dulcie smiled across at her and said, 'Hello, are you new? How are you settling in?'

The woman stopped mid-dart and greeted her. She had unnaturally black hair and heavy eyeliner. Her lips quivered and she blinked rapidly.

'Fine, fine thanks.' she straightened up. 'I'm Ivy. I've been here for a couple of weeks now and I'm just getting to know everyone.'

'Sorry to have missed you so far. I'm Dulcie but most people call me Ceci. The children started it.' Dulcie didn't see the need to state how long she had been there. 'Are you living in the chateau itself?'

'No, I've got a wooden lodge through the woods. I've improved the heating and done it up. But, erm just going to feed the chickens at the moment. I must go,' and with that, she hopped off.

In a positive mood, Dulcie was amused by her odd behaviour. She would see more of her at the community meeting. She chuckled shaking her head slowly and then realised that she was sauntering in the same direction as Ivy. When Dulcie rounded the corner of the chateau she found Ivy standing with her back to her, head bent to confer with Jane. Jane spotted that Dulcie was approaching. She broke off the conversation and peered around Ivy.

'Ready for your stint in the kitchen?' she called over.

'I am.' Dulcie said slowly. What was she up to? In all the time that she had been in the community, she had never forgotten her turn on the cooking rota.

'Well, that's alright then. I was just saying to Ivy that we need to make sure there are enough eggs. By the time it's your turn to cook, I'll be planning a big shop. When you are in the kitchen make a note of anything that's getting low, could you?'

'Yes, that's fine,'

'Well done,' Jane said. Dulcie growled quietly to herself, it grated. Jane acted as though she was in control and managing the other members.

As Dulcie drew level with them, Jane added, 'And you are helping the caravan family.'

'Roger and Sheila? Yes. Ziggy was a bit upset about school. I'm sure he will be OK.'

'That's nice,' said Ivy nodding.

'Yes, you are a marvel with the children. It's what you do, I imagine.' Jane said with a smirk. What was she implying?

Then Jane laid her hand on Ivy's arm, 'I've had a very busy life Ivy. And my experience in local government taught me to look out for everyone in the community.'

Dulcie had been gradually edging sideways and almost paused to comment but she decided to leave the rest of the conversation to Ivy. She gave a small wave. 'Well see you later.'

A tension headache was building. So it was time to take refuge. She strode purposely in the direction of the gatehouse, head down and arms swinging. When she looked up there was a figure in the distance.

Is that…it's Gilles. . . She felt her heart quicken and she walked even faster to greet him.

As she drew nearer, she could see that he was carrying her cat in his arms. Oscar saw her and began to squirm to get down. Gilles couldn't hold onto him, and Oscar streaked off towards the cottage.

'Bonjour, one of the ladies in the town saw him trying to stalk her chickens. She hadn't seen him before. I thought he was yours, so I said I'd bring him home.'

'Thank you, I don't think he's been as far as the town before. He stays around my vegetable patch. I would have been so worried if he hadn't come back. . .and you came all the way back here for me.'

He grinned in answer, 'It was a good reason to see you again Ceci.' She felt warmth rush to her face. He was good company, but despite his talk about gossip, she couldn't imagine that he really saw her in a romantic way.

'Well come in, and I'll put on some coffee, that's if you've got the time.'

He nodded. Once inside, Dulcie rushed to drop papers into the bin, tidy paintbrushes to the back of the table and grabbed a pile of folded clothes to carry into the bedroom.

She called behind her, 'Please, sit down.' She felt caught out but told herself he wouldn't care how tidy she was.

When she returned, he was leaning against the sink and gave her a piercing look. 'Tell me, is something wrong, Ceci?'

She was about to reassure him when his concern touched her. She felt her bottom lip quiver and lowered her head to hide her expression. Gilles covered the floor in a few paces and she felt the warmth of his hands on her elbows. 'Ceci. . .' he breathed into her hair.

'Oh, just the stress of meeting residents here and possibly I'm getting paranoid. Now I think about it, I haven't eaten for a long time. I got so caught up in painting.' She gestured to the paintings and let herself fall into one of her fireside chairs.

He laughed. 'Don't worry. I am a good cook.' He deftly lifted a pan from a hook and strode out into the garden. Dulcie was momentarily alarmed at his speed, but she was too exhausted to follow. He returned with a bunch of herbs. She saw him hunting for something but didn't comment. It was such a release to let go and let someone else take over for a change. Soon he grasped eggs, cracked each with one hand and dropped them from a great height into the pan to put together an omelette.

'You French, that's so cheffy,' she said as he handed her a plate and a fork, but her tiredness was soothed by the soft warmth of egg and the crisp tang of parsley.

'Perfect.'

He smirked and washed out the pan before perching on the arm of her chair and quite naturally put his hand on her shoulder. Dulcie caught her breath and then relaxed as she realised that she liked it.

'You know I'm quite used to being alone, but it's at times like this that I'm glad that you were here,' she said.

'I'm glad too.' he looked over at the array of photographs on her wall, 'Your family?'

'Yes mostly of Imogen, my daughter. I'm so proud of her. If you get them down for me, I'll show you who everyone is.' He reached for the framed collage.

She pointed at a picture of an impressive white building. 'This is the Lunar Hotel. Imogen and her friends run it. I stayed to help while they got it going. Imogen has moved into rooms at the hotel, so that she can be there all the time.'

'They are young to run such a large hotel. How old is Imogen?' he said.

'She'll be twenty-five this year.'

'Ten years younger than me,' he said without looking up.

There was a little girl in many of the group photographs. Dulcie pointed to her, 'This is Diana. She is actually Anita's daughter, but they were all living in a shared house when she was born and everyone took a turn at looking after her. It was a happy time.

'I miss Diana. I helped look after her when she was a tiny baby and she has been here to visit me for holidays since.' She smiled and stroked the picture, 'She's a little chatterbox now.'

She noticed his slight frown, 'Oh I mean she talks a lot. Asks a lot of questions.'

'Ah I see, chatterbox. I will remember that word.'

'I miss her, but I still have children to talk to here.'

Dulcie glanced at the inglenook fireplace. She should have lit a fire, the rain had cooled everything down. There was just the loud and deep tick of an ornate clock on the heavy wooden beam above the stove. It set off a train of thought.

'I got that clock just after I arrived at the chateau. I was still living in the caravan outside and working on replacing beams and getting rid of damp in here,' she said. 'It came from a brocante. I can't resist old things. I wanted to tell you about my business idea. You know, I think I could buy French furniture and ornaments at local brocantes and sell them in England.'

His eyes shone, 'You are full of ideas and plans; I like that. French furniture is heavy though, would English people like French furniture I wonder. . .'

'Oh yes, I think so, if I chose carefully and I could paint the very dark objects. They'd like those spindly side tables you get over here.'

'I would enjoy to come with you if you would allow me,' he offered. 'I have some free time after the post is delivered and we can use my car.'

She noticed the mistake in his English. It seemed to happen when he was unsure of himself. 'Thank you, I'd like that.' she said. 'Imogen had a van to move furniture when they started in the hotel business. I don't think they'll need it now. I wonder if I could ask her to bring it to France for me. I'd love to have a visit from her again.'

She felt a charge run through her and, unfortunately, she shocked him as she leapt up out of her chair, 'There's no time like the present. I feel like going down to the phone box in town now to ask her if she'll come.'

He stood too, 'I'll give you a lift in the van and then carry on with my deliveries.'

'Oh, thank you that's so kind. I need to go to the tabac first to get one of those prepaid phone cards,' she looked around the room for her bag, so he bent to recover it from beside her chair. Going out together would make their friendship public knowledge but Gilles didn't seem worried. She gave a small smile; she wasn't worried either.

***

When Gilles parked the van at the end of the street, Dulcie turned to thank him. He gently moved towards her and brushed his lips across her's. She was taken entirely by surprise by the warmth of soft skin. She felt a rush of pleasure intermingled with consternation.

'Things are moving so fast,' she said.

'Live un peu.' Gilles laughed and translated, 'a little. I hope your Imogen approves.'

As she walked along the street, Dulcie wasn't aware of any other pedestrians. She squinted against the late afternoon sun, she felt her pulse racing and her stomach turn over. She didn't know what to think. The thought of Gilles was exciting, but was she acting like a young girl?

Chapter Eight

England

Imogen reversed the white van close to the service door of the hotel and dusted off her hands in satisfaction. She had only passed her driving test a few weeks before.

She caught herself smiling, 1978 was going to be her year. She swung down from the driver's door and heaved three enormous suitcases out of the van, followed by a large easy chair and a cardboard box full of Lever Arch files. She was at the hotel so often that it made sense to move in. The backrooms had been converted into a cosy home. She'd enjoyed transforming one of the bedrooms for five-year-old Diana. But where was everyone?

The reception desk was being covered by Tony, 'You got here in one piece then,' he said.

'Hmm and I'm all moved in,' she looked around for their receptionist. 'What's happened, where's Sharon?'

'She's got a dental emergency, so I'm stuck here I'm afraid or I'd have been there to welcome you.'

'OK, come on a visit when you get the chance. I just need to have a breather.' Imogen backed away then turned to punch in the code to the back office. It was so familiar that she no longer noticed the post-it notes on the noticeboard and piles of letters and booking forms in the in-tray. She slouched in an office chair, legs extended under the desk and momentarily closed her eyes. *If I get hold of Anita now, I'll catch her before she sets off to the theatre.* She turned to the green Trimphone on the desk and dialled Anita's digs in London.

'Could I speak to Anita Tomalty please?'

She could hear rustling and furniture being disturbed, as Anita came to the phone.

'Imogen, I've been wondering how the move's going?'

'I'm in. Tired, but in. It feels like the start of a new era for us. And I did a good job with the van – if I say so myself. Looks like we've got some people interested in buying the old house too.'

'I'll be so sad,' Anita said, 'After all Diana was born there. And has Diana seen her new room yet?'

'No I'll go and pick her up from school in a minute. She's going to love it. So, she hasn't seen the castle stencilled over her bed yet and all her stuff's laid out in there. I'm afraid my room is still a tip, I'm going to sort that out gradually.'

'Great. I suppose as long as you've got somewhere to sleep tonight.'

'Yes speaking of tonight, when do you need to leave?'

Anita's voice altered, 'Now I'm afraid.'

'OK break a leg, as they say.' Imogen heard a hurried 'bye' followed by the dialling tone.

***

Tony swung around the door to join Imogen and Diana while they ate beans on toast. You could only eat so much hotel food - prawn cocktail, scampi, and steak. Diana swung her legs rhythmically and waved her fork in the air as she ate with one eye on the television.

'A letter came for you today from France.' he said handing it to Imogen.

'Is it from Dulcie, can I see?' Diana asked.

'When I've read it,' said Imogen ripping open the flimsy blue 'Par Avion' envelope.

'I spoke to Mummy today. She was just going to the theatre, but she asked if you'd seen your new room yet.'

'Diana nodded vigorously, 'And I'm going to play in it in a minute.'

Imogen scanned over the letter. 'I've meant to ask. . . do we need the van anymore?' she said to Tony and not waiting for a reply she looked over to Diana. 'We might have a holiday in France very soon.'

'Yippee.' said Diana. I'll be able to make dens with the children.'

'Yes and this time, we'll be able to stay in the cottage. It's all done, so we won't be in a tatty little caravan.'

***

Imogen was on duty, hosting a Chamber of Commerce networking event. She planned to work the room and charm people into considering the hotel for business.

'Great to see you again,' a local estate agent, Millie, bustled up to her. 'How's it going, tell me all about it.'

She didn't really want to know the answer, so Imogen just smiled and said, 'Welcome again, glad you could make it.'

Another group arrived, and Imogen watched Millie dive into the middle of them for more effusive greetings. Tony arrived at Imogen's shoulder. 'Everyone's happy?'

'Oh you've appeared,' she pushed him playfully on the shoulder. 'You're a part-timer now.'

Tony grinned while keeping one eye on the incoming crowd. 'Have a heart, it's a long time since I've had a boyfriend. I'm enjoying nesting.'

'You deserve to be happy, Tony. . .' Imogen started to say and then looked intently across the room. There was a new face, a black woman, among the crowd. 'Excuse me, I think it's someone I know.'

It was Lynette from the office, as stylish as ever, she was in a group of people, but looking hesitant. Imogen covered the width of the room rapidly and arrived at Lynette's elbow.

'Hello,' she said softly.

Lynette looked around, her mouth flew open and then her hand flew up to her mouth. 'I knew you ran a hotel, but I hadn't realised it was this one.' She beamed and looked Imogen directly in the eyes, 'Wow this is an amazing coincidence.'

'So, you've joined the business crowd?' Imogen said.

'Yes, after we both left the advertising agency, I finished my distance learning and started training with a solicitors'. I'm here to network for them.' She gave a small laugh and looked at the noisy throng, 'Well I'm networking with you. So glad to see you.' and her eyes showed the truth of that.

'We'd better mingle.' Imogen said, 'but can you stay after and I'll show you around.'

As they worked the room, Imogen stayed close-by, feeling a strong bond with her old friend.

***

Lynette had been given the full tour of the hotel. She met Tony and heard all about Anita and Diana. She was visibly impressed by the stylish decoration. Now that Anita was in a London show and Tony was setting up home with Vic, Imogen missed friendly adult company. In the past, she and Lynette had had the odd lunch in a café, but they had never really seen each other outside the workplace. As Lynette was leaving, Imogen felt a flutter of anxiety that they might not see each other again. She paused on the front step.

'I just wondered, would you like to join me on a day out with Diana next Sunday? I try to get her away from the hotel on my day off. That's if you're not doing anything.'

For an awful moment, Imogen thought that she was going to say no, but after some hesitation, Lynette agreed. Imogen felt a glow of satisfaction when she sat down at her desk to tackle invoices.

***

The Intercom lit up to show Reception were phoning through, Imogen pressed the button, 'Yes Sharon?'

'Someone to see you. Your father.'

With a jolt of surprise, Imogen's automatic response was, 'Oh, thank you'.

She hurried out to the reception area and spotted him before he saw her. She could tell by the way that he was standing that he was tired. When she drew nearer she could see his face looked worn.

'Hello, Imogen dear.'

'Are you alright? What's happened?'

'I'm fine, fine,' he said. 'I just decided to come to see you for a change.' Then he shrugged his shoulders with a smile, 'After all you do run a hotel.'

He was the same, yet different. Maybe he had thickened around the waist slightly and the hair around his temples was beginning to grey. He had always been so staid; Imogen hardly remembered seeing him without a tie. Now he was wearing navy trousers and a salmon pink open-necked shirt.

'Well, of course, you're welcome. Come into my quarters, Dad, and let's sit down together.' Imogen nodded at Sharon, 'Thanks, I'll be busy for half an hour.'

As she keyed in the code for her door, he said, 'You know I should visit more often. I haven't seen your new home here.'

Imogen felt confused to hear this from a father who had always been too busy. 'Well, let me show you around now. You didn't see where I lived before either. I rented a room in Tony's large house. It was furnished, so this is the first time that I've really been able to put my stamp on something. A lot of things are still in boxes.' She looked across at the stack of grocery boxes and tea chests at one end of the room.

'No matter. I think I need a seat,' he said and sank into a wicker two-seater.

'Are you okay?' she said again.

'I'm fit as a fiddle. But I have been struggling. It's all getting on top of me'.

She squatted on a leather pouffe near to him, 'Why what's been happening?'

'Oh, you know,' he waved his hand, 'Selling the house, seeing solicitors about the divorce and then - I've moved into my own flat you know. It's a flat above Alan's garage. Very convenient, they'd originally converted it for their eldest son to use, but then he left home. It needs the woman's touch. Do you have the woman's touch? Your mother did.'

'If you mean a flair for decorating, I'm not sure. Tony was a major influence in the hotel. I can tell you're missing Mum.'

'Don't feel sorry for me. I have ventured into dating. But it isn't the same as having someone there when you come home from work. Someone that you can rely on,' he humphed and his neck sank into his chest. He looked around her living room and kitchenette for a moment.

'Have you heard from your mother?'

'She sends airmail letters from France and I've had the occasional phone call, yes. I think the divorce is a stress for both of you. I wish you'd sort it out soon.'

'It isn't as simple as that,' he said, 'You can't hurry it. Solicitors take their time, and splitting up from your mother is draining -it can take you through the wringer.'

She looked at him sharply. 'Look you're not okay, are you? Would you like to stay the night here, just take a break?'

'To be honest, it would be good not to have to go back to that bare flat and I can easily stay. I've arranged unpaid leave from my company. I'm not sure whether I will ever go back. That's part of a life that's done with.'

Imogen was glad that Ted did stay on for a few days. It gave her a chance to see him as a person rather than just a father. She suggested he try a turn on Reception, but he hated greeting guests so he made himself useful bringing the accounts up to date. Ted was willing to read a bedtime story to Diana, but he looked lost for words when she tried to draw him into one of her games.

Imogen began to wonder whether she should ask him along on her trip out with Lynette and Diana, but by Saturday he said, 'I think it's time I went back to Alan's. Thank you for my little holiday, but if I stay away too long, I will never make a success of my new life.'

'You're quite welcome to stay longer, Dad,' Imogen said.

She saw a smile and then a frown chase across his face, 'Thank you my dear, but I think I've got a date on Saturday night. Better not miss that.'

This news made Imogen feel odd and also sad; he was her father, not a young man about town. But she smiled and gave him a peck on the cheek. 'Well you know you're always welcome.'

***

The day out with Lynette and Diana had been a lot of fun. Diana enjoyed having the attention of two adults. They'd packed sandwiches and a Thermos. Imogen gathered up a plaid blanket from the back seat of the car and carried it in both arms to an area of short grass. It was on a smooth slope running down from the entrance of a stately home. Groups of people were dotted about on the lawns, but they were far enough from each other to give privacy.

There was no chance to have a conversation as Diana kept up a continual prattle, but they revelled in being able to raise their faces to catch the breeze and the weak sunshine. Their relaxation was disturbed by a sharp clack, clack, clack from Diana.

'What're you doing?'

She had decided to dig in the grass and was banging one stone against another, 'I'm making a sharp edge. It's going to be a stone-age knife,' she said while continuing with the rhythmic noise.

Imogen leapt up and offered a hand to Diana, 'Come on I'll push you on the swings,' Imogen was aware of the figure she cut putting physical effort into meeting the momentum of the swing and stretching to push it back again.

No sooner had Diana shouted 'higher, higher,' than she called, 'Stop.' She had seen other children on the climbing equipment and wanted to join them. Imogen strode back to Lynette, flushed with the physical effort. They watched Diana playing and other groups of parents interacting with their children.

Lynette said, 'Luckily I like children.' Then she laughed, 'yes even when their creations involve making irritating noise. I'm used to them anyway. I come from a big family. I've been persuaded to be a Sunday School teacher, so I've taken time off from the children in Sunday school to be here today.'

'I'm not sure that I could take them 'en masse'.' said Imogen.

'My little brothers' noise really got to me when I was studying, I wanted to throw my books out of the window at them sometimes,' Lynette said. 'It's very crowded at our house; we're on top of each other.'

'You know I really admire you for managing to do distance learning while you were employed. You must have a lot of ambition. If you ever want to get away and enjoy civilised adult company come over to the Lunar Hotel.' Imogen said with a slight catch in her voice; she felt that she was pushing for a deeper friendship than Lynette might want.

Lynette's eyelids flickered and she looked away. 'Thank you, though it isn't so much ambition as determination to gain some independence from my family. And I'd love to come and spend some time with you.'

At that moment, Diana came bursting back onto the picnic rug nearly knocking Imogen into the sandwiches as she pushed between the two of them.

'Careful,' Imogen said with a glare. It didn't quell Diana, very little did.

'Can I have an ice cream? Can I? Can I?'

'What do you say?'

'Please,' Diana said planting a very wet kiss on Imogen's cheek.

'My treat, I'll get these.' Lynette uncrossed her legs and lithely pushed herself up. She held out her hand to take Diana's.

Imogen watched them: Lynette's skirt swaying as she walked, her elegant shoulders dipped to listen to what Diana was saying to her. The two of them standing by the ice cream kiosk – we're like a little family of our own today, she mused. Who would have thought, back in the days when Lynette was showing her the ropes at Kent & Minster that they would one day be revelling in a day-trip together?

Chapter Nine

Lynette often dropped in for an evening meal with Imogen when Diana had gone to bed. Imogen collected a tray of hotel food and carried it in, so that they could sit together on the settee and watch television. The conversation had long ago ceased to be reminiscences of their old employment. They had a shared interest in business affairs and legal matters, then one evening Lynette had brought board games with her. They both enjoyed games of strategy.

They had the board on the floor and sat either side of it.

'You are getting better at this all the time.' Lynette said to Imogen, 'I'll soon find it much harder to win.' She eased her legs out from under her.

'I might be getting better, but you're distracted this evening. I can tell. I've been able to plan ways to win without you noticing.' Imogen poured herself more red wine and hovered the bottle over Lynette's glass.

'No, no.' Lynette covered the rim of her glass with her hand. 'I want to keep a clear head for the walk home.' The twilight glowed through the window and lit up her skin to a golden brown. Lynette stood up to draw the curtains and said, 'I'll feel better about being out at night when it gets light earlier.' She sank back to the floor but didn't pay any attention to the game.

'Games need a lot of concentration. Are you getting tired? Tell me, why are you distracted?'

'Oh, I'm not sure . . .' Lynette looked down and then sipped from her glass. She raised her head and looked Imogen in the eyes. 'OK, I suppose it's just that I struggle to do the right thing. My parents expect a lot of me. It's hard, and the younger ones get away with murder.'

Imogen smiled slightly. 'I know your parents are strict. You aren't making a lot of sense, though. Is there something in particular that they push you about?'

'Well, I am expected to be the older daughter. Conscientious at work, looking after the children, fitting in with their views. . . I suppose that's the hard part. I don't feel part of the Church and I have felt the tension even more since I've been doing Sunday school teaching.'

'Mm,' Imogen wasn't sure where to focus an answer. Lynette was describing every area of her life. Still curled up on the floor, she reached up to put on a table light. When she turned back, she realised that Lynette looked as though she was about to burst. It felt like a crisis.

'If I tell you something, I hope you won't judge me. I know Tony is gay and you are friends with him.' Lynette gabbled, 'You see - I like women rather than men. I've known from when I was quite young, but I just thought "That's not how it's supposed to be".'

Imogen sensed that Lynette was waiting for a reaction, 'I see,' she said slowly, 'Thank you for trusting me enough to tell me about it.'

Lynette's shoulders sank and she let out a long breath, 'I haven't acted on it of course. Well there was a girl at school. You know,' she laughed slightly, 'we were on a school trip and we'd wandered off to play in the trees. We had a little kiss, but we didn't talk about it again afterwards.' Lynette began to pack the pieces from the board game into their box and Imogen shuffled nearer to help. Lynette stopped again, 'It's become more of a problem to me since the Sunday school, because I know the attitudes of the Church members. We've got some very outspoken elderly ladies.'

'Do you have to do Sunday school?'

'Oh, you don't know my family, they practically pushed me forward for it. I don't like to let them down. I suppose I've spent years being the type of daughter that they want. I can't imagine not doing that. Are you religious? You've never said.'

'It hasn't played a big part in my life. I sometimes think about spiritual things – but no, not often. We've both had such different families.'

'Well yes,' Lynette had a rich laugh, 'Not least because my family's from Jamaica and your family is rich and white.'

Imogen's heart seemed to stop, 'Well sorry, I can't help where I come from,' she said. 'I'm an only child and I've had to face up to their expectations too, you know. You missed seeing my dad, he stayed here for a short time. I think he's having some sort of midlife crisis, but I'd love you to meet my mum, she's gone off to France to make a new life.'

Lynette's eyes widened. 'I can't imagine that.'

'What, just completely breaking away. Actually, I meant to tell you,' Imogen added, 'I'm going over to see Mum soon. She's asked if she could have our old van now that we aren't using it so much, so I'm going to drive it there.'

Lynette bit her lip, 'I'll really miss you. I'll have to spend my evenings sitting in my bedroom at home and playing solitaire.' Then her tone altered, 'No I mean it. It won't be the same without you.'

Imogen felt secretly pleased. She wasn't sure that anyone had ever missed her before.

'Soon be back, though.' she said. Somehow knowing that Lynette liked women, stopped her from her natural inclination to reach out and rub her shoulder. She would need to go away and think about this new information and question how she felt about it.

'You know I'm really stiff from sitting on this floor.' She picked up the board and helped Lynette up. Imogen excused herself to check that the night porter had arrived.

When she came back, Lynette was in the kitchenette making instant coffee. She carried two mugs into the living room, 'All okay?'

'Yes, he's here and everything is running smoothly.' Imogen held up her crossed fingers with a wry smile.

'And no sound coming from Diana's room she must be asleep by now.' Lynette added, 'How's her mum?'

'She's heading for the stars at this rate. She's in a West End musical now, and she's just heard that the run has been extended. So - fantastic. Not so good for Diana as she only sees her on days off. In fact, I'm going to take Diana with me to France, it will make it simpler for Anita to get on with her career while she can.' She stopped and looked thoughtful, 'She's in Joseph at the moment. Let's go and see it. We could take the train, have a meal out. I'll make sure Tony fills in here. Yes, let's do it.' She suddenly felt exhilarated and clasped her hands together.

'That would cause a stir.' Lynette said, smiling slightly back but in a much more subdued way.

'A stir, why?'

'When we are out together, we draw attention. People aren't accustomed to seeing a black girl being friends with a white girl. Didn't you notice the sidelong looks we got when we were out on the picnic that day?'

'No I didn't,' Imogen thought back to the sunlit park and the ice cream van. Maybe she had been oblivious. 'But I think if anyone is small-minded, we should ignore them anyway.'

'Mm, I like your style.' Lynette nodded at her, 'but. . . I don't think you understand what racism can be like until you've experienced it.' Her face fell, 'I'm sorry it's a downer. Look, let's think about it. People are much more cosmopolitan in London.'

***

Imogen lay awake that night going over everything that had been said. Tony had been threatened with blackmail over being gay, and he'd been horrified. But she and Anita had stood by him and he had made the decision to 'come out'. She knew he had felt liberated by it. He had been worried about clients' reactions and he was still discreet where it served a purpose, but now that he was setting up home with Vic, he was really happy.

Maybe the difference was that Lynette didn't seem able to tear herself out of her parents' grasp. No, I'm not being fair, she thought. She comes from such a different culture and they're very close. I need to support her. Does this alter our friendship in any way? Well, I'm fascinated by what it's like. I wonder how her kiss with her friend in the woods came about.

She felt that Lynette had a strange charisma, a confidence in her bearing which contradicted her quietly spoken manner and hesitancy. Interesting. . . she thought, as her mind fell into sleep.

Chapter Ten

Sunday lunch at the Lunar Hotel went smoothly. Imogen liked to be around in case of emergencies, but the staff worked as a highly trained team. She surveyed the sea of white tablecloths and the waiting staff deftly sliding between tables to provide silver service.

Lynette appeared among the next cluster of arrivals at the door. Was something wrong?

Imogen glided over to the reception desk and intercepted her. 'Everything all right? I thought you were doing Sunday school today.'

'I am, I mean I was.' said Lynette wrinkling her nose. 'Can we go through to the back?' she inclined her head towards Imogen's quarters.

Imogen hid her concern and made Lynette welcome.

She moved a pile of ironing from one of the chairs, 'Come on, sit down. Tell me all about it.'

'Oh no, there's nothing really wrong. I'm skiving off. There's more study to do for work and I just wanted some time to get on with it. I feel really guilty. Can I come and spend Sunday with you?' She looked sheepish.

'There's no need to feel guilty. I'm glad that you feel comfortable here.' Imogen had a feeling of wellbeing. She noticed that Lynette had put her briefcase on the floor and so she carried it over to the table for her.

'It's a haven in here with you,' Lynette said. 'I'm not so comfortable out there though with the Sunday lunch crowd all dressed up.'

'You hold your own. You are always smart.' Imogen's voice rose affronted and she plunked herself down beside Lynette at the table.

'Well thank you.' Lynette smiled. 'It depends on my mood. Sometimes I find it hard to be the only person who looks different. It feels safe in the area I live and with all my family around – strength in numbers.'

'I hadn't realised.' Imogen said, 'Is it very difficult?'

Lynette tucked her headwrap down around her ears, 'I'm afraid yes. I have heard mutters of 'wog' too often when I get on a bus. Sometimes it makes me sad but recently I just get angry. You never know where you'll get it.'

Imogen felt sharp sympathy for her and wanted to make it better. 'Oh Lynette, Netty,' she said softly.

'Oh - a new nickname!' Lynette said with a laugh. 'We have to carry on despite all this. But - get this - when I went for my job interview the receptionist watched me walk in and asked, "Are you the cleaner?" I mean, I was dressed in a suit as well.'

Imogen drew in a sharp breath, 'That was so rude.'

'I've never been sure whether it was deliberate or whether she really was expecting a cleaner. But even if she was, it was unforgivable.'

'Surely that's not at the solicitors' where you work now?' Imogen said.

'Mm,' Lynette nodded her head, 'I still ignore her. She probably thinks that it's me that's being rude. Of course, I'm rising in the company,' she added, tossing her head. 'Well, aren't we getting heavy for a Sunday lunchtime?'

'Oh yes, I should ask . . . have you eaten?'

'I could do with a snack.' Lynette jerked her shoulders upwards apologetically.

'Prawn cocktail and a roast beef sandwich, do you?'

'Mm,' Lynette licked her lips and jumped up to set out her books on the table ready to study. When Imogen came back with a silver tray full of enough food for two, Lynette cleared a space on the table and said, 'No Diana?'

'She's having a day out with Anita. They'll be in later and then you'll be able to meet Anita. She'll like you and I hope you'll like her.'

'I suppose as an unmarried mum, Anita has had to deal with bigots too.' Lynette said.

'Well yes,' Imogen spoke while chewing on her sandwich, 'But she has been sheltered by being with Tony and me.' She stopped and looked at Lynette, 'You know, back then when we decided to open a hotel together, I was still working at the office. I remember going for a coffee together and daydreaming that one day I'd be able to show you around my own hotel. I pictured a dazzling dining room with white tablecloths – just like the one here really. And now I've been able to do that.'

'So you always meant to keep in touch,' Lynette put her head on one side and looked at Imogen. They chewed in silence. Imogen, aware that her mother would have totally disapproved of the way that she was resting her elbows on the table. She looked at Lynette's warm brown skin and thought how tempting it would be to stroke her soft arm. Get a grip, she thought to herself, this must be the result of Lynette saying that she was drawn to women. Oh, perhaps I'm drawn to women, or at least drawn to Lynette. She thought about the implications. Could she take that road? Tony had led the way.

'I can see thoughts whirring in your head Imogen, what's going on in there?' Lynette gently touched Imogen's head.

'Nothing,' Imogen muttered. She was aware that she could really blow it if she let Lynette in on her thoughts. After all,

Lynette was a strictly brought up Sunday school teacher and had already been struggling to come to terms with the issue on her own behalf.

'This is so difficult that I don't know what to say,' Imogen said.

Lynette bit her lip, 'I knew I shouldn't have told you – that you wouldn't be able to deal with it. We were getting on fine and now I've upset everything.'

'No, no you haven't,' Imogen's voice softened. 'it did get me thinking but you haven't upset me in any way.' She grabbed for Lynette's hand. Her knuckles felt boney, she had remarkably long fingers, 'I started thinking after you told me, though. I've thought a lot. I've been on long walks to get it sorted out in my head.' She looked down and stopped.

Lynette tore herself away, jumped up and began pacing up and down the room. 'I'm sorry. I'm really sorry. I couldn't bear it if this changed our friendship.'

Imogen saw the despair on Lynette's face. 'Don't feel bad, Netty. It's me.' Then she forced herself to speak and blurted, 'I think I may have feelings for you that I haven't recognised.'

Lynette stood still and turned to look at her. There was silence.

'Sit down please,' Imogen said, and when Lynette swiftly joined her on the settee, she said, 'I've been thinking about you. . . I don't know whether I am someone who likes women. But I am drawn to you. I feel all warm when I look at you and I admire your wisdom, your determination to do the right thing. . . ' tears hovered at the corners of her eyes. 'I know that if I have feelings for you, it could make your life difficult because you're trying to belong within your family and your church. So I'm just making it all worse for you.' She looked down and wrung her hands, 'I just felt I had to say something.'

There was more silence, and then Imogen felt Lynette's fingertips gently stroke her cheek.

'What does this mean for us?' Lynette said slowly, 'I am very flattered. I like you a lot. You know that. I've always liked you. But what does this mean? It can't go anywhere.'

Imogen clenched her jaw and struggled to reach a place of stillness. 'OK, you are right of course. I'm sorry.'

'No, don't be sorry. I am very pleased that you feel so strongly for me,' Lynette said. 'It's just . . . I feel so close to you too. I admit I feel it intensely, but I have never ever heard of two women being romantic together. Have you?' she lightly pressed her own forehead to Imogen's forehead and held both of her hands. Seconds went by but when she drew back, she said, 'And I want to have a family-a husband and kids. I want them to visit Jamaica. One day I want grandkids.'

Imogen smiled at her. 'I understand. I haven't been looking into the future, but you've got your life mapped out.' She sniffed away her tears and shifted further way on the settee. 'Let's not spoil things. Live for the day, Tony always says. Let's go out and do some window shopping today. I need to find a few things for France anyway.'

Lynette smiled sadly agreeing to follow Imogen back into everyday life.

As they left the hotel, they waved a hurried 'goodbye' to Tony, who looked after them bemusedly. Imogen drove. Sitting side by side facing front in a car made it easier to talk.

'My Dad, he's strict and always certain that he knows best,' Lynette said, 'Mum is the religious one and she's fanatical about it. I think Mum is softer when it comes to her children but unbending.'

'I remember you telling me about your Dad being strict about boyfriends,' Imogen said, 'My parents, I'm not sure how I'd describe them. They were ambitious for me and they can be quite judgemental but. . . since they split up, I think they've been too busy managing their own lives to worry too much about me. All this talk of parents, I think it's because we are thinking about how our parents would take it if we got together.'

Lynette shook her head, 'Not really, because there isn't a lot of doubt in my mind about how they'd take it.' She screwed up her fists on her knees, 'I can imagine they'd try to lock me up.'

Imogen felt closer to Lynette for having had that conversation. Everywhere was quiet on a Sunday so they easily found a parking space. They walked with shoulders touching. She felt that they were a unit. Neither really wanted to browse but they did look into a chemist's window at film for the camera, mosquito repellent and sunscreen.

'It seems odd to be looking at that, standing here in the drizzle.' Imogen said, 'and so frustrating that the shops are closed on Sundays. The desolation of it matches my mood.'

CHAPTER ELEVEN

Imogen hadn't seen Lynette since their walk in the drizzle. It had been an unusually long gap between visits. She became consumed by the agonising thought that she'd said the wrong thing. If only Anita had been around, she would have confided in her. All she could think of was to try the solicitor's office to get in touch with Lynette. If only she had thought to get some contact details. She hung on a bit longer. She knew that Lynette had promised to come to see her the evening before they set off to France. She was beginning to feel nervous at the prospect.

Imogen nipped back into town to organise things for the French trip on the following Saturday. She included small cubes of dried soup; ideal for stopping en route and setting up a primus stove if they didn't fancy going into a restaurant.

Lynette still hadn't come. Imogen, who was usually calm and organised, had an uncharacteristic wobble on the day before the journey. She ticked off items to take to Mum in France: tea bags a large box, English brand toothpaste, a stock of digestive and rich tea biscuits packed around her clean knickers so that they didn't get broken. How many tins of baked beans? They were so heavy. All the comforts from home.

It was the end of the school term, so she had all of Diana's holiday clothes laid out on the bed, clean and ironed. Tony swung through the door with his rucksack. He was going to stay permanently in her quarters while she was away. He stashed the bag on the floor of her bedroom.

'I'm not sure whether I've told you everything. I know upcoming events are on the calendar, but have I told you the arrangements I've already made?' She tapped her lips with her fingertips in thought.

'You made a lot of lists,' he said. 'Don't worry, I can follow the trail of notes on your desk if I get stuck. I hope you can switch off when you get there.'

Imogen nodded ruefully. He grabbed her hand and pulled her towards the door, 'Look come and have a coffee and relax before Diana's home from school. You'll get overtired if you keep on like this.'

She allowed herself to be manoeuvred into a deep-buttoned high back chair in the lounge. It was mid-morning and the lounge was deserted. Tony went behind the bar to prepare a tray with a coffee jug, cream, crockery and he scattered on mint chocolates wrapped in foil.

'You're doing us proud,' she said with a smile and sank further into the chair. 'Will Vic manage without you?'

'I know you were being facetious but actually, you are close to the truth. Vic's never lived on his own. He hasn't said a word, but he looks worried. He relies on me more than I sometimes realise.'

'He could come and stay at the hotel with you.'

He shrugged, 'I think it's good for him to experience the house without me in it occasionally, but yes if he finds it too much, I'll suggest it to him. Are we expecting to see Lynette over, later?'

Imogen's head jerked up in surprise, 'Yes as a matter of fact. What made you ask that?'

'Well she's become one of the fixtures here,' Tony laughed gently, 'I thought that you'd want to say goodbye.'

'She's coming to see us after work,' Imogen said.

'OK, I'll pop in and take Diana for a bit. Give you two space.'

Imogen looked at him and felt irritated. 'What are you saying? She will want to say goodbye to Diana too.' She flushed slightly. It felt as though she had been caught out, but she had nothing to feel guilty about.

Tony paused, looking wary, 'Yes sorry. I overstepped the mark there.' He brought out a notepad and went on to list the events that Imogen had organised for the week and to reassure her that he knew exactly who had booked them and how rooms should be laid out. Imogen barely listened. She was examining how she felt about Tony's assumptions.

A group of businesspeople arrived early for lunch and Tony left to alert the barman. As Imogen piled their cups back onto the tray, she saw a taxi drawing into the parking area and just as it went past the window, she was sure that she spotted Lynette in the rear seat. Her heart pounded. She whipped the tray to the washing-up machine and continued straight through the kitchen to look out of the fire exit. Lynette was leaning in to pay the driver then she turned and saw her.

'Everything alright?' Imogen called across, 'I wasn't expecting to see you until this evening?' She hung on to the push bar but had one foot outside on the tarmac.

Lynette moved nearer and smiled. 'It's fine. I had time off work. I couldn't concentrate anyway, waiting to see you this evening and knowing that you and Diana would be off early tomorrow.'

In Imogen's quarters she sat and opened her hands, palm upwards, 'I'm so used to coming here now it's going to feel odd.' Then glancing around at signs of packing she added, 'I hope I'm not holding you up.'

'No, I've always got time for you. I'd like to be ready by the time Diana comes home from school though. Where've you been? I've missed you.'

Lynette said, 'I'm sorry I felt I needed a bit of time to think, after our last meeting. I have thought about you though.' She leant down to reach an envelope from out of her handbag. 'Here, this is for you. Something to take with you on your journey.' A thick pastel watercolour card made by Hallmark. Imogen dipped her head to read the long verse written in calligraphy.

'No, don't read it aloud,' Lynette said, 'I'll be embarrassed.'

So, Imogen read the rhyming sentiments which began 'You make me ridiculously happy. . .' Something bubbled up inside her and she felt lightheaded. It was a printed card, but she pictured Lynette choosing just the right words, queuing to pay for it, and gathering her courage to bring it and declare herself.

She tipped her head to look up at Lynette. 'Thank you, I'll keep it with me and look at it when I miss our chats together.' She rose to pack it down the side of her case and when she turned back, Lynette was busy filling the kettle and getting out the mugs.

CHAPTER TWELVE

France

The white van trundled through the chateau gateway. It was all Dulcie could do to stop herself from jumping up and down and waving her arms in the air to them. Imogen had phoned from Calais after they'd disembarked from the ferry three days ago. She and Diana had meandered down the country, staying in hotels as they went.

It was thrilling to see them again. Dulcie could see Imogen at the wheel slowly reversing to park by the tall stone wall around the domain. A slim figure in flared jeans, she went around to help Diana to jump down. Dulcie advanced, her arms extended.

'Hello, darling. How are you?'

She ushered them indoors. Imogen wiped her brow, 'Wow what a journey it's been. It was a difficult drive for a little girl like Diana, but she slept a lot of the time.'

'Did you?' Dulcie squatted down to Diana, 'What do you think of France?'

'It's alright. I can say, "Bonjour", "Merci".' Diana said.

'Very good, now I'll get a nice cold drink for you both.' Dulcie had put a bottle of homemade lemonade in a bucket of cold water to keep it cool. She handed glasses to each of them.

She dipped her head to look out of the window at the van, 'The journey was a good test of the van. If it can do that, then you've obviously looked after it. And the seat was comfortable on a long journey?'

Before Imogen could answer, Diana who had been standing quietly drinking, erupted into life, pulling on Dulcie's hand.

'Can we see the castle? Are the children here to play with? Where's your cat?' she said in a childish voice that rose insistently with each question.

Dulcie gave her full attention. 'I think Oscar disappeared as soon as he saw such a crowd of visitors, darling. He'll be back. You'll have plenty of time to see everything. Now, what can you play with? Would you like to have a look through my button box? See if you can find some that match each other.' She rattled a colourful biscuit tin stored beside a treadle sewing machine. 'You will want to settle in. You two can use the bedroom and I will go back to using the caravan again.'

Imogen held her glass, lounging in the chair with her legs outstretched. She was too tired from driving to talk very much but she said, 'We can rough it, Mum. Don't worry about us, we can all stay here and we'll put up a camp bed for Diana.'

They gave up further conversation as Diana talked non-stop about her school and her dancing classes.

Eventually, Dulcie got up to take Diana to the door, 'Come on, we'll go out and unload the cases. Then I'll take you to meet the other children. You'll probably remember Ziggy from last time you were here, but Anise was just a baby then, so you can make friends with her. We'll listen for the sounds of children's voices in the woods.'

***

Imogen, left alone, lugged the cases through to the back room of the lodge and started to wrestle with the metal legs of the camp bed. She failed to hear the sound of someone walking in through the front door, 'Bonjour,' came a man's voice, but she didn't hear that either.

She emerged wiping her hands on the back of her jeans and brushing at her hair, but stopped at the sight of a tall, angular figure in a sky-blue uniform with a soft blue peaked cap. She advanced towards him, 'Hello, can I help you?'

What remarkable confidence he had. He held out his hand, 'Gilles Joubert, bonjour. And you, you are Imogen?'

'I am,' so he knew her name. She breathed more easily knowing that.

'Pardon, Madame.' Gilles said, 'I was hoping to see Ceci. But I am pleased to meet you. Ceci has told me about you and I know she is happy that you are visiting.'

Yes, she remembered that her mother was often called Ceci around the chateau. It was endearing that she'd acquired a pet name here. She wished her mother would reappear, what was to be done with their visitor. It was too much, on top of a long drive. The uniform made her think of a French postman, 'You've brought the post?'

'Not at this time, no. I am a friend,' he said, looking around and clearly not sure what to do next.

'Well, Mum's out,' Imogen said, sinking into one of the chairs. 'Do you want to wait? I'm afraid I'm still recovering from my journey. Mum has just gone to find the children. I'm sure she'll be back soon, particularly if she was expecting you to call.'

'No she was not expecting me,' Gilles said, 'But yes, I will sit.'

There was a pause, then he said, 'I saw your van. Have you a good journey?'

As a hotelier, it was second nature to be welcoming, as a daughter it was not. Imogen already felt out of place and her mother hadn't mentioned Gilles to her.

'Yes it was fine.'

At that moment the door was thrown open and Dulcie blew in. 'Oh, hello. You've met each other. Well, that's good. And Diana is having a lovely time. I waited to make sure that she and the other children had all become friends.'

She slowed as she realised that they weren't responding. 'Time for a good old English cup of tea I think. You too, Gilles?'

'Err no, no. I will leave you to have some family time, Ceci,' he got to his feet, 'I will return later.'

'Okay,' Dulcie felt the tension but was unable to ease it until she'd had time to weigh up the situation. She followed him out to stand on the threshold. Lowering her voice she moved closer to his chest, 'Are you alright? I'd hoped that you two would get on.'

'Yes, don't worry. Imogen has had a long journey,' he said. She felt his hand stroke her upper arm. Their connection was renewed. As he left through the pillars of the chateau gates she stood and waved.

Back inside, Imogen snorted, 'Sorry I wasn't expecting to see the postman. What's going on there?'

Dulcie's back stiffened, 'Not just the postman, dear. He is a friend. Much as I enjoy being part of a community, it has been comforting to have a friend on the outside at times.'

During the next week, Dulcie spent days out with them in the mountains and visiting tourist destinations. It gave her a chance to investigate the best towns for brocantes. She was glad of some time with her daughter. They parked at a recreation area to let Diana run onto the play equipment while they sat at a wooden picnic bench to watch over her.

Dulcie brushed her fingers along the skin of Imogen's arm, 'You've been very quiet. Have you got something on your mind?' she half expected Imogen to comment again on Gilles, but Imogen jerked her arm away.

'Mother. For goodness sake, I don't have to talk all the time.' Then she softened her voice, 'You know I'm an adult now. When I want to ask for your advice, I will do.'

Dulcie sat up straighter. Perhaps Imogen has a boyfriend but I need to wait until she wants to tell me.

'I know, I'm sorry.' she said, 'I'm still finding my feet here, so I suppose I'm looking for someone to feel close to. It'll be better once this divorce is sorted out. Have you heard from your dad?'

'He came over to the hotel,' Imogen said. Dulcie felt surprised; her chest tightened. When she left Ted and went to stay with Imogen and help at the hotel, he hadn't made any effort to come looking for her.

'I think he's a changed person Mum. It wasn't like the old Dad at all. . . or perhaps it was like Dad that I remember from holidays when I was young.'

'So he is more happy and relaxed?'

'No not that,' Imogen stopped and tipped her head upwards narrowing her eyes as though recalling her father, 'he was more real. He was prepared to tell me how he felt.'

Dulcie spoke through gritted teeth, 'And how does he feel?'

'Oh look, Mum, I don't want to get between you two.' Imogen leapt up to go to Diana who was sitting on one end of a seesaw.

***

They were tired when they arrived back at the lodge. The evening had turned cold and they lit a small fire. It was beginning to feel like home to Imogen.

'Come on you, time to get ready for bed,' she said to Diana and Dulcie warmed some milk and conjured up biscuits for Diana's supper.

'I wanted to mention, tomorrow night is the Community meal,' Dulcie said, 'I'm on the rota to help with preparation. Would you like to come to keep me company while I cook? Although I'm sure they would welcome you at the meal, I haven't seen any non-residents there. I think it would be easier if we go off for a picnic together after I've done my share of the cooking. What do you say?'

Imogen got up to put her arm around her, 'Sounds lovely Mum, whatever you think, we'll go along with it.'

Diana was sitting on the floor absorbed in doing dot-to-dot and prolonging supper time by drinking her mug of milk in slow sips, 'What, what are we going to do?' she cocked her head up to look at them.

'A picnic, that would be fun, wouldn't it?' Imogen said brightly.

'Yes, we'll come back to the gatehouse to pick up some supplies once I've finished cooking duty.' Dulcie said. It was a delicate operation to attend to family while still interacting with the wider community, but she was succeeding.

Chapter Thirteen

Dulcie wanted Imogen to become reacquainted with some of the residents, but there was no time to visit the shady woods to see Roger and Sheila. As they left their cottage, they were shocked by a curtain of heat. They had to force themselves to walk through it. The route to the chateau had become a wade through tall, crackly dry grasses. Tiny insects swarmed around their heads. They were relieved to get into the shade of the stucco walls of the chateau. Their feet crunched on the gravel. Dulcie pointed out the modest kitchen entrance.

She led them down a short corridor to a room with high ceilings and walls lined with crazed white-glazed bricks, and blackened grouting. Yet the work surfaces were of modern brushed aluminium on central tables. They contrasted with the ancient arches which housed industrial ovens.

A long-haired single young man, Rolf, and a couple, Sarah and Neal, were tying on aprons and looked up to say, 'hi'. Dulcie noticed with distaste that some large skillets from a previous meal had been left unwashed. It was really too bad. Turning from them and putting on a big smile, she welcomed Imogen and Diana.

'Ta dah, the kitchen.' She took Diana by the hand and led her to look at an enormous inglenook fireplace. Dulcie crouched to child height, 'A long time ago, there would have been a big fire here. They would have put meat up above it to cook. Of course, we use ovens now.'

'What can I do to help?' Imogen said.

Sarah screwed up her face thoughtfully. 'That's very kind. I think we could do with some potato peelers, but we are all organised and I think the little girl will soon get bored,' she nodded at Diana.

'Diana's brought some toys, she'll play at one end of a table.' Imogen rushed to set Diana up on a tall stool. Dulcie organised Imogen with a sack of potatoes and a peeler. She bustled off to pour steaming hot water to clear away the previous night's mess. The group turned to their individual tasks. Rolf was a natural whistler and in time, as others recognised the tunes, they joined in by humming or even singing snatches of the chorus. Diana grew tired of her plastic bricks and sat on the floor playing with a set of bowls and measuring jugs.

Dulcie kept an eye on the wall clock, 'Time to begin frying off onions and start making sauce.' she said, and she turned to Imogen. 'Thank you so much for your help, but I think it's best if you take Diana out to play for a while and we'll do the cooking. I'll join you soon.'

'I'm hungry,' Diana said eyeing a pile of breadsticks, pain au chocolat and brioche in a wicker basket, 'can I have something to eat please?'

'We'll get you something back at the house,' Imogen said.

'Want one of those,' Diana pointed.

'Oh, don't worry. You can have one.' Dulcie said, 'It's good to have something that's authentically French while you are here. While we're part of the cooking team we can have snacks. Gather up your toys. Here's a brioche,' she said, handing Diana a bread bun. 'I'll see you soon, darling.'

Diana skipped, glad to escape the gloomy kitchen and get into the sunshine.

Dulcie accompanied Imogen to the door. 'See you later,' she said as she watched Diana running ahead, lured by the sight of other children. 'Better makes sure she doesn't get too far ahead.'

As they left, she saw Jane and Ivy, who had been standing close together chatting. They turned their heads and took a close interest. Disquieted but not sure why they should have an issue, Dulcie turned back to her three teammates. She felt impatient to get this cooking finished and then, like a child let out of school, she'd be able to join her family. There was a nagging feeling – Jane. I've done nothing wrong; why do I feel wrong-footed?

CHAPTER FOURTEEN

The station was quite a drive away. Having parked the van in the run-down backstreets that surrounded it, they entered through soaring white arches into a grand station hall. Noticing the ticket office across the vastness of the tiled plaza, they dragged suitcases towards the queue.

'Can I remember how to ask for a ticket in French?' Imogen sounded apprehensive.

'Leave it to me,' Dulcie said. 'Now, have you both got everything?' she turned to Diana, 'Shall I buy you a comic from the Tabac?'

'No we'll be okay, it's a waste to buy comics in French. And we have to get through the barrier and over to the other platform in a minute,' Imogen answered.

Echoing acoustics, unfamiliar people. People scurrying like insects. It was such a contrast with their picnic. They had been in an idyllic setting, beside a fast- flowing stream, insects in long grasses tickling their legs, the view of the mountains. They had relaxed knowing that they were far from other people and, while Diana paddled in a stream, Imogen had told her mother about the Lunar Hotel. She in turn, explained her idea for the business. Imogen agreed to help sell items once Dulcie had brought them over to London. But it seemed to be such a long time before they could see each other again.

There was the muffled boom of French station announcements, and she guessed that it meant that the train was imminent

Dulcie swept Diana up into her arms, 'I'll see you soon and say hello to Mummy for me,' she said.

'Oh Imogen,' she almost moaned, 'Have a good journey.' Pressing Imogen to her with uncharacteristic emotion, she could feel Imogen's shoulder blades through her rough linen shift. Dulcie pressed her lips to Imogen's forehead and breathed in her scent. Stepping back to look at her at arms' length, she saw tears in her daughter's eyes.

'Are you really okay, Mum? You know I'm always on the end of a phone.' Imogen said.

'Of course I am darling,' Dulcie put on her familiar business-like tone, 'Goodbyes are always difficult.

She watched them go until she saw their train drawing in. What was I thinking when I decided to move to France, so far away? There was a soreness in her chest; how to heal the gap that they left by their going? She had to turn back to the chateau to make her dream work. It was getting better, she was sending out shoots which grew into the cracks in the chateau walls.

Chapter Fifteen

England

Thankfully Diana had slept most of the last half of the journey. Imogen yawned and wound the driver's window down a crack to help to keep herself awake. Her mother hadn't seemed as settled in France as she had expected her to be.

Imogen had to admit that thoughts of Lynette at home had distracted her. They hadn't been in contact while she was away.

The greetings card wasn't a declaration of love, but it had meant a lot. Anxiety flushed through her body. Lynette had been subject to the influence of her family and may well have thought better of being so rash. Perhaps she won't come to see us? I will have to live with that, Imogen thought resolutely and then felt a twinge of fear. Life would be empty without Lynette.

They reached home after 10 pm. Imogen carried Diana in through the back door of the hotel and straight to bed. She spoke to the night porter and then fell into bed herself. She woke to the insistent ringing of the phone.

'This is Reception. Miss Lynette Williams for you.'

There was a judder in Imogen's chest, 'Yes put her through please.'

'No, I meant she is here for you in reception.'

'Oh, thank you. Can you send her in.' Imogen found herself smiling. She put on the bedside light and then the living room light before unlocking the door to their quarters. I need a comb and I'm wearing a nightdress she thought, I think my dressing gown's still packed.

Lynette's head appeared around the door. She looked solemn as she ventured in.

Imogen opened both arms dramatically and dived to hug her. Lynette's back felt stiff and upright causing Imogen to take a step back.

'Are you alright?' Imogen asked, 'Something must be wrong if you're here at this hour.'

'I just couldn't hold on any longer. I wanted to know whether you had regretted everything that went on between us. I've been torturing myself. But to get that hug. . . well, I'm happy,' said Lynette. Her face was lit up and her eyes wide. Imogen felt indescribable, wild, elation.

'I'm pleased you've come. I've also been wondering how you feel now. I've been thinking about your lovely face.' Impulsively she reached to hold Lynette's face between both her palms, 'Your lips, your perfectly shaped eyes and your chin.'

She let her hands drop when she registered Lynette's surprise.

'I, I don't know what to say, but thank you,' Lynette said.

'Now we must both settle down - Diana's asleep,' Imogen said giggling. 'I feel drunk, though I haven't had any alcohol. Perhaps we should have a secret midnight feast. I'll order some cheese and biscuits.'

'Are you sure? What are they thinking out there? They'll see you in your nighty.'

'Don't worry so much.' Imogen said sitting down, 'But I'll let you go to the door to take the tray. I can't find my dressing gown.'

She phoned the order through and then turned to Lynette quizzically. 'How did you get here, Netty? I'm very happy that you did of course.'

'I caught the bus. I left a note for my family. They will find my coat gone and I suppose they will wonder why I left so suddenly.'

'Netty, you've turned into such a daredevil. You always seemed such a well-behaved and upright person.' Imogen felt breathless. A tapping at the door, and Lynette smoothed down her skirt to go to take the tray.

'She put it on a low table in front of them. 'You're trembling; I'll wrap a blanket around you?' Lynette said.

'So I am,' Imogen looked at the goosebumps all the way up her arm, 'Yet it's a warm night. I'll get my bedcover.'

She reappeared wrapped in a shawl of crocheted squares. 'You look like someone's old granny.' Lynette said, laughing.

'I feel really cosy,' Imogen tucked her bare toes up beneath her on the seat of the settee. She looked into Lynette's deep brown eyes and Lynette returned the look. 'I'm looking into your soul,' Lynette murmured, 'It's a beautiful soul.'

Imogen leaned slowly forwards and touched Lynette's nose with her own. She shook off the crochet comforter and laid her hands on Lynette's shoulders. As if by agreement, they both drew back but continued to meet each other's gaze.

'My family just weren't the touchy-feely type and it feels awkward to feel someone's skin.' Imogen said.

'My family are very huggy, but this is different again, girl.' Lynette shook her head. 'We're on an adventure. For tonight, I'm saying, "seize the day and forget about the consequences".'

Soon there were only cheese rinds and a few crumbs left on the plates. Lynette glanced up at the clock. 'It's past time for the last bus. Are you okay for me to stay here?'

'Of course.' Imogen paused, and then raised her eyebrows, 'You're welcome to share my single bed,' she hesitated feeling awkward and scared of rushing things, 'Of course, you don't have to. I could lay the sofa cushions on the floor and sleep there.'

'Don't be silly,' Lynette smiled broadly, took her hand and made the way to Imogen's bedroom door.

Chapter Sixteen

Light was leaking through the curtains. Imogen woke to the realisation that Lynette was curled up against her back in a single bed. She was suffused with a tingling warmth, could this be real? She wasn't one person but part of a pair. She could hear Lynette breathing regularly, was it in her sleep or was she awake?

As if on cue, Lynette whispered, 'I'm awake, are you?'

Imogen didn't want the moment to change, but she was cramped. She suppressed a yawn, stretched a little and turned over to face Lynette.

'Mm, it was nice to wake up to feel your breasts against my back.' She enjoyed watching Lynette's shy expression and had a strong urge to lean forward to kiss her, but said, 'Is my morning breath okay?'

'It's fine, don't worry. And even nicer than spooning is to be facing each other,' Lynette hutched around to put her arm under her head. 'I still can't believe what we are doing. We'd better not be here when Diana wakes up.'

That was a bit of a downer. Imogen didn't want to think of practicalities, 'Don't worry, it's very early.' she said. Mentally crossing her fingers, she whispered, 'Do you regret all this?'

'No, I'm very happy. Unbelievably happy.' Lynette's eyes shone, and she kissed Imogen on the nose. 'How do we manage this though? At least in a hotel, we are less likely to be noticed.'

'In a crowd, you mean. Yes and I think Tony and Anita will be happy for us, so they'll be our allies. Anita has got some scheduled time-off so we'll see her today. She's desperate to spend some time with Diana.'

'I'm nervous about what she'll think,' Lynette said. 'And what about your parents?'

Imogen could hear her heart beating in her ears. She tried to breathe evenly, 'It's a worry. But we'll get through it. Of course they'll be surprised, but I'm sure I can convince them that this is my life and that I know what will make me happy. You know, I have often felt more comfortable wearing jeans and striding about lifting things. I know that sounds a bit ridiculous, but at those times, I feel I'm taking my rightful role as a powerful person.' She moved her face close to Lynette's and said, 'I'm stepping into my true self, thanks to you.'

Lynette gazed into her eyes. 'I need to gather some of your courage. If anyone at work found out, I'm sure it would be the talk of the office and it'd ruin my career. As for my parents. . . perhaps I'd better not go home.' She screwed her face up tight with a deep frown.

Imogen felt a fierce urge to protect her from the world. At that moment, she felt strong and brave.

'Come here,' she gently kissed her on the lips. 'I want to kiss away all the worries.' She was a lazy cat stretching in a warm bed.

'Mm, that's nice.' said Lynette, 'I will cope. I'll just not tell them what's going on. We'll have to be very careful.'

Imogen wondered whether they could keep that up. She wanted to proclaim that she'd found her person. She wanted to be recognised as a couple, but she realised that only Lynette could predict the best way to handle her own parents.

Lynette rolled sideways and sat up. 'That was uncomfortable. A single bed is too narrow.' She stretched and stepped into the skirt that she was wearing the night before.

They organised the day. Lynette agreed to play with Diana while Imogen drove to the station to pick up Anita.

They arrived back, laughing and bantering while dragging an enormous case between them. Lynette was caught with her legs underneath her on the carpet and with a precarious Mousetrap board set up between herself and Diana. Diana didn't care. She leapt to her feet and bombed across the room, flinging herself at her mother's knees. The game forgotten, Lynette was left to pack it away and to attempt to rise elegantly. There was little time to discuss anything as Anita sat down and listened to a torrent of words from Diana.

Eventually, Diana ran off to retrieve the presents that she had brought back from France for Anita. Imogen glided towards Lynette and put her arm around her waist. She said, 'We've been spending a lot of time together recently.'

Anita looked questioningly from one face to the other.

Imogen recognised it was up to her to be clear. Lynette had a Mona Lisa smile and drew her chin down.

'We are trying to tell you we're an item.' Imogen grinned.

Anita opened her mouth to speak, but was diverted by Diana crashing back into the room with her arms full of boxes. Diana placed them all on the floor in front of Anita, who smiled and winked at Imogen and Lynette before turning to pay attention to Diana.

'Look we'll take a walk and let you two have full use of the floor,' Imogen said, and after checking in with Tony, who was working, they left the hotel.

***

The grass was yellowing and becoming sparse. People were strewn across the park: young men with their tops off drinking beer, families sitting within the boundaries of tartan rugs, mothers with pushchairs keeping an eye on toddlers in the sand. The couple on their stroll a lot less at ease than the other park users. They stayed on the paths and in the shade of trees.

A group of lads caught sight of them and one shouted 'Hello darling,' at them.

Imogen tucked her head down and hurried on. 'No other romantic partner would stand for a stranger shouting 'Hello darling,' at them.' she said through gritted teeth.

'It means nothing,' Lynette said. 'They're not worth it.'

'But don't you see, we're a couple, but no one recognises us as a couple.'

'It's perhaps as well, it makes us safe.' Lynette cast her eyes behind them to check that they were out of earshot. 'And I'm always going to be wary in case I see someone from my family or one of their friends.'

Imogen was frustrated that something significant was happening between them and it was almost as though it were just in her head. They could so easily be just two girls walking in the park. She aimed for a bench beside the path and sat down. Lynette followed wordlessly. They were both involved in their own thoughts and in a place where they couldn't enter into a full discussion. The warmth of the day, the distant sounds of children playing and buzz of traffic cocooned them in their bubble.

'Tony knows all the gay clubs. Maybe we should venture into them now?' Imogen said, 'I can ask him which he thinks we'd like best. Would you dare to do that?'

They paused as an elderly woman came into hearing, walking slowly to allow her miniature poodle to sniff the edges of the path. She looked at them curiously and when she was retreating, they heard her say 'tsk'.

'That may be about race as much as anything. I know her type,' Lynette said. 'I think you're right we might find acceptance and friends if we visited gay clubs discreetly. We'd need to try it. I think,' Lynette looked her in the eye, 'If this is going to work, I can see we need to find somewhere where we can be an acknowledged couple and interact freely, apart from your private quarters in the hotel. I know you think I'm being a wimp. I'm just careful. Out here, where I don't feel able even to let my hand brush yours, I'm longing to kiss you.'

'I'm not judging you.' Imogen said and jumped up 'Let's go home.' She quickened her pace. They walked purposely on hot, dry pavements to the cool sanctuary of the hotel.

CHAPTER SEVENTEEN

France

Home again, Dulcie braced herself to get on with life. Some people were walking away from the gatehouse. She wondered if they had been looking for her, but they didn't turn back. She felt alone, but brought out an exercise book to plan for buying and selling second-hand collectables. She became lost in her work, until the antique clock showed that it was Oscar's teatime. She had a stack of canned cat food and put a saucerful onto the floor with a clink. The sound often alerted him to come running, but he didn't appear. Oh well – cats! She shook her head with a smile. A pity though, this afternoon was one of those times when she would have liked the comfort of having him on her lap and stroking his soft fur.

Several hours later, Dulcie realised that her own mealtime had passed. Where was Oscar? She went into the garden, calling his name. Then she sighted a tabby coloured shape between the rows of beetroot leaves. Was he asleep? He was far too limp to be asleep. Dulcie sank to her knees in silence. She was numb. Her brain resisted thinking about what might have happened. Eventually, she reached out to touch him and his fur was stone cold. A shiver went through her. She burst into uncontrollable tears rocking backwards and forwards as she knelt on the hard earth.

After some time, Dulcie found a cloth and gently wrapped Oscar. He had no wounds. Could an animal have punctured his skin to kill him, or was she so disliked that someone had poisoned him? Was this a warning message from someone? Now pull yourself together Dulcie, she said to herself and took some deep breaths. It wouldn't help to speculate but suddenly she felt threatened and alone. She took a spade and looked around for an appropriate burial site.

CHAPTER EIGHTEEN

People were sitting in two concentric circles waiting for the meeting to begin. There was a cacophony of discordant voices chatting. Dulcie couldn't immediately see any particular friends, although she noticed Rolf, Sarah and Neal from her kitchen shift sitting across the room. She couldn't catch their eyes.

The seats were hard, the late evening sun was pouring through the upper windows and casting a soft light. This meeting had been called at short notice again. Hopefully, it wouldn't go on for too long. She hadn't brought a torch with her to help negotiate the way home. These meetings were a way to make sure that everyone belonged and that everyone had their say, but really some people rattled on until Dulcie felt she had to pinch herself to keep from falling asleep.

Maggie, their founder, ambled to the space saved for her. Then came a round of greetings, everyone got up to hug everyone else. Dulcie sprang out of her seat, her hands came into contact with the sharp shoulder blades of a gangly lad with a tight square jaw who avoided eye contact. She tried to hold her breath to avoid breathing in his. Turning to her other side, there was a middle-aged woman Moira who had arrived recently after her parents had both died. She glanced across the circle; the younger ones seemed much more into all this hugging.

When everyone had resettled in their seats, Maggie began, 'Welcome friends. Look inside yourselves and bring your real self to this meeting so that we can meet each other transparently and acceptingly.'

She adopted a peaceful pose, hands in her lap and contemplated a space three feet away on the floor. A pregnant silence. Dulcie found herself seeking out a patch of blue sky through the high windows. Should I look at my watch or would that show impatience? She glanced around, some of the group looked as though they were considering whether to speak next.

'We need to make decisions.' Jane said standing up and surveying the community. 'We have to decide when to accept new residents and when we are full. How to achieve self-sufficiency, and how much each of us should contribute towards Community meals.' She paused and then said, 'We need an efficient way of making those decisions.'

'What do you mean?' said a young girl in a skimpy grandad vest and flared jeans, 'Don't we just talk and then decide.'

Jane pursed her lips and appeared to tut, 'But we can't spend forever on decisions. So who has the final say?'

Dulcie heard her heart beating loudly in her ear and her eyes slid across to Maggie. Even asking a question like this seemed like a challenge to her position.

Maggie said, 'Ideally I would like us all to agree. After all, when you go with the majority view there are always some people who don't agree.'

'Man, if we could all agree it would be fantastic. I'd go for that,' said Roger leaning forwards and nodding vigorously.

'But how long do you argue and discuss before you get everyone to agree?' Jane's voice became strident.

'That sounds as though you imagine we'd shout each other down.' said Neal mildly. He had been leaning back in a relaxed pose, but now he shifted in his seat.

Jane turned her whole body to address him, 'You are interpreting what you think I mean, rather than putting your own point of view forward.'

Neal looked at the ground and said no more.

Was anyone else going to put a point of view? Dulcie had a sinking feeling that they were beginning a long debate on how to go about debating.

'Could we wait until we have to make a decision and then decide at that time how we want to work it out? I mean I am uncomfortable with deciding now. For me, it might depend on what the decision is about.'

'I appreciate your diplomacy Ceci. I can see you are uncomfortable with open debate and you are trying to head it off.' Jane answered and Dulcie shrivelled, she recognised passive aggression.

Maggie intervened, 'Maybe by taking each decision one at a time, we can deal with them in bite-size pieces.'

There were smiles around the room and murmurs. 'Right good one,' said Roger looking satisfied and taking Sheila's hand.

'I enjoy this group. I believe we will get there.' said Neal.

'Yeh,' Sheila looked directly across at Neal, 'we are very supportive of each other. You know, we talked about Ziggy being bullied at school? Well, it's cool now. We can be amazing when we work together.'

Jane leaned her upper body forward. 'Hmm, good,' she said. 'So.' She straightened her back and raised her head as though about to make an announcement. 'some of you may know that Ivy and I have witnessed food being misused. In fact, food that belongs to the community was being taken out of our kitchen.' She looked around self-importantly.

Ivy raised her hand tentatively, 'I'd like to add to that,' and then she said more quietly, 'Because I think some of us are a little short of money and can only just afford the amount we contribute to the food budget.'

'Hang on now, before we talk about this, I'd like to know who you saw taking food?' Rolph asked.

'What have you seen?' Sheila put her head on one side, her hair falling over one shoulder and addressed Jane, 'Is it some of the kids messing about?'

Jane refused to be drawn, 'It isn't for me. Maybe we should leave the thief to identify herself.'

'What?' Roger looked around the room rolling his eyes.

There was another silence, during which Ivy took out a paper tissue and sniffed.

'We reach an impasse,' commented Neal.

The young girl in the grandad vest raised her hands in frustration, 'Yeh now we all feel that fingers are being pointed at us.'

'Well, you've pushed me into it.' Jane shook her head in irritation and stood up as though ready for battle.

'Please take a seat, Jane,' Maggie said, 'and explain what this is all about.'

'Ceci, well Dulcie, gave some food to young Diana while she was staying here. So not only did the food come from our kitchen, but it was given to a non-resident.' Jane said. 'We have rules and they need to be kept.'

Dulcie felt a sinking in her stomach. She gulped. How did she deal with this?

'I think I can agree with that. I saw it,' said Ivy.

At this Jethro, a gruffly spoken bearded man who sat in the outer ring said 'Yes there's something in that. We are paying for the food.'

'Perhaps we need some rules about limits for outsiders?' someone else added.

'Yeh, now that could cause a problem. How many outsiders do we have at a time and how much of our resources can they use?' Jethro came back into the conversation.

'I'm a little surprised that you didn't discuss it with us,' Ivy spoke now directly to Dulcie.

'Yes,' Jane's face was twisted with malice, 'We weren't being petty, you see I believe it will become a greater issue as the community grows. What have you got to say for yourself, Ceci?' and she gestured to Dulcie and stepped back as though handing her the floor.

Dulcie looked at the people in the ring. All this over brioche! Could she feel comfortable and at home here ever again? She checked to see how Maggie was dealing with it. Maggie wore a slight smile but her eyes showed that she was disconcerted. Okay now is the time to speak up for yourself Dulcie.

'When,' her voice came out louder than she'd expected it to and she cleared her throat to start again, 'When I arrived here, I was shown around by someone called Katy.' She took a deep breath and slowed down her delivery. 'Unfortunately, Katy is no longer in the Community, but she told me that when you are on cooking rota, you are welcome to take food. At that time, people did it without a thought.'

'No one remembers,' Jane heckled, but Dulcie refused to acknowledge her.

'I will speak,' she said suddenly raising her voice and clenching her fists. 'I gave a child a brioche, yes. I see this community as my home, my family. I wanted my daughter from England and our little girl to see our community, but our picnic on our own – that was prepared in my own quarters.'

Someone made a low hiss as though of disbelief. Dulcie registered the sound, but she was determined to make the most of her chance to address them.

'There are ways to sort out misunderstandings and problems. Ways of putting your point without accusations.' She looked around the room, and then tears came to her eyes, 'I don't want any more to do with this.'

She pushed her way to the end of the row of chairs. She was vaguely aware that people in the row were disconcerted. She heard Maggie saying weakly, 'Can I just say,' and then more loudly 'Ceci' but by that time Dulcie had flung open the door and was outside.

She wished that she hadn't left like that, but she didn't want them to see her break down. She could hear them - mob, a pack. She was breathing fast, but they weren't going to give chase. She made her way home. She was alone. This is the culmination of her doubts about belonging to the community. Human nature gets in the way of making a sharing community. There was no reason to stay. She would be relieved to go back to England.

Chapter Nineteen

She had to get away. Now she suspected that Oscar's death had been sabotage. The gatehouse was comfortingly familiar, but she was reliving the conflict. She longed to share her thoughts with someone, but she couldn't bring herself to tell Imogen about it. There was Gilles, but this wasn't the time, it was time for bed. The darkness of her bedroom was inviting, even though she dreaded lying awake and worrying. After a glass of red wine, she slept soundly.

The next day she decided to blank the problem out until she could deal with it logically. It was her way; she had survived a lonely marriage for years by blanking out thoughts and running on autopilot. Not one person had visited after the conflict to offer support, and that hurt.

The business idea was a positive, so she made a start by going to a brocante close to the town. It was a success. Gilles arrived while she was unloading the boot full of vases and mirrors and carrying them to the house. He parked the post office 2CV van in the shade of trees just outside the entrance and hurried towards her, shading his eyes from the sun.

'You're a sight for sore eyes,' she realised that she must look hot and dishevelled.

He looked briefly puzzled but said, 'ça va?'

'I'm very well thank you,' then she lowered her head and admitted, 'Well that's not completely true. I'm having a hard time.' She gestured to the pile of picture frames, 'But look, I'm buying beautiful objects.'

He nodded in approval and turned to the boot, sweeping up the last pile of items himself, and followed her into the house.

'Thank you,' she said. 'I'm piling them all in here,' and she indicated her bedroom.

'How can I help you? You look unhappy,' he said softly. She sat down on one of her easy chairs and he took the other.

'Trouble at 'Le Manoir de Calme'. I need to be busy and stay away from the place.'

She glanced down and contemplated the rug. She didn't want him to see what was in her eyes. He reached out and covered her hand with his own.

'Oscar, my cat. I found him - dead in the garden,' she said. She heard a small reaction from Gilles, but didn't look up. 'You are the first person that I've told about it. I miss him so much, poor little cat. I don't know, but I'm beginning to suspect foul play. I haven't spoken to friends here.' She shrugged.

'And then, just when I was at my lowest, there was trouble at our Community meeting. I was attacked. Well, practically called a thief.' She went on to describe the events at the meeting. 'Perhaps I shouldn't have given a brioche to Diana, but it was always acceptable for those who were working in the kitchen.'

'Mais, c'est a small thing. Brioche. . .it would be stale by the next day anyway.'

'Well, maybe the brioche was just an excuse. You see there's a woman here, Jane, she has taken a dislike to me. She was ring-leader and I was shocked that everyone else seemed to pile in against me.' Dulcie huffed a small laugh. 'Ironic eh, it was me who advised Ziggy to be brave. Well, I did stand up for myself in the meeting, but then I ran out - let myself down.'

'No,' his fingertips guided her chin towards him and he kissed her cheek gently.

'Oh Gilles, you are a comfort just as I really need it. It's amazing, we've suddenly grown close. We need to think about where it's going.' She sat up straight and put on a mock teacher tone, 'After all you are just a boy.'

'I hope that isn't what you see, Ceci. I am not so much younger than you,' he moved his face closer to her again. If she didn't relax toward him, it would have left him looking silly. But why would she push him away? She admired the way he was prepared to risk rejection. She leant into him and he cupped her chin again. This time, continuing the movement to put his hand around her back and wrap her in his arms. Her heart beat more rapidly. Again he brushed her lips with his. Her senses were awakened. His lips explored her face and she relaxed into it. She kissed him with an abandon that carried her back to the feeling of being a young, vulnerable girl. Maybe she could be that with Gilles.

What seemed like hours later, Gilles pulled back to gaze at her. His eyes were blurred with emotion. 'I don't want to rush you, Ceci, but I have a great desire for you. I want to be here for you.'

She was overwhelmed.

'Let me into your life, Ceci. You want a life outside this place,' he cast his eyes around the room, 'and I can support you.'

Dulcie smiled, 'Thank you Gilles. I'm sorry for dismissing you as a boy. My heart is beating so fast, I can't think or even breathe,' she automatically pushed a non-existent strand of hair away from her face.

Gilles seemed to understand, 'You've had a busy morning. Rest now. Let me help at the brocantes, my darling.'

He leaned forward in his chair with a sparkle in his eye, 'I will be back this afternoon and we can go out in the van. Together, we will manage larger furniture.'

Dulcie was caught up in his enthusiasm. 'Thank you that would be wonderful.' she said. He stood up, smiled broadly and briefly trailed his fingertips over her shoulder as he left. Dulcie felt an after-tingle long after he had gone.

She suddenly felt brighter. Things might work out. Put the Chateau into perspective. She looked down at her lap. Her once beautifully manicured hands were now rough from work and beginning to look older. There's still life in me yet though, she thought, jumping up to check her hair in the mirror.

***

By the time she heard him knock, she felt pleasantly refreshed. He knew of a large brocante sale some way away. The straight roads led them across rural open spaces and they listened to the van radio. The rhythmic music relaxed them. Dulcie found herself swaying a little, in time. Giles drummed out the beat on his knee, while Dulcie joined in, tapping her fingers on the steering wheel. They looked at each other and laughed. Once there, they were fortunate to find somewhere to park along a side street.

It was exhilarating to explore a different town and with interesting company. The tree-lined main street was transformed by a crowd of people continually moving between, around and through sales pitches. There was so much jostling and so much to see that it was useful to work as a pair.

They passed a busker playing the accordion. Gilles stopped to listen, something Ted would never have considered. Dulcie stood beside him and let herself lean her head against his shoulder, feeling the rough flannel of his shirt under her cheek. She wanted to freeze the moment, or photograph it to savour later, but eventually, she said, 'Come on- we have business to do.' Gilles laughed and tossed coins into the musician's collection box. It put them in a holiday mood.

Dulcie spotted an elaborate hat-stand. 'The English adore those. Anything ornate,'

The grizzled seller with a cigarette permanently balanced between his lips spoke quickly despite the cigarette. Dulcie felt a twinge of irritation that her language skills weren't up to the challenge.

'Could you speak to him please?' she asked Gilles. With the hat-stand supported on his shoulder, they moved on.

'What a coincidence – hats.' Dulcie called out to him, as they arrived at a stall which had an array of jewellery and accessories. They stopped to examine it, and she tried a string of beads, admiring the effect in the stallholder's mirror. Gilles tried a cap, pulled a face and swept it off. The next was much too large. He knew it and struck a pose in the mirror. They caught the stall holder's disapproval and edged away. Dulcie realised that she hadn't felt so light-hearted for a long time.

Their feet were aching, and their throats were dry when they reached the farthest edge of the market. They stopped beside a triangle of benches under dappled shade but even so, Dulcie thought longingly of all the pavement cafes they had seen. But what would they have done with their haul? Gilles stayed beside the stacked purchases while Dulcie retraced the road to collect the van.

They had a solid dark wood wardrobe and other large pieces that she would never have managed without the tail lift on the van and Gilles's help.

As they strapped the furniture securely to the sides of the van, he grinned at her 'We work well as a team.'

Driving away from the town, she said, 'I sometimes find it difficult to deal with stallholders.'

'You are hard on yourself; it will get easier,' he said. Yes, perhaps she was just tired.

The trip had been tiring, but it helped her to dismiss thoughts of the chateau. As soon as she thought of returning home, she felt tense again.

'Glad to get a drink,' she said.

'Ah, refreshment. The farm of my parents is not far from here, bah I think we need to rest now though.'

Dulcie turned and looked at him. He was right, she felt ill-prepared for a social occasion. 'So tell me about your home?'

'We were a big family, so we have a big farmhouse. The others left home, never to return, but I did. It works because I don't stay in very often. I use it as somewhere to sleep.'

The van entered a seemingly endless rutted road which travelled over undulating hills. They drove past rows of vines neatly tied up to wires. The landscape looked as though green railway lines were curving over upturned dishes.

'Vineyard country. Are there vineyards on your family farm?'

'Ah, oui. It is good soil for grapes up here, but on the lower land we have a few pigs and poultry. My father is still healthy and he knows farming. My mother is a strong woman, too. She loves England. She has kept photograph albums of her time there. I think she would like you.'

'You do? Wouldn't she mind the age difference?'

She wondered if he had heard. He didn't answer. The road was climbing. It wound through several tunnels as the Pyrenean lowlands neared their peaks.

Sun was streaming in through the driver's side window. Her hairline felt sticky. She drove with one elbow out of the window.

'It ought to be getting cooler towards the end of the day, the sun's going down.' she observed, but the sun still raged. She gestured for him to pass her a newspaper from the floor and balanced it on her shoulder to avoid her skin burning.

'I wonder what the hold up is?' They drew to a stop close behind the bumper of a boxy Renault 12, 'There's something blocking the tunnel ahead. Is it worth turning around?'

Gilles gently laid his palm on her thigh, it was hot and heavy. Without thinking, she glared at him and he quickly withdrew it. He said, 'The road is narrow, and if we turn around, we will have to go hundreds of miles out of our way.'

'You know all of these roads?'

'Yes, for years I've visited cousins, grandparents, and friends. I've travelled all over these valleys.'

'Then you belong here.'

'It is home. I have lived here all my life except when I went to England.'

'We're so different. I don't feel as though I belong anywhere. My parents split up and my father moved to the country. I went to a finishing school in Switzerland, so I lost touch with old friends. And now I've left England. . .'

'I hope soon you will belong here. Our old traditions will be yours.'

She looked at him as though for the first time. 'I feel so close to you Gilles, yet I'm so far away.'

'What do you mean?'

Was the sun getting to her? Why would she spoil what they'd got? 'Oh I don't know. I don't even know you.'

The cab was airless. 'Shall we open the doors, it doesn't look like we're going anywhere.' She wafted the newspaper as a fan. 'You and I are so different. Of course, your family - are they Catholic? I wonder if your parents are expecting you to produce babies.'

'I suppose they are, but it will be my decision. If anything, they might not like for me to see a woman who is divorcing. Our religion is very, the English phrase, strait-laced. But they will get used to it. They have to.'

Dulcie sat quietly for a moment. They watched three or four cars emerge from the tunnel on the other side of the road.

'Maybe we're moving on now,' she said.

He shot her a worried glance, then his expression cleared, 'Oh the traffic.'

But it wasn't moving. The passenger door of the car in front shot open and a woman went to the back seat to deal with a small child. She took him out and hung him over the verge for a wee.

Gilles attempted a laugh, 'Let's hope we don't start moving at this time.'

Dulcie glanced across at the child. 'Gilles, I'm past all that. I'm not too old to have children but it's not what I want. My time is over. I came here with my dreams and I want to live a little before I become a granny myself.'

His voice was sad. 'I think, that you wish that you hadn't kissed me today.'

She hung her head as she wasn't sure of her answer.

He noticed and said, 'Well, I am sorry. Perhaps I should not have done it.'

They had just had such a carefree time in each other's company. Dulcie felt perturbed. She opened her mouth to speak, but at that moment, car engines began to start up - they were away.

They drove in silence. Dulcie felt the tension, but she was tired. Two brocantes in one day had probably been a bad idea. When they reached the chateau, Gilles seemed tired too.

She got out her house key, 'Well, see you soon. Thank you for coming with me.'

He looked stricken, 'Yes, it is late,' and he in turn made for his car.

Chapter Twenty

On opening the door, Dulcie gasped. There was the back of someone's head. He was sitting in one of the easy chairs. Her heart was pounding. He had heard her and he moved. Dulcie was on the verge of turning and running when she realised that her husband Ted was standing up to meet her.

She went weak, 'What on earth are you doing?'

He cleared his throat, 'I'm sorry, I've surprised you.'

This wasn't an explanation for invading her house, after all the grief that he had put her through.

'How dare you just come in here. How did you get here?'

He moved a few steps towards her, 'Oh, don't be angry Dulcie. I arrived a few hours ago, and I had to ask around for you. Someone let me in.'

He had different clothes, smart- casual colour-coordinated. Even the fact that he'd discarded cravats and tweed jackets made him look completely different.

She noticed his large suitcase placed on the rug in front of her fireplace. She felt furious.

'Now, for old time's sake,' his voice was pleading, 'There's still a lot between us. I thought I should see you in person. All these solicitors' letters just make things worse.'

She sighed. 'It's been a very long day. I would prefer you to warn me when you decide to suddenly turn up. You rarely turned up when we were together, and now you've travelled across the channel. Just let me sit down,' she slumped into the chair.

'You look all in. Stay there and I'll put the kettle on. I think you need a nice cup of tea.'

This infuriated her further. 'You can't just walk in here and offer me a cup of tea in my own house. You've tortured me with letters threatening to leave me penniless. You aren't welcome here.'

'OK, OK,' he put his hands up in surrender and backed further towards the sink. 'I understand you must feel that way. I was going to visit our friends in Carcassone and I thought I'd come to see you on the way,' he turned to get cups down from hooks . . . 'I'm sorry I didn't write to warn you. I originally arrived just after lunch and imagined that I'd have a civilised chat with you, and carry on to them. It didn't work out.'

Dulcie contemplated him. He looked jaded and he moved like an old man. 'No don't use up the English tea,' she said irritably. 'There's some instant coffee in the cupboard there.' She nodded up towards the dresser.

There was a pause, just the tinkle of china and a teaspoon clinking against it. Ted handed her a cup and sat down himself. The sustenance was welcome. Dulcie kept quiet. She could feel the trickle of a warm tear running down one cheek and she didn't want Ted to realise it.

He started to speak.

'What?' Dulcie barked out at him without looking in his direction.

'You've made a good job of decorating this place. You were always good at making a home, Dulcie.' he said softly, casting an eye around the room. He turned his full attention to her, 'I haven't liked what's been happening with the solicitors. To be honest, I've been miserable.

'Life threw me up in the air and I landed in a tangled heap. One minute you were there and the next you'd gone. What on earth happened, was there anyone else involved?'

'Humph, you're a fool. Why should there be? I just couldn't take that life anymore.'

'You should have given me a chance to talk about it. It was such a shock for me. For a while, it didn't sink in, and I just carried on. But I was lost and bewildered.'

Dulcie had sometimes wondered how the break-up had affected him, so she was prepared to listen. 'But you didn't come to find me, did you?'

If he had raced after her and pleaded with her to go back, she probably would have capitulated. She took a sip of coffee and watched his reaction.

'I'm sorry I wasn't able to take it in or take any action at first. In the beginning, I wanted to make sure that colleagues at the Bank didn't find out what had happened. I kept up a front. Just sorting things out without you to do it.' Ted looked troubled, 'I'm sorry I know when we were together you felt ignored. I relied on you though. Since you left, I dated a few people. It's a shallow and depressing experience.'

'You don't get it do you?' she said through gritted teeth. 'I was stuck in the home, providing a backdrop for your precious career. Being the hostess, socialising on your arm, but you'd become a stranger. You never bothered even when I made a fuss.'

'I don't want to get into an argument about the past, but you did scream at me. I remember you ripping my newspaper out of my hands.'

'Yes' said Dulcie, 'well, I don't want to be that person anymore. I had to save myself.'

'So you went to stay with Imogen and then you were off to France.' Ted looked around the room again. 'What's your plan?

It's a bit basic, isn't it? I couldn't believe it when I realised you have an outside lavatory.'

Dulcie paused, feeling indignant, but then had to admit that it was basic.

'There's so much more to life. You know, here I can walk out of the door and through woods.' She was going to say more, but then she remembered that this had turned out not to be such a paradise. She no longer felt safe and accepted. She sighed heavily and cast her eyes around. 'Look I've got a van full of stuff to unload and I haven't had a meal yet.'

'Can I help? But maybe it would be better if we tackled the unloading in the morning when we both feel fresher.'

This made Dulcie sit up. 'You were expecting to stay?'

'Not quite, I had hoped to go on to Carcassonne today. Gerald and Amanda are half expecting me there, but they knew that I'd planned to call in on you first. The plan hasn't turned out well. I can probably get into a hotel in the nearest town. I'll get a taxi. May I use your phone?'

'I don't have one. You could walk to the town.' Dulcie said and then glanced down at his case. Ted chewed his lip. She knew she was being mean. 'I don't suppose it would hurt. We had a camp bed when Imogen was here, I suppose you could put that up.'

Dulcie dragged herself out of the chair and plodded over to the kitchen area. She took out ham and the ingredients for a dressing. 'If you want to help, you can pick something as a side salad from the garden.' She threw the words over her shoulder. Obediently he was gone.

Blessed peace. Her emotions were in turmoil. As she whisked the oil and vinegar, she felt overwhelming resentment but it was mixed with relief at seeing a familiar face.

Later they sat opposite each other at her tiny table and red wine mellowed them both.

'I think we were both in the trap.' Ted suddenly said, 'I was brought up to work to provide a big house and the lifestyle to match my position. Well, you know the life we lived, it was stressful for me. And we knew people - but I don't think we had many real friends. Perhaps we lost sight of ourselves as human beings.'

'It's wonderful how you can suddenly paint yourself as a victim. You were never at home. Was there another woman?'

'There wasn't another woman. I did have drinks with someone from work once, but that's as far as it went. I didn't have time to complicate my life any further, for goodness sake. Was there another man?'

Dulcie felt oddly flattered that he thought there might have been. That was the second time that he'd mentioned it. It was an important point to him.

'No, I was busy being a mother and socialising with other mothers. That side of my life was shut off,' she tailed off realising that this could be taken as a criticism.

Ted reached across and put his hand over hers. It felt warm and firm. Sadness washed over her. Why couldn't they have had some intimacy while there was still something to save.

She felt calmer. There was an easiness in sitting with someone who had been familiar to her for years. It was easy to forget for a moment, that they had been through the acrimonious split. 'Since I've been gone, how have you been?'

'Oh. . .I've seen a bit of Imogen.' Dulcie knew that, but Imogen hadn't given anything away. 'Yes,' he cleared his throat, 'I got lonely and miserable. Once they knew, my manager at the bank was accommodating. They gave me time off while I sorted myself out. After the house was sold, Alan and his wife let me rent an apartment over their garage. It didn't feel like home. I can't do what you do with a house.'

Dulcie smothered a yawn of exhaustion, but she was transported back to her old life. 'Their son's flat.' she said.

'Yes, a bachelor pad,' he half laughed and went on, 'I tried the life of a bachelor. People did some matchmaking but it was hell. What do you say to these girls when you know very little about them? I found myself discussing 'Teasmades' with one woman and then wondered if she thought I was being suggestive. He went into an exaggerated mime to illustrate the story of his apologising, ' "oh I didn't mean a Teasmade for us in the morning," ' he waved his hand in the air vaguely, ' "you know I meant in general." She gave me a filthy look and walked off.'

Dulcie laughed at this.

Ted said, 'But tell me about your business. I know Imogen drove the van over for you.'

'You will see my stock tomorrow morning when you help unload,' she said, and then hesitated, 'that's if you are prepared to do that.'

The side of his mouth raised in a quirky expression that was the old Ted.

'Now I really do have to go to bed.' she said.

CHAPTER TWENTY ONE

Ted joined Dulcie in heaving furniture out of the van. They cooperated by taking one end each of solid oak chests to lift them. They stood some furniture on its end in the lean-to greenhouse. 'It's only temporary,' she said, 'I'll soon have it over to England and get the sales going.'

'I didn't expect to find you doing such physical work. Do you really need to do this?' concern showed in his expression.

'Of course I do you old fool,' she said, 'Its all about our marriage split.' But she nudged him in the ribs with an elbow which belied the aggression in her words.

'We'll see what we can do,' he said quietly.

Dulcie instantly felt lighter, but she also had a twinge of discomfort. He was speaking awfully like a father and she didn't want to be patronised, she just wanted her fair share. They took the smaller ornaments into the house and Dulcie ran a steaming bowl of soapy water from the geyser. She let Ted wash each item and took a tea towel to dry them and lay them carefully on newspaper. This was too much like the early days of marriage when they had worked as a team.

'I had thought of using Imogen as an excuse for coming to visit you, you know.' Ted said. 'But we haven't really talked about her.'

'Are you worried about Imogen?' Dulcie's thoughts went to the Yorkshire Ripper.

'Yes and no, she's a clever young woman now and she is confident in what she does. I admire her but when I visited, I couldn't get close to her.'

'She was always such a daddy's girl – that is, when she saw you.' Dulcie glanced over at the photos of Imogen on her wall.

He turned away from the sink to face her, 'Maybe she is just growing up and away, but perhaps we should find out what's going on with her.'

Dulcie looked away and said 'Hmm'. She felt that he was accusing her of deserting their daughter. 'I did have quite a chat with her when she was over here. But I admit I've been distracted recently. There are some problems in the community.'

'Really?' He raised his eyebrows. 'I genuinely thought that you'd chosen the perfect life for you. One where you are at one with the earth and with the community.'

Dulcie briefly told him of Jane's battle for power in the meeting and her fears about the significance of the cat's death. She managed to show very little emotion. She had become the old Dulcie, but his voice softened when he said, 'Oh I'm sorry to hear that. What's at the heart of this Jane's dislike.'

Dulcie pondered, maybe she hadn't considered Jane's motives enough. Typical of Ted, she thought fondly, he thinks things through. He plays life like he plays chess. But he was still talking and looking concerned, 'We've both been suffering then.'

She sat down. 'Yes I'm glad that I spoke up for myself, but I don't need this hassle. I'm going to leave here and make another new start.' Suddenly everything felt heavy and she knew that she sounded weary.

Ted's face brightened, 'There's just the slight possibility then,' he said indicating in the air a tiny space between his thumb and finger, 'that there may be a second chance for us. After all, we've both learned a lot since the split. I, for one, would put my relationship with you as a higher priority. You gave me a real scare when you ran off.'

'You make me sound like a young child. But Ted, we still see each issue from different perspectives, don't we? You know, I'm willing to listen and learn from what happened to us. As for a second chance,' she paused, 'I'm not sure about that.'

'Well, my dear. I am going to take a walk down to the phone box in the town. I'll get in touch with Gerry and Amanda so that they know not to expect me just yet.' He frowned and narrowed his eyes, 'If that's alright with you, of course.'

'Yes, it's okay. The company will be a help,' she waved her arm lazily in his direction and closed her eyes.

Chapter Twenty Two

Dulcie drifted off to sleep the moment that Ted left for the town, but she woke to a low rattling roar. Possibly a motorbike? She eased her aching body out of the chair and got to the door in time to see two people dismounting. There was Jeannine, the cleaner from the hotel, and a man in a waxed jacket and boots. They were both removing motorbike helmets and hanging them on a Peugeot motorbike. They caught sight of her and Jeannine advanced smiling.

'Ceci,' she opened her arms to her and went in for a double-cheek kiss of greeting. She gestured to the man behind her to come forward and introduced him, 'C'est Christophe.'

'Bonjour Madame,' Christophe said.

Jeannine smiled broadly with such good humour showing all of her wonky teeth. She said, in French, 'I wondered how you were. We enjoyed having you at the hotel. Did you like it? That evil Claude asking you to leave. It wasn't fair.'

'I'm pleased to see you again,' Dulcie said when there was a chance to get a word in. She smiled at Christophe but couldn't help wondering why they had called.

'Come in,' she added.

'Oh, non Madame, we've come to tell you about an accident.' Jeannine laid her hand on Dulcie's arm. 'Do not worry, but as I was leaving work this afternoon I saw a man near to the telephone box in the square. He was not well, not well at all. I got off my bike, a bicycle you understand, not the motorbike.' She glanced at Christophe's motorbike. 'I offered to help him. He was pale in the face and grimacing in pain. I held him under the elbow and sat him down. I used the phone box to call for an ambulance. They drove him off to the hospital. He asked me to let you know what had happened. You know him? He is English.'

Dulcie felt trembly and had to force herself to concentrate in order to speak clearly. 'It's Ted from England. We've been married for years. Thank you. I must go to him.'

Jeannine took a step back and laid her hand across her chest. 'Husband - I see. You must be so shocked. What can we do?' She looked to Christophe. 'It would be difficult to use the motorbike.'

'Thank you. I'll go to him, but I'll use the van. Thank you so much for helping him and for letting me know.'

'Of course,' said Jeannine, 'and when all is well. You must come to meet me at the hotel and tell me all about this Ted.' Dulcie felt her firmly clasp her forearm. Jeannine was a good woman. She watched them replace their helmets and drive off before preparing for her own journey.

***

What on earth, Ted thought. He was half asleep. He awoke fully when he stretched out an arm and felt the cold metal of a hospital bed frame. The sheets were smooth and cool. He was propped in a half-upright position on a soft surface.

He opened his eyes and observed other men in beds opposite but it occurred to him that they would be French. No point in making conversation then. Terror swept over him. I need to be at home, where I know people. I've got myself into a fix. I should hold onto Dulcie now that I'm gaining ground with her, she was always capable of looking after me.

He drifted back into sleep, to be woken again by a youngish man in a white overall. He indicated needles and Ted realised he'd come to take a blood sample. A male nurse – unheard of! And I feel powerless. I can't cope with having my blood taken, I wish Dulcie were here now. Has someone told her where I am? Is there a phone? Maybe I can get in touch with Imogen? Before he could ask, the young man left.

Another awakening and this time he noticed an attractive young nurse swish past pushing a trolley. She didn't glance in his direction, but she had luscious swinging black hair just like Anna, his current girlfriend. Well, maybe not current. They always find a reason to drop me and I left a message to say that I was coming here. She's probably moved on already. Now stop it. I must stop feeling sorry for myself. I'm an old fool if I ever expected Anna to last. She was too young and full of energy. He remembered Anna's eccentric and colourful clothing and the way she dared him to act as though he were thirty again. But I'm not young, he thought, it would never have worked. I was turning into a sugar daddy.

Where are you when I need you, Dulcie? Yes, he acknowledged, she is like an old slipper. He chuckled to himself, I'd better not let her ever hear me say that. I've got such a great affection for her. She'll be here soon. I know she will. And he drifted back into trusting sleep.

***

What visiting hours would the hospital have? Dulcie hadn't been into the nearest large city and she didn't know where the hospital was. It was difficult to think.

She picked up some bread, a chunk of cheese and some fruit and put them into a canvas shoulder bag. She may need to wait around for a while. The journey by van would take about twenty minutes, but she had no idea how to find the hospital.

She would have welcomed the chance of a sightseeing trip if she hadn't been far too anxious about Ted to notice the surroundings.

As she neared the suburbs, she hit urban roads with lines of trees on central reservations. There were rows of parked cars under the trees in the shade. From the van's high cab, Dulcie could see a long way. She drove across a bridge and glanced sideways at a broad glittering river.

There were signs for a hospital, so she followed them. The hospital was an enormous cube and dazzlingly white in the brilliant sunshine. She cruised its car parking area to find somewhere to park. Finally, a driver reversed out of a space so she waited to use it.

Dulcie contrasted this ultra-modern building with the Victorian edifices in England. Through the sliding doors, the reception desk looked more like the entrance to a luxury hotel than a hospital. After some challenging conversations with reception staff to find the correct ward, Dulcie approached a line of lifts and was swiftly carried to the third floor. Another world from the traditional France that she inhabited. There was Ted in a bed behind a toughened glass wall. She gave a small wave and he smiled weakly at her.

'So, what happened?' she said as she pulled up one of the moulded plastic visitor chairs.

'I still don't know what hit me,' Ted said, 'I felt a strong tightness and panicked, then this woman dialled a number and before I knew it I was being taken into an ambulance. I just had time to tell her where you were. I must say, the French hospital system is incredibly efficient but I'm so relieved you've come.'

Covered in a maze of coloured wires attached to machines, he looked exhausted. He was diminished by the fold of white sheet across his chest and the strange equipment.

'So it's a heart problem?' she asked. He had no chance to answer as a woman in a white coat carrying a clipboard arrived and in rapid French asked to sit down.

Ted's French was not good enough to follow a conversation so Dulcie responded to her. The woman identified herself as a doctor and confirmed with Ted that he was happy for Dulcie to be involved.

'We still have tests to do, but I don't think that Monsieur Best will need to stay in very much longer.'

Dulcie leaned forward in concentration, 'So he can go home?'

'We have a very good café on the ground floor for you to wait, if you can take Monsieur Best home after his tests,' the doctor said, and she went on to describe the ideal recovery for someone who had had a minor heart attack. Ted looked perplexed. Dulcie laid a hand on his arm, 'I'll tell you all about it in a moment.'

The doctor was impatient to carry out more procedures, so Dulcie quickly summarised.

'Can I come back to yours?' he asked.

'Of course, we'll work something out. I don't know whether you will be well enough to carry on travelling to Gerald and Amanda's at the moment.'

Chapter Twenty Three

It was so unusual to see Ted, framed by her ornate cast-iron bedstead beside the bedside table with pretty glass ornaments, an open novel and her alarm clock. Asleep, his head was tilted back and mouth slightly open. His medication intruded on her bedside table, pushing her belongings to one side.

He woke up and peered into the middle distance with narrowed eyes and brows drawn down. Then he focused on Dulcie's face as though seeing her for the first time, and his expression was full of emotion. She felt an echoing prickle in her eyes and looked away quickly. Everything had happened so fast. When she turned back to him, Ted had already sunk into sleep.

∗∗∗

One of the conventions of the community was that residents should declare overnight visitors. It made sense for the security of the others. Dulcie thought about it, but she hadn't visited the chateau itself since the community meeting.

Her insides quivered as she walked over there. It was something that had to be done. Maggie and Jane had adjacent apartments, on the ground floor near to the meeting hall. Dulcie knocked and entered Maggie's room through double wooden doors, which led straight into a stylish open-plan living room. Despite medieval beams, the room had trendy long low sofas, a teak sideboard with smoked glass display shelves, and a glass-topped coffee table standing on thick cream carpeting. Maggie had the one and only telephone in the manoir. Maggie herself sat in a higher upholstered chair. A bit like a throne, thought Dulcie but practical for an elderly person with creaking joints.

'Come in, Ceci, you are always welcome. I was hoping to see you after the difficulty in the meeting.' She smiled and beckoned Dulcie over.

A distant door slammed and Jane appeared with a pile of folders in her arms. She nodded, 'Dulcie, hello.'

Dulcie moved a leather seat over to sit close to Maggie, while Jane deposited her paperwork onto a nearby desk. 'I wanted to let you know that my estranged husband, Ted, has arrived from England and he'll be staying with me for a while.'

Jane curled her lip, 'We know. It's been a day or two, hasn't it?'

'It hasn't been long at all,' Dulcie said, 'and he's been taken ill. He won't be joining in any of our activities. I hope that the residents will understand.'

'I'm sure they will,' said Maggie,' you are well-liked here Ceci, people are always very understanding,' and she glanced at Jane as though indicating someone who was understanding.

'Of course,' Jane agreed with a tight smile, 'however, Ceci we were just about to get on with some of the business of the community. So if you'd excuse us. . . '

'But I do have some business to do. I need to ask about leaving here.' Dulcie said. Maggie looked startled while Jane raised her eyebrows and went back to the table for her papers.

'Leaving here for good?' she brought across one of the large ledgers and stood close to where Dulcie was sitting. 'We'll need to find what type of agreement you signed when you got here, whether you can recover anything of your deposit, and how much notice you need to give. You must realise, it's going to take us some time to recruit someone new.' She looked across where Maggie was frowning and biting her lip.

'I thought that everyone had the same type of agreement. When I arrived, they were made with the whole community present.' Dulcie felt her hands growing sweaty and wiped them down her thighs. She was ignored. She stood up and stepped closer to Jane. Jane flicked through pages in an attempt to find the year and month that Dulcie had arrived. She was running her finger down lists of figures. It looked a mess. Ducie saw that all the relevant paperwork had been stapled to the pages: receipts, bills, invoices. She noticed a few names of local traders, the large cash and carry, but also a quirky logo of arrows circling the globe. It looked just like the logo on her so-called payslip, from the Hotel Chez Inez. That same logo appeared with remarkable regularity. Why would the chateau be trading with the hotel? Jane noticed that Dulcie was standing close by and fixed her with a glare.

'Never mind. It's quite a time-consuming search. It might even be in a previous ledger. We're busy, so I will be in touch.' Jane said and waved Dulcie away.

Maggie's mouth opened slightly and she frowned at Jane. In a kindly tone she said, 'You have a visitor anyway, so maybe it will be best for you to go back to him, Ceci. Maybe we could get together later. How does that sound?'

As she walked back to the gatehouse, Dulcie reflected that this encounter hadn't settled anything. While Jane held all the records, she wouldn't be able to trust them.

***

She looked in on Ted when she returned. He was lying awake. She collapsed down to sit on the edge of the bed.

'Oh, Ted,' she said shaking her head slowly, 'that was difficult. I feel isolated here. The sooner I can organise leaving, the better it will be. And it's such a pity, as I was beginning to make this gatehouse feel like a home.'

'You've been to speak to the community then?'

'Well to the leadership, I've given my notice in now, but it looks as though it's going to be a while before I can leave.' She looked at him and was surprised at how drawn he looked, 'That's just as well as you need time to recuperate.'

'You look tired.' he said and patted her hand.

'Well, it's more that I'm worried. There's something terribly disquieting going on in the community now. I don't know what it is. I need to think about it.'

'Look I'll shift over and you can lay your head down here.'

Dulcie looked at the plump pillow and pulled her shoes off to lie down. No, damn it. It was her bed. She pulled off her clothes and fell into bed. She felt the heat from his body and smelt his familiar 'Old Spice' smell. Eventually, she pulled the covers over herself.

Chapter Twenty Four

As Ted recovered, Dulcie began to devote her time to the invalid. She closed her mind to her money worries as her business had stalled. He sat at her small kitchen table with a breakfast boiled egg while she finished her coffee.

She noticed that his jaw had lost some of its definition and his eyes were dull.

'You really must take some exercise. We need to get you strong,' she said.

'I somehow can't get any motivation.' Ted said.

'It's glorious outside. Finish that, and I'll set you up in some shade in the garden. You can watch me weed the vegetables and we'll take a little stroll each day.' Dulcie left him to it and dragged a small table from her store of French furniture in the lean-to, followed by a folded deck chair that was stored in the caravan within her hedged garden.

He shuffled out, holding a book. The air was alive with the sounds of birds and the slight rustle of leaves in the breeze. Dulcie hurried back into the house to bring sunglasses for them both. She needed some peaceful time in the garden too.

Both settled, she raised her face to the sun, closed her eyes and basked in the warmth. 'Who would have thought, that we'd be sitting together here.' she said, 'It's such a different life than the one we had mapped out.'

Now that he was well enough to go outside, she realised that he could plan to move on and she found herself feeling dismayed at the idea. Yes, she would miss him.

She sensed Ted turning to look at her as he dropped his book onto his knees.

'This seems like paradise to me. I'm just beginning to wind down and think more slowly. I look back . . . I wasn't awake to what was going on in my own life. You were very valuable to me my dear, but I took you for granted, I know I did.'

She heard the 'my dear' and her teeth were on edge. She understood that he meant well. 'Well, thank you, Ted.' she said.

'Yes, things went so smoothly when you were around, and I felt that we fitted into society as a couple,' he added.

'Our life was a testament to my good organisational skills. But I'm sure there are more creative ways of using skills.' She smiled across at him in case he thought that she was levelling more criticism at him. 'I'm beginning to realise that it wasn't your ideal life either. By leaving, I gave you a chance for a new life too.'

Ted reached across and sought out her hand. She felt his thumb circling the skin on the back of her hand. 'But you don't realise how much you were missed. Since you left, I've felt exposed and alone. It was as though you'd died and I was in mourning. People at work gave me pitying looks and didn't know what to say. I could tell they were wondering what I'd done wrong. I don't think I did so much wrong, did I?'

How to answer that? Dulcie had felt let down, but perhaps he had been unable to give what she wanted. He had been too wrapped up in his own world. We are all the result of our upbringing; his parents were like that too.

He continued, 'After you'd gone, I think I had a bit of a breakdown. I couldn't function. I left work on a long break and obviously as you know, I had to deal with the solicitors. They are like an army ready suited-up to enter a battle. And you know I was the one who worked every day and that resulted in our prosperity, so I do deserve to keep some of what I provided.' Her silence seemed to have led him back into his original combative frame of mind.

'Once I was on my own, I tried to work out how to pick myself up. I modernised. You perhaps noticed . . .much more coordinated. I stopped asking the barber for such a severe short back and sides. I approached a dating agency. No mean feat I'll tell you, the unnerving women that run these places - all pearls and twin sets. They look at you as a biological specimen in a Petrie dish. Some of the dates were extremely awkward.' he laughed slightly, 'Well you know I can't converse about art, feminist politics, drama.'

It was hard to make a new life, and she supposed that he hadn't asked for it. She was curious, as this was a path that she had never considered taking. 'Didn't you get on with any of the women then?'

It did work out in the end. I saw a girl called Bronwyn for six months. She was stylish, and I enjoyed getting to know her set.', 'But then she dropped me, for absolutely no reason. I was even more depressed then. That was about the time that I'd moved out into Alan's flat. So life seemed pretty empty.'

He paused and looked towards the chateau for a while as though deciding how much to tell her, 'Then there was someone called Anna. She is a bit out of my league I'm afraid. You know those women, very self-assured and full of energy. I suppose she has charisma. Not sure why she was dating me. She isn't that much younger, but she isn't a worn-out old thing like me.'

He's looking at me like an appealing puppy, Dulcie thought. What is it about him? He really wants me to save him from something. A stab of resentment went through her. She didn't want to rescue anyone anymore, but she stood up and looking down at him kindly she said, 'You need to build yourself up again. Come on, we'll try a little walk in the shade of the woods.' She held out an arm to help him up.

As they moved off, they failed to notice Gilles, who had parked the post office van on the road outside the grand gateway and was rounding the hedge towards her vegetable garden. He hung back and looked carefully. He didn't know Ted, but the couple's body language was certainly close as they strolled arm in arm.

Chapter Twenty Five

The routine of Dulcie's days soothed her. She spent mornings with Ted in the garden. He looked on while she tended rows of vegetables. She would take rests for cool Stella Artois sitting beside him under a tree with only the sound of bees floating between plants to disturb the silence. In the afternoon she took the van out to visit sales or worked in the lean-to, while he took a gentle stroll in the hills.

She hadn't seen Gilles. She still felt the bubbling delight that she'd experienced when they were together. At times she rehearsed introducing him to Ted, but as days went by she surmised that he must have had second thoughts after their discussion in the van. Well better to find out now that the relationship wouldn't work. It was easy to think that, but she still felt a sore ache inside when she wondered where he was now and what he was thinking.

What about Jane? She loathed to let Jane get the better of her. She had a hunch about the peculiar logo that she'd spotted on so much of the paperwork. It looked so much like the Hotel Chez Inez logo that she wanted to go to check out what the connection could be.

The hotel lobby was, as before, deserted. She could hear a distant vacuum cleaner. Dulcie knew that Jeannine would be a friendly source of information so she followed the noise. She spotted Arlette in the second-floor corridor. She was sorting bundles of sheets from a trolley and didn't see her. Arlette was more senior than Jeannine and so could be closely involved with Claude. Dulcie turned back to the lift entrance to give Arlette time to disappear. When the coast was clear, she continued to follow the drone of the cleaner. Yes, there was Jeannine's back. Jeannine screeched when she turned to find Dulcie standing just behind her.

'Sh, Shh,' Dulcie couldn't help being amused but held her finger to her lips.

Jeannine clutched her hand to her chest dramatically and puffed out her lips. 'No need to be secretive,' she said, 'Arlette would not mind you visiting us.'

Dulcie edged closer so that she could speak in a quiet voice. 'I don't want everyone to know the reason for my visit. I feel that I can trust you, Jeannine.'

Jeannine lolled on the edge of the bed and reached into her pocket for a wrapped toffee. 'Want one?'

'No, thank you.' Dulcie said sitting down beside her. I've come for your help, really. There's such a lot of conflict at the chateau now that I think I'm going to have to leave.'

'Oh,' Jeannine looked sad and was about to speak when Dulcie went on, 'I know people in the chateau don't come down to the village a lot, but I saw a logo,' and she pulled a drawing of the logo that she had seen out of her pocket. 'Is it the hotel logo?'

Jeannine leaned back resting her palms behind her and nodded slowly, 'It is.'

Dulcie felt her pulse quicken. 'Okay, can you think of a reason why it would appear on official papers at the chateau?'

'Yes, of course, Claude buys supplies from the chateau, oh at least twice a month. All of the vegetables that you can grow, but also some tinned foods, coffee beans, sugar, even scouring powder for the baths and disinfectant. There would be paperwork.'

'I see.' Dulcie decided to act as though this was unsurprising. 'Of course. Which of us does he deal with? Have you seen the person?'

'I don't deal with supplies, you understand, but I have seen two women. One is short and blonde; a little dumpy. The other has very dark hair. We could ask Claude for their names.'

'No,' Dulcie shook her head for emphasis, 'I don't want to talk to Claude about it at the moment. I'd like to find out all I can first.' and she smiled at Jeannine in thanks. 'That's a second time that you've helped me, Jeannine. I hope I can help you one day.'

'I see you as a friend,' Jeannine said shrugging.

'Thank you, that means a lot to me.' Dulcie clasped her hands. 'I'll let you get on before Arlette comes along to complain.'

She left the room and moved swiftly down the corridor. She daren't risk the area around the lift again, so holding onto the bannister, she trod carefully on the back stairway. One more thing, did she need written proof of trade between the hotel and the chateau? No the books at the chateau were their own proof. Just a short distance across the tiled floor now, to get to the door of the hotel and away.

As she passed the entrance door, she saw that customer area on the pavement was now half full of people, and a waitress was weaving between the tables. Her initial thought was, just act casually and stroll away, until she thought that she recognised Ted's back. He was sitting at one of the tables talking to an animated dark-haired woman.

Dulcie hesitated. He hadn't mentioned coming to the town. As far as she knew he never visited there. Looking across at the pair, this seemed more than a casual discussion about the weather or a business meeting. The dark woman was animated, and Ted was nodding his head in reply. No harm in greeting them, in any case she needed to check that it really was him.

She looked down to check that she was at least tidy, before accosting a strange woman. She was wearing an emerald green cheesecloth blouse with a stylish scarf tied around her hips. That added to her confidence but she was still a little reluctant to do this. The woman seemed to sense that she was being observed, so Dulcie was forced into making a move.

Dulcie glided between the tables towards them, smiling a greeting.

'Bonjour,' she called, a few paces from the table. Ted turned and saw her for the first time. His eyebrows shot up and his mouth dropped open. It turned into a half-smile that didn't reach his eyes. With practised ease he raised an arm and beckoned her to the table.

'Dulcie, there you are. Come and meet Anna. Anna is English.'

Anna paused with the arms, that she had been using to gesture with, still held in mid-air. She lowered them slowly. Dressed in black with a silk scarf flung around her shoulders, she had full lips, intense brown eyes and volumes of dark hair. Her face changed in an instant from startled caution to thoughtfully scan Dulcie up and down. She extended her hand to Dulcie.

'Hello, Anna.' Dulcie said and then turned to Ted, 'I wasn't aware that you had friends from England here.'

'No, when Anna realised how long I would be staying, she came over to find me. She didn't know that I'd been ill. We knew each other for a while in England.' He cleared his throat, 'Since you've been gone, you understand.'

'Of course,' Dulcie said and waited for them to say more.

'I have heard all about you.' Anna said. 'I'm interested in what made you come over here. Poor Ted had quite a shock when you went, or so I gather. I've been there for you though, haven't I?' her voice changed as though she was speaking to a baby and she leaned into Ted and touched his arm. Ted smiled at her without looking up at Dulcie.

This was awkward. They had been separated so Ted had a right to see whomever he liked, but he had led her to believe that he'd been lonely. She would not consider having any kind of showdown in the hotel, 'Well I'll see you back at the house,' she said.

How long had Anna been in France? How did she know where Ted had gone? If Ted had left her with the address, then he must have planned for her to join him? Perhaps he had telephoned Anna and asked her to come. Dulcie couldn't believe that she had allowed herself to mellow towards him, to trust him.

When Ted finally arrived back at the house, she was ready for him, and her anger had built. He avoided her eyes but said, 'I'm sorry, it must have been a shock for you to see Anna.'

'I don't understand,' she said. 'How did this Anna know where you were?'

'I left her Gerald and Amanda's contact details in Carcassone. They must have told her where I was. Dulcie, you can't blame me for her arrival. I assure you I didn't engineer it.' His voice sounded pleading and irritated Dulcie.

'But who is she?'

'Remember I explained that I'd been dating. Anna is someone that I've been dating.'

'What and she came all the way here to find you? That hardly sounds like a shallow relationship and someone that you had a nightmare trying to chat with. Because that's what you told me had happened when you dated. Ted, I just want to tell you, now, how I feel. I'm shocked because I let you wheedle your way into my home and into my new life. I'd even begun to take your needs into account. It feels like a betrayal.' Dulcie was annoyed that she had begun to cry and she swiped a tear away angrily.

He looked downwards and sideways and sighed deeply. 'What can I say to you?' he took time to think and then nodded. 'Look Anna is a really nice woman. You saw her. She's younger than me and I didn't expect her to see anything in me.' He sighed again and waited for her response.

'No that's not what I mean. Anna and I did get on well, but I've had experience of being turned down by a lot of younger, more glamorous women and I expected that to happen with her too. I didn't expect that she'd follow up and come to see me in Carcassone. I'm as surprised as you are.' And there his eyes became brighter and he allowed himself a slight grin.

Dulcie didn't miss that, 'So, you're flattered.'

He moved close to her and put his arms around her. Dulcie welcomed him while feeling tempted to push him away. He carried on in a soft voice, 'You and I have grown closer in the last few weeks. We've rediscovered our relationship, and you have been so caring.' She looked up at him. His eyes were soft and wrinkled with kindness. 'I'm so grateful for this time that we've had.'

'So am I,' her tone of voice echoed his.

'But I think it is time I went. I need time to think things through.' he added.

'Dulcie felt confused, 'Where are you going to go?'

'Possibly on to Gerald and Amanda as originally planned. Will you be OK?' he said as he went into the bedroom.

She didn't answer. She sat down to try to think it through. She needed more information to understand it.

Ted must have whipped his clothes and toiletries into a case, because he emerged remarkably quickly. 'I'm sorry, Dulcie. Let's keep in touch.' He brushed past her on the way to the door.

She had time to say, 'OK, I've got their number. We'll talk some more.' She followed him to the door to watch him leave, feeling numb and weary. As he got to the pillars of the gateway, a small red Fiat drew up and Dulcie saw Ted open the boot and load in his suitcase. She peered at the driver. It was Anna. So, he hadn't gone for thinking space, he'd gone with her.

'Bastard,' she yelled after him, but the car was leaving.

Chapter Twenty Six

She had lost everything: Gilles, the community, Ted, even the cat. What did she do to deserve to be abandoned? Where could she turn for safety and a shoulder to cry on: Imogen, England. It was a subconscious need to retrace her steps, back to England as this new life had obviously been a false move. So, go back to the fork in the road and take another direction. Blink away the tears and hold your head high, she thought, before grabbing a bundle of tissues and crying into them.

Imogen was hours, if not days, away. The van was full, old and slow. No, she would take a fast train to Paris Montparnasse use the metro to the Gare du Nord and carry on to the channel ferries. It was going to take more than one day. She braced herself for a long trek.

Dulcie rapidly pulled an overnight bag from under the bed. She threw underwear and toiletries into it. Miraculously, there were some English pounds in the drawer with her passport; fate offering a helping hand. She walked to the railway station, pausing to look back at the turrets of the chateau with a sharp tingling in her chest that threatened to rise to her eyes. There was no imminent train to Paris so she was forced to stop and sit on a waiting room bench. She was forced to think. Could this really have happened? She had begun to feel so close to Ted and so full of hope that they belonged together.

Two days later, Dulcie stepped out of a taxi at the Lunar Hotel. Her shoulders sloped from carrying her bag, her fringe was lank and greasy, her make-up had worn off and her mouth tasted sour. She paid the driver and looked up at the building. The white frontage gleamed in the midday sun. Nothing had changed on the outside, but Dulcie had never seen Imogen's quarters in the hotel.

Imogen was behind the reception desk. Dulcie saw bewilderment, pleasure and then concern flash across her face when she first saw her mother.

She moved out from behind the desk and rushed to her. 'Mum, what are you doing here? Has anything happened?' she said.

'I need to tell you, but only after I've had a rest. I haven't let myself feel yet. I'm just trying to keep it all in, darling.' It was such a relief to see Imogen that Dulcie felt her lip tremble. Thankfully, Imogen took charge, called a member of staff to cover the desk and led her by the arm.

'Come and see where I live. We'll get you settled down. How long have you been travelling?' Imogen said as she opened the door.

A hint of pot noodle wafted through, as Dulcie followed her in. Dulcie had half expected to see Diana. She was surprised to see an eclectic living room and a self-possessed young black woman, sorting through a briefcase of papers. She leapt up and began to rapidly collect the papers, randomly stuffing them into a briefcase.

'It's okay you don't need to go.' Imogen edged around to stand between the two, 'This is my mum. Mum,' she said, turning towards Dulcie, 'meet Lynette.' Dulcie was surprised by Imogen's dramatic introduction and Lynette's confusion. Maybe this was a hotel staff member, it was difficult to know, but she filed the mystery to the back of her mind. Lynette shook her hand formally but then left. Dulcie sank down onto the wicker sofa. To her consternation, she finally allowed her face to fall. It was too difficult to keep up the front any longer.

'What is it?' Imogen said. It flooded out. It was easy to tell her because she knew the people at the chateau and she knew Ted so well. As she spoke, she realised that it would be hard for Imogen to hear. Imogen cared about Ted. In fact, Imogen began to look more and more worried until she was biting her lip and had tears in her eyes.

'I'm sorry to lay all this on you. I'm so tired, can I just go and lie down?' Dulcie said.

'Yes of course,' Imogen took her bag for her and led her into the bedroom. The curtains were still drawn so the room had been shaded from the sun, but the bed was unmade. There were clothes and bags on pegs, on the chair, and on the floor.

'Um' Imogen made a half-hearted attempt to remove things.

'Don't worry.' Dulcie pulled up the bedcovers and launched herself on top of them. She closed her eyes. 'I'm too tired to care.'

'Okay,' Imogen breathed, 'see you in a while.'

* * *

Waking slowly, her eyes were still closed but she was aware of not being asleep, of sore hips and a dry mouth. Dulcie forced her eyelids to open. She was lying on a candlewick bedcover on a single bed. Where was she? Oh yes, Imogen's room. She took it in. She didn't recognise the dark coloured cardigan hanging on the knob of a cupboard or the rucksack on the floor. Imogen was growing away from her. Things change. Imogen had probably gone back to work.

'Hello.' She tried speaking it. 'Hello,' she called a little louder.

* * *

Torn between hearing her mother's story and wondering how Lynette had taken the sudden interruption, Imogen was relieved when her mother went to bed. She rushed through to reception.

'Sharon, Lynette came out here. Has she left?'

Sharon turned casually. Imogen wished that she had kept the tell-tale urgency out of her voice.

'No, I think she's still in the back office. She said she was going to use a desk in there. Is that alright?

'Oh, yes of course, thank you.' Imogen smiled reassuringly.

Head bent over the desk, Lynette was still working on papers. She partially looked up when the door opened.

Imogen's heart leapt. She took the office chair beside Lynette's. 'I was worried about you. I thought you might have gone.'

'Does your mum know anything about us?' Lynette looked wide-eyed.

'She's going through so much of her own stuff, I don't think she can take in what else is happening. When Dad went to France, he called on her and they got back together. Now he's gone off again with a girlfriend. I don't know what to think. What's he playing at?' Imogen shook her head and then shuffled her chair closer to Lynette to draw her into an embrace. Lynette's warm cardigan under her palm, it felt right to be closely joined. They could get through anything. After a moment of silent holding, she stroked her cheek. 'That must have been a shock to you. It was a shock to me too.'

Lynette let out a breath, 'So you weren't expecting her.'

'No of course not,' Imogen felt a stab of hurt. She drew back to look at her, 'I wouldn't do that to you. I'd have told you.'

'So what are we going to do now?' Lynette looked down at her hands, 'I am worried about spending more time with my parents. They would get it out of me somehow. But now it's difficult here too.'

Imogen gathered her strength and made herself think clearly. 'I need to give Mum some space to get over her problems, but I'm going to be upfront with her. Even Sharon is beginning to realise that there is something between us, so we need to put on a brave face.'

'Fight the good fight with all thy might.' Lynette quoted, smiling.

What a complex situation. With that one comment, Imogen realised that she was dealing with all of Lynette's religious background and in a very public arena. But she knew that she could trust her friends and she had fingers crossed that in time, her mother may stand behind them.

'Come here,' she coaxed and pulled Lynette forward, firmly wrapped her in her arms for a deep kiss which pulled them out of their immediate surroundings and back into their own bubble.

Chapter Twenty Seven

Showered and rested, Dulcie looked down at the area below the window where groups of guests were sitting under parasols with their drinks. She was calmer. Imogen had found her an ensuite hotel room and it was such a luxury after years of using an outside toilet and carrying her washing equipment across to the chateau when she needed a bath.

All the people below seemed connected, whereas she felt alone. At one time she'd helped out in the hotel, but it was now fully staffed and she'd just be in the way. She thought back to France. Her real work was there. There was still a van full of furniture and she would need to go back at least once to sort out her house. No, stop it. Take some time out and look after yourself, she told herself and resolved to go for a walk, buy some magazines and then have as long as she liked lying on the bed, doing nothing, talking to no one.

Over the following week, Dulcie caught up with life in England. It hadn't changed since she'd been away. She recognised that English people were standing up to the onslaught of IRA bombings and going about their business despite the danger. Each month brought some new atrocity in the newspapers. The heightened awareness of unattended luggage had reached the Lunar hotel.

In rural France, Dulcie had felt cut off from the wider world. The politics of the chateau had been all-consuming. The hippie culture of the chateau wasn't a strong trend in England anymore; Britain was getting tougher. Dulcie almost felt like a tourist visiting her home country, so where did she belong now?

Darling Imogen worked too hard. Dulcie had hardly seen her but it was also a relief to be left to her own devices. Even Diana was away with her mother, but now that Dulcie had rested, she was looking forward to having some days out with Diana and meeting up with Anita again.

One morning, as she finished breakfast in the dining room she saw Imogen talking to a waitress. Dulcie lingered by her chair rather than interrupt, but then moved forward to catch her as she was leaving. Imogen didn't hear her approach above the murmur of voices and clink of cutlery.

She touched Imogen on the shoulder, 'Hello dear, have you got any time to do something together today or maybe tomorrow? I'd love to have time for a good talk together. I think I'm going to have to go back to France to sort everything out there soon.'

'Sorry Mum, I've been so busy. I should have organised something.' Imogen led the way out of the dining room. When they reached reception, she said, 'I could come with you to scout out shops for your French antiques.'

'Thank you that would be lovely, but,' Dulcie paused, 'I would like a really good heart- to- heart. I've had time to gain my equilibrium and now I need to mull it all over with someone.'

'Let's go for a drive out for the day and maybe find a little café somewhere then.' Imogen began to move towards the door to her own quarters, 'I'll just go and get changed out of business clothes.'

'Okay, I'll wait out here.' Dulcie waved towards the side door and took a seat at one of the outdoor tables. There was a pleasant breeze and bright sunshine. Who could feel miserable on such a nice day? She noticed a movement. A little black and white cat was sliding through the table legs.

'Hello,' she cooed gently. He was wary but ventured towards her and wound himself around her shins, she heard the beginnings of a purr. Memories of Oscar doing the same thing came back to her, but then the memory of his limp body. She shook her head, determined to move on from sadness.

They had undisturbed privacy in Imogen's Ford Escort, and the low burring of the engine was a comforting backdrop to concentration. As they drew out of the hotel exit, Imogen twisted in her seat to watch for traffic and Dulcie let her concentrate. They followed a road away from built-up areas; past suburban rows of houses until there were more hedges and fences between properties. A sharp click click click of indicators as they came to a roundabout and Dulcie relaxed, letting Imogen choose the route.

'I'm pleased to see the hotel is successful. So how have you been?' Dulcie ventured after a while.

'I'm fine.' Imogen took a quick glance towards her mum, 'I'm happy Mum.'

'That's good. I was worried, as you seem quite preoccupied and very busy. I worry that you are investing everything in your work. All work and no play, you know. . .'

'I'm fine, tell me about you.'

'Coming here put everything in perspective. I'm bitterly disappointed about the way it worked out in France. I'm disappointed in myself too. I let myself down by not getting more involved and insisting on being heard, but everyone seemed against me.

'It's awful,' Imogen said, 'You got on so well with them all and helped out with the children.'

'I know, you'd think at least some of them would have stuck up for me.' Dulcie stopped speaking for a moment and looked out of the car window to regain her composure. 'They all let me down. I can't believe how Jane has been able to take over.

'I've been thinking, just before this all happened, I discovered that Jane had been selling off food from the chateau. No wonder she always emphasised difficulties between the town and our community. She wouldn't have wanted us to hear of it from there.'

Imogen said, 'And you were able to mix with the French. That could have made you a threat to her, you know. Being able to mix with the locals, will help you to build a good life there, Mum.'

'Yes, I know. Maybe I could carry on the brocante business, but move out of the commune. She has ruined it for me. How dare she criticise me. What she's doing is fraud. I should expose her for what she is, but I've lost my confidence since this whole situation with your dad.'

I've heard from Dad, I thought I ought to let you know.'

Dulcie heard a loud heartbeat thumping inside her ears. What had Ted got to say now?

'He's back in England. He didn't actually go on to see your friends in France at all.' Imogen went on, 'He's in a bit of a state actually. He feels awful about leaving you like that. From the sound of it he got caught up with this Anna and she swept him away.' Imogen sighed heavily, 'I don't understand it. I knew he was dating Anna regularly, but I didn't think it had been anything serious. Strange that she'd travel across France to get to him.'

'Don't make excuses for him Imogen,' Dulcie knew that her feelings seeped out making her voice sound strained.

'I think this Anna must have seen him slipping through her fingers and then decided to catch him. It was hard to be supportive over the phone, knowing what he'd put you through. Remember, he may have done well at work, but it doesn't make him clever in his personal life. He's been weak, and I think he regrets it.'

Dulcie thought she would explode with both hurt and anger but she didn't want to upset Imogen, particulary when they had the chance of a day out together.

She changed the subject, 'I can see it's difficult for you. While I'm here, I'd like to see some of Diana. That will help my mood, I love being with her. I could take her out and treat her. Perhaps I could take her to school for you some days.'

Imogen pulled the car into a rough gritted car park in a country park open to the public. They walked together, Dulcie carrying a cardigan over her arm in case it was windy up on the high rocks. They picked their way through bracken dotted with sporadic low bushes and spindly saplings. The path wound its way around the base of a large rock. It looked like a series of enormous boulders balanced on top of each other and infilled with plant growth. The path then climbed up the sides, and after much effort and puffing, they attained the smooth surface on top. There was complete silence. Dulcie stood and surveyed the town laid out like a model far away. The sky stretched wide; blue with wisps of clouds.

'Time for a rest?' Imogen said, sitting close to the rock's edge.

'I'm tempted to dangle my legs over the edge, but maybe that's too scary,' Dulcie said, sitting down beside her.

They both took a moment, lost in their own thoughts. A flock of birds rose below them disturbed by some animal.

'Mum, I kept wanting to say something in the car,' Imogen began. 'Now we're alone I want you to listen so that I can explain properly.'

'I'm listening,' said Dulcie slowly, wondering what was coming.

'You asked if I was happy, and I am. In the past, I envied people who had someone there for them. I never saw anyone that I admired enough to want to be their permanent girlfriend.'

Dulcie said nothing but she began to smile, it sounded as though Imogen had at last found a boyfriend and her imagination started to move ahead.

'The thing is Mum. You saw Lynette in my living room when you first arrived. I think you may have guessed something already. I've always admired Lynette for her quiet good sense. She seems so centred. When she turned up at the hotel one day, I was completely drawn to her.'

'What?' Dulcie didn't realise she had spoken.

'Yes, we took a while to get to know each other. I was fascinated by Lynette. She has changed my life and made it so much brighter and more thrilling. So I hope you can be pleased for us.' Imogen stopped and looked at her mother, shyly.

'My goodness. I don't know what to say to you.' Dulcie wiped non-existent sweat from her brow and blinked, 'So she came to you and sought you out?'

'No, it wasn't like that. She was here for a meeting,' Imogen rushed on, 'I know it's going to be hard for us. I've seen how Tony struggled with it, but we think we can be discreet and still be happy.'

Dulcie gave a little laugh, 'Imogen what are you thinking? I think you're right, you have been lonely but why can't she be just a friend?'

'Because she isn't just a friend.'

'You are living in a hotel that's very public and Imogen, not just another woman, but a black woman.'

'I'd have thought better of you.' Imogen's head jerked.

'She seems perfectly nice. It's just there've been those National Front marches and all that trouble recently. And I imagine that her upbringing must have been different from yours, wouldn't there be times when you don't understand each other?'

Imogen was becoming agitated. Dulcie valiantly looked inside herself for the right thing to say. She took a deep breath, 'After meeting so many different types of people at the chateau and breaking away from my marriage, I do know that there are other ways of living your life. I suppose I'd just like you to be sure of what you are doing.'

She smiled at Imogen and lightly touched her arm. 'Think carefully in case this is a phase that you are going through.' Dulcie saw Imogen flush and felt anxious that their relationship could be damaged. 'What am I saying, I've seen you think carefully about life and make good decisions. I'm sure this is one of them. I'm looking forward to getting to know her.'

Imogen flushed. 'Thank you, I knew I could rely on you.'

Dulcie drew a sense of peace and invincibility from the vast panorama of the natural world contrasting with the tiny insignificance of the town. 'Our petty problems are so insignificant in the scheme of things,' she said, 'but if I want you to do what you believe is right for you, I must do the same for myself. I find it hard to know how to relate to your dad now. You say he's regretting it. I'll try to accept that, but it's difficult, after all I've been through. I think he and I need to talk'.

'Yes, I hope you will do that,' Imogen stood up and wandered over to the other side of the plateau to survey the view in that direction. 'You must do what you think is right about Dad. Poor Dad.'

Chapter Twenty Eight

Back at the Lunar Hotel, they saw Anita's Mini in the car park. 'Diana is back with Anita, come on. Let's go and see them.' Imogen said.

As they walked towards the hotel, Diana burst out of the building with Anita closely behind. Her face was lit with excitement and she had already started to speak as she covered the ground between them.

'I've been to the seaside. Look. . .' she was holding out postcards. 'We stayed in a caravan, like yours,' she said to Dulcie. 'We went on the sand.'

'Okay, okay,' Imogen took her hand, 'come on let's get inside.' She laughed across at Anita. 'I take it you had a good time? Shall we sit in the lounge and I'll get drinks for you?' Imogen led them through the hotel and they sat down on leather chesterfields bracketing a low glass coffee table. Imogen disappeared for a moment.

'Lovely to see you again Anita, how was your theatre run?' Dulcie said, but there was little time to discuss that as Diana insisted on showing Dulcie her postcards.

Imogen returned with a tray of drinks and handed Dulcie a letter. 'This just arrived for you Mum. It's dad's writing.' Dulcie didn't respond, but she took the letter and pushed it straight into her pocket to examine later. She watched Imogen take Diana onto her knee to hear more about the holiday, and she wondered who else knew about Imogen's new relationship. She had to tread carefully. If she didn't Imogen might always remember that her mother hadn't supported her.

As they went their separate ways before dinner was served, Dulcie called back to her daughter, 'Do you expect to see Lynette tonight? If she does come, can you call me? I'd like to meet her properly.'

***

When Dulcie finally returned to her hotel room, she sighed heavily and sat on the bed. She was tempted to lie on it but remembered the letter that she'd put in her pocket. She ripped it open.

Dearest Dulcie,

I don't know what you think of me. I'm very sorry that I left you so abruptly and I hope that you can forgive me. I'm back in England now and thinking of those times that we had in France together. We had a chance to feel carefree. I grew very close to you. I hope that you felt the same about me.

I miss you dreadfully. I think, despite my mistake, that there are still some miles left in our marriage. Can you bring yourself to give us another chance?

I know I've got some explaining to do and I would like to do it in person. Say the word, and we can arrange to meet. I suggest somewhere in town away from the hotel, what do you think? It would give me the greatest pleasure if things turned out well between us and we could

*go and tell Imogen together. I know she'd
be pleased.*

Your darling Ted.

Dulcie dropped the letter on the bed. Inexplicably, she burst into tears. What possible explanation could he have to offer? Of course, perhaps he doesn't know that I saw him getting into a car with Anna. Is he still with her? She picked up the letter to read again for clues. It seemed important to meet him and hear what he had to say. Her heart started to beat fast and she wasn't sure what to do next. It was convenient to be able to phone down to reception for help. Tony answered, back at work again.

'Tony?' she said breathlessly.

'Yes, how are you?'

'Well, I'm alright, it's just I need to get in touch with someone. Can I have a look at the phone directory in the office and have you got any bus timetables? I'll be right down.'

CHAPTER TWENTY NINE

Lynette arrived through the back door of the hotel. She looked distressed. There was a cloth bundled around her forearm, and she clasped it with her other hand to hold it there. Imogen immediately took her into her rooms and made way for her to sit down. Lynette crumpled into a chair.

Anita and Diana were playing together at the table. Diana noticed that something was wrong. Her eyes went big and her lip trembled.

'It's OK, don't worry,' Lynette reached out to the little girl and attempted a weak smile.

'I'll take Diana. We'll go out to the park and let you sort yourselves out,' Anita said with a worried look.

When they'd left, Imogen enveloped Lynette in her arms. 'You're hurt, what's happened? I'll wet a cloth and clean you up,' she broke away towards the kitchenette.

'No don't fuss, Imogen. I just need to get over it.' Lynette let her head fall back onto the chair back. 'I want to rest.'

Imogen knelt beside her on the floor and gently unwrapped the cloth. She was shocked by the amount of blood, but it was now a trickle rather than a gush. She tried to give Lynette space by just holding onto her hand. They were silent with only the burr of the fan in the background. They both looked up as the door handle moved and Dulcie walked in on them. She gasped and sat down heavily on the sofa.

'Hi Mum,' Imogen said, 'I'd meant to call you but we're in the middle of something at the moment.'

'I can see. I'll be back with the first aid box,' and Dulcie swept out.

Lynette looked at Imogen questioningly. 'It's okay she knows. I told her today and I think she might understand,' Imogen said.

When Dulcie came back she gently ministered to Lynette, wiping away smears of blood and tears. 'We need hot sweet tea for shock,' she said.

Imogen brought the tea as Lynette explained, 'I'd got off the bus and was walking to our house when I heard the most awful racket. It was people swarming along the street towards me. I was so scared, my heart started thumping and I just froze.'

She shuddered, 'It wasn't dangerous at first because there was a three-deep wall of policemen surrounding the marchers. In fact, at the edge of the street, local kids were copying the marching, but then I saw the banners and heard what they were shouting. . . it was the National Front. I knew I had to get out of there, but when I turned to run the other way I realised there was a great roar coming from that direction too.'

She put down her cup, which rattled as her hand shook and she spoke more rapidly, reliving the scene. 'There were protesters in that direction too. I felt trapped, so I made for an alley across the street. It all happened really fast. There were bottles and plastic flying through the air. I felt sorry for the police horses - they were caught up in the middle of it. A policeman grabbed me,' she sobbed. 'But then he was tackled by a couple of youths and I fell to my knees.'

'Oh, your knees are scraped too,' Imogen reached for the cotton wool to bathe Lynette's knees. Lynette carried on, 'Yes someone started to drag me along and the next thing I knew I was in the alleyway. I could see a line of police moving behind a wall of plastic shields but luckily, I was out of the way in the alley. The person that took me there dived back out. I wanted to get as far away from it as possible and somehow I managed to stagger home.'

'Oh thank goodness someone helped. Who was it?' said Dulcie, 'You poor girl. No wonder you're in a state.'

'Well it wasn't so easy. I didn't really know what was going on. When I got indoors, my little brother was the first to see me. He got hysterical - wailing loudly. The dog started to bark. That brought everyone running. I realised I'd cut my arm and it was pouring. Dripping blood all over the floor.' Lynette stopped and drank her tea. She closed her eyes for a moment, but then took a deep breath and started to speak again.

'Mum fussed around me but they were all saying "What happened? Where've you been?" I began to try to tell them but then it all blew up. Mum got angry; I know she was probably scared for me, but she said, "This is what comes of going out all the time. We never see you.".'

Dulcie could empathise with Lynette's family, but her heart reached out to her. Lynette went on, 'I told them that I often come to this area and the Lunar Hotel, but it didn't help. Dad lost his temper and everyone else cleared out of the way. He was shouting, "We never see you nowadays. You're not our daughter anymore." It seemed like they were blaming me for being caught up in a riot. I was shaking and I couldn't talk to them. I ran out of there, back into the street.' Lynette paused as her tears overcame her, 'I know they're upset, but I couldn't get through to them or explain anything.'

Imogen put her arm around Lynette's shoulder and Dulcie sighed. 'This is so dreadful. I can't believe it's happening in England. Look I'm going to leave you two to get over it, but I think you ought to get that cut seen to – it looks deep.' She stood up to leave, but then hesitated by the door and half turned. She wanted to reach out with some warmth.

'It's hardly the time, but I don't know whether there will be a better time. I just want to say Lynette, Imogen told me that you two are together. At one time I would have been more shocked, but I've seen a lot recently.' She gave a short laugh. 'Anyway, welcome to the family dear. I hope you'll grow to see me as a second mother,' and with that, she left.

Imogen relaxed, her heart leaping. You could always rely on Mum. But then she turned her thoughts to Lynette. 'Alright Netty,' she whispered as she gently kissed the top of her head. 'I think we ought to drive you to hospital.'

***

Sitting in the lounge ostensibly relaxing with a magazine but waiting for Imogen to return, Dulcie noticed a plump black woman in reception. She was smartly dressed and wearing a hat of the type that Dulcie herself would have worn before her change of lifestyle. She appeared to be looking around for someone. Dulcie took a guess that she was related to Lynette. As she approached her at reception, she overheard the woman asking for Lynette.

'Excuse me?' she said 'May I interrupt? I'm Dulcie Best,' she smiled and held out her hand to shake the other woman's, who looked startled but reciprocated.

'Vanessa Williams,' she said with a slight movement of her head which made her gold earrings shake. 'I'm sorry, you are?'

'Well, I'm the mother of your daughter's friend Imogen. Imogen is part of the management here.'

Oh, okay, do you know where Lynette is? We're worried about her,' Vanessa said.

'I can imagine you would be, but don't worry she is being looked after. They've driven off to the hospital to have her cut looked at. I'm not sure whether they'll both come back here or whether Lynette will go back home, but why don't you come and have a coffee with me?'

Vanessa raised her eyebrows. She took a few steps to one side. Dulcie realised that she needed to be persuasive and hurried on, 'From one mother to another, I think we ought to talk.' Vanessa pressed her lips together tightly but gave a curt nod. Dulcie showed her over to the leather chesterfields and they sat side by side, feet tucked under the seat.

'So, what's going on?' Vanessa said, 'Lady, I'm sorry but we've found out that Lynette comes here when she should be at home. She let down the church. She used to be a Sunday school teacher you know.' She shook her head, her eyes blazing.

'Our two daughters have become very close. Imogen explained that they've been spending time together.'

'Hmm, I've imagined worse than that. So I'm pleased,' Vanessa smiled at Dulcie for the first time, 'I didn't know they knew each other, but at least she has a friend.'

'Yes I think they make each other very happy,' Dulcie said.

Vanessa looked at her quizzically, 'What are you saying?'

Dulcie didn't feel that it was her place to tell Lynette's mother what was happening, but she'd come this far. 'I think they mean a great deal to each other. I imagine that they may decide to live together. I won't say that I wasn't shocked. At first, it was a bit of a surprise for me. But if it makes them happy . . .' she trailed off, noticing that Vanessa had let her mouth fall open. 'I think Lynette's a lovely girl, a credit to you. And if you get to know Imogen, you'll find out how responsible and sensible she is.'

Vanessa gulped, 'If you are saying what I think you are saying, it cannot be. Jesus Lord, I'm begging you are not saying that.' She looked into the distance and stopped speaking altogether. Her jaw tightened, 'She will bring shame upon us all.'

Dulcie felt at a loss. She wanted to affect a good result for Imogen and Lynette's sake, but she sensed that now was not the time to argue. Vanessa was still getting over the shock.

'Mrs Williams, may I call you Vanessa? We are both mothers. I'd like us to be friends.' Vanessa looked distracted. Was she wasting her breath? 'I lived with my husband for a long time and I was miserable. It took many wasted years for me to realise that you have to make hard decisions to save yourself. I would hate Imogen to settle for a loveless marriage for the sake of appearances.'

Dulcie felt she should keep talking while she had the advantage. 'You haven't seen them together but when you do, you will recognise how right they are for each other. I just want them to be happy.'

There was a moment's silence before Vanessa shook her head as though trying to shake off all this new information, she said, 'No one is going to agree with two women living together. How could they manage?'

'I understand what you are saying,' Dulcie thoughts strayed to her own doubts about a budding relationship with a young Frenchman, 'but sometimes you have to ignore all that and follow your heart.'

'For real,' Vanessa said, 'but it's not natural, is it? What about having children?'

'I know,' Dulcie said. This woman was going through the same thoughts as she did. 'Imogen is my only daughter and I'd love to have grandchildren.'

Vanessa met her eye. They seemed to understand each other. She said, 'I'm glad that I've got a big family. So you've only got the one.'

A crowd of guests pushed through the door at that moment and made for Reception with a lot of noise. It disturbed the intensity of their meeting.

'Yes, I've just got Imogen. But she does like children. She looks after a little girl Diana, a lot of the time. And I love to see Diana,' Dulcie felt herself growing tearful, she didn't want to cry. Vanessa patted Dulcie on the knee and Dulcie added, 'And of course, I'm very proud of Imogen setting up this hotel with her friends.'

'Lynette is working in a solicitors'. What she does, I don't know. Too much concentrating on careers, I think,' Vanessa said.

'It isn't the same as it was in our day,' Dulcie nodded.

'It is the same for us. We are Church people.' Vanessa brushed an imaginary piece of fluff off her skirt. 'I don't know. I'm glad to meet you but I am going to need some time to think about this before I talk to Lynette. I don't know what her father is going to say.'

The hotel was getting busier as people arrived with reservations for the restaurant. 'I need to get home.' Vanessa said.

'Mm, I understand. Naturally, it's so unexpected you need to take it in. Shall I get Lynette to phone you if they come here?'

'We don't have a phone. Better to give us some time anyway.'

'I hope we meet again?' Dulcie said with a question in her voice.

Vanessa swiftly pulled Dulcie towards her in an embrace that tipped her hat to the back of her head, 'Thank you. I know you mean well,' she said readjusting the hat and stood up to leave. Dulcie stood and watched her as she left through the main doors. She finally turned to look around the hotel and noticed the receptionist watching them. There was a flutter in her stomach. It had been a short meeting, but it felt like she'd just been through a battle.

***

It was dark. Imogen eased the handbrake on gently to avoid jolting Lynette, who was sitting tensely upright with her arm in a sling and a dressing on her leg.

'Is this the place, here?' Imogen pulled up in front of a neatly cut privet hedge and a small wooden garden gate. She peered to see the house number, but it was hidden in the shadow of a porch. Everything took on the unworldly yellow of streetlight. It turned the front lawn into a muted mustard green.

Lynette moaned, 'I think the pain's worse. Yes, we're here.' She glanced up at the lit windows of the house. 'Can you come round and help me out?'

Imogen opened the passenger door from the pavement and leant into the car to support Lynette as she eased her body around to bring her feet onto the pavement. 'I'm not sure this is a good idea. I think you should have come back to mine. I'm going to wait here a while in case you need to run back out again,' she said.

'So what do you think, you're doing?' a voice came from behind her. Imogen stiffened and turned. She saw Lynette's mother for the first time. But Vanessa was ignoring Imogen, she was speaking to her daughter. 'I can hardly believe what happened tonight. If I had not seen it all with my own eyes. You didn't once think about what you were doing to the family.'

Lynette held out her hand to her mum. 'I'm sorry Mum.' Was this a general apology? How much did Lynette's mother know? Vanessa was still standing close beside her and now she turned her attention to her. 'So, you're Imogen.'

'Yes, I am. Er pleased to meet you, Mrs Williams.'

Vanessa tsked, 'What a pair you are,' she shook her head. 'I've just been speaking with Dulcie. She's a very nice lady, but I don't know what to make of you two. I don't think you should be meeting your father tonight, girl. You go back home with Imogen.' She looked Imogen up and down and said gruffly, 'I trust that you're going to look after her.'

Imogen was vaguely aware of the movement at one of the curtains in the downstairs bay window of the house. Vanessa turned and saw it too. Vanessa rushed to say, 'Me, I don't understand. But you will always be my daughter. I pray that you will come to your senses. Now you two go. I'll tell the family that I've sent you off to get better.' She looked significantly at Lynette, 'I'm going to speak with your father.'

'Thanks, Mum,' Lynette said, and Vanessa leant into the car arms stretched to reach for her. After a hug, she turned to Imogen, 'Now go.'

As the car pulled away, Lynette said, 'That was awful, just awful.'

Imogen took a glance to her left. Lynette was quietly crying. She placed one hand over Lynette's.

'Soon have you home. We've got the rest of our lives to sort this out,' she said.

***

It was late when they got back to the hotel. Neither felt ready to settle down to sleep. They tried the television just in time to catch an announcer signing off and suggesting that viewers tune in to BBC radio.

'We'll do better than that, I'll put on Radio Caroline.' Imogen said. 'Lynette, please stay with me. Even if your parents had been happy, I would want you to stay with me. I know that it's you that I want. We belong together.'

Her face was full of anticipation. Lynette couldn't help smiling. 'I hope we can manage this, but yes Imogen, yes, yes.' She leaned back against the sofa and reached up with her good arm to caress Imogen's cheek. Their eyes locked.

She pulled Imogen down to her, 'I could look into your eyes forever,' she whispered into the warmth of her neck. 'and I trust you, I know that I will always see the truth there.'

Imogen's heart beat fast. She caressed the back of Lynette's neck, feeling her warm soft skin. She revelled in the thought that they were together. Their kiss, when it came, was gentle and yet firm. Lynette's hungry response made Imogen feel weak at the knees, 'I love you.'

Lynette's lips stopped moving. She placed her palm on Imogen's chest, 'Sorry what did you say?'

Imogen said it louder, 'I love you.'

'I love you too,' Lynette answered, 'It's good to hear it. We'll have to go through a lot. I hope you are ready for it, but I know that everything is going to be alright.'

They stayed comfortably entwined until the early hours. Planning could wait, but Imogen felt brighter in the new knowledge that they would face the world together in the future.

Chapter Thirty

France

Gilles got up early to leave the house before his parents were awake. He couldn't face them in the mornings. He avoided the bars that he would normally frequent with friends in town. Talking about it made it worse. The English have a term 'heartbroken' and he could feel it. It was like a huge crack down his centre.

People scarcely noticed him when he was withdrawn. No one shouted 'Bonjour' or 'Salut' across the street, and he was glad.

He dropped off mail to the reception counter of the Hotel Chez Inez. He was there just as a group of staff were leaving after their shift. They crowded to get out through the main door, so Gilles fell in behind them.

'You should have heard them, it was disgusting,' Jeannine was saying through her giggles, covering her mouth coyly. 'Our lady guest had invited him to stay. It went on and on. I was blushing.'

Another woman whacked Jeannine on the arm, 'You didn't hear it. I don't believe it,' and she laughed.

Gilles moved as close to the women as he could to try to overhear more.

'It is disgusting, and in the middle of the day too. We could have walked in on them,' Arlette joined in, 'and Jeannine tells me that the old pig has a wife up at the chateau.'

There were lots of snorts at this. Gilles made a snap decision to interrupt. 'Excuse me, are you talking about the old man who was a visitor at the gatehouse?'

'What?' They all turned around sharply and looked irritated. Only Jeannine stopped to speak to him while the others moved ahead. 'Yes, that's right. Do you know Ceci?'

'Yes, I used to talk to her. How is she?'

'I haven't seen her for a while. This is the old man who was taken ill in the street here some time ago. He was whisked off to the hospital and he asked me to go up to the chateau to tell Ceci about it. Poor Ceci, she said he was her husband. But he came down to the hotel and stayed a few days with one of our guests here. Some husband, huh.'

'Yes, yes, a bad business.' Gilles agreed with her. 'I can always rely on you for the gossip, thank you.'

Jeannine looked pleased, but then less so when she realised what he was inferring. He strode back to where the van was parked, his postbag thumping against his side. One thought, go to Cici to apologise for staying away, and be there for her, whatever she was going through.

On drawing up to the chateau, he sensed that the gatehouse was deserted. But maybe she had just closed the curtains to shut out the world. He tried knocking and calling, but there was no response. Disconsolate, he glanced around. The vegetable garden was beginning to wilt through lack of water. She must be gone. His hopes had been raised only to sink once again. He couldn't leave it there. She had needed a friend and he hadn't been there for her. Now what had happened to her?

Remembering the overbearing Jane, he decided not to ask at the chateau. At the risk of being accused of trespassing, he thought he'd just take a look around and gather information.

Gilles took a wide arcing path through the shady woodland where he was less likely to be spotted.

With a thud, a large weight hit his shoulder and he was on the ground. It felt as though all the air had been knocked out of him. He opened his eyes to a close-up view of a grubby child's leg. Gilles felt the child dig a knee into his stomach to launch himself off again. 'Ha, ha,' came a childish voice from the distance as the kid ran off into the woods.

Still lying in the dirt, Gilles saw a hippie making his way over, 'Aw man. That was bad.' he said, holding out a hand to help Gilles to his feet. When they were both standing, he added 'Hi, I'm Roger.' He raised a palm in greeting.

'These kids!' Roger shook his head, swinging rats' tails of hair. 'That dude's a friend of my own kid, too.'

Gilles dusted down his uniform trousers, 'Thank you for your help.' He reached out to Roger and then thought better of it, withdrawing his hand 'I'm Gilles. . . I came here looking for my friend, Ceci. You know her?'

A smile spread over Roger's face, 'Ceci yeh I know her. She's real cool.' Gilles was still slightly overcome so Roger explained, 'A great lady.'

'Ah yes, I agree.' Gilles nodded, 'I am worried about her. Has she gone?'

'Yeh man. . .There was a big blow-up in our meeting, and she got upset. . .I was there. It wasn't cool. But she left before she could find out – Sheila and I, we called for another meeting a few days afterwards and we discussed what had happened to Ceci. We asked the meeting whether they really wanted to leave it like that. She was a shining light, man, and it had upset everyone. Everyone wanted her to know how much we backed her. Y'know we wanted to go to see her but she had a visitor, so. . . then she was gone.' He flung his hands in the air in a gesture of futility.

'So where would she go?' Gilles said.

'I wish we knew man. It's unfinished business. But hey, she will be back.'

'She had relatives in England, and I know the name of her daughter's hotel. Bah, but she may have gone to Paris. . . her daughter would know.' Gilles said, almost to himself.

'If you do get hold of her, tell her we all miss her. She was great with our son Ziggy.' Roger grabbed Gilles by the shoulder and Gilles gasped, but Roger meant no harm. 'We love her, send her our love and tell her to come back.'

Gilles felt a jolt of hope that Ceci had everything to come back for.

Chapter Thirty One

England

Dulcie checked on the weather. It was a typically English overcast day, so she decided to throw a mac over her arm. She was dressed up to meet Ted and she had butterflies in her stomach. There was just time to pop in to say goodbye to everyone before getting the bus.

Dulcie had the keycode to the hotel office, but once in she saw that Imogen was busy on the phone. Imogen looked up and waved an arm to beckon her over.

'Okay, but she's here now. Wait a minute.' She covered the receiver with her hand and whispered to her mother, 'A call for you from France. Here's the phone, I'll leave you to it.'

Dulcie took it. A male with a French accent was speaking.

'Hello is that you, Gilles?' Dulcie said, her heart leaping, 'I don't understand, how did you get this number?'

'I remembered the hotel name and voilà, International Directory Enquiries. I was asking Imogen if she could tell me where you were. But there you are.' he sounded delighted.

'Is everything alright over there, this must be costing you the earth?'

'It is alright now, dear Ceci. I am sorry that I stopped visiting you. You know, I saw that you had someone staying with you and I thought that you wouldn't want me to visit anymore. Now I know that I should have been there for you. I have missed you.'

Gilles went on to tell Dulcie what he had learned at the Hotel Chez Inez. 'Jeannine is your friend, you know Ceci.' He said, 'she would like to see you again.'

Dulcie wasn't thinking of Gilles now. When he gave her the news of Ted's behaviour, she was so shocked that she couldn't concentrate. Recognising the odd silence, Gilles went on to tell her about the supportive meeting at the chateau community. 'So a lot has happened. It is good news, no?' Then he passed on Roger's message. 'Tell her we love her. So, I hope you will not be sad and please come back to us very soon.' His voice lowered, 'please come back to see me very soon. I have been desolé without you.'

A silence. 'Hello, Ceci?'

'Yes, yes I'm still here.' Dulcie felt at her most vulnerable. She had a choking feeling at the bottom of her throat and wasn't sure that she could trust herself to speak without her voice breaking. 'Gilles, I thought you'd given up on our, our relationship. I don't know what to say.'

'I hope you did not mind that I phoned?' Gilles sounded hesitant.

She knew she sounded strange, 'No, no, of course not. It's a lot to take in. And Gilles,' she put some feeling into her voice – to try to get a message across the telephone line, 'I've thought of you too, thank you. I will come back very soon. I'm going to talk to Imogen and make arrangements to travel.'

'That is very good,' Gilles said with a smile in his voice.

'See you soon, Gilles.' Dulcie said, full of emotion. 'You lovely man.'

She put the receiver back onto its base and sat without moving in the office.

CHAPTER THIRTY TWO

Travel

Well, Ted's apology was such a waste of time. She would not be meeting him. Now there was nothing he could say to win her over and it was too late to get a message to him. Ha, she took satisfaction in the thought that he would be waiting in vain.

She was eager to get back to France and impatient to see Gilles again. He had a lot about him, and she wondered why she had let it drift just because Ted was around. If only she had had the confidence to ignore their differences. She had been frightened that he may find it too difficult in the end and reject her. Dulcie pictured Imogen and Lynette; if Imogen could stand up for the person she loved, against all odds, then surely her mother should be able to do the same. She rushed out for the bus into town. She had to make it to the travel agents' before closing time and organise a flight to Biarritz.

***

Dulcie felt alive again – writing on flimsy blue airmail paper. Writing lightly to avoid damaging the tissue, she kept the letter to Gilles simple: just the time and date that her flight would arrive. She slipped it into an envelope bordered in blue and red and addressed it to the Joubert's farm.

She packed and got herself organised.

'I've loved having you Mum, and we will certainly visit, won't we?' Imogen looked fondly at Lynette, who nodded and smiled. Dulcie abandoned her reticence about overt displays of affection and threw her arms around them both, ending by crouching beside Diana. She flourished a Basildon Bond airmail pad and a pack of coloured pencils.

'This is for you to write on and make little drawings. I will look forward to you sending them to me in France.'

Imogen saw her off at the main entrance where her taxi was waiting. As she left Dulcie said, 'Say goodbye to Ted for me, won't you? He has to find his own way now.'

Flying was still a novelty. There had been a holiday to Spain once with Ted, but this was only her second flight. Dulcie liked to be prepared: travel pills and a paper bag full of sherbet lemons to suck on take-off and landing. She sat beside the window, squashed close to the wall to avoid the rough, tweed sleeve of the man next to her. She needed to separate her mind from England and start to think of France again.

Biarritz airport was tiny, so Passport Control took no time. How quickly you forget the extremes of temperature in France. As she walked through the exit doors she was hit by a wall of heat.

She shaded her eyes. There he was – Gilles was bounding across the pedestrian crossing towards her. He halted in front of her, his face alight and took both of her hands in his. Dulcie was both happy and apprehensive. They had had such a shaky start.

He noticed her hesitancy, and said quietly, 'Bonjour?'

What was wrong with her, Gilles had been there for her throughout everything. 'Bonjour Gilles,' she reached her arms out to him.

He was so tall. She had to reach up to him. She hadn't pictured this moment and it was overwhelming. It was wonderful, but they were in a thoroughfare. Dulcie pulled away, laughing despite herself. She reached again on tiptoe to kiss his cheek, 'Live a little – as you say, and thank you for finding me.'

Gilles concentrated on road signs and changes of lane as they left Biarritz but once they were on a major road they began to exchange news. Dulcie told him that she'd discovered that Jane had sold food from the community. I think it's for her own gain - nothing has ever been said about it. But just after Jeannine confirmed it, I found Ted sitting with Anna, so the whole thing went right out of my head.'

'Everything happened at once. I am sorry you had to endure it on your own.' Gilles shook his head. 'Do you think anyone else was involved at the chateau?'

'That's the tricky part. I'm not sure who Jane's allies are. But I feel more confident to face her now that I know the community want me to be there. It's made all the difference.'

'I'm glad,' Gilles took his eyes off the road, 'How do you think she will react?'

'Once she realises that she has been found out,' she paused, 'I'm afraid that she will find a way to attack me. But really, I think she will want to leave and if she doesn't do that, surely she will have to retire into the background, and let us all carry on as we were.'

'You are a good person Ceci and, now I have met Roger, I can see that the community is where you belong.'

'Yes, but the community needs fixing. Somehow we have to make sure that someone like Jane can't take it over, for their own ends. We should become more at one with the town in the future, too. Invite them in and break down barriers.'

'Excellente,' he said, 'and as the town mayor, I can help with that.'.

Chapter Thirty Three

France

Pushing the front door of the gatehouse open, Dulcie breathed in damp, unloved air. She rushed to throw the curtains back and exclaimed over her neglected house plants.

'My mother, she has sent us a quiche and we can pick something from your garden to go with it,' Gilles followed her in with a cool bag. 'You must be tired.'

'I'm just so thrilled to be back. Gilles, this feels like home. You feel like home.' She rushed to him and, now that they had their privacy, she threw herself into his arms with abandon. Moments later, she admitted hunger, 'I want to see Roger and Sheila. Let's take the lunch there and have a picnic.'

She changed into the light, floaty clothes that she had adopted in France. When they walked hand in hand over to the family's caravan, Dulcie realised how dry the grounds of the chateau had become. But there were still so many flowers – scrubby lavender bushes and an intense dash of yellow from flowering broom. She breathed in the scents of the clear French air. She wanted to dance for joy. Sheila was sitting on the steps of their caravan hulling strawberries into an enamel mixing bowl.

'Hello, where's the family?' Dulcie called picking her way through woodland undergrowth.

Sheila stood up to greet her, 'Hey, this is far out. Good to see you Ceci, and this is Gilles.' She put her bowl on the floor and met Dulcie halfway. 'Roger will be back soon, he's doing some logging work and the children. . . well, Ziggy's at school and Anise has started nursery school now.'

'How marvellous for them. And yet I was looking forward to seeing them again,' Dulcie said, 'I want to thank you and Roger for supporting me. I was so overcome when I heard about the meeting.'

Sheila unfolded stools for them. 'We felt it was important. A step in getting the community on the right track. I was shocked at the way we let you be persecuted. I think we guys were too surprised to be able to act, in that first meeting – that's why we held another.'

'Thank you,'

Roger drove up in a battered truck and, for a man who moved slowly wherever he was, he joined them quickly.

'Hey dude,' he grasped Gilles's hand, 'Glad you did it.' Then he gave Dulcie a loose hug.

Sheila took their offerings and set about making a picnic. 'There's another community meeting next week. I hope you will come? Then we'll be able to move forward as a group. It's a pity we won't see the first changes.' Sheila smoothed her hair down over one shoulder. 'We're going to England to visit for the summer solstice.'

Dulcie felt a stab of disappointment. 'I didn't realise you had plans.'

'Yes, but we won't be gone long.' Sheila smiled encouragingly, 'My parents pay our fares so that they get to see their grandchildren. We like to go to Stonehenge to see the sun come up. It's like a pilgrimage.'

Gilles said, 'I'm sorry you're going. I think Dulcie will need your support at the chateau. Things have to change.'

Dulcie was surprised that he had interjected. Maybe their relationship gave him a stake in the community or maybe he was interested because he was the mayor?

'Yeh,' Roger was filling his pipe, 'Maggie is having trouble leading the group now. A few of us have noticed. Things will have to change.'

'We'll support you if you want to take a central role, Ceci.' Sheila said, 'I'm freaked out at the idea that Jane is going to take over everything. You should have been at the meeting, there was such a strong feeling for you.'

Chapter Thirty Four

'I will come with you to see Maggie. I will speak as the mayor as well as your friend.' Gilles said, and it felt good to know that someone would be there to support her for a change. Dulcie kicked off her shoes and completely relaxed.

'As my partner?' Dulcie felt she was challenging him, but it was important to know what their relationship was now. 'I'll have to tell her about Jane's trading with the hotel,' she said.

'Yes as your partner. I would like to, make a home with you here,' he said airily with a glance at her to gauge her reaction, 'and then I think we need to talk about the community. If people are on your side maybe we could broach changes to the way the meetings run and decide on more help for Maggie.'

'Poor Maggie, she has put so much into this place. She started it all; it must have been a struggle.'

'Yes my family talked about her I remember, I was young when she arrived. People thought she was strange and then a ragbag of people joined her.'

'It's important to preserve memories of how the chateau community started and to honour Maggie. But just for now, we need some sort of system so that no one can cheat on the finances again,' Dulcie sat up, her eyes instantly wide. 'And if this place is going to be worth living in, we want to make sure that everyone is valued and everyone has a say.'

'You are a woman like me. You believe in the philosopher, Rousseau. I am passionate about his ideas of human rights and obligations.'

'Mm, you must tell me more about him.' Dulcie laughed now. She thought she remembered something about Rousseau. So religion may divide them, but politics may join them.

***

Maggie's face lit up when she saw Ceci.

'Welcome back. Bienvenue,' she added for Gilles' benefit. 'I wanted to talk to you Ceci. It seems that as a community, we let you down.'

Jane was standing at Maggie's shoulder. She had a tight smile as she said, 'Quite so and keeping the community in good spirits is very important to us.' She sat down, and the others naturally followed suit. Dulcie was on a low, wide cream leather chair. She stretched her forearms along each arm. The leather felt soft and cool. Gilles sat on a similar chair at the opposite side of the rug.

'Well I want to begin by explaining that I've brought our mayor with me, because he and I plan to live together in the future. Hopefully, that will bring the chateau and the town community together.'

Maggie turned to fully face Gilles. 'That's so gratifying. It will be a great advance for us. And of course,' she looked now at Dulcie, 'I hope that isn't the only reason you got together,' she laughed gently, 'I'm very happy for you both.'

'Thank you.' Dulcie, for a moment, felt full of emotion. Maggie was like a mother to her. She moved on, before Jane had a chance to jump in. 'I know how much you have done for us in the community,' Dulcie said, 'and so it's important for me to sort something out. I have had time to think while I've been away. I'll come straight to the point.' She rested her gaze on Jane, 'Jane I believe that you've sold off food from our community kitchens to the Hotel Chez Inez. I'd be interested to hear what you have to say.'

Dulcie risked a sideways look at Maggie, 'Were you aware of this?'

Jane jerked her chin upwards and her eyes widened. There was a short pause.

'Well, I'm not sure why you would believe that,' Jane glanced at Maggie sitting alongside her. 'The whole community pay for our stores and it wouldn't make any sense for me to sell them on,' she pursed her lips and frowned then said slowly,' . . . oh, I occasionally collect goods on behalf of the hotel when I'm going to the cash and carry. They've sometimes helped us out that way too. Maybe that's what you are thinking of?'

Dulcie could feel herself flushing as she realised that Jane was trying to wriggle out of it. 'I see. But you had a pile of papers – invoices, receipts – from the hotel all pinned to your accounts book. I saw them last time I was here.'

'Ceci, this is getting unpleasant,' Maggie said.

Jane tutted, 'Really, I volunteer my work for this community, but I draw the line at being accused. I categorically deny that I've done anything with community food. If you want proof of that, I'll bring the account book here.'

'So it isn't stored in this room anymore?' Maggie asked her.

Jane turned to address her, 'No I decided to transfer records into a new book and take the older ones away for storage. But I can easily bring them back.'

'Well, please do Jane and then we can clear this up,' Maggie clapped her palms flat onto her lap.

Dulcie deemed that this was the best they could do for the present, 'And then I'd like a chance to thank the community for their support and to plan for something joyful to bring us all together.' Dulcie said.

'Something joyful,' Maggie tapped her fingers on the arm of the chair, 'like a feast or festival?'

'What about a fancy dress party?' Jane spoke up.

'This could be a chance to invite the people of the town,' Gilles said.

'Of course, we'll put it to the community meeting. It sounds an excellent idea,' Maggie said.

Gilles calm voice chimed in, 'I admire your far-sightedness and willingness to look into the future, dear lady. I know, from Ceci, that you are well loved. I think the community owes it to you to consider your future as well as its – our own.'

Tears sprung to Maggie's eyes. 'Well' she shifted forwards, 'I will make an announcement calling for a meeting immediately.'

* * *

Returning to the gatehouse, Dulcie felt a glow of achievement. When they had a chance to sit down together Ceci said, 'Thank you for your support Gilles, 'although I'm so disappointed. I feel as though I'm back where I started with Jane.'

Gilles sat down and steepled his fingers in thought. Dulcie stopped working to join him on the fireside chairs. He said, 'Now she knows that she is being accused, she is going to destroy the evidence. So, how to prove it?'

Chapter Thirty Five

Roger and Sheila strolled in together and sat close by. Roger raised his hand, 'Hey Ceci.'

Sheila smiled from the other side of him. Dulcie relaxed a little. Maggie arrived just as the noise from the crowd had reached a crescendo. Eventually, there was a hush as people became aware that she was waiting. Dulcie's mouth felt dry.

'I'm calling on you all to welcome Dulcie to this meeting. There have been regrettable difficulties, but I hope that Dulcie will feel at home again here and withdraw her notice to leave.'

'Hear, hear,' came Jethro's deep voice and there were a smattering of claps followed by clapping from all of the group.

'And I want to welcome Gilles Joubert, in his role as town mayor, but also as he will be a member of our community as Ceci's partner.'

Dulcie was gratified that she'd welcomed him so publicly, and she flushed slightly, she looked around the room and realised that she knew all these faces.

Dulcie simply said, 'Thank you Maggie, I would like to stay.'

Maggie went on, 'I know that many of you would like to have more information on finances. The amount that each resident contributes varies according to their accommodation agreement.'

It was time to intervene before the discussion became a dry financial report. Besides what Dulcie wanted to highlight had direct bearing on finances. She felt lightheaded, but she made herself interrupt loudly enough to be heard and to sound determined.

'Maggie, there's something that I need to raise urgently before the residents discuss finances.'

Maggie faltered, 'Yes? Well if it can't wait,' she said.

'Wait a minute,' Jane glared across at Dulcie, 'you need to wait your turn.' Having admonished Dulcie she looked pointedly to Maggie.

Dulcie knew that she had to take control. She stood up and took a step forward so that she held the floor. 'I am passionate about the community, and I long to see us working together. When I arrived here Maggie explained her vision,' she waved her arm towards Maggie, 'correct me if I am wrong Maggie, but it was of a place where there was no hierarchy, a place where we supported each other as family and where each contributes what she or he can.'

'That's right,' said a voice and Maggie nodded.

Dulcie lost her impetus for a moment, 'Well. . . now that Jane has begun to help Maggie that ethos is being diluted.'

She was surprised that timid Ivy spoke up, 'This sounds like a personal attack.'

Hearing that, ignited the passion in Dulcie's chest. ''It has become personal for me. You were there when I was attacked in one of these meetings.' Hearing this Ivy looked away. 'If, and I say if, someone is given the role of deputy then the system should be completely transparent. I discovered that having taken our money to pay for the community meals, Jane has been selling off food to a local hotel.'

'Maggie stood up, wringing her hands and blinking rapidly, 'Please Ceci. You know that Jane has already denied that accusation.'

'Bear with me, Maggie. I first became suspicious when I saw the Hotel Chez Inez logo on financial papers in Jane's account book. I went down to investigate and learned what had been happening there.'

Dulcie noticed that Jane was red in the face. Jane opened her mouth as though to say something, but she didn't.'

Dulcie strode across the room, which caused a collective rustle of movement. She opened the door, to admit Jeannine. 'This is Jeannine she has worked at the Hotel Chez Inez for two years. She has seen our van arrive at the kitchen door and food being unloaded. Can you show me who brought the food, Jeannine?'

Jeannine stood tall and solemnly pointed to first Ivy and then Jane.

Some onlookers seemed stunned but an elderly woman at the back said, 'Oh come on, let Jane and Ivy defend themselves.'

Jane said, 'I think I told you we sometimes bought food for them at the cash and carry. We were helping them out with transport.'

'Non,' Jeannine said,' I talked to our chef. He has said many times that you sold food cheaper than he could buy it anywhere else.'

No one said anything until Roger broke the silence 'So what have you got to say now, Jane?'

Jane stood up with tears leaking down her cheeks. She brushed a sleeve across her nose, 'Say, I haven't got anything to say. I have put a lot of work into helping Maggie, but now you will have to do without me. I can't stay here. I'll be leaving the chateau altogether.' She walked out and Ivy hurried to follow her.

Jeannine sat down on a chair that Gilles had carried over for her.

Maggie said, 'Well' she took a deep breath and momentarily swayed before grabbing the arm of her chair, 'I owe you an apology, Ceci. You've uncovered an important drain on the community's wellbeing.'

Dulcie felt a rush of exhaustion but gathered herself to say, 'Thank you Maggie, but I couldn't have done this without Gilles and Jeannine.'

Maggie screwed up her face, 'I'm afraid that I let this happen. As I get older I find I need help with the administration of the chateau and so I haven't been overseeing it properly. I'm sorry, everyone.'

There were murmurs of concern from the group.

'And,' Dulcie added, 'I'd like us to try to join with the French. We've transplanted ourselves here, but what do we offer them? Could we invite the townspeople to one of our community meals or even hold an event for both chateau residents and townspeople?'

'We never have because of the language barrier,' said Rolph.

'You saw Jeannine speak just now. Many French townsfolk speak some English and you will pick up French,' Dulcie answered. Jeannine nodded enthusiastically.

'I approve wholeheartedly of your suggestion Ceci,' Maggie said, 'but in the spirit of community I know that it isn't up to me to either agree or to dismiss your ideas – it's for the people to speak.' She swept her eyes over the crowd.

Suddenly someone stood up and started to clap, others joined until the whole room was on its feet. The noise was overwhelming, and some had tears in their eyes. Ceci mouthed, 'thank you' in several directions and then sat down heavy with emotion.

As the sound died down, Maggie called out, 'We all have strong feelings. I want to leave now to speak to the two women that have left the meeting. Shall we take a break?'

She made her way out and others stood about in knots. Dulcie's arms and legs felt shaky. A crowd gathered around them. Each person wanting to acknowledge what she had done or to thank Jeannine and congratulate Gilles.

'You are part of us and you've done a lot for my family and for the community.' Sheila said, 'don't be shy.'

'We really need to welcome you back,' Neal gave her a warm hug. Dulcie was overcome. She might, at one time, have been uncomfortable with this outpouring of love but to her surprise she felt good. This was what she had hoped for, when she first read about a commune in France.

*****

Christophe's motorbike was on its stand just outside Dulcie's garden. Jeannine and Christophe were in the lodge.

'C'est Fantastique,' Jeannine said. Christophe sat on the floor, cross-legged in front of Jeannine's chair.

'Thank you for bringing Jeannine,' Gilles said, and handed each of them a glass of red wine. They raised their glasses high, 'Santé. Good health and congratulations.'

Gilles perched on the arm of Dulcie's chair while they told Christophe what had happened. 'I'm glad that I could help,' he said. 'What will Claude say?'

'He will have to buy food at the correct price. I have no love for Claude,' Jeannine said, 'and I wanted to help you both of course.' She nodded to them and sipped from her glass again.

When they left, Gilles and Dulcie accompanied them along the moon-lit garden path and stood to wave as the motorbike roared away. Once it had disappeared Gilles turned to Dulcie and took her in his arms.

'I've been wanting to do this for some time.'

She lost herself in the moment; all focus on his closeness. 'What a wonderful evening.'

As they turned arm in arm to go back inside bats flittered across the inky sky. They stopped to watch them. Gilles held up a finger, 'Wait there,' he said and sprinted to her lean-to.

She didn't welcome any more surprises.

'Cover your eyes,' he warned her.

'What?' Dulcie said partially irritated but beginning to enter into his silliness. 'Come on Gilles I don't like having my eyes closed.'

She felt him close to her. There was something furry against her waist. She opened her eyes in surprise. There was a tiny, fluffy black kitten with shiny currant eyes looking bewildered. She felt as though she could float away with joy. 'Oh, he's so small, such tiny paws and little ears.' She turned to Gilles, 'for me?'

'For you and perhaps another reason maybe for you to stay?

Dulcie's heart melted. He was, perhaps, the only person who had registered how deeply she had felt the loss of Oscar. Tears sprang to her eyes, 'What shall we call him, or her? I know – Rousseau.'

'He laughed, 'I like that.' He collected a cat bed from the lean-to and followed her indoors.

Dulcie fondled the little bundle and then gently placed him onto the floor. 'I'll let him explore his new home.' Rousseau took a few faltering steps and then disappeared beneath one of the chairs.

'It's strange for him. He will soon make it his home,' Gilles said, 'And now, sit down for something more serious, my darling.'

Dulcie didn't like his change of tone, but mesmerised, she sat.

'I know you don't want to be rushed,' she opened her mouth, but he shushed her, 'and you know that I like to have plans,' he said, grinning. 'I have money saved and I would like us to buy one of the apartments in the chateau itself. We would have more room and be close to Maggie as she gets older. But Dulcie.' Now she knew that he was serious. He had never used her proper name before and she felt a thrill of delight at hearing plans for their future.

He fell to one knee, in front of her chair. 'Will you consider marrying me?'

She couldn't keep the smile away, and yet she knew that marriage was an enormous commitment and that she couldn't jump in hastily.

'Come here,' checking for the kitten, she slid down onto the floor beside him to nuzzle his neck. 'It's early days, but of course I will consider it, you lovely man.'

He smiled and began to say, 'I will show you that you need me in your life. Nothing worth having is easily won.' before she stopped all conversation with her passionate response.

DIANA'S STORY

BOOK 3

Chapter One

Diana had lived in the Lunar Hotel all her life but, its white painted exterior shone in the dim evening, and she dreaded its unfamiliarity. Builders had invaded, and everything was different. At least, now on a weekend; all was quiet.

'Sure you want me to come in with you?' her friend Clare pressed closer to her as they walked.

'You're scared, aren't you?' Diana marvelled, 'It's only an empty building. Don't you want to find out my exam results?'

' 'Spose so. Though we won't be able to have a holiday together now whatever your results are – not now I'm going to have to retake mine.'

Diana pulled the key out of her jeans pocket and forced the heavy double doors open. The builders had torn a huge hole in the wall behind the reception desk and there were bare wires where wall lights had been. The carpets had been cut away in places, and in other areas they were dusted in chunks of plaster. Diana's steps sounded hollow as she raced across the floor to deactivate the burglar alarm.

'There's the mail,' Clare pointed to the floor behind the door. Diana dived for it and shuffled through a pile of brown envelopes to find the one addressed to her.

'Let's open it inside.' The hotel's private quarters seemed different too. The washing up bowl was turned upside down in the sink and there was a peculiar stale smell. They went through to her bedroom where a New Kids on the Block themed duvet set was folded neatly on her bare mattress. The magazines that she had been reading a week ago were strewn across the desk. She flung herself across the bed to lean up against the wall and took a deep breath before ripping open the envelope. It could be life-changing. Her chest felt fluttery.

'French A, German A and English B'. Wow, she jumped up and only consideration for Clare, who had been disappointed by her grades, stopped her from prancing around the room waving the results in the air.

'Well done,' Clare said, kicking the toe of her Doc Marten against the skirting board.

'Thanks, but I'm sorry. I know it's totally shit for you.' Diana sat back down with a sigh, 'D'you think you could come to France for just a short time.'

'No, mum and dad won't pay for me to go on a trip now. But I am pleased for you, Di. It means that you'll be able to get into your first choice,' she put on a broad smile, 'Sheffield Uni. That's so cool.'

'Yes,' Diana said quietly. 'though I applied because everyone expected me to apply. I don't know whether I want to go now.'

Clare smirked and jabbed her in the arm, 'Now you're scared.'

'Me, never. I just need time to think what I want to do. It was cool staying with your family, but now I think I want to see Mum in London. I want to see her face when I tell her about my results in person. I might not even need a degree for what I want to do. Who knows, I might follow in Mum's footsteps and be an actress.'

Clare looked vaguely interested, 'D'you think you could? You'd better warn Imogen and Lynette that you aren't going to join them in France, then,' her face fell again. 'Mm, my name is mud at home, but I'd better go back there and talk about what I'm going to do.'

For Diana, it now felt vital to set off immediately and she needed to get herself organised. Clare was right; she had better phone Imogen with her results and explain her plans first. They would have been waiting for news. 'Aww, well don't go yet. I'll phone France, and then we can get going. You'll walk me to the station, won't you?'

So she made the phone call to Imogen. Imogen was staying with her mother, Dulcie, and her mother's French husband. There were shrieks of delight and the receiver at the other end was passed around from person to person.

'I'm so proud of you darling,' Dulcie said. Diana lapped up the praise. Dulcie had always acted as her surrogate granny.

Lynette, Imogen's partner, was the last to speak to her. For a while, Diana had had a prickly relationship with Lynette. She could always rely on Imogen, and when she was little they'd done everything together. Once Imogen moved Lynette into the hotel, she had sometimes felt a bit like a spare part.

Lynette's firm views on how young people should behave had caused some tension too, but now Diana felt a rush of warmth when Lynette said, 'You go, girl! We're proud of you. Have you told Anita yet?'

'I thought I'd visit mum to tell her rather than just phone.'

'Great idea. We'll see you soon then.'

Diana's rucksack was already full because she'd used it to stay at Clare's. She bent and shuffled the contents around a bit and flung dirty knickers onto the bedroom floor. On the bottom shelf of the bookcase she spotted her money box. She felt it had been waiting there forever for just this occasion.

'Hey dude, are you sure? Won't they go mad?' Clare raised her eyebrows. Diana paused. Yes, she was sure. She struck it against the side of the desk until it smashed. Clare muttered,

'Wow.' Diana knew she was facing her greatest challenge, no one else realised what was in her mind.

They set off for the station with linked arms. Their differences were what drew them to each other. Clare had a comfortable house and a close relationship with her mother and father. Diana had been loved and cared for, but her family had been pretty fluid. As an actress, her Mum Anita, had returned to the Lunar Hotel whenever she was 'resting', Imogen and Tony who jointly owned the hotel formed a warm surrogate family when she was little but then Tony met Vic and they had moved out together.

Clare stood still in the middle of the pavement. 'I'm going to turn off here.'

This marked the end of summer with Clare and the beginning of her travels. 'Say thank you to your mum and dad for me.'

Clare spoke into her chest, 'I. . .When will you be back?'

Clare was suffering and Diana felt a pang on her behalf. 'I don't know. I suppose I'll come back in time for Sheffield.'

'Let me know how you get on won't you.'

Diana felt a heaviness in her chest but forced herself to ignore it. She threw her arms around Clare. 'Goodbye. It's like losing a sister.'

Clare had tears in her eyes. 'I know.' She looked quickly away, 'See you soon.'

<h1 style="text-align:center">CHAPTER TWO</h1>

Diana sank into a window seat on the London-bound train and stashed her rucksack on the floor by her feet. She caught sight of her own reflection in the train window: a young woman with pronounced cheekbones, strong jaw and thick brunette hair chopped in a blunt cut bob. She didn't want to be conceited, but surely she could follow her mother's footsteps with those looks. Maybe there'd be the chance to find out in London. She caught the reflection of a youth on the opposite side of the carriage looking at her, and quickly pulled her shoulders back and her stomach in.

Time to think. Glimpsing suburban back gardens reminded Diana of Clare's family. She remembered when they were young, in a paddling pool, making dens and playing rounders with Clare's dad. Sometimes it had been painful to see Clare with her dad. Would her own dad have been jokey with her or strict?

Tony and, later, his partner Vic had been the men in her life as she grew up, but she still wanted to know what her birth father would think of her. Would he be proud of her exam results? She had tried asking about him, but Imogen always said, 'ask your mum'. Well, she wanted to get closer to her mum, but whenever she'd raised the subject of her father, Diana had sensed that she was treading on risky ground. All she knew was that he was called Pete and he hadn't been involved at the time of her birth. She filled in the gaps in her knowledge with daydreams. Maybe he'd been drawn to Anita because she was an actress. Perhaps if Diana followed in her mum's footsteps, he would notice her name being advertised in theatres and be drawn to come to see her, too.

She read the billboards and shop names as they streamed past. Then she almost stopped breathing. On a rail side hoarding, there was a glamorous picture of her mother beside the name of a play. 'Starring Anita Tomalty'; her mother looked enchanting. Diana smiled in recognition. It seemed to be a sign.

Diana was well travelled, so she was surprised to feel butterflies in her stomach when her foot landed on the platform in London. It was a hard, polished surface under a vast cathedral structure with a soaring glass roof. The city. She became part of the crowd all moving in the same direction while keeping her eyes upwards, ready to follow directional signs.

The underground platforms were crowded; people stood too close. It made the hairs on the back of her neck rise. Then there was the anticipation as she heard the rush of air hissing when the tube arrived and then the whistle of brakes. How long would it take to get across London? Should she have phoned ahead?

***

She emerged from the arched exit of a tube station and noticed the sky. She'd have to hurry. It had turned a deep purple-marine, shading to pale around each streetlamp. She just had to get her bearings, she was pretty certain that she could remember the right direction to turn to get to her mother's flat. Her mother, Anita, lived on a pleasant street of three-storey terrace houses lined with residents' cars. Golden light seeped onto the road from rows of windows casting the doorways into shadow.

Diana screwed up her eyes to make out the building numbers. At last - the right one.

They had spent time together but it never felt enough. She had a hazy memory of school holiday visits when they'd arrived at the front door happy but exhausted after a day out at Chessington World of Adventures. It had deteriorated since. The paint was cracking. It was just an ordinary door on an ordinary street. She rang the number for her mother's flat.

'Hello,' a deep voice came from the crackling intercom.

Her heart missed a beat at hearing a stranger. Her voice came out as a choke, 'Hello I'm looking for Anita Tomalty'.

'This is the right place. Can I give her your name?'

'It's Diana, her daughter.'

A hesitation, and then, 'Push the door'.

She felt an itching in her throat at the smell of pine disinfectant. The door opened onto a flight of stairs with wrought iron balusters. Diana's feet sounded on the painted wood. Happiness welled up in her at the sight of a string of Indian bells hanging beside a door on the second floor. That was her mother's style. As she knocked, the door opened inwards. Diana smiled in readiness, but then faltered when, instead of Anita, it was an office block of a man in a black open-necked shirt tucked into denim jeans.

'You'd better come in,' he said, standing aside.

She edged past him, uncomfortable in the narrow hallway. She sensed him locking the door behind her. Her mother, Anita, was perching on the arm of a sofa in the small lounge. It appeared that the houses opposite were peering in through the swagged curtains of the windows. Anita rose to greet her, elegant as always, but Diana noticed her narrow wrists and that her hands were slightly trembling. Anita smiled.

Affection showed in her eyes, 'What are you doing here, Diana? I thought you were travelling to Imogen in France?'

She looked so tiny. Oh, to wrap her mum in her arms. But Diana felt inhibited in the presence of the stranger.

'I just . . . I don't know, I just really wanted to see you. And I've got the results of my exams.'

Anita's voice brightened, 'Oh wow. . . results. So, come and tell us about them.' She threw her arms out towards Diana.

Diana noted the 'us' and glanced between the two of them.

'Oh um, this is Gary, my new manager.' Anita inclined her head towards him.

Gary stepped forward, 'Well hiya Diana. I've heard a lot about you.' He went for a high five. She wasn't expecting that. His palm was fleshy and hot. Then Diana felt him touch her elbow as he manoeuvred around her to sit in the farthest corner of the room.

Anita sat back down and patted the seat beside her. 'Let me hear more. When did you get your results?'

Diana sat close to her mother and could feel their shoulders touching.

'I just found out this morning. Two As and a B so I can go to my first choice university – Sheffield. I didn't think I'd do so well in French and German, so it's really cool.' She watched her mother for a reaction.

Anita threw her head back and laughed. 'Well done, you deserve it. Your exam results are the first step to a marvellous future. Now you can relax. You've got time for a well-earned holiday before you go to Sheffield.' She put her arm around Diana's shoulders and gave her a squeeze.

Diana felt her arms relax at her mum's touch. She wasn't sure about going to university; it seemed like years out of her life, but she wasn't going to spoil this precious moment. So no discussion of career choices and which ones required a degree. She looked down and stroked the sofa's fringing.

It was a good time to try to renew their connection, 'Mm' she nodded, 'and what are you doing? How is your play?'

'We're just in rehearsal at the moment, so no late nights . . . thank goodness. I'm going to be Queen Elizabeth the first, would you believe? I'm experimenting with ways to play her at the moment. I see her in a lonely fight to maintain her royal dignity as she gets more worn out with court politics. She was a queen for a long time, you know. I'm enjoying getting my teeth into it. There are fewer roles available for mature women, but thanks to Gary here, I still get some interesting jobs.'

Gary smiled briefly, but then he reacted to a series of electronic notes. Diana and Anita turned to watch him as he leant over and hauled a brick of a black plastic mobile telephone from a side table. He pulled out an antenna and put it to his ear, 'Yeh mate, what can I do you for?'

Diana smirked at his Yuppie status symbol. She and Clare always laughed at pretentious people. She looked to see if her mum would share a giggle.

Gary walked out, still talking. Once they were alone, Anita leant towards her, 'So now what's happened? Won't Imogen be expecting you at the chateau?'

'I phoned her with the results. They were all pleased over there, but I wanted some time with you before I went to France.'

'Aww. . . that's lovely. Of course, you're welcome to stay for a while. I'll be quite busy, but maybe we can find some mother-daughter time – go out for a meal together perhaps.'

It was what Diana wanted to hear. She felt a yearning to be a little girl again and to be held. Gary reappeared and replaced the mobile phone with a flourish. 'Right, drink anyone?' he beamed at both of them.

CHAPTER THREE

Diana was woken each morning by the sound of Gary and Anita moving around in the bathroom and kitchen. It felt easier to stay in the warmth of her bed than to worry about getting in the way of their morning routine. It was cosy to imagine that she was, at last, in a normal family with a mum and dad getting on with their lives. By the time she emerged, they had left the flat.

She was used to organising her life around studying, but now she was cast free with no timetable to follow. In the first few days, she explored the flat: sneaking a biscuit from a tin on a top shelf of the kitchen cupboard, reading the invoices on Gary's desk, flipping through books in the bookcase.

She peeked into Anita's bedroom. Half of the wardrobe was given over to Gary's clothes. He had made himself at home. His socks were strewn across the floor. Anita's side of the room was neater. She had an ornate chest of drawers and an altar to cosmetics. Tucked in the corner of a drawer, Diana found a heavy photograph album. The binding was splitting through age, and when she delicately turned the pages, there were black and white photos fixed on with tiny cardboard triangles at each corner. Most of them featured two little girls. Someone had written on the black cardboard in white ink 'Anita and Maura' and occasionally their ages had been written below. She remembered Maura was her mum's sister, but she'd never met her. Maura had emigrated to America. Tucked into the back of the album was the yellowing Order of Service from her own christening. She wondered about that time and how Anita had coped with being a new mum. She can't have been much older than Diana was now. There was a wooden bead necklace with a cross attached. It was looped around the back cover of the book. Running the smooth beads across her palm, she realised that it was a rosary. Anita's mother had been from Ireland and no doubt she was Catholic. Diana felt a yearning to understand her background and to be more involved in Anita's life.

***

She spent her days wandering around city streets, first those local to the house, and then she travelled further afield by tube. One day she took the Tube to the theatre district. She felt a prickling of emotion as she remembered her mother talking about all of these theatres when she stayed at the Lunar Hotel. It had been like a mythical story, but now it was real.

Her stomach twisted up as she wandered from one theatre to the other. She wondered why it disturbed her so much, but it was nearly lunchtime, so perhaps food would help.

She stopped outside a corner shop cluttered with advertising boards. There was a copy of 'The Stage' among a display of newspapers and journals on a table outside. It was like fate calling. She nipped in to buy a copy and a couple of cheese rolls. The midday sun was warm, so remembering a tiny park surrounded by railings that she'd passed earlier, she made tracks to it. The sun filtered through the leaves of trees providing perfect dappled shade. She sat down on a bench tucked away in a corner, and spread The Stage across the wooden seat. Her mother's world in the paper beckoned to her and she became wrapped up in it. Eventually, she grew aware of a figure entering the park gate. It was probably time to move. She took one last look at the opportunities in the back pages.

"Auditions this afternoon at the Shaftesbury Theatre" she read:

"While preferable, no training required and you don't need an agent."

Her heart beat faster, this was her chance! Would there be time to get there? She was obliged to fold away the paper, anyway, as the newcomer arrived at the other end of the bench. She pulled an A-Z out of her rucksack and held it for reference while she jogged along pavements and around pedestrians to get there in time to register at the audition.

Oh, no. There was a queue of young people trailing all the way down the street. It was off-putting, but she'd come this far so she may as well join them now. She stood just behind the last girl in the queue and looked over the rest. Everyone had dressed to get noticed: wide-legged trousers, ripped denims and mesh tops. She caught smatterings of nervous chatter, mostly about audition pieces.

Someone further up the queue said, 'We've been waiting an hour and a half, and it's hardly moved.' Diana's heart sank.

The girl nearest to her said, 'Like your crop top.'

'Thanks,' she was glad she'd put on crop-top and pedal pushers that morning. The girl was all in black and her eyes were made-up for the stage. 'You look good too.'

She let the conversation drop while she tried to remember a speech or a song that she'd learned in the past. By the time the queue reached the door, her feet ached. A sense of camaraderie built among the people in the queue. There was a hum of voices by the time they entered the building. Diana watched from the wings as the girl in front gave her sheet music to the pianist and belted out a song.

***

'Next,' came the shout. In response, she ran out with a fixed smile. She arrived at the pianist's side and whispered, 'What have you got? How about something from West Side Story?'

'Name,' came the impatient voice from the stalls. She tried to find her voice to say her name loudly, despite a dry throat. Could they hear her? The first note played, and Diana launched into 'There's a place for us.' She was far too high and adjusted key mid-song. She noticed an arm wave from the stalls, and the piano stopped.

'OK, next,' came the long-suffering tone.

Diana's breathing speeded up, and her chest tightened, but she stood for a moment longer clutching the warm wooden corner of the piano.

Her thoughts were racing, and she blurted out, 'I'm not really a singer, I act.' There was no response, 'I'm the daughter of Anita Tomalty.'

Still silence, and she felt eyes on her. So, she turned and tried to maintain a dignified walk offstage, but it had turned into a dash by the time she reached the wings. She tucked her head down and marched right on out of the theatre. The traffic outside had stopped at the lights, so she rushed headlong across the road to the pavement opposite. She knew that the next stage of the process would be 'call-backs', but they wouldn't be calling her. In her blind panic, she crashed into the corner of a wall and bit back a yelp. She couldn't shake off her humiliation and hardly noticed where she was walking.

After some time, Diana stopped walking and shivered. The sun had faded now, and the sky was the pale grey of threatening rain. She wished that she had brought a windcheater. She was by the slow-moving tarnished silver of the Thames. Remembering the A-Z in her bag, she sat down on a wall. The cold stone beneath her discouraged staying for long, but where was she? She couldn't help crying as she looked across the dull water. Time to pick herself up, after all, she had money in her bag and people who cared about her. She took a deep breath and set off along the embankment with her shoulders back and head held high.

Just ahead there was a youth huddled on the slabs. He had set out a rug under an arch of the bridge. She was unnerved. She had to go that way. Glancing around, there were a few people behind her, but they were at a distance. He wasn't looking at her; his head was down. 'He's not going to bother you', she told herself, she looked straight forward and quickened her pace.

Just as she drew alongside, he muttered, 'Spare change?'

His voice was such a tiny murmur that Diana retrieved a cheese roll from her bag and handed it to him. It made her realise how lucky she was to have somewhere to go. It was busy above on the high road, and taxis were passing at speed. When she saw one displaying the lit 'To Hire' sign, she stepped forward to hail it.

Chapter Four

Diana let herself in the front door of her mother's building. Anita and Gary should be at home by now. She was struck by the stillness of the flat. It was as though there wasn't anyone there, and yet she sensed a presence. She was right. They were both sitting waiting for her in the lounge. Her mother was holding herself tensely on the edge of her chair. Diana had been racing home to be comforted, but she suddenly felt sick. She was exhausted.

Anita's voice was tight, 'I'm afraid we know where you've been.'

Diana paused, 'Oh.' She looked from one to the other. She wasn't sure why they were annoyed.

'You used my name. . .' Anita's voice built in strength, 'well, didn't you?'

Ah, so Mum had heard from someone at the auditions, but Diana felt confused. Had her mother wanted to deny that she had a daughter? She couldn't bring herself to ask.

Instead, she said, 'Yes, I'm sorry. I panicked, and I suppose I thought it might help.' She sat down beside her mother, 'You don't mind, do you?'

Anita looked across at Gary and raised her eyebrows. He shifted in his seat, 'Well it's not ideal, is it. We're trying to manage Anita's image and the way her name is used.'

Anita sprang up, 'Look it's not just that, Diana. You're supposed to be having a break before you go to study. That's what I want for you. I want you to have a better future. If you'd had my life as a child in a single-parent family, never knowing whether there would be enough money, you wouldn't so carelessly throw away your chances. You've seen how I've struggled. You should know show business isn't easy. I can't understand why you'd want to dabble in it?' She shrugged quickly, 'From the sound of it you aren't very good at it, anyway.'

Diana felt a physical pain in her chest. This was her own mother and yet she was trying to crush her. She had always believed that, even when they were apart, there was a thread of affection connecting them. She had even expected Anita to be proud that her daughter wanted to follow in her footsteps. She felt her lips trembling and tears pricking in the corners of her eyes.

Anita hadn't moved. She was poised as though waiting for an answer. Diana knew that she needed to defend herself, 'I know I'm not a singer. Going to that audition was a mistake. But I can act. I take after you.' As she said that, she was hit by a flashback of being on the stage that afternoon.

Anita answered immediately, 'You could do anything you want to do. Don't be such a fool.' She sprang out of her seat and swept her hand across her forehead. In a defeated voice, she added, 'I've got so much going on at the moment. . . having you here is just too much.' Anita half turned away, 'The next time I hear from you it had better be by telephone from France,' she said through gritted teeth. 'You hear me.' She left the room, and the door flew shut behind her.

Diana stood in the centre of the room. She couldn't make sense of any of it.

Gary coughed gently, 'Look give her time; she's tired, she doesn't really want to upset you.'

Diana sat down on the sofa. It felt warm from her mother's body. She drew her legs up and shrank into the corner of the seat. The stress of the whole day overwhelmed her. Her chest felt full, and she gave in to sobs; great heaving sobs. Her tears came, and her nose began to run. She wished that Gary would just go and leave her to her misery. He seemed to feel obliged to do something. Without warning, he joined her on the sofa.

'We can talk about it. Maybe I can launch an acting career for you. Don't worry. I'll talk your mother round.' Diana stopped crying. She must look terrible; she looked around for tissues. He shuffled nearer, 'You've got your mother's looks, you know.'

She began to listen, could he really see her mother's glamour in her? When Gary leant closer, she could see his deep pores and dark stubble. He smelled different – sweet and tangy like he'd been standing over a bonfire. She tried to breathe it in. He was slightly taller, causing her to look up. She felt his lips brush hers. It felt electric, and it was a shock. He pressed his lips to hers. It made her head spin. Perhaps she did have the same effect on men that Anita had? She lost herself in the moment and took the comfort that he offered.

Suddenly she felt a sharp movement of air as the door was thrust open. They parted. Anita in a dressing gown, her usual elegant chignon strewn in auburn curls around her shoulders and her cheeks flushed, stood with horror in her eyes . . . 'What on earth?'

Diana was too stunned to speak; she looked from her mother to Gary and felt guilty.

Anita paced in front of them, her face twisted. She grabbed at Gary's arm, but despite wrenching at it, he stayed seated.

'How could you?' she screamed and then she turned on Diana, 'And you. Do you do everything to spite me? Go on get out, I can't bear to look at you.'

Diana flinched. Was Anita going to hit her? No, she turned her attention back to Gary. Diana darted around her and headed for her bedroom. She shut the door firmly behind her and sat on the floor with her back to it, half afraid that Anita might push her way in. She heard thumps and bangs, muttered voices - then silence. She focused on the legs of the bed and a leather pouffe that was in her eye line. Perhaps she would be more comfortable sitting on the pouffe, but she didn't move. Daylight was fading, but she didn't bother to put the light on. She was getting sore from sitting on the hard floor. Everything had gone so horribly wrong. She felt alone. She often felt alone. Imogen seemed so far away. She missed Clare, but Clare would never be in this position and probably wouldn't be able to understand. Hovering at the back of her mind was her own father. She was broken inside and he could make it better.

Diana had been sitting so long that it was difficult to ease her folded legs into a standing position. Feeling numb, she slowly gathered clothes into her rucksack, took one last look around the room that her mother had given her, and left as silently as she could. As she reached the bottom of the stairs, she thought she heard a sound like 'Diana' from above, she paused to listen. No, it was nothing.

Streetlights turned the sky from black to deep blue, but the windows of Anita's flat were in darkness. Diana's heart beat fast. She had to think, and think quickly. She headed towards a McDonalds that she had passed regularly in the last week.

'Just a cheeseburger and coke please,' she handed over the money. 'And excuse me, can you tell me what time you close?'

The bald-headed man kept his concentration on the till, 'Eleven tonight,' he said, barely moving his lips. She scanned the Formica tables and red bench seating, choosing to sit as far from the window as possible. She imagined that someone could be watching from the dark outside. There were only a few customers at the tables, and all were alone. She fidgeted with the plastic lid to her drink and the straw while she thought about her options. Of course, Imogen's mother Dulcie and her husband would welcome her in France. Her sensible voice said that she should go there, but no, she felt drawn to search for her father. She had always envied Clare for having a father. Fingers crossed, somewhere out there, her own father might be eager to meet her.

Her mouth went dry. How could she reach him, especially after so much time had passed? Who might know something and be prepared to tell her about him? About Pete, she at least knew his name. Actually, there was Tony. When she was born, he had been at the Lunar Hotel with her mother and Imogen. He must know something. Now he was living in the country with his partner Vic. She should go to them first.

She looked up as she sensed that the man behind the counter was glancing over at her. 'Looking for a job? There's one going here,' he yelled across.

'No, no thank you.' Diana wondered what made him ask, 'I'm going the right way for Victoria coach station, am I?' she pointed in the opposite direction to Anita's flat.

'Yeh, just get the tube at the end of the road,' he said and turned away.

Diana hurried out. She needed to phone ahead. She wondered what time the last coach left. If she missed it, she could only think she'd be spending the night on a bench.

Chapter Five

As the coach was leaving the outskirts of London via the Edgeware Road, Diana fell asleep. She only woke when other passengers stood up to gather their hand luggage. As they crowded into the aisle, ready to leave the coach, she uncurled and stretched. The coach drew up to a marked bay in a bus station. She pulled down her rucksack from the rack above the seat, while a group of people stood beside the coach waiting for their bags from the hold. Once she had clambered down the steps, she scanned the area for signs of a familiar face or car. There was Vic, standing with his hand raised to attract her attention. He loped across to her with a worried look on his face.

'There you are. Great to see you,' he patted her on the back, 'we're over here.' He waved towards a substantial car, one of the later Ford Sierras with the curved headlights.

Diana slung her rucksack on the back seat beside Vic and got into the front. She knew that she should be grateful to them for setting out to meet her at short notice and yet inside she felt a deadness that prevented her from responding to them. Tony was in the driver's seat, his face lit by the bus station lighting and the coloured lights on the dashboard, 'This is an unexpected pleasure.' He leaned across to kiss her, 'I want to hear all your news.' He drew the car away and out onto the main road.

She was glad she'd had a chance to relax on the coach before having to face cross-questioning.

Pausing at a junction to turn, Tony leant forward to look both ways, 'Thought you were going to France,' he said, 'but of course, we're pleased you've come to see us at last.' He took a swift glance her way, 'Does Imogen know where you are?'

'Oh, I spoke to her from the hotel, but I'll have to phone again.' She covered her mouth as she stifled a yawn.

He left a few moments of silence. She watched the curve of the road and realised that they were gently climbing.

'Are you okay?' he said, looking over at her.

'Yeh, it's just been a lot of travelling. I had a bit of a row with Mum,' she said, feeling the pain all over again.

'It'll be a mother-daughter thing. You'll both come around in the end.' His voice seemed to be drifting a long way away. She wondered when to mention that she was going to look for Pete, but she felt herself beginning to fall asleep. It was so warm in the car. Should she try to stay awake? It was too tempting to drift, so she hoped that they would understand.

Later, Diana only vaguely remembered staggering out of the car and into Tony and Vic's kitchen. She jerked awake again when their spaniel, Bruno, launched an over-enthusiastic welcome at her. She flopped down at the pine kitchen table and bent to pet him, while Tony made her some tea and Vic went to make up the bed for her in their spare room.

***

Diana had been dreaming that she was running along the road, waving and shouting as Pete drove away. It was heart-breaking, didn't he know that he was her dad? He didn't stop. It took a moment to force her eyes open and to realise that it had been a dream. She didn't recognise the bedroom. A traditional cottage dormer window was set into the roof, and yet the interior was modern. Vic would have had a hand in the minimalist taupe and cream decoration. Tony had a more traditional style. Diana considered swinging her legs out of bed and stowing all her clothes into square wicker baskets set in an open-fronted chest. Was it worth unpacking? She felt lethargic, and besides, she hoped to be setting off again as soon as possible.

She couldn't hear any movement, so she slipped out of bed to see where Tony and Vic were; her bare feet on an unfamiliar wooden floor. The garden below was bordered by an old red brick wall which followed the curve of the road beyond it. The lawn was surrounded by tall bushes, their straggly branches swaying in the breeze. She noticed Vic, down to her left, he was in shirt sleeves and taking food to a small flock of chickens. She'd better go down and start her day.

Tony was in the living room with his feet up on the coffee table, watching breakfast TV. 'Just get yourself some cereal if you want,' he said, 'and there's a cafetière of hot coffee.'

She brought her cereal in from the kitchen. 'Erm it's OK to eat in the living room, is it?' she gestured to the bowl.

'Yes, yeh you make yourself at home. We'd like you to see it as another home.'

She wanted to remember that feeling. There was such a history between them all. Tony, Imogen and her mother Anita had been housemates before she was born and they'd agreed to bring her up together as a surrogate family. Imogen's mother Dulcie had come to help out too, before she moved to France, and she acted like a granny. Tony had often taken the father role, so Diana worried about his reaction to hearing that she was going to seek out Pete.

The room was warm. A cast-iron wood-burner and low ceilings meant that it would be cosy in the winter. She sank into a floral linen sofa. A shaft of diffused sunlight lit the dim room. After a comfortable pause, while she ate her cereal, he added, 'Vic's going to be glad of your company, to tell you the truth. I'm busy overseeing building work. We're converting a corner shop into a bistro, and I try to keep an eye on the contractors at the Lunar Hotel too.'

Diana knew that her face fell. He wouldn't be around very often. She wondered when she would be able to introduce questions about her father, 'Are you going today?'

'No, I try to stay at home on the weekends.' He gave her a warm smile.

She'd rather speak to Tony on his own, but she could hear Vic banging about in the kitchen. Then he joined them. He had changed into fleece-lined slippers, and he was struggling to carry in an unwieldy bundle of Sunday Times and supplements. Vic was slightly older than Tony and more reserved. When he sat down, it felt as though she had a comforting elderly uncle beside her.

Her indecision ended; before she could hesitate further, she said, 'I wanted to talk to you. I've been so busy with exams, and now I feel that I'm at a crossroads.' She hadn't planned the next words. How to put this? She looked at Tony, 'I know you were there when I was born. At the hotel, I mean. And. . . I've decided that I want to find out more about my father.'

She saw a shadow cross over Tony's face. But she was committed to carrying on now, 'I understand how people feel. He didn't treat Mum right, so I know Mum and Imogen don't want to tell me much. But I need to find out what he's like for myself. It's my life and my relationship now. Can you help? Do you remember much about him?'

'Humph,' Tony flushed and sat forward, clasping his hands together. 'I met him, yes. But I've got to tell you I don't think this is a good idea.' He sat in thought and shot a look across to Vic.

'But perhaps now she's an adult?' Vic began.

'No,' Tony interrupted. 'You see, if the girls aren't telling you anything, it isn't my place to go against them, anyway.'

Diana found it hard to hide her feelings. She had a sour taste in her mouth.

He met her eyes and said in a soft voice, 'I'm sorry. I know it's not what you wanted to hear. But don't let it spoil your visit. We don't get to see you very much, so why don't you have a bit of a holiday here?'

He was being so unfair. It was up to her to make her own decisions, but she said no more. There was an uncomfortable silence.

Vic seemed to force joviality into his voice, 'Well, it's an important time for you, I should think. About to go to university. Are you looking forward to it?'

'Oh yes,' she realised this was a chance to shine in Tony's eyes again, 'I had the results. Two As and a B. It means I can get into my first choice university, if I want to.'

He didn't notice the qualifier. 'Oh well done,' Tony said.

'Yes, congratulations,' Vic added.

CHAPTER SIX

Vic carried two cups of coffee while weaving between metal tables and pushing chairs out of the way with his thigh. Diana was sitting holding Bruno's lead. Vic nodded towards where the counter assistant had been standing only moments before, 'She's OK to let the dog lie under our table. If we want anything else, I'll need to go back up without Bruno.'

The café was empty, so they'd chosen a large round table sitting in the bay window. It looked over Long Helsham village green with its bus shelter and phone box. Vic took a seat opposite Diana.

'Well, now you've had the full tour what do you think of Long Helsham?' he asked.

'It's lovely. I like the mixture of different types of houses with rough natural areas in between. I'm not sure that I could live here, though.'

'I suppose a village isn't busy enough for teenagers. A lot of them move to the city to work.'

Diana ignored the word 'teenagers' as she felt older than that. 'Couldn't they live at home and travel daily?'

Vic piled spoonsful of sugar into his coffee, 'There's only one bus each day and two on market days. And they're timed to attract shoppers.'

'You've chosen a bit of a backwater then.' Diana said, 'Sorry, I didn't mean to be rude. You must like it.'

'Now we've renovated the cottage I'm hoping it will be the way that I imagined it. I want to get to know people a bit more. There's a village hall, so there're whist drives and the local amateur dramatics.'

Diana felt sad that he hadn't achieved his dream after all. 'It must be difficult with Tony being away a lot.'

'I'll be more involved when the bistro is up and running. He'll do the cooking while I do front-of-house. Well, for a while at least, until we can afford to add more staff.' His shoulders slumped. He looked down and toyed with his teaspoon. 'But yes, at the moment I sometimes feel lonely. I find myself watching anyone who passes by our cottage and looking forward to meeting delivery people.' He gave a sad laugh.

Diana felt choked up. She had imagined that Tony and Vic were living an idyllic life. 'Aww. . . I'm sorry. I bet things will get better when Autumn comes. There'll be bonfire night, then village pantomimes and carol singing.'

He grinned and reached down to rub Bruno's ears. 'Oh yes, don't worry about us – eh Bruno? It takes a while to be accepted into village life I think, but actually, I am meeting the dog walkers.' He lowered his voice and looked around, 'I'm not sure whether I ought to tell you this, but I absolutely understand you wanting to find your dad. You know, I've got a family that I don't see.'

'Oh, I didn't know. Were your parents upset about you being gay?'

'No, it's not that, but I had a wife Barbara and two children.' He pulled out his wallet and showed her a worn photograph of two children aged about six and eight. 'I stayed in the marriage for a long time. Barbara was . . . well, I can't fault Barbara. She was clever, and she had an outgoing personality. I was glad to have her with me socially to events where wives were invited.

She looked good. And when the children were born, I fell in love with them. They were just so cute.'

Vic's eyes shone. 'Michael, he picked things up so quickly, and he had no fear. He'd just wanted to have a go at everything. And then when Nicola came along, I thought I couldn't love another child as much, but', he shook his head slowly, 'oh she was so funny and such a huge personality - I miss them.' Diana noticed his eyes crinkle and water, 'I don't know what they're like now.'

'How long is it since you saw them?' she asked.

He bit his lip, 'Oh a long time,' he launched into an explanation, 'You have to understand. I fell for Tony when we worked together. I didn't even know he was gay. I knew that I was gay, and I thought I could fit that part of my life into odd times when I went to gay clubs. I was even a drag queen. I was quite popular.' He stopped and looked at her with raised eyebrows and struck a pose.

Diana laughed. Vic seemed to want her admiration, but then his face fell again. 'In the beginning, I enjoyed Tony's company, and I didn't think it needed to go any further, but well,' he shrugged and said archly, 'You can't fight something like that can you darling?

My life turned upside down. When I told Barbara, she was devastated, and I felt awful at causing all that. The children were upset. They could see the state she was in. I was torn between looking after the family and wanting to see more of Tony. Then the decision was taken out of my hands; she upped and took the children to her mother's. That would be about twelve or thirteen years ago now.'

He turned abruptly to stare out of the window. Diana turned and looked too, to give him time to gather his feelings. 'I had some wrangles with Barbara about seeing the children, so I haven't seen them often. There were too many times when she promised that I could see them and then let me down.'

Diana took another sip of coffee, not realising that she'd let it go cold. Ugh, she gulped rather than spitting it back into the cup. She was calculating the passage of time. Twelve or thirteen years ago she would have been seeing her mother in the school holidays and spending time in France with Imogen's mother.

'They must be quite old now,' she said.

'Yes, Michael is older than you. So, you can imagine, now they're older I hope they will come looking for me.' He rested his elbows on the table and held up his crossed fingers. 'I know they will.'

'Oh my God, how awful,' she said.

'Yes, missing them feels like a physical pain and I have to try to forget it. It eats into me. But that's why I want to help you.' He sat up and clasped his hands together. Bruno beside him thought they were about to leave and sat up expectantly. 'If I can help bring one parent and child together. . .'

Diana leant forward, resting her arms on the table, 'Ah, did you know Pete back then?'

'No, but Tony told me that Pete threatened to 'out' him. Why? I don't know. I think he wanted to have some hold over him. It doesn't seem that long ago, but attitudes were different then. Tony didn't want everyone knowing.'

Diana went very still. She'd expected to hear that Pete had treated her mum badly, but she'd had no idea about this. 'I can't imagine anyone disliking Tony,' she said in a subdued voice.

'No, he is rather likeable isn't he,' Vic said, 'but that was what prompted Tony to 'out' himself and start a new life. Tony told me that he actually went to confront Pete at his office.'

Diana jumped to the edge of her seat at this, 'Ah, so Pete had an office. Where was it?'

'You know I'm not sure dear, but I do know that he ran a boat trip business around the rivers and canals. I'm not sure what the business was named. It might have been under his name or owned by someone else.'

Diana's heart was beating fast. So little to go on, but she was determined to use the information somehow.

Bruno stretched his lead to stand guard at the window. A cat sauntered across the road, and he began an excited wiggle and small barks.

Vic stood up, 'Time to move, I think. But if you go looking for Pete, you will let me know how you're getting on, won't you?'

Vic called through to the back, 'Thank you,' as they left the empty café.

***

In the following few days, Diana slept late in the mornings. With time on her hands, she even wrote to Imogen and told her where she was. Vic cajoled her into joining him on long dog walks in the afternoons, exploring the surrounding woods and fields. He coached her on what she should say to Pete and to consider all his possible reactions. She decided that she would reassure Pete that she wasn't there to judge him. She wanted to get to know him as a father, but it was important to hear his side of the story, eventually.

'I won't want him to feel bad though,' she enthused, 'I need to tell him that I've had a good life. You and Tony and the others made really good Christmases for me. I loved everyone gathering together at the hotel.'

'Yes, that's the point Diana, you make your own family. The gay community is like that too. People get together and fall out again just like in any family, but there's a sense of belonging. You know, that's how I started finding my real self. When I got into drag, it meant that I could act out all the behaviours that I wasn't able to do as a straight man.'

'I don't think I've seen you do a drag act; I'd love to see it.'

'Maybe one day.' Vic's mind had moved on. 'Tony isn't really into that. He gets passionate about cooking and our holidays are our outlet.'

Chapter Seven

Vic stood on the grass verge as Diana made her way to her seat on the bus. She felt a pang of sadness at waving goodbye to him and to Bruno. Diana mouthed 'Bye' through the window at the last sight of him as it pulled away. The country road was too uneven and had too many bends for her to be able to read; she visualised the path ahead. Vic's story was an insight into how a father could feel about being estranged from his children, and it made her more determined to find Pete. It wasn't just her quest, she might be fulfilling an ache for him too.

As the bus reached the outskirts of the city, she paid more attention to scenes outside the window. The streets of Victorian shopfronts were shuttered and strewn with litter. As a child, she had often visited this city, but as they drew into the bus station, it was different. There were new pedestrian-only areas, large new shops, and new concrete underpasses; but the canals and rivers were much the same. She followed the course of the river, past an out-of-town shopping centre and riverside office blocks until the landscape opened out. The road ran parallel to the river. There was a pub teeming with lunchtime customers. The gravelled car park overflowed onto the road, which was lined by parked cars.

Narrowboats and cruisers were moored along the river. Diana stepped across an area of rough grass to get nearer. She noticed large boards placed on the bank advertising 'Mystery

Boat Tours' and 'Sunday Lunch Boat Trips'. There was tarpaulin tied over the top of one boat. The next vessel along the towpath was more substantial, and it was served by a path leading to a wooden booking office. The office seemed to be open, so she went to sneak a quick look through the window. She could see a figure inside. She knocked and tried the door.

It was part office and part storeroom. A young man in a heavy fair-isle jersey wearing wellingtons stood with his back to the door. He didn't fully turn to face her.

'Yeh, can I help you. 'Fraid we aren't running today.'

He oozed aggression, so Diana looked instead to an elderly woman with tightly permed steel-grey hair. She sat at an Amstrad computer, flicking through a notepad, but she was observing Diana.

Avoiding eye contact with either of them, Diana said, 'I'm not interested in a boat trip at the moment. I'm looking for someone called Pete. I've been told that he was definitely working around here in the early 1970s.

Fair Isle jerked his head around, 'Pete in the 70s, eh. So, what's it to you?'

Diana's mind raced to work out how to get him on side. He could know something. She couldn't think of a non-committal answer, so she avoided the question, 'Were you around here in the 1970s?'

He fully turned to face her and lowered his chin, 'How old do you think I am?'

She drew in a quick breath and turned instead to the elderly woman, who pursed her lips and looked away. Diana lost her nerve. Instinct told her that she was on the right trail, but maybe there was another way.

'Sorry. Sorry to have troubled you.' She turned and left, crunching across the gravel outside the shed. Then she strode through the rough grass towards the road. There was a comfort in being around other people. 'Maybe if I ask in the bar? I wonder how long the landlord has been here.' But her bravado had temporarily deserted her. In the pub, there was a sour smell of beer. She was used to the Lunar Hotel bar, but she had been in very few public houses. She went to stand quietly alongside the men lining the bar. Thankfully, a pretty girl of around her age was pulling pints while keeping one eye on customers, and she took pity on her.

'Hello, can I help you?'

Diana asked for a shandy.

'Lager shandy or bitter shandy?' Even that was fraught with questions.

Diana took her glass through to the lounge bar and sat at a low table by the window. While turning a beer mat from corner to corner, she considered her next move. Was this going to be a wasted journey? Perhaps she should check the time to make sure that she didn't miss the bus back to Long Helsham. No, there was plenty of time, time to waste even. Drinking slowly, she was left with just a drop of shandy in the base of her glass when the woman from the booking office entered the pub and stood in the doorway scanning the bars.

Clearly, she recognised Diana and bustled up to her table, sliding into the seat opposite.

'I wanted to catch you,' she said quietly.

Diana didn't react immediately. The woman laid hands with raised veins and brown spots onto the table, and she moved one hand to place it over Diana's. Her skin felt cold.

'I'm Betty from over the cabin there,' the woman said with a jerk of her head towards the river, 'Now, tell me why did you want to see Pete?'

Diana realised that people weren't going to give out information without knowing why she needed it. 'Nothing bad. It's just that I know someone from his past.'

'Well,' the woman leaned in to her, 'I've always believed in wimmin helping other wimmin,' but then she raised her head and looked around, 'Oh I'm parched. It's bin quite a day in that damp shed.'

Diana recognised that this might be a hint. 'Oh, I'm sorry, can I get you a drink?'

The woman acted flustered, 'I really wasn't hinting, but that's ever so kind of you. I'll have a large gin and tonic please, lemon no ice.'

When Diana placed the drink in front of her, Betty looked up and smiled, 'Cheers, and pleased to meet you love.'

Diana said, 'And you, I'm Diana.'

'I'm sure you've a good reason for wanting to find Pete. Course there might have been other Petes at that time.'

'This one ran a boat business, and I know he had an office,' Diana was quick to add.

'This one still owns boats here, but you won't find him here anymore. He handles his businesses at long distance. Mind you, you din't hear about him from me.'

Diana's mind cleared and she grinned.

'Are you his mother?'

Betty chuckled and took a large gulp of her drink. 'Bless you, no.'

There was a kind of disappointment in hearing the answer. Diana suddenly felt a bit silly, 'Oh it's just that I. . .'

'That's okay dear. I bet you wonder what I'm doin' here. I live upstairs. I've got rooms. So, this is home to me. Well,' she shrugged, 'It's always been a bit of a home to me, the nights me mam use' to leave us kids playing outside while she was in here.'

'I see,' Diana recognised that Betty was sharing a bit of her life with her, 'so, you're one of the locals. You must know most people. Do you know where I would be able to find Pete?'

'Well, I can give you his address. He lives right outside the city now. But whether you'd find him, I don't know. He doesn't let just anyone in. 'Ere, have you got a pen and paper?'

Diana found a pencil in her bag and felt around among the pleats of her jeans to find the pocket. Luckily, there was a scrap of paper folded many times, and she smoothed it flat on the table. Betty licked the pencil, 'now let me see. 'Fraid it's a house name, not a number.' She wrote carefully in spidery writing.

'Thank you,' Diana's heart leapt, 'I can't believe I've finally found him. If it is the Pete I'm looking for.'

'His last name is Lawrence.'

'That doesn't help me, because I never knew his last name,' but she mentally rolled the name around. If life had taken a different turn, she would have been Diana Lawrence. What would Diana Lawrence have been like?

'Must be important – if you've come looking for someone, with so little to go on.' Betty looked at her sideways.

Diana blurted, 'I think, I think he may be my father.'

Betty's face softened, and she gently placed her hand on Diana's forearm. 'Ah, well take it slowly love. Go slowly and listen to all that you hear.'

Chapter Eight

Diana felt fortunate to find a Betty. She knew the ropes, and introduced Diana to the pub landlord so that she could enquire about a room for the night. She decided that she would stay and set off, to find the address that Betty had given her, first thing in the morning. Diana threw her rucksack into a corner of the room. It wasn't luxury, but it served its purpose. She had decided to save some money by missing out on breakfast. She spent more time in the bar chatting to Betty about changes to the city, as she knew she wouldn't see her again.

It was so tempting to hitchhike, but she had been warned over and over that it was a bad thing to do. How likely was it that something would go wrong? But a voice inside her, sounding remarkably like Imogen's, absolutely refused. Instead, she had used even more money getting to the central bus station again and then taking one of the infrequent buses that travelled out of the city, stopping at every village. Doing this alone made her tense and she wished that she could have called on Clare to join her. If she thought about it long enough, she wondered what she was doing there. The scenery was a diversion. The bus wound through a natural area of rocky crags and steep wooded valleys. She asked the driver to point out the right bus stop, but she still travelled on the edge of the front seat in case he forgot.

When she alighted, the village setting took her breath away. It really felt that she was on a quest in a fairy-tale village.

But the cluster of grey stone cottages with moss covered roofs were jarred by high-end Mercedes and Porsches parked nearby. Did Pete fit into this community? She may be about to meet him. She froze with the dread that he would reject her, an intruder in his life. Subconsciously she probably feared him. She felt dizzy and reached out to hold the post of a road sign for support. Looking up, one of the arms read 'Sunnyside'. That was the name of his house. With a name like that he must be a good-natured optimist.

She trekked up a single-track road pressing close to the hedgerow to avoid cars. Fortunately, few cars used the road at that time of day. She stopped at the summit of a rise sighting an outcrop of grey buildings bounded by dry-stone walls. Could this be Sunnyside? This was her father's house.

What did she look like? She found a brush from her bag and pulled it through her thick mop of hair. Think about anything rather than what could happen now. On a white metal sign, she read the name, 'Sunnyside Caravan Park.' She huffed a laugh at the irony on this overcast day.

She felt a bit queasy and tried concentrating on something ahead. There was a tall Scots pine beside the buildings – she tried thinking of that. She even considered turning and retracing her steps.

When she moved closer to the walls, a Doberman loped across the distance between the house and the five-bar gate in front of her. His glinting eyes never left her. He ranged backwards and forwards across the width of the gate, giving short sharp barks that rang out in the still air. Diana's insides were quaking but she steeled herself to stay immobile.

There came a man's shout from over by the buildings. A slightly built man strode towards them. His trendy Brad Pitt curtains of ear-length hair and fake tan didn't fit with the image conjured up by his battered Barbour jacket and wellington boots.

He snapped an order to the dog who immediately lay at his feet.

'Yes, can I help you,' he had a slight Midlands accent.

She wished that she'd planned her first words. There was a pause while momentarily nothing would come and then she managed to say, 'Hello, I'm looking for Peter Lawrence. Are you Peter Lawrence?'

'Yes, that's me,' he looked at her expectantly.

Diana took a deep breath, she just had to go for it. 'I'm the daughter of Anita Tomalty,' she stopped again, 'And I think you might be my father.'

'Diana is it?' he said.

She felt slightly lightheaded. How had this been so easy? He didn't seem at all discomfited. It was as though she'd commented on the weather.

He looked her up and down, and grinned, 'As stylish as Princess Diana but more beautiful. I'd been expecting you. You called at one of my offices. You'd better come in then,' and he grabbed the dog's collar and opened the gate to her, 'don't worry about Caesar here. Once he knows you, he's alright.'

Diana flushed. She could feel tears hovering in her eyes. He hadn't questioned her. He didn't seem to doubt that he was her father. 'I've always wondered about you. It's so cool to finally meet you.'

He grasped her hand as though in a handshake and cupped her elbow with his other hand. 'Well, you're here now and welcome. I can see it's taken you back. Come on,' he put his palm at the small of her back, 'walk with me and we'll talk. I'll show you around. Around the grand estate,' he humphed a laugh. Caesar bounded off to investigate the smells in some bracken and Diana found herself hurrying to keep up with Pete's pace. 'So, what does Anita think about you coming here, then?'

'She doesn't know about it.'

'I see,' he gave a slow smile. 'Well, anyway, you did a good job of tracking me down. How did you find me?'

Diana remembered Betty's warning and waved her arm airily, 'Oh, I talked to people who were around at the time I was born. I've always wanted to get to know you. It's been a gap in my life. Lots of people around, but not my real father.

'So, I've just finished my exams and my life is about to change. . .It's crazy I know, but I didn't feel that I could move on without seeing what you thought I should do.'

He didn't immediately answer, and she didn't know what else she could say. It felt awkward because she needed cues from him. She didn't know how she felt now that she'd met him. They had reached the brow of a hill.

She looked up and saw the picturesque stand of Scots pine and a church spire in the near distance, fading to hills in varying shades of grey and, even farther away, the indistinct grey blocks of the city. 'Wow,' she released her breath, 'You've got quite a view here.'

'Thank you. I like it,' he grinned, 'but tell me about yourself. I know you did well in your 'O' levels. The school published the results in the paper.'

Diana was stunned but nodded her head as though not surprised at all, 'So you've always kept an eye on me.'

'That's right,' he continued to have a closed-lipped smile, 'but I thought best leave well alone. I couldn't take on a family in the early days, I was young and making my way, right?'

'But since?' Diana worried that she was challenging him far more than she had meant to, 'I'm just wondering that's all. I've been happy. I had a good childhood.'

'Good, but yeh, since then I didn't want to rock the boat. I don't think they wanted me in your life. Anyway,' he stopped and turned to her, 'you're here now, and I'm very pleased to see you. You're an adult, so it's a better time now. Let me show you all this,' and he jerked his head at the land around them.

Just over the brow of the hill were the pale roofs of caravans, but he pointed to the stone buildings. There was a barn, a farmhouse and a collection of low outbuildings. She admired a small rose garden bordering a paved area. He unlocked the barn doors, 'This'll be open later on.'

The enormous interior was dim. He stepped through the door onto a richly patterned carpet. They were surrounded by one-armed bandits and further in, snooker tables and a plastic ball pit.

'It's quite a money-spinner.' He strolled up to the snooker table. She followed. He picked up one of the balls and weighed it in his hand thoughtfully 'So why now? I've got to ask - I wonder what you were expecting from me?'

Diana suddenly felt dizzy. She reached out for the corner of the table. He was bound to be wary, he hardly knew her after all, but she began to relax in his company.

She took a deep breath, 'I don't know. I've finished my A levels. I was going to go to France to join Imogen, but I was going with my friend Clare, and she can't come now. I wish I could get on better with Mum. She's wrapped up in the theatre and I suppose I wanted to know who you were and what you'd think of me.'

She looked at him and realised that it was like talking to a stranger, 'I got an 'A' in French and in German and a 'B' in English at A level. So, I've got a place at university,' she said, standing up a little straighter. 'I'm not sure what to do with my life, and somehow I thought I'd have a better idea once I'd met you.'

She glanced around the amusements and wondered what she was doing here. 'I had this silly idea that you must rate actresses like Mum and perhaps I should go into the theatre, but,' she bit her lower lip, 'I tried that.'

'So have you worked out how you'd get through university? You'll have enough to live on, I mean.'

'Yes I'll get a grant, if I go.'

He touched her elbow, 'It's okay, I'm naturally cautious. Got to be really – when you're in business.'

He put the ball down firmly and turned to walk back to the door. 'An actress hmm,' she heard him say over his shoulder, 'Not much money in that, but there's always scope to use your acting skills in everyday life.'

He led her across the paved area to the farmhouse. The sun had come out from behind clouds, and it felt warmer. He waved to one side as he walked, 'That's the camp shop there. . . and the laundrette. Come in and meet my wife, Elaine.' He was smiling now.

Elaine was alright. 'She's pretty', Diana thought. Elaine hung back, but her smile seemed warm and genuine. Diana had to lean forward to hear her soft 'hello.'

Pete didn't explain who she was, but perhaps he'd told Elaine when he heard that Diana was looking for him.

'Hello. I hope you don't mind me just appearing like this.'

'Elaine doesn't mind, do you?' Pete said before Elaine could reply.

Elaine explained that she was about to finish cooking. Her voice grew louder as she spoke. She was clearly a favourite with Caesar, who stuck to her side.

'You'll stay for a meal?' she asked.

***

There was a formal dining room. The smoked glass dining table was already set. Elaine brought in an extra placement for Diana and then lifted a dish of lasagne onto a table mat in the centre of the table. The reality of being at her father's house to have a family meal finally hit Diana. She thought gratefully of Vic and even Betty, who had helped her to get here.

'Do you get involved in the business too?' she asked Elaine.

'No, not really. I have plenty to do here. I'm 'general help',' Elaine said but without softening it as a joke. 'Everyone gets put to work here, even Caesar. As a guard dog,' she added, this time with a laugh.

Pete used serving tongs to lift salad leaves out of a bowl, and then passed the bowl to Elaine. 'Diana's just got her 'A' level results. See,' he jabbed his fork towards her, 'I always thought my family were clever. It's just I didn't get the chances.'

Diana found herself babbling on about school and Clare and then telling them all about her visits to France.

'My daughter travels. So what music do you like?' Elaine asked Diana.

'Oh I don't know - Alison Moyet, Queen, David Bowie, all sorts really.'

'Mmm,' Elaine nodded knowingly, 'My daughter Kim, she likes Madonna.'

Diana nodded, 'Will I get to meet her?'

'She works in the family business, so she comes over quite a lot,' Elaine said. Diana noticed that Pete reacted to this by sitting up a bit straighter and puffing out his chest.

He began, 'Let me tell you a bit about me and the business. See, my upbringing had a lot to do with me ending up in business.' Elaine settled back and sat quietly, watching them both. Pete went on to tell her more about how he'd started boat trips and publicised them with local businesses. He alluded to expansion in recent years to work across Europe.

'It sounds exciting,' Diana said dutifully though she couldn't imagine how it all worked.

'I see you brought a bag with you.' Pete nodded at Diana's rucksack in the corner of the dining room. 'Why don't you stay?'

'Well if that's no trouble?' Diana looked across at Elaine.

CHAPTER NINE

Diana had felt welcomed into the heart of the family, but the next day was like the first day at a new school. She woke up to a silent house. It was all so strange. She peeped through a crack in the curtains. The view and the expanse of sky were amazing.

She felt restless and quietly made her way down the stairs, walked barefoot on the wooden floor of the hall and found the living room. As there was no one around, she sat on the edge of their cream leather sofa unit. She picked up a magazine from the glass-topped coffee table and leafed through it. It was some local business magazine, and the only pictures were photographs of people shaking hands as they received awards.

It was time for breakfast TV. She looked across to the enormous television sitting in a mahogany cabinet. Would it create too much noise if she slid the cabinet doors open? She took the risk and found the television controller. Maybe she could watch something with the sound turned down to a whisper.

A shuffling movement outside the room gave Diana such a jolt that she almost dropped the controller.

'Another early riser,' Pete said as he walked in, 'I always get up and do a few hours in the office before breakfast.'

'I hadn't realised you were around,' Diana said and stood up awkwardly.

He didn't seem to notice, 'I was thinking last night, I'd like to show you where I grew up. Shall we do that today? Come on, we'll grab something to eat and then I'll drive you over there.'

***

Diana was glad to be wearing trousers when she hoisted herself up into the front of Pete's Land Rover after closing the gate behind them. She relished a drive out with him. The trappings of his business all around them were intimidating, but in the car, they were on an equal footing.

They drove onto the city ring road. 'So if you hadn't stayed with me, where were you going? Pete said.

'I think I'd have gone back to Tony and Vic – to their cottage, and then on to France. I haven't been there this year. It would be nice to see them all.' She remembered that Vic said that Tony had been to see Pete and so she added, 'Do you know them?'

'I've met them yes, a long time ago.' His voice softened, and she could only just hear him over the sound of the engine, 'Imogen wasn't my greatest fan. It was different in those days. Seems like a lifetime ago.' She felt warm towards him and resolved not to pry anymore.

They were in suburban sprawl, passing a Working Men's Club, a pub and carvery, a double-glazing showroom. The treelined streets had houses all of the same brick design – street upon street of council houses. Pete pulled up outside a semi-detached house with a long front garden.

'See the path and the garden gate,' he wound down his window. 'One of my strongest memories is walking down that path in my knee socks and short trousers on my way to school. My mam used to look out of the window and wave.'

She looked. The house had a front door set back in a tiled porch, and she could imagine his mother waving out of the bay window. 'Did you have brothers and sisters?'

'There was my mum, and my gran and me. Gran was my dad's mother, but Dad died just after I was born. We managed when I was little but when mum got ill, gran took over looking after both of us. It shouldn't have affected me at school, but I felt different. The other children had lots more toys, and they went to places at the weekends. I'm not blaming anyone.' He looked at her as though realising that she was there for the first time, 'It was just the way things were.'

He reached up and brushed a stray hair away from the edge of Diana's mouth. 'you know you look a little like her. Some of your expressions. She'd have loved to have met you.'

'She'd be my granny. I wish I could have met her. What was she like?'

'She was very kind. Her name was Dorothy. When Gran died, it upset her not to be able to manage. She had MS, you see. But she got enjoyment out of life. We used to play board games on a Sunday.'

'I don't know a lot about MS,' Diana said.

'No, well it meant that I often took time off to stay at home. I did all the washing, housework, shopping. I wanted her to have a good life, but sometimes I resented it. Most of the lads in my form at school had plans. They applied for apprenticeships and went to college, but I'd not got the education behind me. So Diana,' he looked at her with a softening in his eyes, 'I don't want you to judge me. I did the best with what life threw at me.'

She looked again at the house and now imagined Pete as a youth. 'That's so sad. Of course, I don't judge you.'

He went on, 'Mum had just died, when I found out that Anita was pregnant. I couldn't deal with anything. Anyway,' he sat up and swiped at his eyes, 'it seems to have turned out for the best. You've had a good life. You've turned into a wonderful young woman. I wish Mum could see you.'

Diana felt herself beaming. Everything was going to be alright. 'Could we ask to go in?'

'I don't think so. There's no reason. My bedroom was up there, the window above the front door. Come on,' he said, putting the car into first gear and accelerating away.

He pulled into an impressive gateway. It had the appearance of a park with specimen cedars and ornamental trees.

'The cemetery,' Pete said. There were rows upon rows of graves, Diana thought of a housing estate of gravestones. He had no trouble remembering where he was going and parked.

'Mum's just here.' he said.

'Do you want me to come with you?'

'Mm, I'll introduce you to her. I want her to know you.'

It was reassuring to see their names, Frank Lawrence. His wife Dorothy Lawrence. It made them real in Diana's eyes. They were far away from traffic noise and she was glad that they were peaceful.

Pete said, 'I didn't know I was coming here. I'd have brought flowers.'

It seemed such a pity not to be able to bring them anything. Diana looked around for a stray daisy, but the grass was well manicured. Then she remembered her yin and yang pendant and drew it from out of her sweatshirt. 'Can I leave this for them?'

'Thank you, I think she'd like that,' Pete said solemnly.

She briefly touched his hand, 'I'll go back to the car and wait 'til you're ready to come.'

It was locked, so she leant against a nearby tree. She could smell the scent of fresh-cut grass. A breeze caused an ever-moving dappled shade. A pigeon cooed. She looked over at Pete. He was leaning over the grave. He'd been there a long time. When he walked back to her, he was visibly upset. She couldn't think of anything to say that would be any use.

Back in the Land Rover, he said, 'She lived in a home at the end. That's my regret. I wasn't able to look after her. If it had happened now, Elaine and I could have had her to live with us.'

Diana leant back against the headrest on the way home. It had been an emotionally exhausting visit.

She turned to look at him, 'Thank you for taking me to see your past. It means a lot. It feels like I've missed a whole section of my life, when I could have been part of it.'

He was silent for a few minutes, and she began to feel alarmed. Had she said something wrong? Then, 'Well,' he said, 'You can be a part now. I've set up several businesses, and as you know, Kim already works for me. If you want to work for me too, we can build it up together.'

She felt a tingle run through her, she guessed it was warmth towards him. He must be pleased with her – not least because, in some way, her arrival gave him his mother back.

Chapter Ten

In the following days, Diana shadowed him as he dealt with paperwork to learn about the business. She lived in a state of heightened tension – marvelling at the sudden change in her life and anxious about measuring up to the challenge. At times, she wondered how her mother was and whether Imogen was getting impatient for her to arrive in France. She wasn't worried. She was sure that Vic would tell them that she was okay if they asked him.

Pete had suggested she put in a morning stocktaking. She was left in a windowless concrete-floored room. A low moment - it was cold and lonely, but she was determined to impress her father with the speed and accuracy of her stocktaking. She had been given a pencil that was too soft; it blunted as soon as she used it. If only she had brought a radio with her. At least she had remembered to wear a watch; it was just after eleven. Too early to break for lunch. She leant against the racking. Surely stocktaking wasn't that important? But maybe Pete was testing her stickability, or maybe he wanted to keep her out of the way? No, she unconsciously shook her head so that her hair swung out to brush her cheek. She didn't want to start being negative.

She turned again to the cans of beans, tinned pies, tinned stew, she realised that they were in ordered rows so she could estimate amounts by eye. This was going to speed up her progress. Suddenly she was flashing through the racks. Elated, she locked up the shop and strode back to the house. There was no sign of Pete's Land Rover outside, but she could hear Elaine in the kitchen. She would make use of the extra time by doing some office work.

The office was familiar to her by now. A heavy computer, leather desk pad, letter opener and calculator were laid at neat, right angles. Pete was a stickler for order and had everything filed away and labelled. He must have been in a hurry as he'd left his Filofax on top of the printer, which was sitting on a small table beside the desk. She couldn't resist swivelling on the office chair and leafing through the Filofax. The calendar showed meetings with unfamiliar people and organisations. So, she didn't know all about his business yet.

Under that day's date, it showed that he was going to be at Felixstowe. He wouldn't be back for a long time then. She listened for Elaine again and then decided to take a good look around.

She found receipts in a drawer. He was meticulous in keeping receipts. Looking at the items, he was a big spender. Just as she thought that she'd seen everything of interest, she came across a brown envelope full of newspaper cuttings. She carefully withdrew them. There were headlines:

'Actress's love child.'

'Anita Tomalty sensation.'

'Nightclub ejection for Anita'

'My secret shame – Anita'

Her heart started a loud thump. She shouldn't be reading these things about her mother. There were also small gossip column mentions of her mother and even magazine pictures and critiques of Anita's red-carpet fashion. It revealed her mother's world. Wow, Anita looked so young in the pictures.

So, Pete had followed their lives. She felt uneasy and thoughts raced around her head. Then why hadn't he come to find her? All of the clippings signified that he was obsessed with Anita, so why hadn't he stayed with her? She had completely forgotten that he had caused problems for Tony and she should investigate that too.

She had been so lost in reading the slips of paper that she didn't even hear Elaine approaching. Elaine stood in the doorway, looking aghast.

Diana felt a jolt of guilt and was about to apologise when Elaine said, 'Oh no. He doesn't like people being in here on their own. Come on out.' Elaine took a step away and spoke from the hall, 'I'm not even allowed to go in there. Don't let him find you.'

Elaine's horror was infectious. Diana tried to remember what order the cuttings had been in and hurried to put them back into the envelope while being delicate enough not to leave a trace that she had been there. She slammed the drawer shut, sprang up from her knees and followed Elaine.

She gulped feeling guilty, but hadn't realised the severity of what she'd done, 'I'm sorry, but he didn't have the drawers locked,' she said.

Elaine was sitting in the living room by this time, 'Well at least he's still out.' She said in a soothing voice. 'Pete has a lot of different businesses and it's important not to mix them up, that's all.'

Diana felt relieved and sat down too, 'Sorry again,' she muttered, 'I hadn't thought about how I must be changing everything by being here.'

Chapter Eleven

As Tony slung his raincoat over the coat peg, he could smell the dog bed below it. The smell of home. In the kitchen, he laid his briefcase down on the pine table. Weariness made his arms and legs feel heavy. On autopilot, he checked that there was water in the kettle and clicked the switch down to set it working. He rubbed his aching shoulders and sat at the table, head in his hands.

He had been at the bistro all day. The electricians had gone ahead channelling in plug sockets before consulting him, and now he had to work out how to get things altered. They were already behind schedule in converting the kitchen, and every extra week cost more on the mortgage. He wondered whether Vic had been in touch with the printers to place an order for flyers.

Wait a minute; it was very quiet, where was Vic and why hadn't he heard Bruno?

Vic was out with the dog. The answerphone was flashing. He pressed Play.

'Tony, Anita here. I'm worried about Diana she left here late one night and I was sure she'd gone to France, but Imogen says that she came to you. I'm frantic. We had words, and I need to talk to her. Can you pass the message on please?'

Then there was a peep, she had been timed out.

He had told Diana it would be one of those mother-daughter things!

Another message and this time it was Imogen's voice, 'Hi Tony, Hi Vic. Hope you're well and that the hotel refurbishment is going well. Just phoning because Anita seems upset about Diana. I know she saw you, but we were expecting her here. What's going on? Let us know – did she go back home to the hotel? Speak soon.'

Oh, that's all we need. I'm sure Diana wrote to Imogen. He picked up the phone to call her.

'Hello,'

'Allo? Gilles speaking. Is that Tony? Comment vas-tu?'

'I'm fine merci, just in from work, but I got a message from Imogen.'

'Okay, I'll pass the phone to her,' Tony heard a murmur and crackle.

Imogen's voice, 'Hi, thanks for getting back to me. Is everything alright with you?

'Yes, it is with us - but I'm surprised that Diana isn't there. She left here about a week ago. I've been at the hotel, and she isn't there. The hotel's still half-finished I'm afraid.' He looked out of the kitchen window hoping to see Vic walking down the drive. The light was growing dim outside, he would need to close the curtains in a moment.

'So, she isn't there.' Imogen was beginning to sound just like her mother, 'Well I hope she gets in touch soon. I had Anita on the phone. She's distraught. I know Diana's got a lot of common sense, so, fingers crossed, she's okay wherever she is, but it's worrying not to hear anything.

'Erm, I'm wondering whether to come home, but you know, I'd hate to do that. It's a long time since Lynette and I had a real holiday together. Poor Lynette needed to switch off from work. I wish I'd taken her away sooner. We are just adjusting to the slower pace of life here.'

'Yes, 'course you need a holiday. And you don't want to see the Lunar Hotel, the state it's in.' Women, they were easily upset. He stood up and lifted a mug out of the kitchen cupboard, while he spoke, 'Have you asked her friends?'

'Yes . . . Clare, her best friend, hasn't heard from her. Should we tell the police?'

'I think we're panicking unduly. It's not as though she'd made arrangements to be anywhere at a certain time, so she isn't really missing. Kids, they don't realise that people are wondering where they are. Look I'll ask Vic if he has any ideas and we'll start looking for her. Don't worry; she is on holiday after all.'

Oh, well thanks, Tony. I knew we could rely on you.'

Tony brewed himself some tea. The house was cold, how long had Vic been out? On reflection, perhaps he should worry about Diana. She had seemed to be in a disturbed mood when she was here, and she had talked about seeing her father. That was all he needed. He'd better make another call.

'Hi Anita, I got your message. I'll look for Diana. Don't worry; she's got her head screwed on.'

'Thank you, Tony. Have you any idea where she is?'

'She came to see us and stayed for a while. She asked about her dad so she could be trying to find him.'

'Oh no. I hope I haven't driven her to that. It would be a disaster.'

'Yes, I know. I did warn her off.'

'I'm sorry. I bet you'd put all that behind you. He's the last person that you want to think about. I would come to see her, but it's difficult here.'

'Aww, are you OK? I haven't heard from you for ages.'

Anita lowered her voice, 'He isn't here now, but he'll be back any minute. I'm having problems with Gary. He seems to think he can control me. He may be good at getting work in, but I'm not going to let him push me around.'

'No,' Tony felt a shiver run through him at this news, 'Do you want me to come over there. I'm surprised that you haven't thrown him out already.'

'No, I'd rather you found Diana for me. Gary behaved badly while she was here. I'm afraid I was too upset about my relationship to think about her.' She sounded tearful, 'I'm just exhausted. I've been working too hard, I think.'

'Perhaps you'll be able to get away from London – and Gary – for a while.'

'Yes, it's what I need. You know, I was thrilled that she came to tell me about her exams. She's done so well, hasn't she? But instead of getting closer to her while she was here, I lost my temper.' Anita's voice changed, 'Did she tell you about it? She left without saying goodbye.'

'She mentioned it, but she seemed preoccupied with what she was going to do in the future more than anything. It can't have done any lasting damage. She knows she's loved.'

'I've worried about my career so much, but now I want to come back and live near to you all. You all feel like family.'

Tony knew how driven Anita could be and he could only guess at what Gary had done. 'I'll be glad when you get back, and we can look after you. Look I'll go and get something to eat and talk to Vic and then I can work out a plan of action.'

'OK, thanks, Tony. You're a star.'

'Bye, love.' Did he hear a sob in her voice; his heart went out to her.

He put the phone down and paused thoughtfully. How could he help? Tony bounded up the stairs to check whether there was anything left in Diana's room that might be a clue as to where she'd gone. He sat on the bed and looked around, but it was pretty bare. One of her socks was lying in a corner. Teenagers! He picked it up and rubbed its softness against his cheek.

There was a thump downstairs. It sounded like Vic coming back. Tony shouted, 'Hello' and heard an answering call.

Vic was full of energy, draping his scarf over a peg and peeling off a knitted jacket. Bruno raced across the tiled floor, wiggling his 'welcome home' dance. Tony bent to detach the lead and appreciate the attention.

When he straightened up, Vic lunged at him arms spread, 'Welcome home, my darling.'

'Woah, woah,' Tony laughed and stopped for a serious kiss. Vic had grown stubble throughout the day and felt raspy. He still delighted in the knowledge that they'd achieved their dream life together. But then he pulled away to talk.

Vic got in first, 'We've been asked round to the neighbours' tomorrow evening for a barbeque.'

'Well that's great, but I might have to make my excuses.' Tony noticed Vic raise his eyebrows, 'No wait a minute. I've heard from Imogen and Anita, they don't know where Diana is; they're worried. I'm going to have to go and look for her.'

He noticed a haunted look on Vic's face before Vic turned his head away.

'What?'

'I'm afraid I gave her some hints about how to find her father.'

Tony felt a surge of tension rise in his chest. He knew Vic's motives, but he was furious and hurt and desperately worried all at the same time

Vic winced, 'I'm sorry, you can probably guess why I wanted to help her.'

'I know, I know, you were relating it to yourself, but it isn't the same at all, you bloody idiot. If she's anywhere near him, then I need to go and sort it out.'

'But he ought to have a chance to know her. Surely he won't be horrible to his own daughter?'

'Won't he?' Tony said, clenching his fists until he felt his nails sharp in his palms.

Chapter Twelve

Pete was sitting waiting for the ferry to arrive. Kim should be on it with quite a small group. She had two women travelling in the car with her and another three had travelled as foot passengers.

There were double yellow lines all around the port, so they always arranged to meet in the terraced streets of Parkstone. The streets were lined with cars all down one side and were so narrow that they shut out the sky. Rows of sash windows overlooked the road; some had been modernised with aluminium frames. He pulled out a newspaper as though on a stakeout.

It was a rare moment for him to sit and reflect. He could hardly believe that Diana had arrived in his life and that she had so quickly weaved herself into his affections. 'She's had such a different background', he thought; 'Imogen and Anita will have influenced her with their values. I'm overjoyed that she's come to me and she's so like Mum. I want her to know me. Will she understand my life? That's the point.

'Elaine, how's she taken it? She knew I had a daughter. Yeh, Elaine's been a good girl. She'd never go against my wishes anyway.'

He always knew when she was upset. She had been hurt in the past. It was that that drew him to her. She was like an injured baby bird in his hand. He'd picked her out from all the women that he knew.

When he was young, he'd always been angry. He knew, now, that there was no reason. Most things went his way. He had an office; it had no expensive frills, but it was his command centre. Everything was controlled from there. He was building a strong reputation at the golf club. He was known as the man who got things done. Years ago, his ex., Anita, had been a nagging annoyance, and he'd tried threats to be sure that she would get rid of his baby. Then he picked up the paper and saw a birth announcement, 'Diana Maura Tomalty, daughter to Anita Tomalty.' Well, at that time he'd been determined that she wouldn't trap him.

Pete had made his choices, but at that time, he was an unhappy young man. He was transported back to those days. Busy all day, his only chance to think had been at the end of each day. When he had relaxed as the hot water poured over his back in the shower, he'd play out his regrets. If Mum had been alive, she would have been ecstatic about Diana Maura. He would have liked that. Did the newborn look like him, he'd wondered. Should he visit? No, idiot! He would not jeopardise the future.

You might think he had it easy, but this business was tricky. When he was an up and coming young man, there was always someone trying to muscle in on his patch. Gotta be tough. He had just finished his jiu-jitsu practice session. He decided to drop in on the office. He was always wary about who might be waiting in the narrow passageway which led to 'Angels Massages'. This time there was a figure there. Adrenaline pumped, and he went cold. He automatically looked behind him. An empty street there. Drawing nearer, he realised that the figure was a woman holding a furled umbrella. She was a petite blonde, he was filled with relief, 'You gave me a heart attack standing there darlin'.'

She rounded and seemed as disconcerted as he had been. 'I was just deciding whether to go in,' she said in a warm low voice. 'I probably won't. You go ahead of me.' and she waved him to the door.

Pete thought quickly. He lowered his tone, 'Did you want Angels? We won't bite you.'

He offered her an arm and she accepted as though clutching at someone saving her from drowning.

The poor little thing was shaking. 'Come on through, and we'll get you a nice cuppa tea.'

He opened the door for her, and she allowed herself to be shepherded through. Whatever she said was inaudible.

He could tell that she was well-spoken, so he wasn't sure what made him speak roughly, 'C'mon love, let's get you inside,'. Betty was just behind the door. She had probably realised that something was going on outside in the passageway.

'Two teas Betty, please?' he said as he rushed his visitor through to his office. Betty pulled a face but made no answer.

'Now,' Pete said, taking his seat behind the desk, 'tell me all about it.'

The young woman had gathered herself, 'I was just considering turning to prostitution, would you believe?' she said and placed her handbag on the floor beside her feet. 'I'm Elaine,' she stood up to reach across the desk to shake his hand.

'Pleased to meet you Elaine, you can call me Peter.' He watched her legs cross and her feminine hand movements as she explained that she'd just lost her job. 'I'm on my own bringing up my daughter. I have been for the last ten years. But it's got worse.'

Somehow Elaine had raised Pete's spirits. 'Let me see what I can do to help,' he said. Betty came in with the drinks, and he introduced Elaine as 'a friend of mine' who would like a job. 'Perhaps you could show her how you run the place?'

He had arranged for Elaine to meet him again for a meal on one of his boats. When she left, she looked so much happier. He remembered smiling all the next day. Sometimes fate dealt you a good hand. Life was hard, and Pete wanted some security.

Elaine, at first, had been more of a liability than he'd expected. Once past the dating phase, she confided that she had a mess of financial difficulties. His heart melted, and he asked her to move into his city-centre flat. When he had asked her to live with him, it was like taking in a rescue dog. Her gratitude ensured that she was strongly loyal.

Of course, there had been Kim as part of the package. When he'd been introduced to her, they'd all gone for a pizza.

'Hi,' he'd said. Kim had tossed her head and rolled her eyes. Pete had pressed his lips together and, at the time, said nothing; but he wasn't used to this kind of disrespect.

'Ah, teenagers. I hope you can be friends in time,' Elaine had said.

'I'm sure we'll get along just brill.' Pete had dealt with worse than her. He remembered Kim had been fascinated by his fast car and she loved going out to restaurants and even to the Rocky Horror Show.

He could see Kim had the same streetwise willingness to work that he had had when he was younger. She was a bit rough around the edges, but she was shaping up. He wasn't sure of her loyalty, so he had decided to keep an eye on her.

Elaine made sure that everything was as he needed it. She didn't get involved with his business anymore, but occasionally Betty visited her at the flat.

When Kim finished school, she kicked her heels around the city. He was scornful that Elaine had no control of her.

Pete remembered the day that the exam results were out, he'd walked in on Elaine crying. Reddened eyes were unattractive.

'No qualifications?' his mouth twisted.

She shook her head.

'Straight up? None? Where is she now?' he thumped down into his favourite chair and put his feet up on the coffee table.

'Well hardly any, but she's not bothered. She's gone off to see her friends.'

'Well, if she's not bothered,' he raised both of his hands in a gesture of defeat.

'She's going to end up in a dead-end job and get nowhere.' Elaine sniffed, reaching for a tissue.

He was getting impatient with this and threw out the solution, 'She can work for me.'

It didn't ensure peace. Elaine's chest heaved and her head jerked up, 'What, you want her to be a whore.'

'No, no,' he was surprised by her vehemence, 'she's family. I'll make a job for her as a business assistant. I'll explain her new role to her when she gets home.'

'But we aren't family, are we?' she argued, 'we aren't married. I am solely responsible for her future and,' she paused, and tears sprang into her eyes again, 'I'm scared.'

Pete smiled at the thought and sprang up to comfort her, 'Go on then gel,' he'd said, nudging her in the ribs, 'Marry me.'

Her eyes opened in amazement, 'You mean it?'

'Yeh, I mean it. Marry me.'

Pete's prolonged visit to his past was interrupted. He noticed a burly man stepping out of a front door, advancing three steps down his path and swinging open the tiny wrought iron gate to the street. He approached Pete and rapped on the driver window. This could only mean trouble. Pete lowered the window.

'Yeh,' Pete made it a growl.

'Can you move mate? I've got me wife coming home in a minute, and she's going to need this space.'

There's always one, Pete thought with a sigh. He built up bile and forced out, 'Fuck off. I'll move when I'm ready.' He pressed the control to raise the window. He was irritated with the thought that this could escalate, even though he was well able to look after himself. The man turned back to his house, swearing loudly and threatening to go to the police. Pete knew he was within his rights, so he turned on the radio and ignored him.

But he knew something was bothering him. His last few nights' sleep had been disturbed. He bit a hangnail and leant to select another radio channel. He knew what the problem was. He was worried about hanging on to Diana now he'd got her. After all, Elaine and Kim only had him to look out for them, but Diana had the whole network of Anita's group of friends. At the moment, Diana didn't know all about his businesses. It wouldn't be wise to let her know any more business secrets until she'd come to understand his world view. He could imagine that Imogen had sheltered her from facing any hardship. It had given Diana a trusting naivety.

A tiny red car pulled up alongside him, blocking the roadway. Kim, at last. She got out into the road, and he opened his car door.

'Bit of a tight squeeze in the car. Some of the women came in as foot passengers, and I picked them up on the Harwich side. Can they have a lift with you?' She shepherded three young women out of her passenger door and, like chickens released from the coup, they made their way over to the pavement. A pretty brunette, an older, taller woman and another with straggly mouse-coloured hair, who looked like she needed a good feed. Oh dear, was Kim out of her mind? Oh well – he gestured to them to get in and got back into the driving seat with a sigh.

CHAPTER THIRTEEN

Tony parked the car in a lay-by at a safe distance from the buildings on the hill. He walked the last mile through the woodland that surrounded 'Sunnyside's boundary wall. If he could be sure that Diana was in there, he planned to get over the wall and into the grounds. He would dodge behind the caravans to get close enough to attract her attention. He just wanted to speak to her. If she could reassure him that she was happy there and that she didn't want to leave, then fair enough.

Few windows were facing in his direction, so he would be able to stride across the tussocky grass to reach the front door unobserved.

He picked up a branch and trailed it behind. It might be some protection in case of attack. His heart thumping, he approached the farmhouse door. He hadn't expected to see an electronic camera and microphone. He comforted himself that Pete wouldn't recognise him after all these years, no one else apart from Diana would know who he was. He pressed the buzzer.

There was a crackling, and his image appeared on the camera. 'Hello' came an unfamiliar woman's voice. He heard a dog bark in the background.

He deliberately made himself appear bumbling, looming up to the camera and stuttering, 'Err I'm here with a survey.'

The door immediately opened, and Diana appeared. She looked wide-eyed but had the presence of mind to shout over her shoulder, 'Can you hold Caesar? It's okay, I can deal with it.' and then to Tony, 'I could see it was you, so I said I'd answer. What're you doing here?' she said urgently.

He leant in so that only she would hear, 'Is Pete around?'

'No he's gone out. It's just Elaine and me – she's his wife.'

He laughed with relief, 'It's good to see you. You've had everyone worried.'

'Oh, there was no need. I thought Vic would tell everyone where I was, if they needed to know.'

Tony straightened up a bit, 'Well we did need to know. I want to know whether you are staying here of your own free will. Are you happy? You aren't being pressured into anything that you don't want to do, are you?'

She took a glance behind her, 'I'm okay here. I know what I'm doing and I'll get in touch when I can.'

'Okay, okay,' Tony backed away, hands up, 'I just need to be able to tell your mother and Imogen and Lynette.'

'I promise I will phone or write so that everyone knows how I am,' she said and smiled reassuringly.

They both reacted to the clattering of dog claws on a wooden floor. Tony hoped the dog was still under control. 'See you do. You know we care about you.'

She flapped her hand close to her stomach to usher him away surreptitiously. 'Thanks, but it's easier if I go now.'

He turned to leave.

Diana looked worried and put her head on one side, 'You do understand?'

Tony nodded and then in the voice that carried, 'Well goodbye. Do get in touch.' As he stalked away, he felt disturbed. She said she was alright, but it didn't ring true. He remembered how he too, had felt capable of looking after himself when he was young. He understood, but he hoped that she wasn't being over-confident.

Chapter Fourteen

Elaine raised her eyebrows at Diana as she let go of Caesar's collar. 'So, was that one of your friends?'

'Yes, I suppose I should have let people know where I was.' Diana laughed, 'Geez, he was a bit dramatic though.'

'Yes, I heard him ask whether you were being pressured into anything. He wondered if you were safe.'

What was Elaine getting at? Had Tony's visit offended her? Diana shrugged, 'And I'm with my own dad. I'm very comfortable.'

'Are you sure?'

It was Diana's turn to raise her eyebrows, but Elaine had turned away. Elaine was okay; Diana enjoyed her company. Diana offered to take Caesar for a walk. As she strolled around the country lanes with him, she almost hoped to see Tony again, but he had gone. She spent the rest of the day in the house with Elaine.

They were spending a peaceful evening together until Elaine raised her head to listen. The front door opened and they heard people coming in. Elaine sprang up to greet them in the hall. Pete appeared, followed by a willowy girl with short, dyed blonde hair. She seemed a few years older than Diana, although she didn't have much make-up on. She was wearing a skinny t-shirt and jeans. The girl slid around Pete and sat down on the sofa.

Pete made an announcement before picking up the television controller to turn down the sound, 'Kim's been away working in Europe for a while. Now she's back.'

Elaine reappeared with a drink for Kim, but Kim barely acknowledged it. Her eyes bored into Diana. Her chin jutted out as she said, 'Pete told me you'd be here. He's asked me to help you if there's anything you need to know about the business.'

'That's the way, girls,' Pete said, sitting down in between them. He got out the map, 'Come on, Kim, show Diana where you've been.'

'Um,' Kim bent over it, 'let's see, I started over here,' and then she pointed to each town that she had visited.'

The study of a map drew Diana in, 'But what do you do when you're over there?'

'OK, I'll explain it,' Pete leaned back legs and arms spread, 'Through all my business connections here, I get to know quite a few lonely but respectable businessmen,' he dipped his chin in emphasis. 'So, I set up a marriage introduction service. They know me, and they know I'll be discreet.'

He smiled then went on to say, 'Then we need to find the right kind of girls from across Europe who want to come over here to marry. Girls who live in deprived areas are keen to come to England, and they jump at the chance of marrying a businessman. Kim here,' he put his hand on Kim's shoulder, 'she's good at making the first contact and they see her as a friend. Then Kim leads the group travelling together and explains how things work in England.'

He shifted to look at Kim, so Diana turned to hear her view, but she just said, 'Uh huh,' and looked towards the television.

He ignored her and turned his attention to Diana.

She said, 'Wow' and took a deep breath. 'All that travelling sounds like a dream job.'

'Yes,' Pete gave a broad smile that made Diana feel warm and relaxed, 'Eventually, you'll be able to go with Kim. You won't need to go to university. There are more opportunities here than you'll ever get through academic work.'

'Have you already been to any of these places?' he asked, pushing the map further along the coffee table towards her.

Diana shifted along the sofa, and as she did, she glanced across to where Kim sat impassively, apart from a slight curl on her lip. Diana felt a jolt but tried to show no reaction. The memory of that expression would burn into her. Maybe Kim was feeling jealous. A painful lump arose in her chest. Kim was already established as the daughter of the family. She worried that if Pete found her wanting, he might prefer Kim. I'll try to fit in with everyone and win Kim over, but I'm going to need to watch out for her, she thought.

They spent the rest of the evening around the television and, on the surface, there was harmony. Elaine disappeared to the kitchen, and for a while, Kim vanished too. Diana lost concentration on the programme. She was picturing Kim standing by the sink plotting against her with Elaine. But no, she should avoid getting paranoid. She had done nothing wrong. She expected Elaine would be sympathetic to her daughter, but surely, Pete wouldn't be as easily swayed.

CHAPTER FIFTEEN

Pete was a perfectionist. Elaine giggled when Diana noticed how long he spent in the bathroom each morning, 'It's the hair spraying.'

Diana could well believe it as she noticed him repeatedly smoothing his hair when he was preoccupied.

'One day he even ordered the music CDs by musical style – so don't move them!' Elaine sniggered behind her hand. At that moment, Pete walked into the room and stood just behind her.

Diana noticed Elaine go white, and her brain raced to try to think of a way of easing the situation.

So, she said, 'We'd just noticed your music collection. I was telling Elaine that I liked Donny Osmond and she's making fun of me.' She matched the story with a woebegone expression and a pout. Pete seemed mollified, and Elaine shot her a grateful look as she edged out to the kitchen.

By the time that Kim appeared for the evening meal, the incident was forgotten. She seemed to be busy every day and left the house early in the morning.

'Think you could take Diana with you tomorrow?' Pete asked while passing around bowls of Angel Delight.

Kim gave an 'mm,' and a slight nod.

'Yeh, I think it's time she learnt the ropes from you.'

Diana was still unsettled. She wanted to fit in, and she wasn't sure whether she made the grade. She felt a frisson of excitement when she went up to her bedroom that night. She could learn to model herself on Kim. What should she wear? Kim always wore leggings and oversized jumpers, but that wasn't Diana's style.

***

Kim was eating the last of her toast when Diana walked in the next morning. Kim sighed.

'S'pose I'd better wait for you.'

'No, don't worry. I often miss breakfast anyway,' Diana tossed her head and caught a glimpse of herself in the mirror. She looked cool.

'C'mon then.'

Kim leapt into a little Japanese runaround hardly waiting for Diana to get into the passenger side before roaring off. They swung around the country roads. She barely slowed down for the 'Stop,' signs on suburban roads. Diana sensed Kim's intense engagement in driving, so she avoided starting any conversation. Was it a deliberate ploy to avoid chatting? She was interested in the inner-city scene: colourful shop fronts crammed together in terraces and then rolling areas of open grass around high rise flats. Diana noticed women in hijabs, young people gathered in groups and elderly people leaning on sticks. She lurched against the seat belt as the car drew to an abrupt stop outside a printing shop.

'Shall I come in with you?'

'Can if you like,' Kim muttered as she opened the driver door. While Kim stood at the counter, Diana sat in a row of chrome chairs arranged in front of the plate-glass window. She saw Kim hand a file over the counter before joining her.

'What are you getting printed?' Diana asked.

'It's a catalogue. It's taken months to collect all the photos to create a glossy catalogue of brides.' She turned to face her and stuck her chin out, 'It's an unusual business, but it's not illegal, you know.' She folded her arms across her chest and leaned back with her head against the window.

'No, no, I hadn't even thought it was.' Diana said, 'Are they doing them while we wait?'

'No, they've gone off to get some leaflets I dropped off last time. It's to advertise membership. Pete hands them out to his contacts.'

The printer returned. Kim leapt back up to pay by card and carried away a bundle of leaflets. As they stepped out of the shop, Diana asked,

'Where're we going now?'

Kim looked irritated that she was being questioned. She strode to the driver's door and got in. Diana joined her in the passenger seat.

'Do you mind me tagging along?'

'Aww no, I don't really. I'm just tired, I suppose. It makes a change to have someone to talk to.'

Diana reached to take the leaflet bundle from Kim and stow them away in the glove compartment, but it was full of empty crisp packets and coke cans. She was taken aback but didn't show it and cleared what space she could. On impulse, she turned to Kim,

'I just want to get to know my dad. You see, I've wondered about him since I was little. I'm not trying to muscle in or get in the way of what you do.'

Kim acknowledged that she'd heard but started up the car.

Diana carried on, 'I might not like working for Pete, dad, . . . who knows. I had other plans and I could still do them.'

Kim turned her head slightly, 'What plans?'

'I've got a place at uni, to do languages,' Diana said quietly. 'My languages might help you talk to the girls.'

'That's it. You go girl' Kim gave a sharp laugh, 'No, I like that you've got something about you. But your languages probably won't help unless they're from somewhere in Eastern Europe.' As they drove on, she explained, 'I'm going to do some visits. Girls that come over here can stay in the caravans at the site, but after a while, I get them somewhere to rent.'

'You've made friends with them?'

Kim stopped, and with one eye watching for traffic lights to change, she said, 'It's more like part of my job. They get jittery if they don't get a husband straight away and especially if they don't know much English. I want to make sure that they're still okay. Let them know that we're still working on it for them.'

Chapter Sixteen

At the next stop, they got out on a narrow street and stood on the pavement to wait at a front door, until it was yanked open by a smiling young girl. Kim instantly painted on a bright smile, 'Diana, this is Jana.'

Jana moved sideways to let them enter. Kim led the way, and Diana tried not to show her reaction to the room ahead. It was full of belongings: boxes, vanity cases, chairs, files, rucksacks and suitcases, stacked precariously around the room. A restricted space had been cleared to allow access from the front door to the door into the back room.

Jana in the doorway ahead frowned anxiously, 'Can you walk around the the...'

'The clothes horse,' Kim supplied the phrase.

'Ah, the clothis horse.'

They edged sideways through a circuitous pathway. The second door opened onto a room with a threadbare rug and a sofa along one wall facing an unlit fire. Kim and Diana sat on the sofa while Jana picked up a stool to sit opposite.

Diana pulled her jersey across her body and hugged herself.

'I sorry, I can offer a drink? Will be warm?' Diana noticed Jana's red nose and rheumy eyes. Either she had been crying continuously, or she had a streaming cold. Deciding not to take a chance on germs, she said, 'No thank you.'

Kim leant forward to peer at Jana's face. 'Are you alright?'

'Oh, yes. I've just got a cold. I feel ill,' Jana sniffed loudly, pulling a balled-up tissue from her ribbed sweater sleeve.

'Hmm,' Kim said sharply, 'have you taken anything for it?'

Jana looked up in surprise and then shrugged, 'I not know what. I not know where to go.'

'OK,' Kim jumped up, 'I'm off to the chemist.' She strode back to the door, 'I'll be back soon.' Her voice softened, 'we have to look after you, you know.'

Diana, momentarily lost for words, smiled at Jana. She cast her eyes around the room, wondering how much English she understood.

'Did you learn English at school?'

Jana smiled back, blankly. 'Drink?'

'Oh no, thank you,' Diana shook her head, 'but don't let me stop you getting one.' She added, 'have you been in England long?'

I have been here since three. . . four weeks.' Jana frowned to herself, 'Kim, she bring me here.' Jana pointed ceilingward, 'Lucie and Eva they have been here long time.'

'So there are three of you,' Diana nodded encouragingly. Jana said, 'You are a friend of Kim?'

'Yes, no, well I've known her for a few days.' Diana said. 'Does she visit you a lot?'

Jana shrugged again. 'She comes to help us. We look for husband. Lucie is going to be married.' She smiled again, 'But Eva. No one chooses her? She is sad now. I am sad for her and . . .' her words came out in a rush, 'I am worried now. Maybe it happen to me.

'I am not happy now. I had saved money to come here. I want a good life and a good husband. Now I worry that it will happen to me. I no want to be in house of girls.' She leant towards Diana with a look of compassion, 'You got a husband?'

Diana felt like an imposter because Jana seemed to assume she was in a similar position. She cleared her throat, 'No, but I have family here.'

As though she hadn't heard, Jana went on, 'How I get money? You see, how you get job with no English? No one want you.'

Diana felt overwhelmed and unable to think of anything that could help. She thought of all the things that she'd learned in the last few days. 'What is Eva going to do?'

Jana had shut down and blankly said, 'Saw a man. Who know?'

'Man?' Diana asked, but Jana had closed her eyes and sunk into her chair.

Diana looked around at the tobacco-tinged the wallpaper and the 1940s tiled fireplace with a dark empty grate. Her own feelings echoed Jana's depression. In the beginning, Diana had imagined that everyone benefitted from the marriage agency.

Diana hadn't heard anything, but Jana must have had acute hearing; she sprung away like a conspirator, 'She comes back,' and Kim returned.

'Here you are,' she dumped a chemist's bag onto a small coffee table. 'Make this up with boiling water and drink every four hours.' She held up a packaged medicine bottle, 'and take this, it'll dry up your cold. Stop your sniffing. And put some make-up on for fuck's sake, you're letting yourself go.'

'I'll be back. See y'later,' and she gestured to Diana to get up and follow.

'Nice to meet you,' Diana added as they left the room.

Chapter Seventeen

Eventually, Kim pulled up at the end of a terraced row, where there was a greasy spoon café. They stood side by side at the glass and chrome food counter to order.

At the table, Kim played with the salt and pepper pot. She poured salt onto the brushed chrome tabletop and traced patterns in it. Diana felt irritated but didn't comment.

She decided to speak in the hope of diverting Kim, 'Is this a typical day for you when you're back in England?'

'Yeh,' Kim paused and looked thoughtful, 'What about your mum, what's she like?'

'She's an actress. You might have heard of her - Anita Tomalty.'

'Mmm,'Kim tilted her head, 'What has she been in?'

'Mainly theatre, but you might've seen her on TV in ''Tenko'. She was one of the women in a prison of war camp, and she's had some parts in soaps.'

'Maybe I have then, is she quite old now but glamorous?'

'That's right with long red hair.'

Kim scrutinised her, 'Maybe you look a bit like her – the high cheekbones. You don't look like Pete.'

Diana felt a stab of pain on hearing this. 'Oh, I don't know, I think the shape of my face might be a bit him.'

Kim laughed, 'You think a lot of him, don't you?'

She forced herself to laugh back, 'It's awesome. At last, I've got a father.'

Kim was hard to read; she seemed both friendly and prickly. She didn't reply immediately. She looked out of the window and said, 'I haven't seen my father for years, but it's his loss. He left Mum and started a new family with someone else. I don't know, I might look him up sometime.' Kim lifted her chin and looked Diana in the eyes.

Diana remembered Vic's hurt. She met Kim's eyes and said, 'It is his loss. Look at you travelling across Europe. You're getting on with your life.'

Kim gave a slight smile. 'Hard on Mum though.'

'Yes, how did your mum and Pete get together?'

A shadow passed across Kim's face. 'Oh, I don't know.' She returned her fingertip to the spilt salt. 'I'm not sure that it was any great love, but she always seems to need some fella. Pete's been good to me, though. When his business does well, I do well.'

'Elaine seems nice.'

'Yeh, she's not bin a bad mum. She has her moments, and I've stuck by her. She's coping at present.'

Diana leaned her forearms on the table. 'Is she though? She seems a bit overshadowed by Pete.'

'Their business, not ours.' Kim's head snapped up, but she gave Diana a look that softened her answer. It was perhaps a sore point, and Diana decided not to say anymore. She felt sad for Kim. Their lunch had arrived on the counter and she sprang up to bring the plates over.

'Anyway' Kim said, squeezing tomato sauce all over her bacon roll, 'shit music isn't it?' She shouted across to the counter, 'Can't you put on something decent?'

The lad in a stripy apron behind the counter gave a gentle smile in acknowledgement and carried on working at the coffee machine.

'What music are you into?' Kim bit and chewed while waiting to hear from Diana.

'Oh, the usual. I've been busy at school so I listen to Radio One when I'm revising. I used to hang out with my friend Clare - at her house mostly. I lived in a hotel, which wasn't a great place for us to hang out. We went to a few gigs together.'

'How about electronic dance music, eh? You can just switch off and get lost in the beat.'

Diana had barely listened to that type of stuff. 'So, that's raves isn't it? Have you been to a rave?'

'Wow, yeh. It starts as a kinda treasure hunt. You get your tickets and then it's a hella adventure to find it. There's an easy vibe at raves y'know? No matter who you are: black, white, rich, poor, everyone's just into the sound.'

'Yeh, you need a car to get to them,' Diana commented.

'Come to one with me. You'll love it.'

'What do you wear?'

'Don't be a wimp. No one cares. Just something that lets you dance. Jeans, shorts, hoodie . . .'

'Thanks,' Diana felt herself beaming despite not wanting to appear uncool. Things might work out with Kim after all.

Chapter Eighteen

Diana was up for a carefree night out. It would be an adventure with Kim just as she had had adventures with Clare in the past. They rolled up outside a large warehouse set back from trees on the edge of an industrial estate. She followed Kim's lead, remembering not to ask too many questions that would annoy her. Kim had been right, there was a carefree atmosphere and those going to the rave were friendly and chilled.

Boom tung tung, boom tung tung permeated the site and bounced in Diana's ears. The sweet incense swirled around her as she steered a way through the throng of bodies. For as far as she could see, heads bounced randomly to their own different beats. Kim disappeared into the crowd and came back with some pills.

'Here you'll need these,' she said into Diana's ear.

Diana hesitated. Kim must have done this before, she thought, and Diana didn't believe in being one of life's observers, so she took the plunge. Kim shouted to her over the noise and waved a pair of white gloves in her direction. Nearby groups were voguing. Diana noticed a boy, or maybe it was a girl, in a loose-fitting mustard-coloured shirt and a boy in tightly fitting white silk trousers making flamboyant hand shapes as they danced with gloves on. They were highlighted like puppets in the dim light. She tried it, but she was so hot and sweaty that she soon threw off the gloves and then she threw off her jacket. She marvelled at this new experience. It was totally rad. She could understand the pull of the beat, the sound enticed her body to meld into it.

How long had it been? Hours. Time had stopped and floated away in the dry ice fog. Kim danced rhythmically beside her all this time. She turned to her now, but there was no longer any Kim. No matter. Kim could certainly look after herself. Still stomping, she gradually worked her way through the crowd towards the entrance.

Outside the fresh air assailed her skin and hit the back of her throat. She felt more morning-alive than she had ever felt. She was still part of all of the happy groups of people. Other individuals had trickled outside too. She made her way across the rough turf to look for the car. Fortunately, metallic, Japanese vehicles like Kim's were uncommon, so she spotted it easily. She would have loved to fall into the car, but Kim was nowhere to be seen. She may have to go back into the throng to find her. She ambled closer, leant against the cold steel door frame, and dipped her head to peer in. There was someone or something on the back seat. It was Kim curled up. When Kim noticed the movement, she turned her head to look at Diana.

'Get in,' her arm beckoned lazily.

Diana slid into the driver's seat just in front of Kim's legs and reached through the seats to her.

'Are you OK?'

'Yeh, yeh, I'll be awight in a minute,' Kim winked and heaved herself up on her elbow. 'Shoulda taken more. I came down too early.'

Of course, Diana remembered now, it was only because she'd taken something earlier that she'd been able to manage intense hours of movement. She tuned inwards to listen to her body. She still felt a bit wired but on the cusp of exhausted.

'Will you be OK to drive home?'

Kim groaned, 'Oh no, not yet.' She swung her legs down to sit upright on the back seat. 'It's Sunday tomorrow so they'll be sleeping in. It's better if we arrive back, late morning. We don't want Caesar's barking to wake them.' She looked around stupidly. 'Wish I had something to drink.'

Diana grabbed a bottle of water from the glove compartment and passed it through to the back. They took it in turns to take a swig.

Greater numbers of people were walking past the car now, some still dancing to their own internal beat, and some looking for their cars. They watched as those cars that did start got stuck in the mud. It didn't seem to be a problem for long. Good-natured volunteers crowded around the rear of each stranded car to push. The helpers came away laughing covered in an icing layer of mud.

'Cool, we'll be able to watch the sunrise,' Diana said, and they sank into silence. But she felt twitchy. Whatever she'd taken couldn't have worn off yet. She hated being bored, too.

'So, tell me more about these girls. Where've you been in Europe?'

'Oh, you know. Prague – there's a great rave scene there. But I've been all over.'

'So once the girls want to sign up with us, who pays for their glossy pictures. We do, I suppose?'

'We just rent a photography studio, and I take the pictures, but yes we pay for the glossy brochures. What's with all the questions?'

'I'm trying to get my head around it. What do the girls do all day while they wait for a husband to take the bait? And what happens if someone they don't like wants to marry them?'

'They don't have to do it, but they'd be fools to turn down a well-off husband.'

Diana had caught Kim at an opportune moment to probe for the truth; her heart began to race. 'Are all the girls pretty?'

Kim shrugged.

'Well, what happens if no one chooses a particular girl to marry? What does she do then?'

'They should go back, but they don't,' Kim shrugged again and then threw herself back to rest on the headrest.

Diana was distracted by a group of lads who were walking close to the car. One of them, wearing a back-to-front cap and denim dungarees, thumped on the roof of the car and gave a whoop, but it was all in good spirits. Diana, on impulse, copied his yell and lifted her t-shirt up to her neck, exposing her lacey bra. She heard more hoots, as they all passed. She was excited at the effect she'd had.

Kim sat up straighter and slowly shook her head. 'You shouldn't be let out. What are you doing?' She glared at Diana, 'The trouble with you is, you've had it too easy. You don't know what it's like in the real world.'

'I'm learning,' Diana said in a small voice.

Kim clenched her fists. 'The girls who come over and don't make good marriages. . . they get filtered down to the bottom. They're left behind. They had hope, and suddenly they have none. They get work alright,' her eyes flashed, 'they get work in one of Pete's brothels.'

Diana went cold. 'Wha. . .'

'Yeh, you're thinking about the boats and the marriage business,' Kim crowed, 'but how do you think he got the money to start out with boats? Ducking and diving that's how. Sucking up to the oily men with power.' She had raised her voice, but now there was silence.

Diana needed time to take it in. She glanced at Kim and saw her breathing heavily. 'Here have some more water.' She handed a fresh bottle over to the back seat. She felt like crying. 'So you're saying that Pete, what – manages brothels. Does he force the girls to work there?'

Kim sighed and said in a weary voice, 'He finds girls who are desperate and who haven't got much support anywhere else. He only has to give them a few encouraging words and make them feel special, and they're grateful for it.'

'You make it sound like he sets traps.'

'I'm sure he'd be just as happy if these girls found well-connected husbands who'd be in his debt, but prostitution is an equally good option as far as he's concerned.'

Diana was horrified. Had Anita been one of his 'girls'? She wanted to run to her mother and ask. She wanted to protect her mother. If Anita had been involved, Pete could be blackmailing her over it.

'I don't know what to say. It makes me question everything. What about your mum? Was she one of his workers?'

'Mum hasn't gone into detail about her past, but yes, I guess so.' In the dim light of dawn, Diana could see tears glistening in Kim's eyes. Even Kim could be emotional, especially when it was about her mother. Diana felt closer to her.

'It doesn't have to be like this. We could help Elaine start a new life and get a proper job. She's not an old person yet. I could get my family to help you both.'

Kim sounded defeated, 'Don't. How does anyone get a job when they have no legitimate work experience? I've never paid National Insurance, so I don't think I could claim benefits. You think you can just leave this world – as if! I've seen girls try, but the fear that someone will find out that they were 'on the game' haunts them.'

Diana felt her jaw tense. She wanted to brush away these obstacles. 'Elaine looks downtrodden. She can't go on like that. Let's do something about it together, now.' She grabbed Kim's hand and looked her in the eyes. 'Imogen brought me up in a hotel. So that's somewhere to live. I bet she could give Elaine a job there. And you, if you want. He can't hurt you, not if we go to the police.'

'Thanks for worrying about Mum. You're a good kid. I'm not going to lie, you've got me thinking, but you're wrong. I'm fine. Pete doesn't treat me badly, and Mum has got a better life now than she ever expected to have. He looks after us.' Diana felt doubtful, and she could see that Kim knew that, but Kim didn't continue trying to persuade her. She reached for the car door handle. 'Listen we need to drive home, then have a shower, and we can think the whole thing through later.'

Chapter Nineteen

Diana and Kim were like dreary sloths at Sunday lunch. Pete stole occasional glances their way. He didn't ask them what was wrong, but Diana noticed that his jaw was tense. She wondered if she was in disgrace.

She couldn't help seeing Elaine with new eyes; searching for clues to her past in her present self. It was hard to look at Pete: a man who viewed women as commodities with less worth than men, yet she believed that he'd loved his mum. So she wondered, how did he really see her even though she was his daughter, and what did he think of Anita? The realisation came that his outward charm masked a darker self.

Even though she had been up for a few hours now, her eyelids still felt weighted. At the end of the meal, she made her excuses and went up to bed. She meant to lie on top of the covers and read, but, within moments, she had drifted off to sleep.

She awoke with a start. Was it night-time already? The room had grown dark. The half-opened curtains revealed that the darkness was caused by a sky of threatening clouds. She chafed her bare arms with her palms. She was chilled. How long had she been asleep? The digital clock showed 15:00. So where was everyone?

She could hear voices rising downstairs. Pete sounded agitated. Were Elaine and Kim in trouble? Her arms and legs were as heavy as damp sandbags, but she forced herself to move first her arms and then her legs. She gently eased her bedroom door open and peeked down the stairs. The voices seemed to be coming from the office. She tiptoed onto the top step to get near enough to hear. With one hand pressed flat on the wall and using the other to grip the bannister, she could rest the toes of each foot at the sides of each step to avoid creaks. By easing herself down each step, she reached the halfway point down the stairs, where she was able to hear.

Kim's voice, 'It's what you wanted, isn't it?'

'But a rave. . .'

'You asked me to show her the ropes, and you should be glad that I had my eye on her. I couldn't believe she turned so fast. She's not like us she's still wet behind the ears; she thought you were Father Christmas and Batman all in one.'

'Well – she's my daughter. So now she knows more, is she shocked?'

'It was a surprise. She's determined to save us from you. She talked about the police.'

'The police. Didn't you tell her that there's nothing illegal in a mail-order bride business? There's nothing wrong with it. I blame you, Kim. It's what you've said to her. If I'd told her, she'd have understood.'

'Oh, so it's all my fault, is it? She was bound to look down her nose — little Miss Posh.'

Pete raised his voice, 'Don't come that with me. She isn't posh. She just needed to understand.'

'Tell her yourself then. Explain.'

Silence.

His voice dropped, she could hardly hear him, 'We need to tidy things up a bit in the businesses. That's all. She hasn't gone to the police so far, so she could calm down again.'

'Huh.'

'We just need time. I can't lose her.'

'Why not?'

Pete's angry voice again, 'Why not? – That's what you want isn't it'. There was a squeal of pain. Diana heard a flurry of noise and Kim emerged in the living room doorway, panting and dishevelled. She looked up and spotted Diana on the stairs. Pete appeared behind her and immediately followed Kim's gaze. In an instant, he used both hands to push her. Kim went sprawling across the hall floor as he launched himself up the stairs at Diana.

Diana turned and scrambled for the top of the stairs but felt Pete's grip around her ankle. No sounds but panting. She felt him pulling at her ankle, and her body jarred as it was dragged over the carpeted stair edges. His weight was on top of her and took the breath out of her lungs. Her arms were pinned to her sides. She kicked out, but it was useless.

She heard Kim's voice, 'Give 'er what for. Little know-it-all.'

'Get out Kim,' Pete said, 'Just get out if you know what's good for you.' Diana's thoughts raced. While he was distracted by Kim, could she slide away from him? He was too heavy. There was a scrabbling noise, and the front door slammed as Kim left. Diana's fleeting thought was that Kim had chosen to put her own selfish needs first.

Pete lurched sideways and yanked on her arm to drag her down to the bottom step. He held her by both arms. His grip was surprisingly firm, and his face was too close to her's. She tried to avoid looking at him. His features were twisted in anger.

'Get off. How dare you,' she screeched as loudly as she could, perhaps Elaine would hear and come running. 'You're supposed to be my father.'

Pete's nostrils were flared and he was breathing hard. He gasped out, 'You haven't given me a chance. You didn't give me a chance. You've ruined it.'

She couldn't speak, her mouth filled with saliva, and her tongue felt enlarged. She gulped, 'Ruined what? The disgusting way you use women? Did you treat my mum like that?'

In a low, determined voice, he said, 'You don't know anything about anything. I've not even seen her.' She was amazed to see tears in his eyes, but he was still gripping harshly – tears of anger. 'I've fought for everything I've got. You're my daughter! You could have been a part of it.'

Diana was trying to understand his reasoning. He'd put her in a different category from all other girls. You can't split off the way you treat women. He was her father, and she hated the idea of letting him down, but how could she give up on those poor girls. She couldn't let it go on. Looking around the hallway, could she struggle to distract him. Would she be able to bite him? Where was Elaine? Surely, Elaine wouldn't let this happen?

'Dad', she tried, 'What are you doing? I can't believe you're hurting people. You can run a business without that.'

He sat and faced her, still holding onto her upper arms. His chest noticeably rose and subsided. 'Who am I hurting? I've built up a good business and I reward loyalty. You could have a great future with me.'

'Can't you stop the illegal parts?' she didn't believe that he'd listen, but she had to try, 'I wanted you to be proud of me,' tears came to her eyes, 'but instead, I'm ashamed of you.'

He gritted his teeth and gripped tighter, 'Don't judge me, Diana.'

'I can't stay if you do this. I can't be part of it.' She desperately tried to think of a way to explain why it was wrong and how it repulsed her, but her desperation about their relationship took over, 'I want us to be a proper father and daughter.'

Silence. 'So what is it. . . . you don't agree with? The girls who make their money out of prostitution?' She thought, was it that? No, it was more, 'I don't agree when they have no other hope. If they want to do it, it should be their own decision. Then they need to take responsibility for it.'

'It is their decision.'

'But you wait until they have no friends or relatives for support and then you present them with that option as though it's the only one.'

He shook his head vigorously, 'Point is - what are you planning to do about it?'

She bit her lip, 'I don't know. I don't want to be the one to cause you trouble. . . why does everything have to be so complicated?' She couldn't help but give in to crying.

'You need to trust me,' his voice softened. 'You're right, at the beginning I was bending the law because it was the only way, but perhaps I can phase out the business that you aren't happy about.' Pete screwed up his eyes, 'I feel for people. I worry about my girls. Some of them come to me when they're upset. I've even lent them money. And look how happy Kim is working for me. When you know a bit more about the world you will understand, it isn't black and white.

'I had to survive on my own wits. I had to learn how the world works and who to get to know. There were no introductions for me, and I had no money behind me.'

He loosened his grip now, and tension slackened as they sat on the carpeted steps.

'Look, my mother was in a lot of pain, and she used to get depressed at what she couldn't do. She wanted a life for me and she knew she was letting me down. I see you in her.' He reached to stroke her cheek.

'Didn't she disapprove of what you got into?'

'She would have. She had to go into a home in the end, though. It wasn't like she could come checking up on me.'

Diana began to believe, to hope, that she could help him to change. He wasn't all bad. She remembered to ask, 'But what happened with Tony?'

'What?' he faltered, 'You've changed the subject completely. Who is Tony?' he said.

'Just before I came here, I saw Tony and his partner Vic. I heard that you'd threatened to 'out' Tony years ago.'

'Oh, Anita's friend. I hardly remember it to be honest.' He shifted slightly and looked away. 'I wasn't ready for Anita being pregnant. I was only a lad meself. Tony got between the two of us. We were sorting it out. He should have kept out of it.' He looked at her with a soft look in his eyes, 'Of course, this was before you were born. If I'd had the chance to see you and to hold you, I'm sure I'd have fought to be a part of your life.'

This explained the cuttings that he'd kept hidden. Her heart went out to him. He'd been a young boy with none of the family that most people drew on for security and backing.

He put his forehead to hers, and she felt his hair tickle her skin, 'All that time not knowing you. You are so precious to me, now that I've had that chance. I don't want to lose you - not again.'

Diana's heart melted, 'You won't.'

He pulled her towards him. She leant her head against his chest. She could hear his heart thumping.

'Sure?' he whispered. 'And we'll see what we can do about cleaning up this business a little.'

She sat up and found some tissues in her jeans. Diana wiped her eyes and offered some to him; then he blew his nose. She couldn't help smiling at him now. Maybe they were beginning to understand each other and to grow closer.

'What about Kim?' She remembered his argument with Kim and the slap that she'd heard.

'Oh, she's jealous. She thinks you've moved into her territory, that's what it is. I'll talk to her. Win her round. She's a bit of a loose cannon at the moment.'

Later, back in the bedroom, Diana hugged herself and considered all that they'd said. She felt a true warmth towards him as a person now, not just towards him as a 'dad' symbol. Perhaps she could bring Anita to see him. Maybe they could finally go some way to being a united family.

Chapter Twenty

There was a new closeness between father and daughter. She sensed that they walked in step. He started to say 'cool' just like her, and she began to pick up his obsession with tidiness. Kim had been despatched on another European trip soon after the weekend of the rave. Pete took Diana everywhere with him. She was now fascinated to learn more about brothels. Were the girls who worked in them just like her or had they got a different outlook on life?

Pete kept control of each of the businesses by dropping in at arbitrary times. He took Diana along to the boat business. She was introduced to 'Fair Isle', his name was Lee.

Lee walked up the path towards the car to meet them as they parked on the road nearest to the booking office. He seemed diffident.

'Well this is an enthusiastic welcome,' Pete smirked. Lee scowled and looked down. Pete laughed and nudged Diana.

'He's not happy because we didn't bring Kim,' then he raised his voice to Lee, 'She's too good for you son.'

Lee said nothing but Diana noticed his sidelong look at her. She felt sorry for him, it must have been annoying to have an audience for this encounter.

Diana was prepared to see Betty when they entered the hut. Remembering to exercise discretion, she didn't ask where

Betty was. Lee lifted a stackable stool from a corner so that his visitors could sit beside the office desks.

'So, we need to plan for the next introduction event,' Pete pulled out a file of papers and ordered them in a row across the desk. 'You clean and smarten up the boat,' he looked up at Lee, 'I'll leave a list of men and Betty can send out the invites.'

Pete turned to Diana and said, 'Kim is always at the introduction events because she knows the girls. They get glammed up, and we lay on nibbles and drinks so that men here can meet them for the first time. You attend it with Kim. It's just a babysitting job really so you'll enjoy yourself.'

Diana couldn't imagine it. Whereas she might have clung to Kim for a lead in the past, now she was dreading meeting up with Kim again. She noticed a subtle brightening of Lee's expression. Perhaps there was something between them, although Kim had never mentioned him.

CHAPTER TWENTY ONE

Diana loved the idea of a party, but this was different. She felt responsible for it going well, and anxious that there was something 'not quite right' about the whole thing.

She hadn't asked how partygoers indicated that they were matched up, but when the group of girls surged onboard, she noticed a clutch of coloured cards tucked into their evening bags. A tall girl hung back to adjust her sling-back shoe. Diana asked her what the cards were.

'You give them to the men that you are likely to meet again,' the girl had said with a flick of her hair as she hurried after the others, 'you'll need to get some too.'

She had expected a formal cocktail party, but it was much more fun. Two colours of strobe lighting danced across the two floors. The upper floor was a balcony furnished with tables overlooking the dance floor below. She went up to the balcony so that she could have an overview of what was going on. It was quieter up there. Hanging over the railings, she could see the crowns of everyone's heads. It was a useful way to observe without being observed. The girls all looked glamorous in every colour of long and short dress. How could they afford them? Already, a fug of tobacco smoke surrounded them in mist, which was highlighted by beams of the strobe lights and then blended back into the dark again.

She spotted Jana. Her make-up was so sophisticated that she almost missed recognising her. Jana was standing in a group of girls who were keeping close to each other. They looked nervous, but as she watched, they split up in different directions and targeted individual men.

Diana knew she should be mingling and checking that all was well. The buffet table looked wonderfully tempting too. She swung down the metal stairs to join the throng. She couldn't hear what was being said over the sound of the beat. The only way to be heard was to speak into someone's ear, so those who were having conversations were thrust into intimacy. Were these men really so easily flattered? To Diana, it was obvious that the girls were playing a role and laughing over-enthusiastically at whatever the men said. Some of the music wasn't bad. She found herself moving in time with 'Love Shack.'

A man in a suit approached, 'Wanna dance?' He was tall, she had to look up uncomfortably to see him.

'No, no thank you,' she shook her head to get the message over. The strong smell of tobacco and beer and the movement of the engine underfoot was making her feel queasy. She didn't fancy anything from the buffet anymore. She had trouble making her way through the crowd. People didn't hear her say 'excuse me'. Where was Kim?

Over by the buffet, there was a sudden clatter and female gasps. She craned her neck but there was a crowd gathering and she couldn't see what was going on. Surely this was the job that she was here for. By gently pushing, she managed to get herself to the area of the incident. The music ceased, but the roar of mingled voices was almost as loud. The tall girl that she'd spoken to earlier was lying in the middle of the group, her dress ruckled up and her legs ungainly. Diana's heart missed a beat.

'Give her air,' she yelled at the people nearest to her while looking around again for Kim, but there was no sign of her. Diana pushed herself forward, catching the back of her hand on someone's sharp bracelet. She knelt beside the girl. Her eyes looked odd and she had a twisted expression. Was she having a stroke? Was she breathing? Suddenly the girl jerked and focused her eyes on Diana. The girl attempted to struggle to her feet and once in a kneeling position, she hit out wildly at the legs of the people surrounding her. A space cleared and people began to turn away.

'Are you alright?' Diana said.

The music started up again and drifting groups edged back around them intent on the food. She would have helped the girl to her feet, but her flailing arms were a danger. Kim appeared at her shoulder.

'What's happened now?' she sounded irritated. Diana wasn't prepared for a shouted discussion and ignored Kim. She concentrated on helping the girl to rise by offering her an arm.

'See if you can get your balance.'

The girl looked disorientated. Potato salad was splattered down one side of her dress. When she stood up, Diana beckoned her away from the crowds and led her into the galley. She steered her towards a stool.

'Do you want me to get someone for you?' she asked.

The girl shook her head. Diana wondered what she could do next. She grabbed a cloth to wipe down the girl's dress. If it had happened to her she would have wanted to have a friend with her. Rows of sparkling glasses were stacked on trays beside them. Diana seized a glass and held it under the tap.

'Look, what's your name? You must have come with someone.'

'I'm Chiara,' the girl said, taking a sip from the glass.

'How are you feeling now?'

'Okay,' Chiara finally became aware of her. 'Why what has happened?' She looked down at her clothes and gasped. 'What's all this? Did someone throw this food at me? I can't join in the party looking like this.'

Diana realised that this might be an ideal opportunity to get off the boat and speak to Betty in private.

'Don't worry, I'll look after you.' She bent to look at Chiara and said, 'We'll get off. Some fresh air will help too. Wait there.'

She left the galley and hunted around for Kim. Now that she had a plan, she didn't want Chiara to wander off and remove her excuse. She spotted Kim, edged close to her then spoke into her ear.

'Chiara isn't well. Can you get the crew to pull in? I need to get her off the boat.'

Kim briefly nodded and said, 'Get her to the deck and wait for me to speak to them.'

***

The evening air hit them like plunging into an icy lake in spring. As soon as the rumble beneath their feet ceased, Diana grabbed Chiara's hand and shouted.

'When I say 'Go', jump.'

She landed on the hard-packed towpath, jarring her knees. Chiara, by her side, looked relieved to be on land. The boat was chugging away. Diana felt released. She guessed that walking in the opposite direction to that of the boat would eventually lead back to the boarding area.

Chapter Twenty Two

As they walked, Diana glanced at Chiara. Tears were streaming down her cheeks.

'D'you want to talk about it?'

Chiara shook her head, 'I don't know. It was the lights. I still feel strange, but I was glad to get away – some of those men weren't very nice.'

'That makes two of us. I'm glad to get away too.' Diana strode out with even more vigour.

'Chiara was struggling to keep up in high heel shoes.

'But I worry what will happen now,' she stopped to take a breath, 'If I don't get a husband.'

Diana didn't know what to say. This was all new to her, and she couldn't think her way through the maze of 'what ifs'.

Betty was sitting in the booking office. She barely looked up, 'Back so soon?'

Diana pulled out a stool for Chiara and threw herself down on an office chair. She turned to Betty, 'Yes Chiara here wasn't well. She needed to get away from the noise and flashing lights.'

At this, Betty stopped working at the computer and got up. 'I'll put on the kettle.' She shook her head. 'The poor girl.'

Chiara sat for a short while and then said, 'I don't want to stay here until they come back – thank you for helping me, but I'm going home.' She smiled at Diana, 'What about you? Are you going to be okay?'

'Yes, I'll be fine,' Diana nodded, and as Chiara left she called, 'Good luck, Chiara.'

When she had gone, Betty moved to sit closer and placed her hand on Diana's arm, 'So you found 'im then.'

'My dad, yes, I did, thank you. I've been getting to know them all, but it's made me freak out a bit. Everything's different.'

Betty chuckled, 'Yes Pete's got his own way of doing things, he's not too bad, mind. You'll have met Elaine. She used to be around when I worked on reception for Pete. I had a soft spot for her.'

'Yes, she's nice. I'm not so sure what Kim thinks of me.'

'Ah, well no. Kim's alright, but she's been the golden girl so far, getting trained up in the business.'

Diana was sure that was it, and she couldn't blame her. She wondered why Betty stayed around Pete's businesses. He seemed to like a glamorous workforce and Betty didn't fit in.

'She'll get used to you.' Betty continued, 'I'm a bit like a mum to Pete, though I'm sure he'd never admit it. I've got a soft spot for the lad too because he's been good to my Elaine. He did right by her. I was at their wedding. It were lovely, a real happy ending.' Betty's face softened.

'Mm,' should Diana disagree. It seemed a pity to disillusion her, yet she spoke quickly without any more thought, 'Well I don't know,' Diana stopped mid-sentence to change the subject, 'you must know more about the business, but I worry about the girls from abroad.'

'It's their choice. They take a gamble and sometimes it works out for them, and then sometimes,' Betty trailed away. She narrowed her eyes, 'What d'ya mean you don't know about Elaine? You've been there with her, when all said and done.'

'It's just a feeling. I haven't seen Dad do anything bad to her, but she acts scared to do the wrong thing around him. He seems more loving and easy around Kim than he does around Elaine. I don't know . . . ' Diana hadn't analysed the situation until then, 'Kim told me that she was one of the . . .' what did you call them to be polite? 'One of the girls too. So, I realise she's gained security, but she seems more like a servant to me and no, I don't think she's happy.'

Betty bit her lip and sat in silence. Her face hardened. 'I warned Pete that he were to look after her. I've stood by him all these years and kept 'is secrets. He thinks nothing can touch 'im, that's his problem.'

Diana realised she had lit a touchpaper and needed to stand back before the firework went off. Betty fell back again into a silence that Diana didn't feel able to interrupt. Instead, she turned her mind to her own conundrum, Kim. She couldn't help liking her. Kim was fun, but she wasn't sure whether Kim was a loving daughter to Elaine or not. Again, sometimes she seemed to stand up for the girls but was she cold-hearted and scheming inside?

Betty seemed to wake from her trance. 'I need to see Elaine for myself. I know she's in a big house in the country, but she might be better off with me. I don't know. . .' she shook her head to herself. 'I thought Pete had 'is heart in the right place. I know too much for him to cross me.'

Diana had agreed to give him a chance to change things. Now, somehow she'd started something with Betty. It upset her to think that she would cause trouble for Pete. She wanted to be a loyal daughter, but she was curious. She needed the facts to judge, so she said, 'Oh' in a small, questioning voice.

It prompted Betty, 'Oh yes, I've been here so long, quietly getting on with it. I know how he outsources to Albania for fake passports because I'm the one who deals with them. I know how they get here.' She began to speak through gritted teeth, 'I've got a list of all the girls, one way and another. And, I know quite a bit about the favours he's took in return for matchmaking. It'd make your hair curl.'

Betty bit her lip and frowned. She grabbed Diana's forearm with a surprisingly firm grip. 'This could change everything, you know.'

Diana caught her breath, 'Why what are you planning.'

'We need to save them, love.'

'Maybe you're right.' she said slowly, 'Not just Elaine, but all the rest. Though I wonder whether Elaine would thank us. It's difficult, Pete's my dad - he'd think I'd gone against him. Maybe we could change things from within.'

Betty humphed a laugh.

What would Imogen and Lynette say? 'No, you're right. We need to do something.' She felt a sick feeling at the enormity of the decision. She gulped and made herself square up to going ahead with whatever came. 'Fight the good fight with all your might,' popped into her mind.

'So what's the next move? Can we talk to the police?' Diana wondered.

Betty pursed her lips, 'It has to be me because I've got the information.'

Diana was galvanised to move fast before Kim and the girls returned. 'Right, how do we get proof?'

Betty scuttled across to her desk. 'I'll print out lists from the computer, and there are some copies of faxes locked away.' She threw open drawers and rifled through the papers, then held one aloft. 'This is useful.'

The door handle rattled and, almost immediately, Lee strode in. Diana leant forward and propped her elbow on the table to look relaxed. Betty wasn't as successful, she froze.

'I saw Chiara across there. What's been going on?' Lee looked from one to the other.

He spotted a pile of papers beside Betty. It took a moment for him to work out what was happening, then he rushed over and swiped them away. 'Should've known you couldn't be trusted. We'll all be in the shit.'

He flung the print-outs, and they fell to the floor in a flurry of paper. 'Have you been to the police?' he spun from one to the other.

He didn't wait for an answer before throwing open the door of the hut. 'I'm warning Pete. He'll stop you.' They heard him outside and jangling metal.

Diana tried the door. They were trapped. Her alarm was reflected on Betty's face. They heard steel shutters being trundled down over the window and secured at the bottom.

'Least he can't tell Pete quickly.' Betty said, 'We've got the phone.'

'The phone,' Diana leapt to pick up the receiver, but it was dead. They heard a motorbike kicked into action and the throaty roar as it pulled away.

Betty found her voice although it trembled, 'It'll take him fifteen to twenty minutes to get to Pete on that. Longer before Pete comes for us.' Tears were glittering in her eyes. 'We need to get out before then. I'm not sure how ruthless Pete can be, but I don't want to find out.'

Diana forgot her own horror and put her arm around Betty. She knew Pete would be annoyed, but maybe they could remonstrate with him – perhaps even get him to change his ways without involving the police.

It was dark outside. Perhaps someone would investigate the light leaking beneath the window shutters? Maybe Kim could be persuaded to let them out when she came back from the boat, but that would be too late.

'Is there a key in one of these drawers?'

Betty reached for a key from her handbag. Yes, it fitted the lock. Even then, the door rattled but wouldn't budge. 'It's padlocked from the outside.'

Diana's heart was racing, 'Betty, you're no help at all.'

There was no point being irritated she needed to get help. She screamed at the top of her voice, 'Help, somebody, help.' She listened – just muffled traffic noise.

Diana cast an eye around for something to break a window. There was a footstool under the desk. It was unwieldy to lift, but by holding it by one of its legs and using all her might to swing the stool at the window, she managed to crack a pane.

Chapter Twenty Three

Tony was expecting to hear from Anita at any moment. She was determined to see Diana for herself and to mend their relationship. Tony was relieved. He wanted to spoil her for a few days, and hopefully, she would have time to think, away from Gary. He did a few jobs around the house, pretending to himself that it really didn't matter what time she arrived, but he was churned up inside and anxious to start out to see Diana. A car door slammed. It looked like she had taken a taxi from the station.

He rushed to the door, 'Welcome darling,' he held out his arms to her, 'we could have picked you up.'

'You've got enough to do,' she said.

'Well, come and make yourself comfortable.' He waved her into the kitchen.

She removed her lacy fingerless gloves, flinging them onto the table and swept off a navy beret, letting her long red hair swing free.

'Well just for a moment, but I'm eager to go to my daughter as soon as we can.'

'I can imagine. She's been on my mind too. I hope she knows what she's doing,' he said. 'Can I get you anything?'

'Well alright, something refreshing then. Perhaps an alcoholic tipple would be nice.'

Tony played the perfect host while Anita relaxed. 'I think we should set off first thing in the morning,' he said, as he poured the sparkling liquid into a glass.

'I can't wait that long, Tony.' She pushed her hair back with the side of her hand, it was such a familiar gesture for him. He recalled their history. She had been so bubbly and over-the-top when she was younger.

'Can you at least wait until Vic arrives home?' he said.

Her eyelids dipped slightly, she really did look all in. 'Well,' she drew out, 'If you want us to, but it will be dark soon.' He got the message.

They drove up to Sunnyside, but it looked shut-up for the night.

Clouds covered the moon, but they could still see each other by the light of the dashboard. Anxiety scrunched Anita's face. She peered out at the dim shapes of Pete's house and outbuildings. 'She can't drive, so she's cut off from the world while she's up here with him,'

Tony said, 'It's wise to get our bearings tonight, then we'll be able to work out how to approach her later. I'll drive you around Pete's haunts.' Tracking back along winding lanes, they re-entered the city. He drove to a run-down area and toured side streets, pointing out several boarded-up shops advertising Massages.

'The entrances are often down side alleys - more discreet for the punters. I hope I'll recognise which one is his. Of course, it was a long time ago. It could have moved since I visited his office.'

'What about the boating business?' Anita suggested. He negotiated the side streets to aim for the major road and followed signs to get to the waterway network.

Tony pulled up beside the kerb opposite a riverside pub. 'He's got another office somewhere along here.'

They got out of the car. Bushes rustled in the breeze, which moved the clouds across the night sky, revealing the moon. Lights from buildings across the river were reflected in the dark moving body of water.

Anita took a deep breath, 'It's chilly. That's certainly woken me up.'

Tony felt guilty that he was enjoying being a hero for Anita. He strode ahead over tussocky grass and led her across the gravel towards the river. They sensed a commotion from over by a wooden shack on the bank.

He nudged Anita to slow down, 'What's over there?' There was a sliver of light coming from beneath the door.

Anita lacked his caution and hurried closer to call, 'hello?'

There was a crash inside the shed and a female voice, 'Help, someone. We're stuck in here.'

'Stuck?' Anita looked bewildered.

'Is that you Mum?' Diana sounded incredulous.

'Diana?' Anita's face brightened.

'Listen. We're stuck in here. We wanted to go to the police, but we've been locked in. Can you get us out?'

Anita examined the door. 'There are padlocks on here. What about the window?'

'I've cracked one of the panes.' Diana said, 'Can you open the metal shutters?'

Tony rushed over. Something must be securing them. Yes, they were locked too. It would take an angle grinder.

Anita put her cheek to the door. 'Are you alright, Diana? We'll get you out.'

'Thank you Mum. I'm glad you've come. Betty here, has got faxes that we can take to the police, but the person who locked us in has driven off to warn Pete.'

Anita looked desperately at Tony.

'Well we're here now, and if he comes here, we won't let any harm come to you.'

Tony's mind had been struggling for answers. He hadn't got an angle grinder, but he did have a toolkit in the boot. Were there any weak points?

'Stay with them,' and with the sound of his heart pumping in his ears, he raced to the car.

He was thankful for a bright moon. Once back at the hut, he paced the perimeter looking for another way in. He discovered an inlet close to the ground on a side wall. It was a conduit for power cables. He crouched on the grass and dug at the cover with a screwdriver.

Anita appeared around the corner. 'What have you found?'

Despite his effort, he managed to force out his words, 'This might just work. Tell the girls to come over to this corner and see if they can rip away the wall on their side.'

The hole for cables was a chink in the surface of the shed. If he could lever up the bottom board, the rest would follow. He searched in his bag. A chisel gave him more purchase, but he still felt unequal to the task. He could feel the wood giving, but it wouldn't crack. He was conscious of grunting with the effort. It was only when he stopped to wipe his sleeve across his brow, that he realised that there was an enormous amount of thumping from inside the hut and that Anita was screeching in excitement and shouting for help. He had almost prised away the lower board when he heard people advancing from across the road.

'Hey, hey, what's going on?' a well-built man shouted. There were two of them, the other was younger and wore a baseball cap. Tony stood up, and Anita joined him.

She pleaded with the men, 'Please, my daughter and her friend Betty. They're locked in. Can you help rescue them? They're scared.'

'Betty?' the older heavier man said, and then raised his voice, 'That you, Betty?'

For the first time, they heard Betty's voice. 'Yes, it's me. Lee's locked us in.'

The men took a look at Tony's attempt at dismantling the wall.

'I'm the landlord at the pub over there. There're no keys, I suppose?' He stood scratching his head, 'Hold on. We'll help. Come and get my stuff, Keith.' They retreated into the pub. They returned at a run, holding a metal toolbox, a crowbar and hammer.

'Hang on mate,' he called to Tony, 'let's see if we can jemmy the front.'

'If we get the bolt off the front door, it's still been locked by a key,' Tony said.

'Try the metal window screen then,' Anita pointed to it.

The crowbar folded back the metal of the window screen like the unfolding of a paperclip. Electric light from the interior flooded the grass and lit up the rescuers. Diana's excited face appeared.

'Stand back,' the landlord shouted as he pulled on thick workmen's gloves to remove the glass in pieces. Diana shifted a stool over to the window and practically vaulted through it. It took a little longer for them to support Betty to climb over the windowsill. There was no stool on the outside, so Tony and the landlord took an arm each to lift her clear. Betty sank to the ground, still clutching papers in her hand. She looked shaken and one shoe had fallen to the side. Diana knelt beside her to put an arm around her.

The lull allowed Anita to take stock. They still weren't sure what they were dealing with, 'What happened to you?'

'Yeh, if Lee did this to you, the police should know about it,' the landlord joined in.

Diana, still kneeling, looked up at them, 'Yes, Lee's gone to warn Pete to cover his tracks, but Betty has got evidence to show the police to prove what's been going on.'

'OK Betty, m'darlin'. Let's get you up. You can come in and use my phone.' The landlord bent to help Betty to her feet.

Anita looked from one to the other, 'Pete could get rid of his evidence, or he might even get away?'

'We'll drive over there and try to delay him if we can,' Tony frowned and looked at Betty and Diana, 'What do you two think?'

'I need to speak to him,' Diana said, 'I'm coming with you. Now that I know him, it's better for me to talk to him.'

CHAPTER TWENTY FOUR

Diana had never known Tony to drive so recklessly. She was thrown from side to side as he swerved around the bends. The effort of holding on almost stopped her from panicking about what they were about to face. He pulled up at the five-bar gate at the entrance to Sunnyside. His jaw looked tense as he motioned for her to open it. She had to reach right over the rough stone wall to tug at the metal bolt. As she did, a silent streak of dog flew towards her with teeth bared.

Caesar concentrated his aggression on the car; his lips were pulled back flashing teeth. Tony leant out of the window, 'Don't make any sudden movements'.

'I'll go in by myself - Caesar knows me,' Diana called back to him and then crooned, 'Caesar - good boy. You know me don't you, boy?'

She edged her body through the gate, talking quietly all the time. It was a long way to the house. Would Caesar let her in? The fact that he was outside and on guard probably meant that Pete had been warned. They carried on - Caesar and Diana in a slow dance across the grass together.

As they drew close to the kitchen door at the side of the house, Caesar veered off and ran inside. There was no way of knowing who was there, but Diana hoped that Elaine might be in the kitchen.

She hesitated in the doorway. Once she stepped onto the tiled floor, she was sure that someone would be alerted. It was surreal to be creeping into somewhere that she had begun to see as home.

There was a glimpse of her dad through the door between the kitchen and the hall. He spotted her and said, 'What the hell have you done?'

She instantly felt heat – a mixture of guilt and anger.

'Come here,' he said.

Warily she joined him in the hall. Elaine and Lee with Caesar were all there. The atmosphere was charged. Elaine's eyes shifted rapidly between them.

Pete locked eyes with her, 'You let me down badly — you and Betty. I'd have thought better of you both.'

She couldn't catch her breath, 'It doesn't mean I don't care about you.'

'You've just made yourself look foolish. There's nothing illegal in our introducers.'

'What about the effect that it has on the girls,' Diana felt that she was pleading a lost cause.

'Some girls do very well out of it.'

'No,' Diana murmured. She had lost the will to form a prosecution.

He frowned, 'We'll talk about your role in this later,' he turned to Lee, 'Right, let's have a quick review - there's absolutely nothing on us, is there? Our records are secure.'

'Betty's been printing stuff off the computer, Boss.'

Pete almost lost it. He took a couple of strides closer to Lee, his face twisted into a grimace. 'And you let her!'

'I locked her in.'

'You mean like you locked her in?' Pete flung his arm out at Diana. Caesar was growing excited by the shouting, but Pete yelled and waved him off like a gnat. 'I can't believe this. All

I've worked for. . . if she's turned against us, she's going to take it to the police. How do I recover from this?'

Diana was close to tears and she couldn't swallow. Just as she was searching for something to say to mend him, and on the verge of moving into his arms, his head shot up.

He pointed at Diana, 'Caesar, guard.'

The dog leapt to stand alert in front of Diana. She shrunk back. She couldn't tell whether she saw menace in Caesar's brown eyes. When she looked away from the dog, Pete and Lee had both escaped through the front door. Diana's eyes met Elaine's. Elaine disappeared into the kitchen and returned holding out a chunk of meat, calling 'Caesar'. He leapt for it and carried it off into a corner.

Elaine and Diana both rushed for the front door in time to see Pete revving the motorbike. Somehow, until that moment, Diana had believed that Pete would turn a corner or explain it all away. . . her stomach sank.

She was diverted by headlights which appeared from out of the darkness. A four by four from a stand of trees swerved in the direction of the house. The front passenger side clipped the front wheel of the now moving bike. The bike swerved towards the wall of the house.

***

The motorbike was on its side. Pete lay underneath. One of his arms was moving slightly. Tony appeared out of nowhere and tried to lever the bike up by the handlebars. Lee ran from another direction and grabbed the back of the seat with both hands. Pete howled as they eased it upright and manoeuvred it backwards onto its stand. Diana's heart stood still. Elaine jumped forward and gabbled, 'He's hurt don't move him. We need an ambulance.'

Diana thought she saw one racing through the gate, but no, it was a police car. Uniformed police jumped out of the car and took moments to assess the situation. One of them used the radio to call for an ambulance.

Diana was surprised to see Kim slide down from the driver's side of the four by four. She was still dressed in evening wear. When did she arrive? Kim left the car door hanging open and approached the scene. Her hands flew up to her face to cover her open mouth,

'It was a total accident. I didn't expect him to turn in that direction.'

The policeman stepped towards to her, 'And you are?' He flipped open a notebook and ushered Kim away to give her details.

Diana dismissed any idea that it was an accident. The car had aimed straight for him. In the light from the house, Kim met her eyes and looked away.

Elaine knelt beside the still prone Pete while a woman police officer stood beside them both. Elaine had ripped off her apron and had bunched it up to press hard against Pete's ripped trouser leg. Even so, it was beginning to darken with blood.

Only Tony and Lee did nothing. They seemed mesmerised by the scene until an ambulance sped through the open gates.

One of the ambulance staff conferred with the policeman while the other went to Pete's side. Then they unloaded a stretcher and worked on easing Pete onto it. Just as they were carrying him away, Kim made a frenzied dash towards the prostate Pete, 'Are you okay?'

Pete was oblivious to her and Elaine was only concentrating on him. Kim swivelled around to Diana.

'What happened down at the river? Why're the police here?'

Diana wasn't prepared to say anything to her. She was still trying to work out why Kim was there at all. The policewoman took control. 'We'll be able to discuss this inside.'

*****

The lounge became a makeshift waiting room. Diana, Kim, Tony and Lee were seated around the U-shaped leather modular seating area. Elaine joined them, she was flushed, her hair plastered to her forehead and her trouser knees were covered in blood, 'He's gone in the ambulance. I've put Caesar in the utility room. He's whining though. I'll go and check on him in a minute.'

Diana considered sitting beside her to give some support, but she seemed to be too distracted to settle. She looked at Kim; perhaps Kim ought to be comforting her mother.

It was the first time that Tony had been inside the farmhouse. He was sitting right beside Diana, as though having found her, he didn't want to lose her again. She was glad.

Having taken everyone's details, the police established an interview base at the dining room table. Diana was ushered in by the woman police officer.

She smiled conspiratorially, 'We were expecting to find you here. Your mother and one of the workers alerted us. For tonight we'll establish what happened here at the house. There will be more questions later.'

Diana suddenly felt shaky. She wanted this all to be over. She could hear Elaine talking quietly to Caesar in the utility room. It alerted her that others could be in hearing range. The officer heard too and called through to Elaine. 'He seems calm. Can you take him into the lounge now?'

Elaine was all of a flutter, she poked her head around the dining room door holding Caesar's collar, to ask, 'Shall I make tea for everyone.'

'We'll be finished here very soon,' the policewoman said, 'Maybe once we've gone?'

Once Elaine had left it was reassuring to know that the interview was private. Diana still felt ambiguous about 'telling tales' about her father even though it would help everyone else. She recounted what had happened since she and Tony arrived at the gate.

'It would be worth searching the office while you're here,' she added, 'I think there'll be evidence there.'

'Thank you, and we'll interview Mr Lawrence at the hospital. He's your father?'

'Yes, I'd only just found him and we seemed to be getting on well, but then I found out about the women.'

'Must be difficult.'

'Yeh, it was. Is. What's going to happen to him?'

'I think he'll be in hospital for a while. I can't say, but it will go to court. I suppose it's possible that he could be released on bail.'

Diana didn't say anything. Should she build a new relationship with him or did she want to go back to how it was before she ever knew him? Could she even do that? She had promised to give him time to reform, but he hadn't had any time. Would he forgive her? She desperately wanted to see her mother now.

Chapter Twenty Five

Diana's mind was racing with all that had happened that night. Vic was waiting for them back at the cottage and would have fussed over them and made drinks, but all they wanted to do was to go to bed.

Diana was looking forward to falling into bed, but she offered to sleep on the sofa so that Anita could have the spare bedroom. She didn't bother to put on the light and sat in the living room beside a pile of pillows and a duvet listening to the two men and Anita going up the stairs. The curtains were half-open. The moonlight threw a bright window-shape across the floor. She gave a shiver, reached to switch on a table light and drew the curtains. Bruno must have heard her and bustled into the living room, his tail wagging. She made a space for him on the sofa and patted it to encourage him. He wasn't allowed on chairs, but he jumped up all the same. She wrapped her arms around him and buried her nose in his warm fur, taking in his doggy smell.

Her mind took her back to Sunnyside. She wondered whether Kim was able to sleep. Both Elaine and Kim seemed to have switched sides, but who knows. Where had she appeared from and how did she know that something was going on at the house? If there was something between Kim and Lee, he might have somehow communicated with her.

She should try to sleep. It was just hours until morning. She hadn't had a chance to discover how her mother was taking all this, but it gave her a warm feeling to know that she had come from London to find her.

***

When Diana and Anita woke up, Tony and Vic were already busy unloading the dishwasher. Tony said, 'I've decided to visit the Lunar Hotel this morning. We'll leave you here. I want to take a look before we meet the architect for a final check.' Diana felt a sharp pang of homesickness for the hotel and her normal life there. . . 'You'll be able to go home pretty soon. Imogen and Lynette get back this week. I bet you won't recognise the place.'

Diana hoped that she would.

Anita wrapped her arms around Tony's waist and put her head on his shoulder. 'Thank you. You're the best. Shall we take Bruno out for you while you're away?'

'I think he'd appreciate that.' Tony lightly kissed the top of her head. He grabbed a briefcase while Vic tousled Bruno's head to say goodbye, and they made for the door.

Anita popped slices of bread into the toaster. 'Toast for you, too?' They made it in silence.

Bruno rushed up, to sit in a very upright position wagging his tail rapidly.

'No Bruno – I'm sure it's not good for you,' Anita wagged a finger at him and laughed.

Sitting opposite each other at the pine table, Anita said, 'You know, I had trouble sleeping last night for thinking about you. I was so worried when you left London. We ought to talk.' Diana's eyes slid down.

'I can see you don't want to.' Anita sighed, 'look none of that with Gary was your fault. He's selfish and full of his own importance. I clung on to him because he was helping my career, but I need to ditch him.'

Diana felt grateful that her mum was being so honest. She took more bread and refilled the toaster. It gave her a chance to look away while she said, 'Well I'm sorry that I embarrassed you, trying to be an actress. I should have talked to you about it.' She sat down again, this time beside her mother.

'You probably could be an actress. I'm sure you could do anything if you put your mind to it.' Anita squeezed Diana's hand and smiled with tears hovering in her eyes. 'It's a hard life and no one looks out for you but you. I've kept at it. I felt that I had something to prove.'

'Well, you've proved it.'

'Thank you, darling. I hope I have. It's the result of my upbringing. My own mum, God rest her soul, she sacrificed a lot to see me get into acting.' Tears quivered in Anita's eyes, 'Oh, dear this isn't like me' she brushed tears away. 'I hope I've done her proud. Maybe I'll never know when I've done enough.'

Diana said, 'You know mum, I've learned to be independent this summer. I was dithering about my future, but I realise I can make decisions for myself.' She looked down at Bruno while she gathered her thoughts. 'I knew underneath that I was trying to be an actress because I thought Dad would be impressed. But I'm not trying to please him anymore.'

'Yes, you've grown up. I knew Pete was bad news. Maybe I should have told you more about him before, but I didn't want to hurt you. And all I ask is that you are your own woman and you do what you think is right. And Diana. . . she laid her hand on Diana's arm, 'I think you've done that. It must have been difficult.' She put her other arm around Diana's waist, 'I'm proud of you.'

Diana felt a rush of warmth, the touch travelled and hit her heart.

'I still wonder how it has affected Elaine. Her life has been turned upside down. She seemed downtrodden, but she might be worse off now. I don't understand what was going on with Kim. She seemed to love her mother, but then at times, she seemed as bad as Pete.'

'The world isn't black and white.'

'No and not all families are the same. I realise how lucky I've been. Imogen was always there with her common sense, and when she got together with Lynette, it taught me that you should follow your heart, despite anything in your way. Tony and Vic have been reliable and fun to have around and . . . of course, I've always had you too.' She gave a gentle smile. 'You've always been there. I always felt loved.'

'Wow, thank you. That means a lot. Things have been difficult recently. I've been questioning all my past decisions.'

Diana was suddenly alert, 'I thought there was something wrong.'

'Yes, I've been having trouble with my back. I started to live on painkillers, but they're not the answer. It's taken me a while to come to terms with it, but I need to take a break from working. It took me so long to get a career going and I didn't want to lose it. Now the hotel's ready, I'll come back home to Imogen and Lynette, at least for a little while.

Diana felt a pang, 'I didn't realise.' She wished she could have helped but it would be so cool for everyone to be back together again. She had not realised until then that having everyone at home was so important. 'I can't wait to see the new look and everyone back where they belong.' Diana rushed to finish the last of her toast and looked ready to rush off there immediately.

After breakfast, Diana was careful to not even look in the direction of the lead, but somehow Bruno still guessed their plan. He couldn't contain his little whines and even yaps.

'Perhaps a more sedate walk than I would have done at one time,' Anita said, as Diana unhooked the door key to take with them. Outside Diana offered her arm to her mother while holding the lead in the other hand.

They made their way out of the village over a little-used stone bridge which led to fields. The ground by the field gate was muddy, so they had to concentrate on picking their way around puddles.

Once back on the footpath again, Anita asked, 'And what's the future for you? Have you had time to think?' Diana appreciated that this time her mum wasn't dictating her future to her.

She could feel herself beaming, 'I love languages and I want to be able to speak like a native. It was obvious really – I'm going to go to uni after all.'

'Your own decision this time?'

'Yes, now it's my own decision,' Diana nodded with satisfaction.

'Well, that's great. When does term start? It can't be long now.'

'No, it isn't, but there are some things that I want to do before I go. I want to see how they all are. I want to know what Kim was up to.' She took a few more steps and then said, 'and I want to know how Elaine is and the girls that I met.'

'I can see you've got caught up in it, but it might not be as easy as you think,' Anita stopped and scrutinised her. 'You will be going back into a world that you barely understand.'

Diana felt a twinge of irritation. She had been immersed in that world already and emerged unscathed. Anyway, it was unfinished business.

Her mother interrupted her thoughts, 'If you want to see them again, I could go with you, or Tony perhaps.'

A woman in an anorak and walking boots came into view with two small dogs running in circles around her. 'Um, should we put Bruno on the lead before they get any nearer?' Diana felt the edge of the leather lead in her pocket.

'Hello,' the woman was still several metres away, 'Don't worry about the dogs they're all friends.' Her two raced over to greet Bruno. As she drew nearer, she said, 'sorry excuse the smell. Penny's been rolling in something, I'm afraid. Charlie and Penny often go for playdates with Bruno. Are Vic and Tony well?'

'Yes, they're just out for the day.'

'Good, perhaps I'll see Vic later. Tell him Maggie said "hello".' With that, she called her dogs and strode off in the direction of the village. So, Vic had settled into village life at

last.

Chapter Twenty Six

Once back at the Lunar Hotel, Diana's world wrapped around her like a duvet. It made her realise how rootless she had felt over the summer. Now that Anita was back there, Tony and Vic visited more often for communal meals. Diana invited Clare over to join them. It felt as though Diana and Clare hadn't spoken for years, but they immediately regained their old closeness. Diana regaled Clare with her story, while Clare could only tell her that she'd been mooching and revising.

'The grass is always greener. You look at me having a dad, and I look at you with all this,' Clare gestured around the hotel in general, 'and a family group of such different people – but they are always ready to include you in.'

Clare was more than willing to accompany Diana to meet up with Elaine or Kim again. Elaine would never come to the phone, but Kim agreed to come to meet Diana.

They travelled into the city by bus. 'How would you like me to support you?' Clare asked, and added, 'I think you are brave to speak to Kim again.'

'I totally want to have someone there with me on my side. I'm really scared.'

'What after what you've been through!'

'It's different now because I know a lot more of what I'm going into, and I caused all this. I feel a bit sick,' she hunched over.

'You don't look good.'

'Take my mind off it. Tell me about the retakes.'

It was a grey, drizzly day, and when the bus pulled under the roof of the bus station, it got even darker. Diana spotted Kim sprawled on a curved metal bench. She wasn't far from the designated parking bay for their bus route but she hadn't noticed their arrival. She was wearing a leather jacket and knitted beanie hat.

'Look over there,' Diana pointed her out, sharing some of her new world with someone from the old.

People were moving in all directions. Travellers trundling cases looking glum.

They stayed seated as other passengers began to fill the aisle, so they were the last off.

Kim's had folded her arms and was looking at her feet. It didn't strike Diana that she was keen to see them, but once she noticed them, she jumped up.

'Hi, kiddo,' Kim said. This was a new and embarrassing nickname but maybe a sign that Kim didn't hate her for what she'd done, 'Who's this?'

'Hello Kim, I've brought Clare with me. I've mentioned her before.'

Clare nodded and spoke up over the continuous roar of coach engines, 'Hi.'

They sat down and huddled close, to be able to hear each other. Kim focused her attention on Diana, looking past Clare, 'So, you want to see what happened after it all shook down. I can see why you didn't want to come to the house.'

'I wasn't sure about going back there again. How's Elaine taken it all?'

'I know you thought you were helping her. But she relied on Pete. She feels cast adrift now, and despite everything, I think she loves him. So she doesn't see it like you,' Kim paused for a moment and added, 'and maybe like me.'

A pigeon landed on the arm of the seat. Kim waved it away.

'She had a few panic attacks, so in the end we persuaded her to go to the doctor. She'd got into a rut. While she was living up at Sunnyside, on her own a lot of the time, she couldn't see that there was anything else, so it'll be good for her to have a shake-up. I'm not worried – Betty's been visiting her a lot more to help out and to give her a bit of company – and Lee. . .' Kim smiled for the first time, but then said, 'Have you heard any more from the police?'

Diana had been dreading hearing from them, but they hadn't been in touch. 'No, have you?'

'Well yeh, but then I've been more involved than you. Don't suppose you're going to visit your dad in prison either. Do you realise that he could be facing ten years? It was a bit of a drastic way to give my mum a better life, wasn't it?'

Diana felt Clare shift in her seat to lean in closer to her. She was glad Clare was there but, even though Kim was challenging, Diana didn't feel intimidated.

'Ten years, I hadn't realised. But it was something that had to happen because I was standing up for all the girls involved.'

Kim laughed but said nothing. 'I know. You've got some kinda hero complex.' She looked at Clare. 'What do you think of her?'

I'm amazed at what she's done. You helped her though, didn't you?

'Let's just say, I did at times. I could see what it did to the girls, you were right kid. Sometimes it made me feel like shit. But I didn't think Pete could fail and I wanted to keep the business going. I suppose I don't believe that things will get better, like you do. The way I look at it, there will always be someone to take his place.'

Diana was troubled, 'You say that there will always be someone to take Pete's place. So what's happened to the girls?'

'I meant, there will always be someone doing the wrong thing, somewhere.' She reached out to put her arms around Diana. Diana was unsure of her intentions and stiffened. But Kim pulled Diana forward into a rough hug.

'You're too good for your own health. So, you don't need to worry, our girls have all gone to what the police call, a "place of safety". Some charity has got involved. I've gotta say, you and Betty have started something now. The ripples in the pond keep spreading outwards. The police have passed information over to Europe about criminal activity there.

A group of people passed by, parting to avoid the row of seats. A woman stopped to open her bag to get out a folding umbrella.

When they'd gone, Kim leaned in again, 'And I should thank you really. I've talked to Mum and I'm going to run the business for her. Lee will help.' Then she raised her hands as though fending Diana off, 'Chill out, I'm going to concentrate on the boats and the caravan site. So it's all cool.'

'So, apart from Dad, no one's in trouble with the police for being part of the business? Are the police speaking to you? And what about the car going into the motorbike? I mean, are you in trouble?'

'We were just employees in the business. We'll have to see what my solicitor says about it all and about the accident.' Kim looked at her meaningfully, 'The question is, are you cool with me?'

Diana felt a shiver, she had asked herself this. Kim had turned against her, she couldn't deny that.

'I heard what you said when Pete was having a go at me on the stairs, but well, you were caught up in it all.' She felt a warmth for Kim now, 'We had some good times together,' she grinned, 'you were the big sister who took me to a rave.'

'Hmm wish I'd been with you,' Clare said.

Kim shook her head dismissively, 'There'll be others, anyway you can both come on a boat trip sometime. I'll ask Lee to give you a freebie. So, what are you two doing now?'

Diana said, 'I'm off to university soon. Clare's going to be staying back here.'

'But we will keep in touch this time,' Clare said nodding firmly.

Kim looked at her watch, 'Better get going – I'm going to be prison visiting to get signatures swapped over and tap Pete's knowledge about the business. Is there anything you want me to pass on to him?'

Diana had been deliberately not thinking about her dad. Maybe she ought to write to him and explain herself. She hadn't made any decisions about the future, but she went with her gut feeling.

'Tell him, tell him, that I did my best. I will keep in touch with him if he wants that, but it has to be on my terms.'

Chapter Twenty Seven

Everyone had gathered back at the hotel again. Diana loved the new, cream interior décor with touches of jade and blue. Although it wouldn't reopen until the following week, Imogen had started organising the reception area. Lynette was travelling to work from there again. Anita, Tony, and Vic were working on finishing touches. They decided on a dress rehearsal, so one evening they invited a few friends to have dinner in the new restaurant, including Clare and her parents. It was useful as they learned that desserts weren't in the logical place in the kitchen. The evening was relaxed and the hotel began to feel like home again.

Knowing that she would be going away, cast a shadow over everything for Diana, so she stored up these snapshots of family life. On her last evening, they loaded one of the conference tables with huge bowls of pasta and bottles of red wine. They reminisced about the opening of the original Lunar Hotel. Diana had been a baby, so some of these stories were new to her. They had held an opening variety show and invited everyone from the town. Imogen's mother Dulcie had been there helping out at the time.

Imogen described Dulcie's new flat in a chateau in South West France. Dulcie and her husband had been able to lead an original hippie commune into a harmonious and well-organised community with a nursery, school and library.

'Good old Dulcie,' Tony pronounced.

'Next year,' Diana pointed at her mother, 'we will definitely go to stay there together.' Anita smiled in agreement.

'And we ought to have a public relaunch event, now.' Anita suggested and then laughed when everyone took the opportunity to ask her to organise it. Diana was glad, it would give Anita an interest and a reason to stay for a while.

*****

The next morning, they gathered in the car park to see Diana off. Her mother hugged her tightly. She felt so slender and it was as though she didn't want to let go.

Diana felt tightness welling in her chest, 'It's okay. I'll soon be back for the Christmas holidays – will you be here?'

'You bet – Pantomime season.' Anita gave an exaggerated shiver of disgust.

Imogen was doing the driving. There were two cases in the boot, a rucksack and a table lamp. Diana had piled even more belongings onto the back seat.

'You can always come back one weekend and get anything you've forgotten,' Imogen said, slamming the boot shut.

*****

The hall of residence was a 1960s built block teeming with young people. She marvelled at so many people of the same age in one place. The packed environment promised new, exciting experiences. Imogen helped unload and accompanied Diana to search for the warden. Most people had already arrived, but she hadn't missed much. The walls announced that it was Fresher's week. She scanned posters and fliers along the corridors and in lifts as they carried the bags to her room.

Imogen left soon after. Diana was momentarily unnerved. The room echoed. The hooks on the back of the door looked stark and empty, the view from the window was of walls opposite and a slabbed quadrangle below. She sat in the bare room with her luggage piled around her. She would miss Clare all over again, but she forced herself to stop thinking and to begin unpacking clothes into drawers. Rescue came in the form of a girl called Hannelore who popped her head around the door.

'Hello, newbie. Would you like some help to arrange your stuff?'

She didn't need help, but Hannelore did bring her a coffee and joined her later for a chat. Other students on her corridor were keen to introduce themselves. People met in the shared kitchen and drifted along to each other's rooms. Diana grew in confidence and found herself waking up eager for each new day.

***

Six people had arranged themselves around one bedroom; some on the floor. Diana could already pick out those who were live wires, the thoughtful ones and those who would take the lead.

'We were sailing in the Med for most of the summer. Fantastic beach barbeques, partying, playing the guitar, listening to the waves in the evenings. I've brought my guitar with me actually.' Simon, the speaker, said, 'I'll get it' and he stepped over legs and bags to go for it.

A beautiful girl called Caro said, 'I had a gap year, did anyone else?'

'Oh yah, worked my way around Australia. Where were you?' someone else asked. Hannelore had been picking grapes in Europe. A comparison of hostels in various countries ensued.

Diana was squashed beside a girl in a hijab. The girl spoke quietly to her, 'I just had summer with the family. What about you?'

'Oh yes, the same,' Diana said. She felt herself smiling.

FROM THE AUTHOR

I decided to write this trilogy as a way of charting the amazing changes that I had seen since the 1970s – changes that happen so gradually that we often don't notice them.

I've always enjoyed telling stories, but they were off-the-cuff for children. So, now I enjoy writing about people who are learning important lessons in life.

I hope you have enjoyed being part of their world.

I would love you to leave a review. It raises my author profile and provides me with valuable feedback.

You can find out me on www.rosemaryblake.co.uk and you will be able to sign up for my newsletter there. You can also join my Facebook author page @RBlake.author and occasionally I write on twitter @RBlakeauthor

www.ingramcontent.com/pod-product-compliance
Lightning Source LLC
Chambersburg PA
CBHW021222060726
47590CB00005B/1592